DEAD KEEN

ANISE EDEN

TANGLED TREE PUBLISHING

DEAD KEEN

THINGS UNSEEN
BOOK 2

ANISE EDEN

ALSO BY ANISE EDEN

Things Unseen Series

For information, contact the publisher, Tangled Tree Publishing.

WWW.TANGLEDTREEPUBLISHING.COM

EDITING: HOT TREE EDITING

COVER DESIGNER: BOOKSMITH DESIGN

EBOOK ISBN: 978-1-922679-88-8

PAPERBACK ISBN: 978-1-922679-89-5

Dedicated to my sister, Amy, the best sister ever in the history of sisters, because she deserves to have not only books but all manner of things dedicated to her, not to mention songs written and movies made about her. That's just how epic she is.

PROLOGUE

CIARA

ONE MONTH AGO

old. Hard. Rough.

That was the sum of Ciara's awareness: the surface she lay upon, pressing its imprint into her back.

She willed herself to focus. The air was chilled and damp against her face, clinging to her hands and forearms, but the rest of her was shielded by a cloth. It felt soft, loose-fitting. Some quality of the flow of the air or the thinness of the silence around her spoke of spaciousness.

Was she just waking up? But her eyelids wouldn't open, and when she tried the rest of her body, nothing would move. A splinter of worry.

A question tried to form in her mind, but it was like a wisp of fog—vague and constantly changing. Maybe she should just try to enjoy the quiet, the feeling of space around her.

The sound of water drifted into her awareness, lapping rhythmically against a hard surface, lulling her into a deeper state of calm. Clouds of thought drifted further away, unimportant.

Then a jolt—the sound of a sharp click, metal on metal. The tromping of heavy shoes on stone—one pair, then others. The rackety clatter of hard wheels rolling across a hard, uneven surface.

Again, she struggled to open her eyes, but to no effect, as though her will was submerged too deeply underwater to reach the surface.

Questions finally started to take shape in her mind. *Where am I? What's going on?* There were no answers, though, only air swirling in chaos as feet shuffled around her. The people were close enough now that she could feel their warmth.

Who are they? What do they want? Tentacles of fear slid around her chest. Her breathing came faster, harder. Still, her body would not budge.

The feet stopped moving. Someone stood at her head, someone at her feet. The person with the wheeled object came to a stop at her side.

A soft caress brushed across her forehead, followed by a man's voice. "She's definitely out."

But not any man's voice—her boyfriend's. *Max.* Her breathing slowed. Max was there, and he believed she was asleep. His voice was smooth, unconcerned. There must be no need to worry.

She tried again to move, to speak, to tell Max she heard him. But she could not. The tension in her chest tightened a notch.

Two warm hands rested on the tops of her feet, squeezing lightly. "For how long?" a woman's soft voice asked. *Deirdre.* "Are you sure she won't feel anything?"

Her best friend was there with Max. Whatever was happening, she was safe, at least. Once she was able to move, to speak, all her questions would be answered. Maybe she was just asleep, having a vivid dream.

"Relax," Max said—to Deirdre? But Ciara tried to obey.

She heard a soft click, then a mechanical hum. A hand grasped her left arm and rotated it until her palm faced up. It felt perfectly smooth, like a nurse's rubber-gloved fingers. Something cold and wet was spread across the underside of her forearm—rubbing alcohol, judging by the sharp scent stinging her nose. Two cool fingers gently stretched the skin.

Suddenly, sharp pain shot into a pinpoint on her arm near where the fingers touched her. Ciara wanted to jump, jerk her arm away, cry out. But her body remained stubbornly immobile, beyond her influence. *Paralyzed.*

Was she in a hospital, then, and someone was inserting an IV? But with the pricking sensation came a steady vibration. The pain was drawn along her arm in a line like a cat scratch, but slow and deep.

Now, questions slammed into her mind with force

and clarity. *Where am I? What's going on?* Again, she tried to shout, but no sound came. Panic gripped her. She couldn't move her lips.

Max spoke again. "This won't take too long."

Then her arm began to burn, right along the scratched lines. Ciara's heart lurched in her chest. Max and Deirdre must not know she was in pain. She had to find a way to tell them, to make it stop.

With a massive surge of effort, she flung her right arm across her body. Her hand landed on the inside of her left arm, knocking away the rubber-gloved fingers and their torture implement. Life flowed back into her arms, and she began to tear at the painful skin, trying desperately to peel away the offending layers, to stop the burning....

"Ciara!" a man's voice shouted—but not Max's. *Eamonn.* Her now-fiancé.

This time, her eyelids obeyed her command to open. His face was just in front of hers, twisted with worry.

Eamonn's here. Her heart swelled with gratitude and relief. Max was in the past. *Thank God.*

Frantically, Eamonn's hands patted her cheeks, gripped her shoulders. "Ciara, wake up!"

Her eyes followed Eamonn's gaze down to her left forearm. It was a bloodied mess. She looked around her and saw she was sitting on the floor in their bathroom, slumped against the tub. Blood was smeared on the white porcelain, the gray floor tiles, the pale wood cabinet under the sink. And the skin on her arm screamed in pain, felt like it had been clawed off.

"Oh!" She gasped at the intensity of it. "Eamonn, help," she whispered.

"I'm here, Ciara." Careful of her wounded arm, he folded her body against his. "It's okay. I'm here."

CHAPTER 1

NEVE

PRESENT DAY

had never been able to sleep on planes. Still, this was my first red-eye, so I'd held out hope. No luck, however—not even with the lights dimmed and the window shades pulled down. Aching with envy, I watched Con's hefty shoulders rise and fall as he snoozed away in the seat next to me.

Unfortunately, I'd already exhausted all the options for in-flight entertainment. The only thing left for me to do was to create my own.

Con's snoring was deep, like his voice. I could pretend we were having a conversation—role-playing. We were back in the psychiatry unit at Capitol Hill General, and instead of being my colleague, he was my therapy client.

Diving right into the deep end, I murmured, "So I

hear you've just started dating someone. What's she like?"

He answered with another snore.

"Hmm. She sounds harmless, if a bit strange. How do you feel about her?"

This time, the snore was harsher, louder. A revelation of some kind?

"Would you say you're in love with her, then?"

But before Con could snore his answer, our jarringly perky flight attendant popped out from behind the curtain that closed off the galley area. We were seated in the front row, so we didn't get any warning before her sudden appearances. Stopping next to us, she squinted down at me, then at Con, then back at me.

Good grief, did she hear me talking to him? Heat crept into my cheeks.

"Is everything all right?" she asked, her Irish accent similar to Con's.

"Yes, fine. Just wondering, is it Tuesday or Wednesday now?"

"It's still Tuesday in Washington, DC, but it's early Wednesday morning in Ireland. Can I get you anything?"

With a pleading smile, I suggested, "A sleeping pill?"

"Oh, I see." She nodded with practiced sympathy. "Sorry, those aren't on the menu, I'm afraid. If it helps, we'll be landing at Shannon in two hours. We'll come through with breakfast before then, but in the meantime, I can get you a drink if you like."

Our conversation, though hushed, managed to wake Con. "I'll take a drink," he muttered, his voice rough with sleep.

"Good morning, Dr. O'Brien!" the flight attendant chirped. "What can I get you?"

First class: where everybody knows your name. I marveled once again at the quality-of-life gap between my current surroundings and my usual experience in coach.

Con turned to me. "Neve, what'll you have?"

Only two hours until we landed in Ireland, where I would be meeting his brother for the first time at the airport. Better perk up a bit. "Coffee, please. Two sugars."

"I'll take a scotch, neat, please."

"Of course. I'll be right back with those."

As she swished behind the curtain, Con rubbed his eyes, then took his time evaluating me with his "doctorly examination" look. "You didn't sleep?"

"Not a wink. However, I did watch two of the latest blockbusters. They both featured plane crashes."

"Hmm." I loved the look of his wry smile on his sleep-softened face. "So, you're tired, and your judgment regarding film choice is impaired, but you're otherwise unscathed."

The flight attendant returned in record time. She gave me a perfunctory nod as she delivered my coffee but beamed a smile at Con as she handed him his drink. "Just let me know if you need anything else, Doctor

O'Brien, Miss Keane." Then she turned and disappeared back into the galley.

With a sigh, I closed my eyes. I was well accustomed to seeing women give Con "that look." But we were all in such tight proximity. It seemed a bit too close for flirting comfort.

Con frowned over at me. "It's only my second. I won't be driving, you know."

"It's not the scotch." Warmth pricked my cheeks. Con and I had only been dating for a few weeks. I didn't want to scare him off with irrational displays of jealousy. "I'm just embarrassed. While you were sleeping, I entertained myself by having an imaginary therapy session with you, and she caught me."

"Interesting." He tried and failed to look serious, as though I were really filling him in on a case. "Did I say anything revealing?"

"Please, you know that's confidential."

"Hmm. So your body is on vacation, but your brain is still stuck at work." He reached across the armrest and took my hand, a gesture that sent a tiny thrill darting through me. "While we're in Ireland, I'll have to make it my mission to ensure your thoughts of the hospital disappear entirely."

I turned my head away as my blush deepened. "Brave words, considering we're going to be staying with your parents."

"So little faith." He gave my hand a gentle squeeze. "I know we had to put this off for a bit, but I promise to make it worth the wait."

Our trip had been delayed after a CT scan led to an MRI that showed I had not one but two ovarian tumors, one on each side. Since they were smallish and of a type unlikely to put me at risk for serious complications, I would have been happy to get on the plane immediately. But Con and Dr. Mohinder did the good cop, bad cop thing—Con being the bad cop, or at least the "catastrophic thinking" cop—and cajoled me into getting the tumors biopsied before we left. Once that was done, Dr. Mohinder said she agreed with Con that taking a vacation would be better than sitting around at home, worrying as I waited to hear the results. Once I'd scheduled a follow-up appointment with her to take place after our return, we were on our way.

Since the biopsies, I'd only felt the odd twinge of discomfort. But Con had argued that since I was "post-op," I should fly in first class with him—to avoid blood clots, he claimed—and that since he was the one insisting upon it, he should pay for the tickets. He actually needed the extra room to accommodate his metal leg brace. But when it came to me, I knew he was just looking for excuses to treat me without giving me room to object.

Still, with my recent history of panic attacks and my anxiety about taking my first transatlantic flight, I'd decided not to argue. If I freaked out in first class, at least there would be fewer witnesses.

Once on the plane, though, all I'd felt was excitement. There was something intensely intimate about sharing that compact physical space with Con for seven-to-eight hours, knowing that when we landed, we'd be in a different country—his home country. Not to mention I'd be meeting his family.

I stole glances at Con as he scrolled through his phone and nursed his scotch, wincing. *Not top shelf, then.* I smiled to myself, knowing that from the outside, it must look like our taking an overseas trip together was "moving too fast." But over two years of friendship, Con and I had become close—so much so that a couple of months ago, after I was stabbed by one of my patients, he was the only person aside from my parents who I'd allowed to visit me. For whatever reason, I didn't feel self-conscious around Con—not about my wounds, and not about the new anxiety symptoms I developed after the attack. In fact, his presence was one of the only things I found consistently soothing. But a few weeks ago, we had breathed life into the romance long simmering between us, adding a new type of nervousness into the mix.

Then there was the fact that Con had always been less than forthcoming about his personal life, so while he knew practically everything about me, there was quite a bit I didn't know about him. I hoped meeting his family and being in the place he'd grown up would fill in some of the gaps.

"If it helps take your mind off work," he continued, "I've got an email from the hospital. Amos and his friends continue to do well. No lingering issues."

Amos and his friends: the patients at the center of

the chilling drama that had dominated Labor Day week for Con and me. By the time it was all over, Con had rescued me from a kidnapping, we'd both survived threats to our lives, and, by some miracle, we'd managed to thwart an attempt to assassinate the president.

Only a few weeks had passed since then, but those events seemed so distant now. Having a biopsy in the meantime no doubt played a part, as did the fact that I was trying very, very hard to put the whole drama out of my mind. Still, knowing Amos and friends were doing well did make me feel better.

"Thanks, that does help. I'm glad to hear they're okay."

Con tucked his phone in his pocket, then smoothed back a lock of hair that had fallen across my forehead. "Now that you know, I think it's time you put the whole affair out of mind—at least as long as we're in Ireland, with an entire ocean between you and those gurriers. It won't be much of a vacation otherwise, will it?"

I swallowed hard, hoping he didn't notice the quickening of my pulse his touch had triggered. "What's a gurrier?"

"Oh, a lout. Like our lads at Brickhaven."

Ugh, Brickhaven. Just hearing the name of that treacherous so-called think tank raised goose bumps on my arms—and not the good kind. After all, Brickhaven had put Amos, the president, Con, and me in their crosshairs, and they might still be out to get us. I took a deep breath and exhaled slowly, reminding myself what a relief it was to be putting an ocean between us and them. "Okay, well, no promises, but I'll try."

"Hmm." He frowned as he leaned back in his seat. "I suppose that'll do for now."

"Sorry to disappoint." I flashed him a cheeky smile, then closed my eyes before he could reply, pretending to sleep. It must have worked for real, though, because the next thing I knew, Con was waking me with his hand on my shoulder.

"We're here, love. Welcome to my part of the world." He gave me a quick wink and pulled our carry-ons down from the overhead luggage compartment.

I paused for a few seconds, enjoying the warmth that bloomed in my chest every time Con called me "love," his new pet term for me. Then I forced myself into pragmatic gear, checking to make sure we weren't leaving anything important in the seat pockets and trying to swallow a sudden surge of nerves.

We had arrived. Our new adventure was about to begin.

———

Once inside the airport, we entered the line to go through Customs. I gaped at the huge tourism posters displaying some of the country's stunning destinations —castles, cliffs, and so much green.

Other signs stood in stark contrast to those

dreamy images, like those explaining what to do if you were victim of human trafficking. Confronted with such a chilling reminder that we hadn't escaped the darkest horrors of humanity when we crossed the "pond," I was hit by a wave of tension as Con and I filtered into two different lines, for European Union citizens and "others." What if border control didn't let me in for some reason, and we got separated?

Stop being ridiculous, I chided myself, annoyed to discover I hadn't left my anxiety issues at home. Forcing my breathing to slow, I silently confronted my irrational thoughts as perspiration dotted my forehead. Fortunately, once he got through passport control, Con waited for me on the other side of the plexiglass, always staying within sight.

Once I was through, I must have walked toward him more quickly than usual. Con caught me in a steadying embrace. "What happened?" he murmured.

"Nothing, just… nerves, I guess."

Slow, deep breaths. In through the nose, out through the mouth.

He held on to me until we both felt my body relax. Then he placed a gentle kiss on the top of my head. "You sure?"

Embarrassment galvanized me while the sensation of his lips on my hair melted the tension away. "Yes, of course. I'm good to go!" To prove it, I tugged him toward baggage claim.

Once our bags arrived, we rolled our luggage out

into the main terminal. A cheerful voice called out, "Deadeye Con, you ugly fecker!"

Brightening instantly, Con replied, "Flamin' Eamonn, ya mad hoor!"

The next thing I knew, Con and a slightly smaller, leaner man held each other in a crushing embrace. Pulling away, they both grinned widely.

"Christ, look at you," said the man I guessed was his brother. "Can't believe you're really here! Eamonn." He thrust his hand out to me. "You must be Neve. God knows how you put up with this cantankerous bastard. You must be a saint."

Smiling, I shook his hand. "Definitely not a saint."

"I'm not convinced," Eamonn said. "Don't believe a word of what he's told you about me, by the way."

There was some family resemblance between them, but Con and Eamonn must have favored different parents. With bright blue eyes and refined features, Con's younger brother had a natural warmth that put me at ease. Still, I saw subtle signs of emotional strain beneath his good cheer—lines of fatigue around the eyes, a slightly pallid complexion, and the haunted look of someone for whom worry was a constant companion. Not surprising, given that his fiancée, Ciara, had recently been admitted to a psychiatric hospital. It was his request for Con's help with Ciara's case that had prompted our visit.

"He's only told me good things," I reassured Eamonn, which was true. Con hadn't told me much about his family, but he'd never spoken a bad word about them either. The fact that he'd been willing to drop everything and take his first trip home in five years simply because his brother needed support spoke volumes.

I suddenly felt a bit awkward, a third wheel at their fraternal reunion. At the same time, a wave of exhaustion hit me suddenly. A bit woozy, I leaned on the handle of my suitcase.

Con gave me a quick once-over, took hold of my elbow, and nodded toward the exit. "Let's get out of here. I've had enough of airports for one day."

"No worries." Without a word, Eamonn took charge of my bags and led us outside.

Eamonn had come to pick us up in his new sedan. I insisted Con take the front seat, knowing he and his brother had a lot to catch up on. I was determined to stay awake, to take in every bit of Ireland and not miss a thing.

Not far from the airport, I felt every inch the wide-eyed tourist as I exclaimed, "Oh my God, is that a *castle*?" An enormous stone structure complete with towers and turrets rose high into the sky behind a brightly painted roadside pub.

Con and Eamonn exchanged knowing smiles. "Bunratty Castle," Eamonn said. "Ireland is rotten with castles, although this one isn't even that old. Fifteenth century, I think. Still worth a visit, though."

"If you want to eat ribs and get drunk on mead with a crowd of tourists, that is," Con quipped. "If not, don't worry, there are plenty more castles to see.

They're like your water towers in the US. Every town has one."

"Right," Eamonn added, "and you can't throw a rock without hitting a stone circle!"

"That's incredible!" I was hungry to see and hear more, but I bit my tongue so I wouldn't sound too eager. I didn't want Eamonn to think helping Ciara wasn't the main priority of our visit.

A gently curving road took us from Shannon Airport toward their family home in North Cork. Eamonn said the trip to Kilshannig would take a little over an hour, while Con joked that Kilshannig was Irish for "the middle of fecking nowhere."

Whenever we crested a hill or there was a break in the hedges lining the road, I was able to glimpse the brilliant green fields for which Ireland was so famous. Old stone walls, hedgerows, and fences combined to form an intricate web that traced the curves of rolling hills where clusters of cows and sheep grazed peacefully.

With its soft edges and rich colors, the landscape felt welcoming and resembled rural Maryland enough that I felt immediately at home. The road signs written in both English and Irish, however, served as a reminder that we were an ocean away. The brothers indulged me by reading a few signs aloud and explaining some rules of Irish language pronunciation. Observing my enthusiasm, Con kindly agreed to teach me more during our visit.

Meanwhile, as we drove, their conversation kept

returning to the admiration of Eamonn's new car. I tried to keep my eyes peeled so I would see every castle and stone circle along our route, but before Con and Eamonn made it all the way through the topic of fuel economy, their voices and the hum of the road lulled me to sleep.

CHAPTER 2

NEVE

The bumps and crunches of a gravel driveway jolted me awake. Disoriented, I looked up to see Con squinting back at me from the front seat.

"All right?"

"Yeah." I sighed, taking stock. "I fell asleep? I'm sorry!"

"Sorry for what? Jet lag's a bitch coming this way, especially on the red-eye." Eamonn drove up to an elegant two-story home with a stone facade and columns on either side of the front door. Behind the house, the driveway opened into a parking area bordered by a barn and a large garage-style outbuilding. We pulled in between an old blue truck and a newer-looking maroon SUV.

"Do you need a minute?" Con asked. "Maybe grab a coffee somewhere first? Once we step inside, you'll be meeting the parents."

"Oh no, I'm ready," I replied with as much energy as I could muster, although I didn't feel ready at all. I knew I must look exhausted, and I had no idea what state my makeup was in. I popped one of the breath mints I'd tucked into my coat pocket in preparation for this moment.

"We'll come back for the luggage," Eamonn said, gesturing for me to follow.

As stage fright tightened my chest, I reminded myself that I wasn't the main attraction. I could just hide behind Con and blend into the wallpaper. That thought calmed me a bit as I followed the men around the house.

We entered through the back door, passing through a tidy mudroom into a spacious, brightly lit kitchen. Con tried to let me go ahead of him, but I stayed back, knowing it was him they were waiting to see.

A woman who could only be his mother was there first, pulling Con into a tight hug as they muttered softly to each other. A willowy figure in a flowing pantsuit with her long, silvery hair in a loose bun, she had a soft, elegant beauty about her. I could tell she was trying to hold back tears when she finally released him, looking him up and down. Her joy at the sight of him and grief over their long separation showed in her expression as she handed Con off to his father.

Con looked a great deal like the tall, barrel-chested man who gave him a short but strong embrace, then stood back and shook his hand. They exchanged brief words of greeting, and while I sensed some tension there, the love and relief on both their faces overwhelmed it. For a moment, both parents just stared at Con as though they couldn't quite believe he was there, standing in their kitchen.

He came back to me and smiled as he slid his arm around my waist. "This is Neve."

"It's so lovely to meet you!" His mother rushed to give me a hug as well.

"You, too, Mrs. O'Brien," I replied, hugging her back. "Thank you so much for having me!"

"Nonsense," his father said, stepping up and shaking my hand vigorously. "The pleasure's ours. And no 'mister' or 'missus.' She's Imogen, and I'm Jack."

"He means that, about the pleasure being theirs," Eamonn commented. "You're the first girl Con's ever brought home!"

Con rested his hands on my shoulders. "That's right, embarrass me straightaway."

Imogen smiled. "Wait 'til Una gets here on Monday."

Eamonn nodded. "She loves telling the most embarrassing stories about young Cornelius."

"She does," Con agreed, "and you can't believe a word she says, Neve."

"Believe every word," Imogen insisted. "She's bringing her girlfriend too."

"She has a new girlfriend?" Con asked, indignant. "She called me last week, didn't say a word!"

"Not new, actually," Imogen corrected. "They've been together a year."

"Move to America, and everyone stops telling you things," Con grumbled. "Thank God she's sticking with women, at least." Turning to me, he explained, "Una's always had terrible taste in men."

"Ah, leave off moaning about your sister," Jack ordered him.

Imogen scowled at Con. "Yes, no wonder she doesn't confide in you! Yasmine is lovely. We like her very much."

Jack nodded resolutely. "That's right, so don't even think about scaring her off."

"And I'd be extra nice to Una, as well, if you want any of those awful candy bars you like," Imogen added. "She said she'd bring some."

"Black Jack bars?" Con exclaimed in wide-eyed wonder. Thirty years fell off him in an instant.

"And everything else is forgotten." Imogen rolled her eyes. "I've told her they're for dessert only, Cornelius, so don't bother begging for them the second she arrives. She's agreed to keep them hidden until I give her the nod."

"But that's torture!" Con brayed, making everyone smile.

"Fair and just payback for some past sin, no doubt," Jack said, shaking his head. "Partners in crime, the lot of them, Neve. There are still burn marks on the barn door from the fireworks."

"And those were illegal in the eighties!" Eamonn glowed with pride at their transgression.

I turned to Con as my jaw dropped. "I had no idea you were such a troublemaker!"

"Una was behind everything." He held his hands up in surrender. "She'll even admit it. You can ask her when she gets here."

"There you go, blaming your sister again," Imogen scolded. "Your father and I know very well you and Eamonn dragged that poor girl into your schemes."

Eamonn chuckled. "Give it up, big brother. You lost that argument a long time ago."

"That's right," Jack added. "The only thing that saved your arses is that you kept her out of all the fighting."

Fighting? As well as they got along now, it was hard to imagine Con and Eamonn butting heads as kids. But I realized there was more behind Jack's words when Con bristled—almost imperceptibly, but everyone present knew him well enough to pick up on it.

After a brief silence, Jack glanced at his wife and murmured, "Sorry," under his breath. She forced a smile while Eamonn and Con looked at the floor. I wondered what weighty aspect of their past had just been referenced.

But Imogen brushed the topic away, saying, "All right, enough standing around. You two had a long flight. Please, sit down—here or in the front room, wherever you like. I'll make tea."

As the tension in the room eased, the mere mention of sitting down sent another wave of exhaustion crashing over me. I grabbed Con's sleeve as I felt myself start to sway.

He covered my hand with his and scowled. "I think this one may need a lie-down before dinner."

"Oh, that's right," Imogen said, pausing to pat my arm. "Con told us you just had surgery, and with the jet lag…. Well, the guest room is all set up for you if you'd like to take a rest."

"It wasn't really…." *Surgery, or a big deal—just a biopsy*, I started to say, but I decided that might be more detail than they wanted. "That might be good, actually." I smiled weakly. "I'm so sorry. I don't mean to be antisocial."

"Not at all," Jack reassured. "We won't let you miss dinner."

I could sense that while his parents were happy to have me, they would welcome some time alone with their sons. "That would be perfect. Thank you."

Con nodded to Eamonn. "Would you get her things from the car? I'll take her upstairs."

"Sure," Eamonn said, then was out the door before I could object.

Con steered me out into the front entrance hallway and up a staircase to the second level. The house was beautiful, with dark wood floors and decorated in soft blues, greens, and golds. I could barely take in the details, though, because my eyes were already closing.

The guest room was dominated by a large four-poster bed. The mattress called out to me. I collapsed halfway onto it as Con pointed out the attached bathroom and showed me an electrical outlet where I could charge my phone.

"Oh, right," I murmured. "I should call my parents, tell them we got here okay."

"You sleep. I'll call them."

"You're sure?" I asked, kicking off my shoes. It warmed me to know we were already at that stage where he could call my parents on my behalf.

"Of course." Con bent down to place a gentle kiss on my forehead.

I didn't even try to suppress my "besotted schoolgirl" sigh. "Just don't tell my parents that you used to get into fights," I said, trying to broach the subject with a light touch. "It might tarnish the perfect Boy Scout image they have of you."

He didn't take it lightly, however. "I'm the oldest," he said gruffly. "Sometimes I had to take up for Una, but it was usually Eamonn's fault. He's the hothead. I had to come to the rescue whenever he bit off more than he could chew."

"Oh, I see." I knew how seriously Con took his responsibilities toward others, and since he'd come to my rescue before, too, that explanation sounded entirely plausible. That mystery from his past was solved. Still, the topic had put a scowl on his face, so I added, "Well, whether Eamonn's a hothead or not, I think your whole family is lovely."

It worked. He smiled. "Not as lovely as you are

right now, fighting to stay awake just to be gracious. Sleep," he said gently. "I'll come get you for dinner."

"Okay. Thank you. Half an hour before?" I asked, unable to stifle a yawn.

"Half an hour it is."

Several competing emotions battled in his expression. Con still hadn't told me what had kept him away from his home country—and his family—for five years. "Hey," I asked, "how are you doing with all this?"

"Sure, I'm grand." His dismissive tone told me I wasn't going to get anything more out of him at the moment. "You rest. I'll go catch up with my parents a bit."

"We'll talk later, though, right?" I wanted to remind him that whatever might come up, he wasn't on his own.

He smiled again, and through his eyes an impossible amount of affection flowed. "We will. Now stop trying to take care of me and go to sleep. Don't make me say it a third time."

"Or what?" I asked mischievously, but a rush of fatigue got the better of me. I flopped back on the bed, and my eyes shut of their own accord. "Never mind. You win."

"Good girl yourself, obeying doctor's orders," he teased, patting my knee.

"God save me from doctors," I muttered.

The last thing I heard was Con's low chuckle as sleep fell across me like a shadow, pulling me under.

―――――

My head still felt foggy when Con woke me up, and I didn't have the energy to take a shower, so I just freshened up a bit and changed clothes. As I made my way down the stairs, I saw Eamonn and Con standing close together in the alcove by the front door, looking grim and talking in low tones.

"It was terrifying, blood all over the place," I heard Eamonn say before Con spotted me there, frozen on the bottom stair.

"It's all right, Neve." Con motioned for me to join them. "Eamonn's telling me about Ciara."

I stepped closer when Eamonn nodded, a haunted look on his face. "I was just saying, one morning about a month ago, I found Ciara sitting on the floor of the bathroom with the skin on the inside of her forearm mangled. She had scratched herself with her fingernails —nothing sharper, thank God. Still, it was awful, like she was trying to take her skin off." He swallowed hard. "When I found her, her eyes were wide open, but it was like she was in a trance and couldn't see me. I tried to wake her for several minutes before she came to. She swears she has no memory of any of it—not getting out of bed or going into the bathroom, not even of harming herself."

"Janey Mac." Con exhaled the words as a solemn exclamation, then raked a hand through his hair, putting the unruly brown waves into further disarray. "I'm sorry, Eam. That must have been harrowing."

"'Twas a bit, yeah." Eamonn rubbed his face vigorously.

Con placed a hand on his brother's shoulder. "Don't worry. It's a puzzle all right, but we'll get it sorted. I promise."

Eamonn's tension visibly eased. "Thanks. I can't tell you how much I appreciate you coming all this way— both of you." He looked at me and managed a half smile.

"Of course," Con replied gruffly, as though insulted by the suggestion he could have done otherwise.

"I'm just glad we can help," I added to reassure Eamonn that I was all in, as well.

"Right, so." Con clapped Eamonn on the shoulder again and stepped back. "We can talk about this more tomorrow. Ma will skin us if the dinner goes cold."

The atmosphere in the kitchen felt more relaxed than before. I sensed that Con and his family had taken advantage of my jet-lag-induced nap to catch up on some of the overdue family conversations they no doubt needed to have. Judging from their emotions when Con first arrived, their long separation must have been painful for all of them.

Somehow in the previous few hours, Imogen had prepared a gourmet three-course meal. I was grateful for the excuse to eat and drink rather than talk, letting the conversation wash over me. I noticed Con's Irish brogue was more pronounced around his family.

I had a little bit of trouble understanding what they were saying at times, but the others were quick to notice when I looked confused and would clarify things for me. It wasn't the accents that tripped me up, though. It was rapid speech combined with the sprinkling of Irish words and idioms into the conversation. Eamonn taught me how to say "bed" and "head" ("*leaba*" and "*ceann*"), just in case I found myself alone in an Irish-speaking part of the country, got struck by jet lag again, and had to ask for a place to lie down. Con pointed out how unlikely that scenario was, and Imogen agreed, adding that the way Con looked at me, he was unlikely to leave my side the whole time we were in Ireland.

"By the way, Neve, if you need to get away from the boys for a while, we can go shopping in Cork," she offered cheerfully.

"Thanks very much," Con scoffed. "Already trying to steal her away from me?"

"I just might, for a day at least," Imogen countered. "Don't forget, I know how clingy you can be. Remember poor Caroline?"

A rush of heat shot through me, and I pushed it down, chastising myself. *How ridiculous, that the mere mention of another woman from Con's past should make me jealous!* Clearing my throat to ensure my voice sounded perfectly casual, I asked, "Who's Caroline?"

"Ma!" Con threw his hands up. "We were *six*!"

A mixture of amusement, relief, and embarrassment had me biting the inside of my mouth to keep from laughing. Meanwhile, Eamonn and Jack grinned as Imogen leaned over to me and murmured, "They never change, though." Con opened his mouth to object, but before he could get a word out, she stood up and announced, "Time for dessert!"

Jack slapped his knees. "Thank Christ for that!"

Con muttered to himself as he wrapped his arm around my shoulders, and I realized my cheeks already ached from smiling.

CHAPTER 3

NEVE

"Your family is wonderful," I raved as Con lifted my suitcase onto the folding luggage rack he'd set up in my room. "They've been so welcoming."

"That's because they're already dead keen on you." He smiled over his shoulder as he shifted my awkwardly overstuffed bag into place. "No surprises there."

"Please, they hardly know me," I pointed out. "I'm sure they're that nice to everyone. They're such warm people."

"True enough." He came over and sat next to me on the side of the bed. "But there's fake-nice and genuine-nice. With you, they're being genuine." Con reached down and took my hand, tangling his fingers in mine.

I looked down at my hand in his, savoring the sight. "I just wonder why... I mean, it's none of my business...."

He pressed my hand against his chest, drawing my gaze upward. "What is it?"

I shrugged. "It's just that you didn't talk much about them back home. And five years without a visit, that just seems like a long time. If you couldn't afford it, that would be one thing…."

Con dropped my hand onto the bed between us and opened my fingers with his, rubbing the pad of his thumb softly across my palm. "First of all, anything you want to know about me, just ask. The way things are between us now, what's my business is your business."

"Really?" As close as we were, he had always been reticent about certain topics, his family among them. Was he actually giving me an opening to ask *anything*? I stopped short of reciprocating the sentiment, uncertain whether I wanted to commit to answering anything he might ask *me*.

"Yes, really." He leaned forward, his eyes spearing mine with an inquiring look. "That's how I feel about it, anyway."

Dodging his implied question, I gave him a half smile and prompted, "Okay. So…?"

He released my hand and leaned back on the bed. "Well, first of all, you know yourself, we're a bit more used to people emigrating than you are. It's not unusual for Irish families to have someone living abroad."

Over the past couple of years, Con had answered many of my questions about Ireland, filling in gaping holes I hadn't known existed in my knowledge of history. For example, he was the first to teach me the harrowing facts about the brutal social, political, and economic persecution that had historically driven Irish emigration. In the past fifty years, however, he'd explained that more people were coming into the country than leaving. But the year he moved abroad, that trend reversed briefly as many left in the wake of an economic crash. In other words, his family was far from the only one coping with long-distance separation.

"Five years away may seem like a lot," he continued, "but it's not so strange. They didn't come to visit me either, after all." He emphasized his point with a shrug, and I had to stop myself from asking if he'd ever invited them. "Also, before I left, things were difficult, family-wise."

Now we were getting to the real reason.

Con cleared his throat. "First, there was my accident."

I nodded. He had told me about it before. Once, when he was visiting home from college, he was repairing a piece of farm equipment when it collapsed on top of him, causing multiple injuries. His left leg was the most badly affected. He'd had a full knee replacement and had worn a leg brace for support ever since. Con always denied that it caused him any pain, but I knew better. I had often seen him flinch while changing position or grimace when he'd been standing for too long. Just recently, I'd also discovered that he needed to take painkillers on a regular basis.

Still, he'd always told me that he decided early on

not to let the accident stop him from doing what he wanted to in life, although it had put an end to his athletic aspirations. Con had played college rugby, and apparently he was good enough that he'd been scouted by a professional team. But he'd thrived in spite of that loss, finishing his first degree in physiology before pivoting successfully into medicine. Now, Con was a well-respected expert in endocrinology, with a specialty in treating psychiatric patients. That was how we met, working together in the psychiatry department of Capitol Hill General Hospital in Washington, DC, where he'd moved to do his residency.

"It was my fault entirely," he continued. "My father's business is repairing equipment for the local farmers, and I used to help him. That morning, I went off and tried to fix a combine harvester on my own. I knew better than to try to handle it myself, but I was overconfident. Unsurprisingly, it all went sideways."

That was the most Con had ever told me about the accident, and the first time he'd ever told me he held himself responsible. I swallowed hard, waiting for him to say more.

"I stayed here while I recovered. It was hard for my parents to watch me go through that, especially because they blamed themselves. Still do."

"Why?" I almost whispered the word, afraid speaking too loudly would break whatever spell was allowing Con to confide in me.

"It makes no sense, know that first," he said, his

voice rough with frustration. "My father's had depression off and on his whole life. He was going through a bad bout when I was home for that visit. My mother was worried about him. She told me the owner of the combine harvester needed it fixed urgently, but Da hadn't felt well enough to work on it. That's why I gave it a go."

We'd been working together in mental health for two years, and Con had never mentioned his father's depression to me. It must have been a very painful subject for him. I laid my hand atop his as the weight of what he was telling me wended its way through my heart.

"Ma thought it was her fault for telling me about the harvester, and Da blamed himself for being too depressed to work and making me feel like I had to do the job. None of which is the least bit rational, of course. But every moment of my recovery, I could see my pain was raking their souls. I imagine it's hard enough for any parent to watch their child go through something like that, but feeling they were at fault as well? It just added another layer to the pain—for all of us."

"Oh my God." I caressed his arm. "I'm so sorry. I had no idea you went through all that."

Con glanced at me and nodded. "It was bad enough for all involved. I moved out as soon as I was able, finished my first degree, then went on to medical school. But whenever I came home for a visit, I could see the anguish in their eyes when they caught me limping or someone mentioned rugby. I'd moved on, but they simply couldn't. Not while I was still here, anyway—a constant reminder. So when I was offered a residency in the States, I jumped at it. I thought if I put some time and distance between us… well, it would be a relief to be away from them. That's the selfish reason. But I also hoped if I stayed gone long enough, they could let go of the past a bit. Maybe then the sight of me wouldn't make them quite as miserable."

"Oh, Con." He was carrying so much. I encircled his wrist with my hands.

He leaned forward, taking my chin between his thumb and forefinger. As our eyes met, the anguish on his face made me blink back the threat of tears.

"This is why I didn't talk about them much," he explained. "It just… it hurt to be away from them, and it hurt to be with them. But my plan worked, it seems. They're a bit easier around me now." Con gave my jawline a light caress, then dropped his hand and smoothed an imaginary wrinkle from the bedspread.

I was stunned. He had never shared so many personal things with me, and all at once. The moment felt delicate and precious, like a rare flower blooming. Honored by his trust, I searched for the right words. "I didn't sense any guilt or pain in them tonight, just sheer joy at having you back. Maybe some relief, too, I guess."

"Ah, no. That was all you." He shot me a sideways smile. "They're happy I'm home, sure. But they're over the moon about you. They're relieved because I finally found someone. You're proof that I'm not living as a hermit alone in a dungeon somewhere, moaning about my fecking knee and burning origami combine harvesters in effigy."

I smiled at the image. Con was gregarious, extremely well liked, and considered one of the most eligible bachelors in the hospital. "Finding someone" had never been his problem. Plenty of women found *him*, only to be turned away. "How is it that your own family has no idea what a heartbreaker you are?"

"Are you trying to get me to kiss you?" he asked, leaning forward and sliding his hand behind my neck. "Don't think I won't," he murmured in my ear, the warmth of his breath on my skin sending a delicious shudder through me. "I don't care if the whole house hears you moan."

Aghast, I pushed him away. "I do not moan!" I whispered fiercely.

"You do." He pulled away with a glint in his eye. "And I can't get enough of it."

I glared at him, ignoring the heat rising through my body. "I see what you did there, changing the subject."

"I didn't," he objected. "The previous subject had reached a natural endpoint."

As much as I wanted to talk more about his relationship with his family, it was clear he was done for the night. "All right," I said, deciding to be grateful for what he had shared with me. But I didn't want to go back to talking about kissing either, because that might lead to other things that would feel too weird to do in his parents' house. Plus, there was a small possibility that I *did* moan when he kissed me, and I'd die of embarrassment if anyone heard me.

Change of subject it is.

"Well, you *can't* kiss me." I pointed toward an elegant, foot-high porcelain statue sitting on the dresser —the Virgin Mary, wearing light blue robes and looking down at us. "We're being watched."

Although I knew Con wasn't religious, my comment still succeeded in throwing cold water on the hot coals of passion. He glared at the statue. "Yes, here and in every room of the house, you'll find we're being spied on by Jesus, Mary, and any number of saints."

"Well, I think she's beautiful," I said, nodding at the statue.

"I think she's birth control," he replied, and I fell against him, laughing.

We talked for a while longer about the house and the pride his parents took in it. Eventually, I felt my energy starting to flag. Con must have noticed.

"You're fading out. Any other questions for me before bed?"

"Hmm." I mentally scanned the past several hours. "Who's Janey Mac? An ex-girlfriend or something?"

"What?" He looked genuinely perplexed for a moment, then guffawed. "Hah! Janey Mac? It's just an expression. Kind of like saying 'Jesus Christ,' but with more gravitas."

"Ah, okay." I smiled, shaking my head. "I have a lot to learn, so many nuances."

"Don't worry, that's what I'm here for." But all traces

of humor disappeared as Con added, "By the way, Eamonn pulled me aside and invited us to join him when he goes to visit Ciara tomorrow morning. Do you think you'll feel up to it?"

"Yes, of course." Ciara was the reason we'd come, after all, and I knew Con was even more anxious than I was to find out what was wrong, and to help if we could. Her team at the psychiatric hospital was still struggling to diagnose her mysterious illness. As Eamonn had mentioned, she was self-harming, but she insisted she never remembered doing it and desperately wanted to stop. Eamonn seemed to think her ex-boyfriend was somehow to blame, but that man lived in Galway, and Ciara had cut off contact with him some time back. It was an unusual case, that was certain.

Con said that although Eamonn had often turned to him for support in their younger years, ever since Con moved to the States, his brother had never once asked for his help with anything. So when he got the call this time, he knew it was serious. I could tell Con would do anything for his siblings.

"All right, then," he said. "In that case, we should both get some sleep."

My heart sank a little as he stood to leave. "Can I ask one more question?"

"Anything."

I cocked my head to the side. "Deadeye Con?" I asked, recalling the nickname Eamonn had used at the airport.

Con sighed. "Yeah. Nothing too interesting behind that, I'm afraid."

But I couldn't get enough of hearing about his past. "Indulge me."

"Ah, it's just that growing up around here in the countryside, my father loaned Eamonn and me out to neighboring farmers to hunt—nothing exciting, just rats, stoats, and other egg-thieving vermin. I was pretty good with a rifle, or so they tell me. One of the farmers took to calling me Deadeye, and the name stuck. That's all."

"Wow. You've got hidden skills, Deadeye!"

"I'll ask that you never call me that at work." Con winked. "It doesn't quite inspire images of healing. Any other burning questions before I put you to bed?"

Smiling, I stood up as well. "So many. But they can wait."

Con stepped forward and wrapped his arms around me, pulling me into a close embrace. I clasped my fingers around the back of his neck, burying my head in his chest and inhaling the intoxicating scent of him.

"Thanks for coming all this way," he murmured. My whole body softened like warm wax as he pressed his lips to the top of my head. "I know it was a big ask for a first date."

"Are you kidding? Best first date ever, so far. Thank *you* for bringing me!"

There was a smile in his voice as he said, "Goodnight, love."

My very bones seemed to melt. "Goodnight."

Con released me and disappeared out the door with one last look back. I felt the tug of longing—the desire to follow him to his room or insist he stay in mine. But I had good guest manners, dammit, and if his family did have a positive first impression of me as he'd said, I was going to do everything I could to avoid ruining it.

CHAPTER 4

CON

He felt strange. There was no other word for it. Not all bad, not all good. Just strange. Seeing his family again, being home—it brought back a lot of memories, and they ran the gamut from happy to hellish.

By rights, Con should have been wiped out, but he was too wired to sleep. After everyone else was in bed, he went to the study and poured himself a whiskey. The whole house was haunted with memories from the past, and this room was no exception. His father practically lived in the study when he was depressed, sleeping on the sofa—the same sofa Con had occupied those first weeks when he was home recovering from the accident, unable to climb stairs. He stared at that piece of furniture from a wingback chair across the room. Judging from the perfectly neat state of the decorative pillows and the folded blanket lying across the back, it appeared the sofa hadn't been used recently. He hoped that was a good sign of his father's mental health.

Being around the family was like reopening old wounds and soothing a deep ache all at once. Neve was right; there was a lot of love between them. When they'd first arrived at the house, his parents had embraced him so tightly, it flooded him with guilt. Five years apart may have been too long after all. His family had at least pretended to accept the explanation that the only reason he left Ireland was for the residency, and that he stayed away so long because he was building his career and couldn't get away from work.

But it had been hard for him to keep in touch with them like he had with Eamonn and Una. His parents only had a landline and an ancient computer with no internet that they used to do the accounts. They weren't ones to chat on the phone either, viewing telephones as utilitarian tools to communicate only what was necessary—especially on overseas calls, which they insisted were "too expensive" despite Con's reassurances to the contrary.

When Neve had first gone upstairs to rest, Con was glad of Eamonn's presence to lighten the mood as he oiled the rusty joints of his relationship with their parents. They didn't talk about anything too serious, just caught each other up on how they were, with his family sharing news about people they knew in common. Fortunately, his parents were both in good physical health, and his father seemed in high enough spirits. Con was surprised to see how much five years had aged them, though, and he wondered if they thought the same about him. Eamonn still appeared youthful, but the carefree look was gone from his eyes —no doubt due to concerns about Ciara.

Being back with his parents, Con could see his time away had done what he'd hoped: built a carapace over their mutual wounds. That pain was well tucked away now, not raw and forever at risk of breaking through to the surface. He also discovered, though, that the cost of that relief was losing the ease of intimacy they used to share. Now they held each other a bit at arm's length. It grieved him, but if that was the price, he was willing to pay it.

His parents seemed more at ease after their initial conversation, as though some unspoken question had been settled in their minds. Una's arrival Monday would brighten things up further. In truth, Con was delighted his sister was coming. Having everyone there at once—even with some awkwardness—would be a precious thing, and he'd savor every moment. It might be some time before that happened again.

The house looked well, he was glad to see. That they were keeping the place up was another good sign of his parents' health. Neve appeared quite taken with it, which pleased him. Some small part of him had harbored a worry that coming from a city like Washington, DC, she might find rural Ireland a bit small and unexciting.

So far, though, Neve seemed happy to be there. Her mood was cheerful, if a bit subdued by exhaustion. Still, he could tell his whole family liked her immediately. Of course, how could they not? She was an angel, and he loved watching her interact with the other people closest to his heart. Neve's innate warmth, kindness, and complete lack of artifice won them all over, and she didn't have to do a thing but be herself—even her nervous, tired self.

It was a treat for him to sit back and observe while she talked to the others. He never tired of looking at her, and whenever she glanced his way, as though to refresh their connection, it made him feel ten feet tall. If she was turning to him for reassurance, it meant she needed him, counted on him. Neve was leaning on him, and he would never let her fall.

That she'd ended up in his life in the first place, actually cared for him, and agreed to come to Ireland was all proof either of his extreme luck or the existence of the divine. What he'd done to deserve her, he didn't know, but he was grabbing hold with both hands. After all, luck could run out, and his years in medicine had taught him that God was a capricious bastard. He had watched innocents suffer and die while monsters recovered, and not one priest had been able to give him a satisfactory explanation.

Con was mindful, though, that in spite of Neve's enthusiasm for the trip, her panic disorder could be triggered at any time. The last few weeks—months, even—had been quite a trial for her. She'd already suffered an attack of nerves going through Customs. Now, on her first trip outside North America, she was meeting his family while adjusting to the romantic turn their relationship had taken. Neve had some medication to take if it got bad, but he knew she preferred to use breathing and cognitive techniques to calm herself. He'd have to keep a close eye on her, see to it she wasn't put under too much stress so she didn't start to spiral.

He stared down into the amber liquid in his glass, gave it a swirl, and downed the last of it. He shouldn't have been drinking anything, not after the opioid pain meds he'd taken. But he knew there was no way he would get through a day of air travel without them. Even with the meds, everything ached, and pain shot up from his knee through his hip and back each time he moved. One more pill before bed to help him sleep, and then he'd stop taking the heavy-duty painkillers and go back to his usual anti-inflammatories. Normally, he didn't like the way opiates made him feel, drowsy and a bit foggy headed—he liked to keep his wits about him —but tonight, it would be a blessing. He needed sleep. Tomorrow would be an important day, trying to figure out what was going on with Ciara.

It was after five in Washington. He felt the urge to pull out his mobile and check his work emails again, but he fought the temptation. The hospital would call if they needed him, but he doubted they would. His colleague in the endocrinology department, Faraz, was top of the tree, someone he could trust to take care of his patients while he was away. In truth, if he didn't have Faraz there, Con would never have left.

"But if I fell off a cliff, they'd carry on without me," he muttered. It comforted him to remember that he wasn't indispensable—not at Capitol Hill General, that was. No one could fill in for him as Eamonn's brother. Ireland was where he was most needed at the moment, but he was damn glad Neve was there with him. He knew she could help with Ciara, of course, but selfishly, he'd also wanted her there for his sake. Their relationship had just recently transformed into something more than friendship, and he didn't want to risk losing that momentum by being separated for weeks.

However, he wasn't going to be any good to Neve, Eamonn, or anyone else if he didn't get some rest.

Because he knew no one was watching, Con didn't try to conceal his limp or his grimaces of pain as he slowly climbed the stairs to bed.

———

It was a bright morning, but the swish of the tires told of recent rain as Eamonn drove them to the psychiatric hospital where Ciara was being treated. They traveled toward Fermoy along a route that had been improved since Con was last home. Although still curvy and hilly, the road was wider and the surface smoother than he remembered.

Neve had insisted on taking the back seat again, and

he couldn't help smiling as he stole glances back at her. She was listening intently and participating in the conversation but looking out the window the whole time, her eyes glued to the landscape. Whenever they came up over a rise or the hedgerows broke to give her a broader view of their surroundings, he could hear her sigh with delight at her first real glimpses of the North Cork countryside. He was glad they were there in September, one of the top months of the year in terms of weather. Con wanted her to have the best possible experience of Ireland, even if it wasn't primarily a pleasure trip.

Eamonn filled them in more on Ciara's situation as they drove. While her current problems had started about a month ago, he believed their roots went further back. After completing university, Ciara took a job in marketing for the Wicked Games Corporation, an American video game company with an office in Galway. There she met Max, their head designer, and eventually they started dating.

Ciara said she'd made it clear from the beginning that at twenty-two years of age, she wasn't looking for anything serious. But Max was older by a decade, and as time went on, he started pushing for more—to move in together, for example. Then her mother was diagnosed with breast cancer. She decided to move home to Cork and help care for her mother. Since it had become clear that she and Max weren't on the same page, she took that opportunity to break up with him before their relationship went any further.

Ciara didn't like to talk about her relationship with Max, so Eamonn didn't know many more details. But she had told him that Max had a lot of trouble letting her go. For a while after they broke up, he constantly called and texted her, trying to convince her they should get back together. Finally, he seemed to take the hint and stopped contacting her shortly before Ciara started dating Eamonn. Later, however, when Max heard about their engagement, he started up again, this time sending aggressive emails and texts and stalking her on social media. Whenever Ciara told him to leave her alone and blocked him, Max would use a different phone or new account.

"She rarely told me exactly what he'd said, but hearing from him made her edgy and nervous," Eamonn explained, visibly tensing. "I could tell he frightened her. She started losing sleep. Sometimes she even broke out in hives. The doctor said it was due to stress. I finally talked her into giving me Max's number. I left him a few sternly worded messages and threatened to call the gardaí. That's when he finally stopped for good."

"Christ," Con exclaimed. "You never said."

"Well, I thought it was dealt with," Eamonn replied. "Ciara hasn't heard any more from him since then."

But shortly after the harassment stopped, Eamonn awoke to find Ciara in the bathroom, screaming in her sleep with her arm bloodied. He rushed her to a nearby clinic for emergency evaluation. Fortunately, in spite of how bad her injuries appeared, all the wounds were superficial. At first, the fact that Ciara had no mental health history and no recollection of harming herself led the doctor to suspect she fell and hit her head on the bathtub, with a possible concussion or seizure activity. That still didn't explain the scratching, but they thought she also could be sleep walking or have another sleep disorder.

"That's around the time when I first called you, Con," Eamonn said.

"Right." Con remembered the call vividly, when Eamonn had asked if he would be willing to consult with Ciara's medical team on her case.

Over the next couple of weeks, Eamonn took Ciara back and forth to the hospital in Cork for a series of tests. Her doctors investigated various possible causes, including the worst-case scenario that a tumor was putting pressure on her brain. But then Eamonn awoke to the sound of Ciara screaming again. This time, she was slumped over the kitchen table with more wounds on her arm, reopening the same wounds that had just begun to scab over. Again, she had no memory of what happened, but she was holding a bloodied cheese grater.

"All those months when Max was bothering her and she had trouble sleeping, she said it was because she had recurring nightmares," Eamonn said. "At night, she'd thrash about, making noises—screaming but with her mouth closed. It was creepy as hell."

"What were the nightmares about?" Neve asked.

"I wish I knew. I suspected they were about Max,

but when I'd wake her up, she never wanted to talk about them. As terrified as she looked, I decided not to push her. Maybe I should have."

Con heard anguished self-reproach in his brother's voice. "Why do you say that?"

"Because the second time I found her with her arm cut up, she said she'd been having the same nightmare again. I asked her outright if it was about Max, and she froze up—didn't say anything, just started crying. For me, that confirmed it. All of this has something to do with that arsewipe." Eamonn blew out a hard breath. "I haven't asked her about the nightmare again for fear of making things worse. But if I had pushed her to tell me about it the first time…. I don't know. Maybe all of this could have been prevented."

"You can't blame yourself," Con said. "If the solution were as simple as getting her to talk to you about it, she wouldn't be in hospital, baffling a team of experts."

"Maybe." Eamonn pounded the heel of his hand on the steering wheel. "I just can't help thinking she'd get better if only that bastard would feck off back where he came from!"

"Where's that?" Con asked.

"Up his own arse in America," he spat. "No offense, Neve."

"None taken," Neve graciously replied.

"Ciara said he grew up in some weird commune, a free love cult or something."

Con frowned. "Those arrangements always work

much more to the advantage of the men involved than the women, from what I understand."

"That would fit his character, all right."

Eamonn explained that, eventually, they got the results from Ciara's medical tests, and all came back negative. They were relieved to hear nothing was wrong with her physically, but her doctors concluded that unless she had some sort of rare sleep disorder they had yet to diagnose, her problem must be purely psychiatric in nature. It was recommended that Ciara go to Laoch Garr, a nearby psychiatric hospital, for a mental health evaluation.

"I've not heard of Laoch Garr," Con said. "Is it new?"

Eamonn nodded. "Built after you left. It's a private facility, supposed to be cutting edge. They recommended admission for observation, and she's been there for over a week now. They're looking at a few different diagnoses."

"Any idea which ones?" Con asked.

"Let's see… they mentioned depression, a fugue state, something about a 'borderline,' and some other term I always get wrong, but it means multiple personalities." Eamonn added that some members of the team didn't believe Ciara when she said she couldn't remember harming herself. They thought she made the whole thing up to get attention or manipulate people somehow. "But that's complete bollocks!" Eamonn's knuckles turned white as he gripped the steering wheel.

"I believe her 100 percent. She would never.... Ciara hasn't got a duplicitous bone in her body."

"Understood." Con had never met the girl, but he was willing to accept Eamonn's assessment. His brother had been with Ciara for nearly two years, and he'd always been a strong judge of character. If she were manipulative, Eamonn would have picked up on it by now.

Of course, Con also knew well that anxiety was powerful and could do strange things to people. If Ciara was fearful of her ex, it could be impacting her perceptions, including her memory. He didn't know how that might connect to the self-harming, but that was really Neve's department. He was more grateful than ever to have her along. After all, she dealt with these types of serious mental health issues on a regular basis back at Capitol Hill General, and he knew from experience that he could rely upon her insights.

Just before they reached Fermoy town, Eamonn turned down a long, straight driveway lined with birch trees. At the end was a large block of a three-story building with a small car park near the front. The modern-looking structure was surrounded by an elaborate garden with a small pool and fountain at the foot of semicircular steps leading up to the main entrance.

Eamonn pulled into the car park. When his hands fell from the steering wheel, he slumped back against the seat.

Con laid his hand on his brother's arm. "We'll figure this out."

Eamonn nodded. "Thanks." He turned back and looked at Neve. "Thank you both. It just... it means a lot to me that you're here—to both of us."

Con clapped Eamonn on the shoulder. "Jaysus, of course!" It stung him to hear his brother express such gratitude, as though Con's help couldn't be taken for granted. What disturbed him even more was wondering how many times during his years away Eamonn or other family members might have needed his help but didn't want to trouble him by asking.

"I was honored to be invited," Neve said gently from the back seat. "I'm looking forward to meeting Ciara."

That at least brought a hint of a smile to Eamonn's face. Con's heart swelled. Neve was deeply kind, and she always knew just what to say to people.

"Right, so," Con said. "Anything else we should know before we go in?"

"Only that your reputation precedes you," Eamonn said, smiling as their shoes crunched on the gravel drive. "You know one of Ciara's doctors. He was on your rugby team at university, and like everyone else you played with, he's damned terrified of you."

Thankfully, they had reached the building. "You're one to talk, Flamin' Eamonn," Con declared, gesturing for his brother to climb the steps. "That was his moniker back when he was into the rally car racing scene," he explained to Neve, "putting the fear of God in everyone and trying his best to murder perfectly innocent vehicles."

"Innocent?" Eamonn objected as they climbed the steps. "Those cars tried to murder *me*!"

At least Neve was smiling. Once they were done at the hospital, though, Con would have a word with his little brother about how not *every* bit of information about his past needed to be shared with his new girlfriend.

CHAPTER 5

NEVE

We walked through the main entrance and signed in at the front desk. The foyer was a large, round space with double doors to the left and right of us and two elevators opposite where we stood. The receptionist placed a call to a Dr. Boyle, announcing that Eamonn O'Brien "and guests" had arrived.

"That's your old teammate," Eamonn told Con.

"Of course! John Boyle. I remember him well. He was in the class behind me—"

Before Con could finish, the door to our left swung open, and a large man in a white coat swept into the room, smiling broadly. He walked toward us but then pulled back in mock fear when he saw Con. "Eamonn, when you said you were bringing Tarbh on your next visit, I thought it was just an empty threat!"

Then Dr. Boyle and Con both stepped forward, shook hands, and clapped each other on the back.

"Boyle," Con exclaimed, "you haven't changed a day—except for the white coat. That's new!"

"Well, after all the beatings I took from you on the pitch, I was inspired to take up a healing profession," Dr. Boyle said wryly.

Eamonn grinned. "My brother was heavy into the brutality then, was he?"

"Well, I wouldn't say *that*," Dr. Boyle replied, "but he dabbled." He and Eamonn laughed as Con shook his head.

"Will you two shut it before Neve turns tail and runs away from me?" Con stepped to one side, presenting me. "John Boyle, Neve Keane."

"Miss Keane, it's a pleasure," Dr. Boyle said, shaking my hand. "Eamonn told us you were coming. You're very welcome."

"Thank you." In my most anxious moments, I'd feared I might be viewed by Ciara's treatment team as an interloper—or worse, as the "ugly American" coming in and thinking she knew better than everyone else. It was a relief to get such a warm welcome—and delightful to learn yet another one of Con's nicknames. "So what does 'tah-ruv' mean?"

"Ah, Tarbh was Con's rugby name," Dr. Boyle explained. "It means 'bull' in Irish."

"And it stuck because he's so stubborn and bull-headed," Eamonn added.

"Would you stop already!" Con threw his hands up in surrender as everyone else grinned.

Given the purpose of our visit, though, the jovial

mood was fleeting. Eamonn drew a hand across his chin. "How is she today?"

The weight of worry strained his voice. Each incident of self-injury had occurred at night, while Ciara was sleeping. For Eamonn, mornings probably contained an element of dread.

"I'm on my way to find out now," Dr. Boyle said, instantly somber. "Follow me."

He led us through the doors on our right, which opened into a long, brightly lit hallway lined with smaller doors. As soon as we entered, we heard a commotion at the other end and saw a few people scrambling about. We matched Dr. Boyle's quickening pace.

"Eamonn!" The tortured cry came from the end of the hall, and Con's brother broke into a run.

As we drew closer, we saw a slight, dark-haired woman in leggings and a sweatshirt trying to break free from three women in brightly colored scrubs who were holding her in place.

"There's no need for that, now," one of the women pleaded. "We're only trying to help you."

When Eamonn reached them, the women in scrubs —nurses, I guessed—released the woman, who must be Ciara. She flew into Eamonn's arms, sobbing. He held her tightly and pressed his lips to her temple, murmuring softly.

The nurses turned to Dr. Boyle, shrugging and tossing up their hands.

"What's this, then?" Dr. Boyle asked as we reached the group.

Wincing, the nurse who'd spoken made a subtle slashing motion with her fingers and inclined her head in Ciara's direction. I assumed that meant there had been another incident of self-harm. Dr. Boyle had a brief exchange with her in murmured tones.

"They want to lock me in a room and put me in handcuffs," Ciara cried.

"You misunderstand," a nurse with short red hair insisted. She shot Dr. Boyle a meaningful glance I understood well, having seen it many times on our own psychiatric unit. It meant, *We need to take this conversation out of the hallway and into a private space.*

Dr. Boyle nodded. "Ciara, dear, let's find a place for you to sit down. Phoebe, is Therapy Room 2 available?"

"Yes, Dr. Boyle, it's free," the redheaded nurse said.

"Grand. Ciara, Eamonn, shall we?"

"Sweetie," Eamonn murmured, "this is my brother, Con, and his girlfriend, Neve, who I told you about. Is it all right if they come in with us?"

Ciara lifted her head and regarded us with red-rimmed eyes. "Hello," she said softly. "It's lovely to meet you. I'm sorry I'm so...." Her sleeve slid up, revealing fresh bandages on the inside of her left forearm. Quickly, she pulled it back down, covering them.

"No need to apologize, my goodness," Con said gently. "It's wonderful to meet you too. We're the ones who are sorry for barging in at a difficult moment. We're happy to wait out here if you like."

"No." Ciara pulled away from Eamonn's embrace, straightening up. In spite of her distress in the moment, she had an air of quiet dignity about her. "Eamonn told me you were coming to help." She turned to Dr. Boyle. "Is it okay if they join us?"

"Of course, if that's what you'd like," he replied.

"I'll bring tea," another nurse said, stepping away.

"Thank you, Jenny."

Dr. Boyle led Ciara, Eamonn, Con, Phoebe, and me into a room where a few armchairs and two couches sat around a large coffee table. It looked like the type of space that might be used for running groups or family meetings. The rain must have stopped suddenly, because sunlight made the sheer ivory curtains glow, filling the room with warmth.

Ciara curled up against Eamonn on one of the couches. Con and I sat on the other, keeping a professional distance between us, and Dr. Boyle and Phoebe took the chairs.

"All right," Dr. Boyle said in a soothing voice, his eyes on Ciara. "Everyone, take a moment to relax. Tea will be here shortly. Then we can talk."

Ciara nodded, clinging to Eamonn. She calmed as he murmured softly to her and stroked her back.

A few minutes later, a man in blue scrubs knocked on the door. He placed on the table a tray with a teapot, cups and saucers, milk, sugar, and a plate of cookies.

Con leaned over to me, pointing at the plate, and murmured, "*Those* are biscuits."

"I *see*," I whispered back, then bit my lip to keep

from smiling. Back home, Con frequently reminded me that what we referred to as "cookies" were really "biscuits," and substandard ones at that. The brief, light moment felt intimate. It grounded me to be reminded that no matter where on the planet we were or what was going on, we were still "us."

Once everyone had a cup of tea in hand, Dr. Boyle spoke, his tone soft and conversational. "So, Ciara. A bit of a rough morning."

Ciara leaned back and crossed her arms as though to protect herself, then winced in pain and quickly uncrossed them. She lay her left arm down, bandaged side up. "Yes. I had another... *episode* overnight."

"I see." Dr. Boyle stroked his jaw. "Same as the rest?"

Ciara inclined her head toward Con and me and gave Eamonn a questioning look.

"I filled them in," he said.

Looking relieved, she nodded. "The nurse said she heard me screaming. I was sitting on the floor of my room, and she woke me. More scratches in the same spot again. Like always, I don't remember doing it."

"Do you remember having a nightmare?" At Dr. Boyle's question, everyone leaned slightly forward. The tension in the room ticked up a notch.

But Ciara didn't answer. She just squirmed uncomfortably. "Please, Dr. Boyle, I don't know why this keeps happening. I only want it to stop."

Eamonn tightened his arm around her shoulders, and Phoebe shot Dr. Boyle a meaningful look.

"We're going to get to the bottom of this, Ciara, don't worry," Dr. Boyle reassured. "But right now, we have to deal with what's in front of us. One step at a time, all right? I'm told you've had your wound dressed. Are you in any discomfort right now?"

"A little." She looked down at her hands. "Not too bad. Jenny gave me a tablet."

"All right, then." Dr. Boyle nodded. "I'll be meeting with the team shortly to discuss what happened. We'll update your treatment plan. Then I'll come back to you."

Eamonn jumped in. "I'd like Con and Neve to join that meeting, if that's all right."

"If that's what Ciara would like," Dr. Boyle said.

Ciara turned to us. "Would you mind?"

"Not at all," Con said. "Like you said, we're here to help."

"Thank you." She grasped Eamonn's hand.

"Grand, that's settled," Dr. Boyle said. "Ciara, is there anything you'd like me to raise with the team?"

"Please," she said softly. "This morning, the nurses said they were going to put me into an isolation room overnight, one with no windows and the door that locks from the outside."

"We only suggested that it might be a possible next step," Phoebe clarified.

"But I'd have to wear a paper gown," Ciara objected, "and there's a video camera in there!"

"It sounds strange, I know," Dr. Boyle said, "but it *would* be easier for us to monitor you in that room and ensure you don't harm yourself again. We need to give that arm a chance to heal properly."

"I know." Her face twisted in pain. "But if I could remember what happened, you wouldn't have to… you know."

"And it's very upsetting, I know, not being able to remember. It would be just as upsetting to any of us, were we in your shoes. That's why we're investigating every possibility. But if you agree to sleep in the isolation room, it might get us one step closer to figuring out what's going on."

Ciara shuddered. "I just hate the idea of being locked in."

"But you could get out anytime you like," Dr. Boyle reassured her. "There's a call button on the wall. I'll make sure the night staff know to respond immediately if you push it and not to make you wait a moment longer than necessary. You'll have support all through the night, whenever you need it."

"Oh." Her expression softened a bit. "But they said there are some kind of handcuffs too?"

"Safety mittens," Phoebe clarified.

"Ah, right." Dr. Boyle smiled gently. "Those aren't the same as handcuffs, Ciara. You've seen the mittens they put on infants to stop them scratching themselves accidentally? It's something similar. They can be awkward at first, I'll admit. Think of it this way: whatever is happening to you when you have these nightmares, wearing the mittens will protect you from harming yourself."

"Oh, okay. I get it." She tugged at a loose thread on the hem of her sweatshirt. "I'm sorry, Dr. Boyle, Phoebe. I just... I guess I was upset about the new injury, and when you talked about locking me up, it made me think you believe I've really gone *mad* or something."

"Ah, sure," Eamonn scoffed. "No one thinks you're mad, sweetie, and no one's locking you up. If you're willing to give this isolation room and mittens thing a go, grand, but if not, that's all right too. Right, Dr. Boyle?"

"Of course," he replied. "It's up to you, Ciara."

She sighed. "I guess I could try it, if you think it would help."

"It very well may. I appreciate your willingness," Dr. Boyle said. "I'll talk it over with the team, and we'll see what everyone thinks is best." He put down his teacup and looked at Phoebe. "Can we give them the room for a while?"

"Yes. It's not needed for another half hour."

"Good." He and Phoebe stood to leave. "You're all welcome to stay and have a chat, then. If you need more tea and biscuits, just pop your head out the door."

Con and I stood and shook Dr. Boyle's hand.

"Thanks, John," Con said.

"Of course."

Phoebe and Dr. Boyle left the room as Con and I sat down again.

There was a bit of an awkward silence. At least the food and drink gave us something to focus on. I spent the lull in conversation marveling at the masterful way in which Dr. Boyle had managed to not only de-escalate what could easily have turned into a full-blown crisis but also brought Ciara around to agreeing to try the isolation room. Even the tea and biscuits had played a role, creating a moment of normalcy, or perhaps serving as a calming and humanizing ritual. It would be nice if our team could incorporate something like that back at Capitol Hill General. I made a mental note to absorb as many useful ideas as I could while I was at Laoch Garr.

Eamonn looked at Ciara with a mixture of concern and adoration as he stroked her hair. She smiled up at him, then turned to Con and me. "It really is a pleasure to meet you both. Thanks so much for coming. I can't believe Eamonn asked you—"

"Nonsense!" Con cut her off, trying to stop her from feeling any more self-conscious. "I'd never have forgiven him if he hadn't. We're going to be family. If you're having a rough time, there's nowhere else for me to be but right here." His words were filled with the kind of authenticity that couldn't be questioned.

Visibly touched, Ciara added, "Still, Neve didn't have to come...."

"Oh, but she did," Con said, taking my hand in his. "I kidnapped her at gunpoint."

We all smiled as some of the awkwardness melted away.

"I'm happy to be here," I said to Ciara. "It's lovely to meet you and Eamonn both. Anything I can do to help." Unsure what else to say on that subject, I added, "Congratulations on your engagement, by the way!"

"Thank you!" they said simultaneously, exchanging cheerful looks.

We drank more tea and engaged in light conversation about the wedding, which they were planning for New Year's Eve. Ciara brightened a bit. No doubt it helped her mood to focus on the joyful event and her future outside Laoch Garr. But after a short while, an alarm blared in the hallway for several long seconds before it was silenced. It startled us, reminding us of where we were, and why.

Con cleared his throat. "Ciara, Neve and I want to do everything we can to help figure out what's been going on so you can get out of here and back to planning that wedding."

She looked down at her hands, but her voice was clear. "I would love that. I really appreciate it."

Con continued, "It would be helpful for us to hear in your own words what's been happening."

She glanced up at Eamonn, who squeezed her hand and nodded. "Okay. Just promise not to think I'm crazy."

"Don't worry," I said with a smile. "For what it's worth, I have a good bit of experience with that, myself —worrying about sounding crazy."

Ciara half-smiled back. "I'm glad it's not just me." She jumped when there was a knock on the door.

A nurse cracked it open and said, "Sorry to disturb, but we'll need the room here in a few minutes."

"No problem," Eamonn replied.

We all stood and put our teacups back on the tray.

"I think John is about to pull us away to the team meeting," Con said, "unless, Neve, you and Ciara would like to take the opportunity to talk some more?"

"Only if you feel like it," I told her.

Eamonn leaned down close to Ciara and murmured, "She's a psychotherapist."

"I remember, you told me." She smiled at me. "We could go to my room. There's a place to sit, and it's private. No roommate."

"Perfect." I gave Con a grateful look. He knew me so well. While I would have found the team meeting interesting, what I really wanted was to talk to Ciara alone.

In response to some sort of unspoken brotherly communication between them, Eamonn volunteered, "While you two get acquainted, I can pop into Fermoy and get us some of those fancy sandwiches from the coffee shop." He hugged Ciara to him. "If you want, that is."

"Ah, those are so good!" She brightened a bit more. "That would be great. Thanks, Eam."

"No bother." He kissed her hand.

The nurse knocked again, and we filed out. Dr. Boyle was at the far end of the corridor with a small group of people wearing white coats. He waved us over.

"See you soon, girls," Eamonn said.

Con leaned close to me and murmured, "You'll be all right?"

"We'll be *grand*," I said, borrowing one of his most-used expressions.

"Christ, she's gone native," he said with a wink. "Look after her, Ciara?"

"Of course." She appeared pleased to be taking on the role of hostess for a moment instead of patient. "My room's this way."

The men went in one direction, and I followed Ciara in the other. I already felt a kinship with her, not to mention a strong dose of sympathy. I hoped our time together might yield some clues that could help alleviate her suffering.

CHAPTER 6

NEVE

Ciara's room had a large window that looked out over the back garden, with light green curtains and a matching duvet on the bed. There was a desk and chair, a closet, and a door to an attached bathroom, which she shared with her neighbor. On the desk was a notebook and pen. Fluorescent lights shone overhead, but a stained glass-style covering softened their hue. The clinic had gone to some effort to make the rooms as comfortable and homey as possible.

Ciara sat on the edge of the bed and glanced around the room. "Well, this is it. Home sweet home."

"Only for now. You have a nice view." I smiled and nodded at the window as I took a seat in the chair. "Ciara, can I just say I'm so sorry for everything you've been going through?"

She blinked back tears. "Honestly, I worry I really

have gone mad. What if I never get out of here? Eamonn doesn't deserve this."

I rested my hand on her wrist. "First, it's obvious Eamonn is madly in love with you. Second, you *will* be getting out of here."

"How do you know that?"

"Because I know what illnesses look like that require permanent confinement, and whatever you're dealing with, it isn't one of them." Call it instinct, or experience, or a combination of the two, but I felt confident in saying that much. Besides, I knew in that moment it was important to lower her anxiety level, especially when it came to worries about things that might never come to pass.

"Well, that's a relief to hear. Eamonn told me you're a therapist in the same hospital where Con works, right?"

"Yes."

"I guess you'd know better than I would, then." Her shoulders dropped slightly. "It's just frightening to me that no one seems to know what's going on."

"I can certainly understand that." And I did, having a bit of personal experience myself with health issues that were difficult to diagnose. But while I wasn't Ciara's therapist, I wasn't just there for a chat either. It was time to try to find a way around her fears and get to the heart of things. I tried to keep my voice calm and even while also projecting the genuine sympathy I felt. "Can you tell me a little bit about what's been happening?"

She looked down and began to tug on the thread of her sweatshirt again. "Eamonn filled you in, didn't he?"

"A bit, but I'd rather hear it from you, if that's okay."

She met my gaze, biting her lip as though she was trying to decide. After a few moments, she began. "Well, the short version is it's been brutal. It started when Eamonn and I got engaged—no, wait. It really started with me dating Max, my ex." Ciara squeezed her eyes shut, like she was either trying to block out a thought or muster her courage. "I'm a graphic artist. My first job was working in marketing for Wicked Games, a company in Galway that develops video games. I got to be close friends with my supervisor, Deirdre. She was dating one of the conceptual artists, Sean, and he was friends with Max, the head game designer. Max had moved to Ireland from the US to help open the Galway studio."

I hoped the fact that her ex was an American might give me a slight edge in understanding him. "What was he like?"

"I guess you could say he was charming." She looked at the floor as she spoke. "Confident, too—kind of take-charge. I liked that about him at first. The work environment was very pressurized, and when I found it stressful, Max took a lot of things off my shoulders. He decided what we'd do and when, made the arrangements, did the driving—that kind of thing. It was also interesting just getting to know him, seeing the world through different eyes. He grew up on a commune in Oregon, so he had a unique perspective on things."

"A commune? That's an unusual upbringing."

"'Unusual' is one word for it," she said with an eye roll. "It was a 'back to nature,' 'free love' kind of group. His parents founded it. They lived in the wilderness and were into self-sufficiency. But Max said his father made members give him all their money and everything they owned before they could join. Those resources were meant to support the community, but instead, Max's father took most of it for himself and invested it. While Max's family grew wealthy and could afford anything they needed, his father made the other members live in poverty and kept them entirely dependent on the commune." Ciara looked down at her hands. "Max told me it all started to fall apart when one of the members needed an expensive medical treatment. His father refused to pay for it, claiming the commune couldn't afford it. Some other members investigated and found out how rich Max's father had become. The group went after him legally, but before he could be arrested for fraud, Max's father killed his mother, then himself."

"Oh, how awful!" I vaguely remembered hearing about the case, which made the news at the time.

"Max was seventeen when it happened. He had an uncle in the Navy who took him in and helped him establish himself."

"Wow, what a way to start out in life."

"Yeah. I felt sorry for him, but I also had a lot of

respect for the fact that he was able to overcome that tragedy and make something of himself. There were lots of things I liked about him, honestly, and we had fun together. But he was always pushing. He wanted more than I did."

"Like what?"

"To begin with, after just a few months, he wanted to move in together," she said. "I was only twenty-three then, and it was my first time having my own apartment. I didn't want to give up that independence so quickly. So we each kept our own places, but he was always either dropping by mine or pressuring me to come to his. When he started talking about getting engaged, I realized he felt much more for me than I did for him. Don't get me wrong. I did care about him, but I never felt that kind of connection with him, where you just know you want to spend the rest of your life with someone." She peered over at me. "Do you know the kind I mean?"

I nodded. I *did* know. I'd known ever since I met Con two years ago. But it wasn't until I'd broken up with my ex and was single again that I'd finally been able to admit that to myself. It was still early in our romance, though, so I had no idea if Con felt the same way.

"With Eamonn, that connection was there right from the beginning," Ciara continued. "It was immediate. The energy between us just sang." For a fleeting moment, her demeanor changed, all the tension flowing away. "I've never told Eamonn this, but within a month of meeting him, I was looking at diamond rings online. The amazing thing was that he felt the same for me. We were on the same wavelength." Then her shoulders dropped. "Max started talking about engagement around the same time my mother was diagnosed with breast cancer. That's when I put in my month's notice so I could move back to Cork and take care of her. I ended things with Max then, too, and explained I just didn't feel the same way he did. We'd only been dating—casually, I thought—for less than two years, so I really didn't think he'd take it as hard as he did."

As her voice lowered to a whisper, my arms broke out in goose bumps.

"In what way did he take it hard?"

"It was strange." Ciara shook her head. "When I first broke up with him, he remained completely calm, didn't react at all. It surprised me. I thought maybe I had overestimated his feelings for me. But the next day, he acted like nothing had changed, like there had been no breakup at all. He came over to my desk at work, talking about making plans for dinner. He even said… suggestive things to me, like we were still…." She shuddered. "I had to have the breakup conversation with him three more times before he took me seriously."

Although I feared I already knew the answer, I asked, "What happened when it finally sank in?"

"He started calling all the time, sending emails and texts, showing up at my flat unannounced," she said, her voice lowering to a near-whisper. "He didn't seem hurt or angry—no screaming or yelling. It was more like he thought I was being childish, going through some sort of phase, and he was sure he'd bring me back around eventually. But no matter what I said to him, he kept harassing me, saying we were bound together forever and I couldn't escape him—crazy things. He kept harassing me online after I moved back to Cork, but shortly before Eamonn and I met, he stopped. I thought Max had given up. But then, after I got engaged, it all started up again."

I observed Ciara as she shifted uncomfortably on the bed. She reached over to touch the bandages on her arm but stopped short, tucking her hands under her legs.

"Does it hurt?" I asked.

"It's sore, and it itches," she admitted. "But I wouldn't say it hurts. Still, the nurses said if I don't stop doing this, there could be permanent scarring."

"I'm so sorry you're going through this." I could only imagine what it must be like, having so many cuts and scratches layered on top of one another without a chance to heal. I paused, hoping she would feel my compassion and it would soothe her distress. Once she'd relaxed a bit, I took a deeper line of inquiry. "Can you tell me about what happened last night?"

Her gaze dropped to the floor again as she spoke. "Same as before, really." With a sharp intake of breath, she continued. "The nurse shook me awake. I was sitting on the floor, and there was blood everywhere. My arm hurt like hell, and the plastic vase Eamonn brought flowers in was in pieces on the floor. Water and flowers were scattered everywhere. I was holding one of the broken pieces. I'd used the sharp edge…." Ciara's voice lowered almost to a whisper again. "They took two other vases of flowers away, too, from Eamonn and my friend Deirdre. I guess they threw them out."

"Oh, Ciara." My heart dropped in my chest as her distress flowed between us. We sat for a few moments, treading water in the heavy silence. "It sounds like Deirdre's a good friend."

She looked relieved by the change of subject. "The best! We always say we're like twins separated at birth, even though she's a redhead. She's the only person outside my family who knows about… you know." She gestured toward her bandages. "And she's been with me through all my problems with Max. I don't know what I would do without her, to be honest."

"I'm glad you have each other." I smiled gently, but it was time to bring up the thing I knew she least wanted to discuss. "Ciara, Eamonn told us you've been having recurring nightmares. Do you remember them?"

With a groan, she nodded, then dropped her head into her hands.

"I'm sorry. I know it's probably the last thing you want to talk about." I gave her a moment to breathe. "Have you told anyone what the nightmares are about?"

"Not yet." She flopped backward onto the bed and stared at the ceiling. "Not that they don't keep asking. I just don't see how it's relevant."

"It may not be. But the subconscious, where dreams live, is a tricky part of the mind. Trying to figure out your own is like trying to see your back without a mirror," I explained. "If you're having the same dream every time you have an episode of self-injury, that suggests there's some connection there. If that's the case, finding the link could be the key to stopping all of this. If you like, we can look at it together."

Ciara swallowed hard and closed her eyes. "That makes sense, I guess. And I knew I'd have to talk about it sooner or later. I'm just... scared."

"Okay." I slipped into a soothing tone. "What scares you?"

"Well...." She sighed heavily. "Max is in it, and I know this might sound insane, but I'm afraid that even talking about it will give the nightmare power somehow—give Max power over me. Is that crazy?"

"No, it's not crazy," I reassured, "but it's also not going to happen. In my experience, talking about the things we're most afraid of has the opposite effect. Rather than giving them more power over us, it takes their power away."

She cradled her bandaged limb in front of her like a broken wing. "I'm also afraid that once Eamonn and the doctors find out what the nightmare is about, they might believe all of this is happening because I'm still hung up on Max somehow." Quickly, she added, "But I'm not. Not at all! If anything, I wish I could cut Max out of my memory completely, like we never met. I just want to be with Eamonn, to get married and start our lives. And I'm terrified this will ruin everything."

Ciara's concerns about Eamonn's reaction seemed

unfounded. To my eyes, he appeared devoted to her and completely supportive. But I could see that in her emotionally fraught state, irrational fears had crept in. Still, the team needed to know about this connection, at the very least. It could be important from a clinical perspective.

"I've seen the way you and Eamonn are together. I can't imagine the content of a nightmare you're having changing anything between you. He believes in you, Ciara."

She sat up, wiping tears on her sleeve. "You really think that?"

"I do. He even said as much. But you don't have to decide now whether to tell Eamonn about the nightmare. Would you be willing to tell me, though, in confidence? Then we can talk about sharing it with the team, at least."

Ciara nodded slowly. "Yes, I guess I can do that."

"That's good," I said with a reassuring smile. In a situation like this, I knew hypnosis could help. But as a first step, I wanted to see how much she could remember in a fully conscious state. "Just try to relax. If it helps, you can close your eyes. Breathe slowly, and remember, you're not having the dream right now, just describing it. You're safe, right here with me."

"Okay." She closed her eyes and took a few slow breaths.

"Just start at the beginning, and tell me everything you can remember."

"Okay." Her brow creased with concentration. "I

think it's at night. My eyes are closed, but it seems dark, and a bit cool. I hear water nearby."

"What does it sound like?"

"Quiet, gentle. Like it's lapping up against something."

"Okay, that's a good start." I spoke softly and evenly, trying to create a peaceful atmosphere. "What else?"

"I'm lying on my back on something hard… and cold," she said haltingly. "The surface feels rough. I can't get up. I can't move at all, not even to open my eyes. That's when I hear them."

"Hear who?"

"At first, it's just feet walking toward me. Three people. One is pushing or pulling something with wheels on it. I can hear them rolling along the floor. In the dream, I can never remember who the people are at first, even though I've had the same nightmare many times. But then I hear their voices." She took in a shaky breath. "I'm sorry. It just feels scary to even think about it, like I'll conjure them up somehow."

"It's okay, Ciara. I understand, but it's just us here. You're awake and completely safe."

"Right." Her hands clenched into fists again. "Okay. The people walk in and move so one is standing at my head, one at my feet, and the one with the cart is on my left side. That's when I hear Max's voice. He says I'm out. Then I hear Deirdre's voice." Her eyelids flipped open for a moment, as though she was trying to reassure herself that she was, in fact, awake. "She asks if he's sure I won't feel anything. Then Max tells her to relax, that it won't take too long. Then I feel fingers on my arm." She gestured toward the bandaged part of her forearm. "There's some kind of vibrating, humming sound, and fingers on my skin just there, and then I feel a prick, like a needle. I still can't move, can't pull away."

Listening to her speak, I had to take a deep breath of my own. What she described was uncomfortably close to my own experience being kidnapped and restrained by my own boss in the psychiatry unit a few weeks before. Heat bathed me as a wave of anxiety threatened to rise. Gathering my willpower, I shoved it back down into its box.

This isn't about you. Focus, dammit.

Ciara's next words came in a rapid flow. "Then the needlelike point starts moving, slowly scratching my arm, and it feels like the skin is burning. I'm finally able to force myself to move, or at least I'm able to use my right arm. I reach over, knock the sharp object out of the way, and start scratching, trying to stop the burning." Her whole body slumped. "That's it. That's when someone always wakes me up."

"Oh my goodness." I reached over and took her hand. "That sounds terrifying. I'm so sorry, Ciara."

She wiped away fresh tears before they could fall. "I don't feel terrified in the dream, though—not the whole time, anyway. When I hear Max's voice, and Deirdre's, I feel safe. But then when the scratching starts, and the burning feeling...." She cast a despairing glance down at her arm.

"They're people you trust, or trusted at one point. It makes sense that your subconscious might find their presence comforting."

"I suppose. But when I'm in it, I would almost swear it's a memory of something that really happened, not a dream. That's how vivid it is." Ciara peered over at me. "Does any of that help?"

"Absolutely. Thank you for sharing that. I know it was difficult." I squeezed her hand. "One important detail for the team to know is at the end of the dream, when you try to stop whatever implement is being used to scratch and burn your arm."

"Why?"

I took a moment, searching for the right words. "If these episodes of self-injury are triggered by this night-mare—and circumstances suggest there's a strong connection, at the very least—it means you're scratching your arm to try to protect yourself, to end the attack. That's atypical."

"Oh." Her eyes widened. "Why do people usually do it?"

"Well, there are as many reasons as there are people who self-injure. But it's usually a way of trying to cope with overwhelming emotions or thoughts. For example, being numb and wanting to feel something, or trying to push away a painful feeling with a more painful, phys-ical sensation."

"But that's not what I'm doing."

"No, it seems not." I released her hand and sat back. "And it's usually done consciously, but you don't remember getting out of bed or anything else that happens until you're awakened by someone. Has that been the same here?"

"Yes, the nurses say the same." Ciara sat up a bit straighter, her eyes brightening. "What does that mean?"

"I'm not sure, exactly, but it seems likely there's a sleep disorder involved too. That's not a bad thing," I added in response to her look of alarm. "It just means your team has to think outside the box while treating you."

Frowning, she said, "I'm not sure what they think. It seems like some of them think I'm lying about not remembering what happened."

I understood their skepticism, but Ciara radiated authenticity, and her distress over the gaps in her memory was palpable. "If anyone doubts your word on that, try not to take it personally. It's their job to consider all possibilities and look at all the different angles so they can make an accurate diagnosis."

She leaned back, sighing heavily. "I know. It's just frustrating."

"Of course. I can only imagine. But the more information they have about what's happening in your mind, the easier it'll be for them to properly diagnose and treat you. Knowing about the nightmare would help them put everything in context. There's something happening here that's outside your awareness. Your subconscious might be trying to work through something—possibly related to Max, or he could just be a symbol for something else."

Head tilted down, she murmured, "Neve, is there any way you could tell the team *for* me? It might sound less... well, *loo-lah* coming from you."

"It would be better if you told them," I said gently. "You're their patient. They care about you, and they're trying to help."

"I know." She folded her hands tightly in her lap. "But talking about the dream.... It was frightening enough saying it just now, and I feel comfortable with you. I'm not sure I could put all those words together again. I mean, if they want to talk to me about it afterward, that's fine. I'd just rather you tell them. Besides, the way you talk about it makes it sound less mad. Please?"

I *had* offered to do anything I could to help. "Okay, I can do that."

"Oh, that would be brilliant." Relief softened her expression. "Thank you so much. But I'm not sure I want to tell Eamonn yet. Is that okay?"

"Of course. Like I said, we're speaking in confidence. What you choose to tell Eamonn is entirely up to you."

In a conspiratorial whisper, she said, "And it's not just that I worry what he'll think about me, about us. He already blames Max for all this. I just worry that if he found out about the nightmare connection, it would prove his theory, and he might *do* something."

"Do something? Like what?"

"I'm not sure, but something bad. To Max."

Is this another irrational fear of hers emerging? "Because Max appears in a dream you're having? That seems unlikely."

Ciara rolled her eyes heavenward. "Only because you don't know Eamonn. You know Con, though. They both have that temper, although Eamonn says while he's the quick fuse, Con is more like a volcano— dormant most of the time, but you don't want to be around when he blows."

I *did* know Con—or at least I thought I did. I'd never seen anything resembling a "volcano" side to him, however. Maybe Eamonn had been referring to how the brothers were as kids. However, Ciara appeared convinced Eamonn was at least capable of exacting revenge against someone for harming a loved one *in a dream.* That seemed beyond the pale. Still, some small, uncertain part of me wondered who was right about the brothers: Ciara or me.

"I seriously doubt he would do anything to Max." I forced a smile. "But rest assured, I won't say a word to Eamonn. Like I said, I'll leave that up to you." I glanced down at my watch. "I think the treatment team is still meeting. I could see if they'll let me pop in and share this new information."

"Thank you so much, Neve, for being here, and for being so understanding."

"It's my pleasure." We both stood. "Enjoy your lunch with Eamonn, okay?"

"I will." After a moment of awkwardness, Ciara wrapped her right arm around me and gave me a half hug. "Thanks again."

"Glad to help," I said, hugging her back. Then I headed back toward the nurses' station.

I had no idea how the treatment team would react to the information about Ciara's dream, but I hoped it would help them move her case toward a resolution. Like everyone else, more than anything, I wanted to see her healthy, happy, and home with Eamonn again.

CHAPTER 7

CON

Con insisted on driving on their way back to the homestead. The tense, subtle movements visible in Eamonn's jaw ever since they left the hospital indicated he was grinding his teeth; he was in no frame of mind to be behind the wheel.

Meanwhile, a fresh wave of jet lag had Neve passed out in the back seat. Despite her protests that she wasn't tired, within five minutes of leaving the hospital, she was out cold. Con kept glancing at her in the rearview mirror. Her eyes were closed, her perfect cheek resting against the seat belt strap. She was frowning slightly, as though she was still fighting sleep.

As much as he wanted to keep watching her as they drove and indulge in scandalous daydreams about what might happen once his lips were pressed against that irresistible pout of hers, he pushed himself to refocus. In these moments of relative privacy, he could encourage Eamonn to talk about what was on his mind, try to draw the poison out.

As they pulled from the smaller roads onto the motorway, traffic was blessedly light. Con leaned back and stretched his arm out behind his brother's headrest, hoping that if he appeared relaxed, it might help Eamonn open up a bit.

Easing into the conversation, Con began, "So, Laoch Garr appears to be fairly cutting edge, not to mention well run and well resourced."

"You think so?"

"They've created a uniquely relaxed atmosphere, quite homely. It's good that she's getting an hour of individual therapy daily on top of groups. Plus, they have a very high staff-to-patient ratio. John mentioned they even have alternative therapies—massage, acupuncture. I've never seen an inpatient psychiatric facility quite like it."

Eamonn gave a stiff nod. "Best in the country for a problem like Ciara's, we were told."

Con knew what a facility like that must cost. He cleared his throat. "Look, if you two need any help—"

"Thanks, but Calfwood pays well, and her family's chipping in. It's covered."

Calfwood Brewery was the craft beer enterprise in Cork where his brother worked. He and Eamonn didn't typically discuss money, so he was happy to hear his brother didn't have to worry about finances. But Eamonn still radiated tension and outrage. Clearly his mind was elsewhere.

"Murder is it, then?" Although Con asked the question casually, there was no hint of levity in his tone. If, as he suspected, Eamonn was planning on chasing down Ciara's ex, Con wanted to be in on the decision-making, not sidelined because his brother thought he wasn't taking the situation seriously.

Eamonn kept staring out the front window, grinding his teeth so hard Con thought he could hear the molars scraping together.

"She'll get through this, Eam. You both will." A light rain began to fall. Con pulled his arm back and put both hands on the wheel. "John is confident she'll be all right, and I believe him. He's top-notch."

Eamonn closed his eyes and exhaled slowly, as though trying to force himself to relax. He let his shoulders drop and his head fall back against the headrest. "I believe him too," he said, speaking in low tones threaded with intensity. "But, Jesus Christ, I *would* murder that Max bastard in a heartbeat if I could be sure it would get him out of her head."

"Indeed." Con shared his brother's feelings about Max after hearing what Neve had told the team. Obviously, this Max character had wormed his way into Ciara's subconscious, and something about him was torturing her.

Now it was also driving his brother mad with worry. Although she'd expressed reluctance about it to Neve, Ciara had decided to share the details of her nightmare with Eamonn over lunch. Of course, he'd been comforting and supportive toward her, but ever since leaving the facility, Eamonn's mood had darkened.

Con had to hand it to Neve; she certainly knew how to make an impression. She'd slipped in halfway through the team meeting, and when John asked her for her thoughts about Ciara, she had presented a brief but insightful summary of the case as she saw it, followed by the new information about the nightmare—information Ciara apparently hadn't felt comfortable disclosing to anyone else.

Con had worried that since Neve was an outsider and new to the case, the team might not take her seriously, but his fears had been unfounded. Once she began to address them, everyone at the table leaned in and listened. Instead of making them feel like she was barging in and stepping on toes, she'd put everyone at ease immediately with her sincere, understated manner. It was evident to everyone that she really wanted to help Ciara, her kindness and intelligence demonstrated in every word she spoke.

Con had seen the same thing in their work at Capitol Hill General. Neve was so good at her job that she earned confidence and trust without ever having to fight for it. Now, just when he thought he couldn't fall any more deeply in love, he found himself in even greater awe of her, watching her work her magic in an unfamiliar setting with strangers.

A variety of clinical possibilities was discussed after Neve shared her impressions of the case. The meeting ran long as they began moving away from diagnoses of personality disorders and depression and refocused on sleep disorders, particularly parasomnias with dream-enactment. In conjunction with anxiety issues, they also wanted to investigate the possibility of a trauma component. As they considered changes to her treatment plan, the team decided to stick with the idea of keeping Ciara in the isolation room overnight for observation. It would keep her safe, and they just might learn something useful.

The meeting ended around the same time Ciara and Eamonn finished lunch. At Eamonn's request, he, Con, and Neve met briefly with John to discuss the new information Ciara had shared and what it meant for her case.

When he wanted to be, Eamonn was good at keeping his emotions in check, at least visibly. So Con was fairly certain he was the only one who'd seen the precise moment vengeful thoughts had entered his brother's mind: when John asked Eamonn if he knew of any trauma Ciara may have experienced in the past, related to Max.

Now, Con could feel rage emanating from the passenger seat, and he knew his brother needed to be talked off the ledge. "You're right, though," he said. "Even if we bury that shitehawk in the Earth's core, the mind is a complex thing. Smashing his head in might make you feel better, but who knows? It might not help her at all, or it could even make things worse."

"What do you mean, worse?" Eamonn hissed, straining against his seat belt as he leaned toward Con.

"She hates Max! She wouldn't miss him, if that's what you think. She told me herself she wishes she'd never met him."

"Of *course* she hates him," Con interjected. *Christ, he's tense—though understandably so.* "I wasn't suggesting otherwise. I only meant that from what you've said, Ciara is a good person, a moral person. If she felt she was responsible for harm coming to another human being, even indirectly, she might never recover from that."

"That's true." Though the look on his face remained sour, Eamonn leaned back in his seat and crossed his arms over his chest. "That's why I've been trying to think of ways to make his death look like an accident."

Con shot him a hard look. "Ah, that's a great plan. Brilliant. Although you do know, after all that's happened here lately, if that bastard dies any time soon —even of natural causes—they'll be looking at you for it." Since Eamonn seemed only slightly chastened, he added, "Besides, you're hardly a skilled assassin. You'd definitely leave behind some incriminating evidence somewhere, no question. Then you'd end up spending the rest of your life in prison, and where would that leave Ciara? Alone and feeling guilty twice over."

The thought of his fiancée potentially suffering even more appeared to ease Eamonn back into a less homicidal state of mind. "I just want that fecker out of Ciara's head, and her life. And I'd really like to get her some justice."

"You don't even know that he did anything. It's a nightmare, Eam. A dream."

"But John asked me if Max might have done something else to traumatize her on top of harassing her."

"John is exploring a theory. I know it's bad enough that he harassed her. But you don't know of anything else he did, right? Besides, Deirdre's in the dream too. Isn't she a good friend of Ciara's? Would you go after her as well?"

"Feck no," Eamonn said with a huff. "I don't have anything against Deirdre, although the nightmare has me wondering about her, too, I'll admit. But Max, he's done quite enough already to earn a kick up the arse—chasing after Ciara, refusing to let her alone, scaring her. That's enough to make me want to put his balls in a vise." Eamonn gripped the armrest on the door and dug his fingernails into the leather.

"Look, I get it," Con murmured, glancing at the mirror to make sure Neve was still asleep. He recalled how badly he wanted to pummel *her* ex, Stephan, when he found out the bastard had raised a hand to her. He would still jump at the chance if he ever got it, in fact, so he did understand something of what Eamonn must have been feeling. "But you can't touch Max without hurting Ciara."

Eamonn just sulked silently and looked out the window, which was not a good sign. Con could practically hear the wheels whirring around in his brother's head, plotting revenge. He had to offer some alternative that would satisfy Eamonn, if only for the moment, while at the same time keeping him out of trouble.

After considering for a few moments, Con said, "I'll tell you what. I can help you here. First, we need to gather information, put together a proper harassment case for what he did to Ciara. Once you do that, he'll know he can't mess with either of you again without hell raining down. Also, an arsehole like this, he's probably done more bad shite than we even know about. So we investigate him, find out if there's any dirt. If we're lucky, we might even find something that could put him away. In either case, you and Ciara would both be well and truly rid of him."

The silence that followed reassured Con that Eamonn was considering his proposal. Finally, he said, "That might help put him out of her head, all right."

"Right, so." It was decided. Con clapped his hand down on the steering wheel like a gavel. "I just want one promise from you."

Eamonn grunted. "Christ, I'm afraid to ask."

"If we decide there's any extralegal justice to be handed out, you let me handle it."

"Hah! Let you fight my battles? We're not kids anymore, Cornelius."

"No, but we'll always be brothers." Con stretched his arm behind Eamonn's headrest again, speaking softly. "Let's just say, theoretically speaking, that prick's nose gets broken. If you were home with Ciara the whole time, you certainly can't be held responsible. Meanwhile, I could be back on a plane to the States before anyone knows I'm gone, making it very unlikely any consequences would catch up with me."

With a long sideways glance, his brother said, "You're serious?"

"Of course." No matter that Eamonn was thirty-three now, the same age as Neve, Con would always see him as his little brother, his responsibility to shield and protect.

The sound of teeth grinding had disappeared as Eamonn slowly began to relax. "All right. Let's say, theoretically, that something unfortunate does happen to the fecker. If you ever needed that type of assistance over in the States, you'd let me do the honors?"

"Hah!" Con guffawed. Eamonn had no idea what he was offering, with Con and Neve potentially still in the sights of some shady and dangerous forces across the Atlantic.

But Eamonn took Con's response as a dismissal, and his hackles rose immediately. "Fair's fair, Con. You've got your medical license to think of over there, your immigration status…. Besides, I'm no charity case."

"Sure, I know. That's not—" With an exasperated sigh, Con pulled his arm off the headrest and held his hand out to his brother. "All right. Deal."

Eamonn shook his hand a bit more firmly than was comfortable, as though to drive his point home. "Grand. I've always wanted to visit you over there."

"You're hoping something bad will happen to me now, aren't you? So you can mete out some revenge? Thanks a million," he said in mock outrage, pleased to see his brother smiling. "You can come visit anytime. You and Ciara both. You're always welcome. If I didn't make that clear before now, I apologize."

Eamonn nodded. "I knew that. It's just... life, I guess, although I shouldn't let that get in the way. But I knew you were busy with your residency, then the new job."

"Ah, bollocks!" Con objected as he felt a sharp tug on his heart, like someone had threaded a fishhook through it and was trying to yank it from his chest. "Never too busy for you. And never too busy for family. You should come, even if no dirty deeds are required. Have you planned a honeymoon yet? DC is something else. Neve knows that whole area. She could tell you where to go, what to see."

Con caught movement in the rearview mirror as Neve stirred. He'd raised his voice without realizing. He shushed Eamonn, and they both stayed silent for a bit until Neve settled again.

"That sounds great, in truth," Eamonn said softly. "I think Ciara would love that, honeymooning far away from here. And the way you look at Neve, I'd put down money you'll be planning your own honeymoon before long."

"He's getting married, so he thinks the whole world should follow suit," Con muttered as his brother grinned over at him from the passenger seat.

"Yeah, you make all those noises about never wanting kids, too, but you'll be sending me pictures of Con Junior in a couple years here!"

"Now I *know* you've lost it!" Con exclaimed. He'd made it very clear to Eamonn, Una, and his whole family that he had no plans to ever become a father. That decision was subject to change now, of course, depending on Neve's position on the matter.

With regard to Eamonn's comments about Neve and him planning their own honeymoon, though, Con thought, *From your lips to God's ears, little brother.* If he were ever lucky enough to get Neve to agree to marry him, he'd never ask for another thing as long as he lived —not from God, the universe, or anyone. Having Neve as his would be miracle enough.

———

After they'd been home a while, Con stole away to the study while his mother showed Neve how to make trifle. He had to make a call, and he didn't want an audience.

After a few rings, he heard his good friend's voice on the other end of the line. "Hello?"

"Eryk the Viking!"

"Conman the Barbarian!" Eric replied in kind, addressing Con by his gaming handle. Con could tell Eric's wife, Katie, was home. There was soothing music in the background instead of Eric's preferred heavy metal played at top volume. "I wasn't expecting to hear from you while you and Neve were off canoodling in Ireland. What's wrong? Did you piss her off already?"

Although Eric's needling was in good fun, it still

soured Con's mood a bit. There had been precious few opportunities for canoodling so far, and the way things were going, that situation wasn't likely to improve any time soon. First things first, though. "Glad to hear you're not dead yet."

"Uh, yeah, thanks. You too."

Eric was being purposefully vague, so Katie must have been within earshot. Knowing Eric, he probably hadn't told his wife much about the dangerous mess he'd gotten into with Con and Neve a few weeks prior, while she was out of town. Eric's considerable hacking skills had been instrumental in their ability to save the president's life and survive the ordeal. However, until they heard otherwise from the Secret Service, they'd been told all three of them could still be under threat from Brickhaven's "secret society" thugs. Con hoped joking about it first thing had diffused any residual tension.

"So why are you calling me, for real?" Eric asked. "Seriously, did you mess up and you need relationship advice? Because I'd be happy to give you some pointers...."

"You'll be pleased to hear I haven't angered her once on this trip."

"So far, that is."

"Thanks for your confidence," Con said dryly. "While I don't need any pointers, I do need a favor."

"Man, I knew it!" There was some background thumping and rustling. Eric called out, "Katie, be right back, hon," then whispered into the phone, "Just a minute."

Con waited patiently while he heard Eric tromping on stairs, likely retreating to his basement lair.

"Okay, clear," Eric said. "First of all, courage points for asking me for another favor so fast on the heels of the last epic one. Second, if this has anything to do with the last one, the answer is hell no."

"Completely unrelated. Just a little harmless recon."

Eric scoffed. "Harmless? That's what you said last time."

"I didn't say anything of the sort last time. In fact, I remember warning you not to get too involved, but you insisted."

The brief silence told him Eric was conceding that point. "Okay, well, what's the deal now? Is whatever you need illegal in Ireland or something?"

"I hadn't even thought about that, to be honest. Don't cross any lines, though—not with Big Brother watching."

"Hah! Don't remind me." After using his hacking skills to help Con and Neve defeat Brickhaven, Eric had been singled out by the Secret Service for ongoing monitoring.

"I just don't know anyone else with your level of skill, in Ireland or elsewhere."

"Flattery? Really?" Con could picture Eric rolling his eyes. "Fine. What kind of recon are we talking about?"

"The dirt-digging kind."

"Ah. And what kind of bad guy are we looking at here?"

"Hopefully just a sad sack who can't handle rejection—my brother's fiancée's ex. But if there's more dirt there, it would be helpful to know."

"Fair enough. This does sound pretty bite-sized compared to the last favor. How deep do you want me to dig?"

"Just as far as you're comfortable with. And if you don't find anything, it's fine. Just by looking, you'll be helping me stall my brother. He's on the verge of doing something ill-advised."

"Someone who shares your DNA doing something ill-advised? Inconceivable!"

Con rubbed his forehead and waited while Eric enjoyed a hearty laugh. "I'll send you the details, then. Thanks for this."

"No problem. You know I've got your back. Plus, I need a favor from you when you get home, so consider this prepayment."

"Oh, I see."

"Nothing dangerous, just potentially painful. Katie needs servers for a charity dinner at her church."

"Servers?" Con guffawed. "Can you see me carrying around trays of food and drink with my leg? Everyone would be wearing their meals home."

"Don't worry, big guy," Eric replied, and Con could hear the grin in his voice. "You can man the meat station and carve beef or something. Neve can handle serving, right?"

"Oh, you're pulling Neve into this too?" Con was pretty sure she wouldn't object, but he wouldn't commit on her behalf.

"Katie wants to see her—wants to see you both together, actually. She was so excited to hear you two are all loved up. You'll ask her, right?"

"Jaysus." This was sounding worse by the minute. He did owe Eric, though. Fair was fair. Forcing down his inner curmudgeon, Con replied, "I'll ask her."

"Sweet! Thanks. Katie will be thrilled. And I'll call you as soon as I have something on the digging operation."

"Grand," Con said, anxious to end the call before he got roped into any more social events. "Watch yourself."

"Aw, he cares! You, too, man. Say hi to Neve for me. Do all the things I wouldn't do."

"Mind out of the gutter, Viking. Give Katie my best."

"Later, Barbarian."

As Eric clicked off the call, Con released a deep sigh of relief. Now he could tell Eamonn that his hacker friend was on Max's case. That should be enough to keep him near home for the time being, at least.

He poured himself a scotch and settled back into his armchair. Moments of solitude on this trip would be few and far between. Might as well take full advantage, especially since he had some thinking to do—about Ciara's case, how best to manage Eamonn, and, most importantly, how to make sure Neve enjoyed every moment of her trip. Once he was certain she liked his family and Ireland, he would feel more confident taking things between them to the next level. Now that he'd finally made it out of the "friend zone" after two agonizing years, that was something he was bound and determined to do. And the sooner the better.

In fact, he decided it was the perfect time to make another call, this one to Una. Although his sister hadn't made it down the aisle yet, she'd been thrice engaged. No doubt she knew more than he did about diamond rings.

CHAPTER 8

NEVE

t had been a long, full day, but against all odds, sleep evaded me. The room was warm, so I'd opened the window a few inches, letting in a cool evening breeze. Now I lay under the sheet, listening to the susurration of wind blowing through the leaves of the willow tree outside.

I could scarcely remember ever feeling more tired. But my mind was alert and sharp as a pin, churning through thoughts like a laser beam reading an optical disk. *My kingdom for a sleeping pill,* I thought as my brain relentlessly cataloged all I'd learned over the past twenty-four hours.

Number one: I loved Ireland. The landscape was gorgeous, and everyone I'd met so far had been wonderful—genuine, warm, and welcoming. Con cautioned me not to get too rosy-eyed, claiming he was taking pains to present the country in its best light. But even just getting to know different aspects of him by spending time with his family in the country where he grew up was deeply satisfying in a way I didn't fully understand yet. I was confident that would remain the case even if Con did introduce me to the "grotty spots and gobshites," as he called them.

Number two: There was much more to Ciara's case than anyone knew. The way she described her episodes of self-harm, it sounded like some sort of sleep disorder, dissociative episodes, or both. My instincts told me she had suffered some sort of trauma, possibly something Ciara's mind had buried and was now trying to bring to the surface for healing. I'd seen that pattern before. Sometimes, when people were doing well and in a good place, the subconscious would decide they were ready to deal with whatever traumatic memories were previously suppressed. That could lead to a myriad of disturbing symptoms, with their cause remaining a mystery until the memory was brought into the conscious mind and dealt with there. If that was happening to Ciara, what was her trauma, and did it really have to do with Max—possibly Deirdre as well? Or were they merely symbols in her dream? And what about her arm injury? Was that literal or symbolic?

In light of these new questions, I was even more convinced that hypnosis could be helpful. I suggested it to the team, and they agreed. Their psychologist said he would schedule a session with Ciara as soon as possible. I hoped gaining further insight into whatever was haunting her subconscious would help resolve her symptoms.

Number three: Ciara had been dead right about Con and Eamonn. I was resting my eyes in the car earlier when I heard them speaking in hushed tones. Assuming they were having a much-needed talk following the revelations of the day, I pretended to be asleep. I hadn't intended to listen in, and at first, I really couldn't make out what they were saying. However, over time, their voices grew louder, and I overheard enough of the conversation to confirm that Eamonn was itching to go after Max, as Ciara predicted. And while it was clear Con was trying to keep his brother in check, evidently it was not because he objected to the idea of violence in principle. Rather, he was offering to be the bringer of justice himself, should it come to that.

Clearly Ciara knew more about Con than I did, at least in this area. He'd always kept certain things about himself hidden, and I'd been hoping our trip would shed light on some of them. I just didn't expect one of the revelations to be a willingness to exact vigilante violence.

Unsure quite what to do with that information, I jotted it down in my memory, but only in pencil. After all, I didn't yet know what was going on in Con's head during that conversation. Maybe he was just playing along with Eamonn to prevent him from doing something rash. I planned to ask him as soon as the opportunity presented itself.

Number four.

I really didn't want to think about number four, but my brain refused to turn away.

Con didn't want to get married, or at least he was in no hurry about it.

In the car, Con had said to Eamonn, "He's getting married, so he thinks the whole world should follow suit." Maybe he hadn't meant it like it sounded, but I couldn't unhear his grumbled words.

We've only been dating for a few weeks, I chided myself. *Why do you even care where Con's head is on marriage? Yesterday, all you were thinking about was when and how the two of you might finally get the chance to do more than kiss. You don't even know where this relationship is going yet. Slow your roll, Bridezilla.*

But when I heard him speak those words, they landed inside me with the sickening thud of disappointment. Eamonn had also said something about Con not wanting children, but I'd forced myself to ignore that. After all, I had never actively wanted to have children, but that might just have been because I'd never had a suitable partner. So, to weigh whether Con and I might become parents—that question belonged much further ahead in an as-yet-uncertain future.

Upon our arrival back home, I'd been more than happy to put such questions out of my head by helping Imogen get dinner ready while Con disappeared to make some phone calls. In spite of all the new information I was processing, I enjoyed the rest of the evening. Con's family had me laughing helplessly as they tried to teach me a new card game called Twenty-Five. By the end, they finally believed my claim of a complete lack of natural ability in that arena.

Now I had to get some sleep, though. I mentally reviewed the rules of the card game, hoping the effort would finally push my brain over the edge into sleep.

———

I awoke the next day feeling refreshed, which could mean only one thing: Con had let me sleep in. I fumbled around to find my phone. Sure enough, it was a few minutes after 11:00 a.m. I hoped he hadn't gone to Laoch Garr without me.

I threw myself together in a hurry and went downstairs to find Imogen in the kitchen having tea. "Hello," I croaked in my as-yet-unused morning voice.

"You finally got some rest!" She poured me a cup of tea and brought out a loaf of delicious fruit bread they called tea brack. "I'm so glad. Holidays are for relaxing, not rushing around the place like a blue-arsed fly."

Although I agreed heartily, I thought of this trip as more of a working vacation. "Are Con and Eamonn here?"

"The boys went to see Ciara a couple of hours ago," she explained. "Con asked me to tell you not to worry. They'll fill you in when they get back."

"I feel bad for missing them."

"Nonsense! Con told us you work all the time back in Washington." She smiled. "He's eager for you to get a break while you're here."

So Con had made excuses for leaving me behind. He must have known I'd object. Well, there was no point arguing with Imogen on the matter. As I nibbled a slice of tea brack, she chatted away about family and neighbors, perhaps sensing I was still waking up and not fully ready to contribute to the conversation.

I began thinking again about the exchange I'd overheard between Con and Eamonn in the car. It occurred to me that Imogen might help put some of what they'd said in context. As a starting point, I asked her what Con was like as a kid. She said he was very athletic, always out having a game with his friends. But he was also an unusually thoughtful child, taking care of everyone in the family, and he always felt the responsibility of being the oldest.

"He treated it like his job," she said. "He could be quite bossy with Eamonn and Una."

"I can believe it," I said dryly, having collided with that side of Con a few times myself.

Smiling warmly, she added, "So they bickered, like all kids do. But since Con went off to university, they've all stayed quite close."

"I don't have any siblings. I can't imagine what it must have been like with three kids in the house."

"Chaos, utter chaos. They were always getting into some kind of mischief. I know Jack mentioned the fighting, but that wasn't so often." Although Imogen kept her tone light, her shoulders tensed up. "Usually they were doing something like setting off those fireworks near the barn. When Con did get into scuffles, it was usually because Eamonn flew off the handle at something, and Con had to come to his rescue. Always rescuing someone," she added with a wistfulness that made me wonder if there was more to that statement. "I've often thought it was that same impulse that led Con to become a doctor. More tea?"

I sensed there was more to Con and Eamonn's ruffian past than their mother wanted to share, but I certainly wasn't going to push. "I'd love some. Where is Jack this morning, by the way?"

Imogen brightened, her troublemaking boys forgotten for the moment. "He's out for his midmorning walk. He says it's for exercise, but these days it's more of a social activity. He and a couple of his friends who live nearby go walking at the same time every day, so they meet on the road. He says they mainly talk about farming and sports, but I know they gossip away like old ladies," she added with a grin.

Hearing that warmed my heart. Con had mentioned his father's struggles with depression, which it seemed were quite serious, at least in the past. Getting out daily and meeting with friends was a good sign of his state of mind, not to mention that friendship could be a great tonic.

We heard the purr of an engine and the crackle of tires on gravel.

"That must be the boys," Imogen declared.

An air of tension surrounded Con and Eamonn as they walked in the door, shedding their jackets and speaking in hushed tones.

"No need to whisper," Imogen said. "We're all awake!"

"Morning, sleepyhead." Con slid in beside me and gave my knee a gentle squeeze under the table.

"Morning, yourself."

He must have sensed a coolness in my tone because he leaned closer. "I'm in hot water, am I?" he joked as Imogen placed a steaming mug in front of him.

So he knew I hadn't appreciated being left behind. But it was difficult to stay annoyed with him in such close proximity. "It's okay. I know you were just trying to be thoughtful." The smile died on my lips, though, when I saw the looks on Con's and Eamonn's faces. Something was wrong. "Everything okay?" I whispered.

He shook his head as if to say, "Not now."

Their mother passed around O'Hara's tea brack with Dairygold butter—Con's favorite brands, I'd learned.

"Ah, brilliant! Just what I needed. Thank you."

"Yeah, thanks," Eamonn said, absently sipping his tea.

Imogen gave Con a meaningful look. "All right, I have things to do, so I'll leave the three of you to it."

Con nodded at her. "Thanks, Ma. We'll come find ye."

I had never heard Con use the word "ye" before, although his parents often did. He was speaking more like them by the day. I smiled, relishing each chance to discover a new side to him.

Once we were alone, Con began. "So, there's good news and bad news."

Eamonn's expression soured, and I could tell the bad outweighed the good. "What happened?" I asked.

"Well," Con continued, "the good news is Ciara didn't self-injure last night, and she did all right in the isolation room. She said it was strange, of course, and it took her a while to get used to the safety mittens, but she wasn't anxious, and she slept well enough."

"I'm going to kill him," Eamonn muttered to himself. His tone was surprisingly calm, given the content of his statement.

I looked at Con, who rubbed his eyes. I got the sense they had been arguing about Eamonn's murderous intentions—toward Max, I guessed—all the way home.

"Eamonn," Con said, "let's fill Neve in first, at least. All right?"

Eamonn nodded. Sullen, he returned to his tea.

"When we arrived this morning, Ciara was in session with the psychologist," Con explained. "He said he used hypnosis to take her back through her nightmare. Everything went as expected, as far as that was concerned. Ciara described the same details she shared with you. She was quite emotional throughout, but that wasn't the unusual part." Pausing briefly, he shot his brother a concerned look. "After he brought her out of the hypnotic state, she grew quite upset."

"I'm going to kill him," Eamonn repeated, and this time it sounded like a promise.

"We don't really know what happened yet," Con said.

"Like hell we don't!" Eamonn slammed a fist on the table. "He fecking mutilated her!"

When Con placed a hand on his brother's arm, Eamonn leaned back in his chair, eyes closed. Con continued, "It seems the hypnosis session removed some sort of block, and Ciara told the psychologist she *remembered* the events in her nightmare, that they really occurred."

My eyes widened. "What on earth...?"

"She couldn't recall every detail," Con said, "but she's certain it's a memory, not just a dream. Even Deirdre being there—but that's one of the parts that doesn't make sense to her yet. What Max did to her arm, she's not sure, but she did share a few more things that could point us in the right direction."

"Like he's a fecking cult leader!" Eamonn exclaimed.

"He's *what*?" I asked, unable to conceal my shock.

"It's a long story," Con said. "I'll fill you in. But the short version is he arranged real-life experiences for players to go along with the video game he created when he came to Ireland. It's called *Temple of Taranis*, supposedly based on ancient Celtic myths. Ciara said it isn't Wicked Games' best seller, but it has a sizable cult following."

"Like I said!" Eamonn burst out.

"Not an *actual* cult."

"You don't know that!"

I interrupted the brothers' back-and-forth, trying to understand what Con was saying. "Was it something like Dungeons and Dragons?"

"Much more extensive than that," Con said. "Ciara said Max used a sea cave on an island near Galway to host game-themed role-playing weekends for players from around the world."

"Oh, so more like a Ren fair?"

Con and Eamonn exchanged puzzled looks. "A what?"

"You know, those festivals where they recreate a European town from the Renaissance, and everyone dresses in sixteenth-century garb? And there are actors playing certain roles in the town, and music, and jousting, and turkey legs—" Con looked utterly baffled. I bit my lip. "You don't have those here?"

"The Renaissance was a period of crippling poverty and horrible diseases," Con said. "Why would anyone want to recreate that?"

Eamonn muttered, "Actually, I think there's something like that in Dublin."

Perplexed, Con asked, "What?"

"It's called Highland Games, though," he muttered. "Una went last year."

As Con struggled to wrap his brain around that, I brought us back to the main topic. "So with Max, is it more like some kind of full-immersion marketing strategy?"

"Not as such," Con said. "Wicked Games wasn't officially affiliated with these gatherings. They were set up and funded entirely by Max. That may have added to their mystique, since the gatherings could be perceived as truer to the game, untainted by corporate

influences. Evidently, the *TOT* community is quite dedicated. Players paid handsomely for tickets. Ciara said
Max also held rituals in the sea cave, ceremonies he'd
invented. She's pretty sure that cave is where the
memory in her dream took place."

"Oh God." *Poor Ciara.* What torture had Max put her
through? "Wait, what's *TOT*?"

"Stands for *Temple of Taranis*. He was one of the
ancient Celtic gods."

"God of thunder, as in 'everyone has to listen to
thunder,'" Eamonn scoffed. "At least '*TOTs*' is an apt
name for a bunch of grown-up toddlers running around
Galway in capes."

"True, although Ciara said she thought Max took the
whole thing a bit too seriously," Con continued. "The
role he assigned himself at these gatherings was high
priest of Taranis, the most powerful player in the game.
But Max once told Ciara that he felt a genuine spiritual
connection with the thunder god and believed he'd
been chosen to bring Taranis worship back in the
modern age. She thought he was joking, and when she
laughed, he played it off like he hadn't been serious.
But later, when she attended one of the gatherings and
saw Max perform a ritual ceremony, she began to question herself. Now she believes he might have been
serious after all, about all of it."

"Wow," I said. "I guess the apple doesn't fall far
from the tree."

"Meaning what?" Con asked.

"That 'free love' commune Max grew up in, Ciara

told me it was founded by his parents," I explained. "It sounded like his dad was a sort of charismatic leader, but in the worst possible way—exploiting and controlling his followers and taking all their money. If Max really believes he's some sort of priest to an ancient god, and he's growing a following with a high price for entry, it looks like he has some things in common with his father, at least."

"You mean he's a sociopath." Eamonn pounded his fist on the table. "Just the type of arsehole to drug and mutilate his girlfriend!"

"We still don't know what happened," Con said firmly, waiting for his brother to calm down before he turned back to me. "After the hypnosis, Ciara did recall that one night, Max and Sean took her and Deirdre to the sea cave to help them prepare for an upcoming *TOT* gathering. Although she doesn't remember drinking much, apparently she got blackout drunk, because she lost several hours. She woke up the next day at Max's place with her left forearm bandaged—the same area she's been injuring."

"Oh no." A seed of dread sank into the pit of my stomach.

Con stopped and pinched the bridge of his nose before continuing. "It gets even stranger. Max told her she slipped and scraped her arm on the rocks, and he'd dressed the wounds for her. He'd put a transparent bandage on it that he said couldn't be removed for a week, then wrapped the arm with gauze so she wouldn't have to look at the wounds. After a week, he did the same again, but he wouldn't let her look at her arm when he changed the dressing, saying it would be too upsetting for her. When he finally let Ciara remove the second bandage after two weeks, the wounds had healed completely with no scarring. Now, she's convinced the scene from her nightmare is a memory and that Max did something to her arm that night. But because she was impaired by some sort of substance, she can't recall the details."

"So I'm going to find the prick and ask him," Eamonn said, clenching and unclenching his fists.

The air was thick with threats of violence, and with the rage rolling off Eamonn, there was no question in my mind that he was on a knife's edge. I swallowed hard as a feverish heat washed over me.

"Just a minute, now," Con warned. "Before she started injuring herself, you never saw anything wrong with her arm, did you? No scars, nothing, am I right? So none of us know for sure at this stage what really happened. Maybe it is a memory, but distorted—like she scraped her arm on the rocks, and her mind twisted it into the scene from the nightmare she's describing."

Eamonn shoved his chair back as though preparing to stand. "Are you calling her a liar?"

My heart tripped over itself, warning me that my anxiety was spiking. *Stop it,* I ordered my brain. *Calm down. You're not in any danger. This isn't about you.*

"Jaysus, man!" Con grabbed his brother by the wrist. "I'm saying no such thing. I have no doubt Ciara believes every word she's telling us. I'm just saying that sometimes, the mind plays tricks, and you should consider that possibility before you run off to do anyone grievous bodily harm."

All at once, a wave of panic slammed into my chest. As I sat frozen in my chair, all the frightening experiences I'd had over the past few months flashed through my mind. Getting stabbed by a patient. Stephan, my ex-boyfriend, hitting me. Being kidnapped and restrained on the psychiatry unit by my boss. Surviving Brickhaven's threats, and still wondering whether they might come after us again.

I tried to push those thoughts aside and focus on Eamonn, since he was clearly the person in the room who most needed help. But my breathing grew shallow and rapid. *I should move. I should go outside and get some fresh air before this gets any worse.* But I felt glued to the spot, unable to even shift in my chair.

Eamonn hung his head. "I'm sorry, Con. I know you believe her. It's just that before, some of the team thought Ciara was doing all this to get attention. That kind of talk drives me mad."

"Of course it does." Con squeezed his brother's wrist, then released him. "We're all on your side here, though, and Ciara's."

"I know that." Eamonn peered over at me. "Sorry about that, Neve."

As my pulse pounded in my ears, I just smiled weakly and nodded, unable to speak.

Con looked over at me. Right away, his face darkened with worry. "Eamonn, look. You're no good to anyone like this, least of all Ciara. You drink your tea. I'll take Neve out for a walk, show her a bit of the garden while I fill her in some more on the case. All right? Try to relax for a little while, at least?"

Eamonn slumped back in his chair. With an air of defeat, he nodded.

"Good. I'll get Ma to keep you company." Con held a finger up to me and mouthed, "One minute." He slipped out of the kitchen, returning moments later with Imogen on his heels. She promptly began to make a fuss over Eamonn.

Con laid his hands atop mine, which were clutching the arms of my chair. "Join me?" he murmured.

"A little help?" I asked, forcing a smile so no one else would suspect I was in any distress.

Con leaned down like he was giving me a quick embrace, then tilted me toward him, sliding his arm under mine and around my back. He lifted me with ease, and I leaned on him as I stood up.

"Walk with me," he whispered, pointing at my feet. "One in front of the other."

I nodded, thanking God that Con knew about my panic attacks and how to handle them. Holding on to his arm, I shuffled alongside him.

"Back in a bit," Con called over his shoulder. "Taking Neve for the grand tour of the garden."

"Oh, what glorious sights to behold," Imogen joked. "You may run into your father on the road."

"Grand!" Con ushered me out the door. As he walked me around the side of the house to a garden bench, I focused on borrowing his strength and trying to absorb his calming energy.

We sat on the bench, and Con tucked my body into his, wrapping his arms around my shoulders and pressing his lips against the top of my head. Ever so slowly, I started to come back to myself as the anxiety began to ebb.

"I'm so sorry, love," he murmured, stroking my back. "Breathe for me. Slowly now. Slow and deep. That's right. Good girl, you are."

I was vaguely aware that he was speaking to me like a frightened horse, but I didn't have the energy to feel embarrassed. I just focused on following Con's instructions and bathed in his nearness. His unique scent grounded me as I inhaled—sharp, rich, and woodsy, like a campfire just put out. The sensation of being protected by his large boulder of a body also helped.

He tilted my head up and looked into my eyes. "Why didn't you tell me what was going on in there?"

Shrugging, I said, "I thought I could make it stop."

He nodded. "Well, in the future, as soon as you start feeling off, tell me somehow. All you need to do is get my attention. Squeeze my hand, something. All right?"

"Okay," I whispered. Tender feelings for Con bloomed in my chest, warming me. We sat there for what seemed like forever until finally, the aftershocks of the panic attack dissipated.

As the flush of distress faded, I felt exhausted and completely drained. So I was quite surprised when Con's tender ministrations and sheer proximity began to induce another kind of heat. As my paralysis melted away, it was replaced by the urge to move closer to him, then closer again until our bodies touched. But my annoyingly persistent rational mind reminded me that it was broad daylight, his family was just around the corner in the house, and his father could arrive home any minute.

Still, I *could* risk stealing a kiss. That would reassure Con that I was okay, if nothing else.

I tilted my head up until I found his eyes with mine. "Kiss," I whispered by way of giving him fair warning.

But before I could take the initiative, he leaned down and brushed his lips across mine—contact so gentle and barely there, it seemed designed to frustrate and inflame at the same time.

A searing surge of desire drove me upward. "Like this," I murmured, stretching to my full height and capturing his mouth, tasting him. I inhaled his unguarded moan.

Con slid his arms down to my waist, grasping me on either side. Arching over me, now he was devouring. I sensed the restraint he'd exhibited since we first boarded the plane rapidly coming undone. His kiss dove deep, like he was searching for my very soul.

Flames licked up and down my body, and I was overwhelmed by the exhilarating fear that came over me sometimes when we kissed: the fear that the heat between us was so intense, it might spark into flames and consume us both.

But if this is how I'm destined to die, at least I'll die in bliss.

"Ho, there!"

Jack's voice called out to us from the end of the driveway. He must have glimpsed us on the bench. Fortunately, we were mostly concealed by a small yew tree.

Con pulled his mouth away from mine, wearing the savage expression of a man prepared to murder whoever had interrupted the moment—unless, of course, that man was his father.

"Is that you, Con? Neve?"

"It's us," Con shouted back, his voice still rough with desire. He cleared his throat as we disentangled ourselves and tried to sit on the bench as though we'd been doing nothing more than bird-watching.

"Grand! See you inside." Mercifully, his father didn't stop for a chat. I was pretty sure my face was crimson and gleaming with perspiration.

"Christ almighty." Con pushed his hand forcefully through his brown curls. They were still unruly, even though he'd gotten a trim just before the trip.

"Thank you, for… you know. *Calming me down.*"

"Huh," he grunted. "What every man wants to hear after he kisses a woman."

"You know what I mean." I rested my head on his shoulder, threading my fingers through his. "I don't know what happened to me back in the kitchen, but thanks."

"No, that was my fault," Con said. "I knew Eamonn

was worked up. I thought I calmed him down on the car ride home, but I was wrong. Should have taken him for a pint or something instead of subjecting you to that."

I pushed away. "You didn't subject me to anything. Eamonn just feels what he feels. I should be able to handle it."

"Is that so?" He drew a line along my jaw. "So everyone else can have triggers, but you're immune? That's your superpower, is it?"

I didn't think it was a trigger, exactly. I didn't know what it was. I wanted to argue the point, but I knew better than to get into a debate with him while his magnetic proximity was still impacting my ability to form coherent thoughts. It was embarrassing, my lack of control over my anxiety, my attraction to Con—or anything, really. "Can we go back inside now?"

"Is that *really* what you want?" His teasing, suggestive tone in such frustrating circumstances irritated me enough that I shot up off the bench.

"And there I was," he said as he eased himself into a standing position, "just last night, telling Eric I hadn't pissed you off yet."

"You spoke to Eric last night? Well, you can call him tonight and update him."

As I turned on my heel, I both felt and heard a lively smack on my behind. Inflamed again in every which way, I whipped back around only to find Con wearing a broad grin.

"Hey!" My hands flew to my hips, but before I could

raise any further objections, he tucked his arm into mine and steered me back toward the door.

"Go on, get inside," he cheerfully advised. "There's a lewd Corkman hereabouts."

"You don't say," I said, shooting him a sharp look.

But as we walked back toward the house, I had to press my lips together hard to keep him from seeing me smile.

CHAPTER 9

CON

The commotion downstairs woke him, but in truth, Con hadn't been sleeping very soundly. Between the perplexing details of Ciara's case and the provocative knowledge that Neve was sleeping just on the other side of his bedroom wall, there wasn't much peace to be found.

As he headed down the corridor in his robe and slippers, Con stopped outside Neve's room for a moment, pressing his fingers against her door. What he wouldn't give to go inside right now and do what he'd been dreaming of doing with her—dreams he'd finally stopped trying to suppress once she broke up with her ex.

But he could see out the hall window that Eamonn's car was in the drive, and the clock near the stairs read just past 11:00 p.m. Not a good sign.

Sure enough, Eamonn was in the kitchen, looking like he'd been put through the ringer. Their parents sat with him at the kitchen table, their father's hand on Eamonn's shoulder and their mother's wrapped around a steaming mug.

"Con," their father said, clearly relieved at the sight of his elder son. "Eamonn has news."

"I didn't mean to disturb everyone." Eamonn's voice was anguished. "I just wanted to let you know why I won't be by tomorrow morning."

That didn't bode well at all.

"Out with it, then," Con said, taking a seat at the table. "What happened?"

Eamonn had received a call from Laoch Garr after dinner, saying Ciara was in distress and they'd had to sedate her.

"Another nightmare?" Con asked.

"No," Eamonn said, his face twisted with misery. "It's worse. Her arm, it's started to feel to her like it's burning, like someone poured acid over it. They can't find anything wrong with it, but she's in agony. I went over right away, of course." He pressed his reddening eyes against his sleeve. "It helped her to see me, but she was just pleading for someone to do something to make the burning stop. It was so real to her, but she showed me her arm, and there are no burns. It just looks like her usual scratches, healing up okay. Before I even arrived, they tried painkillers, burn cream, numbing cream— they tried everything. Eventually she asked them to just give her something to knock her out, and Dr. Boyle approved it. He said to tell you they've taken skin samples, and they're sending them to the lab, but he thinks it's in her head—not like she's making it up, though. It's real but caused by the mind somehow. Used to be called psycho-something...."

"Psychosomatic?"

Eamonn snapped his fingers. "That's it."

"Right." It was most likely a somatoform pain disorder triggered by the memories that came up after Ciara's hypnosis session, but of course, the team couldn't be certain until they did a full medical workup.

"Do you know what he's talking about?" their father asked.

"Sometimes people develop real physical symptoms in response to psychological distress," Con explained. "We're still trying to understand it, but it's part of the mind-body connection."

Their mother's hand flew to her mouth. "That poor girl."

Con knew that for the patient, the pain was all too real, but if there was no physical cause, it could be very difficult to treat. Ciara would need Eamonn's support more than ever. But his brother had just said.... "What do you mean, you won't be by in the morning?"

"I mean I'm going out of town for a few days."

That was what Con was afraid of. "Like hell you are."

"Don't think you're talking me out of it," Eamonn said, squaring his shoulders.

Con exchanged knowing looks with his parents. Eamonn wouldn't be completely frank with his mother and father there. "All right, but we need to talk more about Ciara, in any case. Front room?"

With a shrug and a nod, Eamonn picked up his mug and led the way into the next room. Con shut the door behind them.

Once inside, Eamonn turned to face Con. His tone mixed with anguish and anger, he said, "You can't deny something happened to her arm now. There's no other reasonable explanation for this... burning thing... feck, I don't know what to call it. But somebody's got to talk to Max and find out what he did to her!"

"Ease up a minute now," Con urged. "I'm not trying to talk you out of anything, but that gobshite can wait long enough for us to sit down and talk this through."

"I'm going to Galway," Eamonn announced, but at least he sat down on the couch.

Con knew this was likely his last moment to stop his brother from doing something reckless. He gathered his thoughts for a moment. "Look, Ciara needs you here. I didn't want to say too much in there, but these somatoform pain disorders, they're very difficult to treat, and a lot of it has to do with emotional healing. You're her rock, Eam. She'll need you around to help if she's going to get better. Don't leave her to deal with this alone."

Eamonn dug his fingertips into his brow. "Don't do this to me, Con!"

"I'm not doing anything to you! I'm offering to help."

"You can help by staying here with Ciara!"

"My being here won't matter to her. It's *you* she

needs, the man she loves, the man who loves her. Not his fecking brother."

Sighing heavily, Eamonn flopped backward onto the couch. "But somebody's got to go talk to that arsewipe. Ciara is convinced he knows something that can help us figure this out, and so am I."

"Stupid question, I know, but have you tried calling him?"

"Yeah," Eamonn said, shaking his head. "He's got my number blocked—not surprising, after my last call to him. But I even tried calling him from Ciara's phone, and he's got her blocked, too, looks like. We even reached out to Deirdre, thinking she'd know how to find the prick. Deirdre's been in regular phone contact with Ciara since she moved away from Galway, but now she's not picking up or calling back for some reason. And neither of them has responded to our emails."

"All right." Con pulled his mobile out of his robe pocket. "Give *me* his number."

"He's not going to talk to you! He doesn't know you from Adam."

"No. But I'd like to call and introduce myself as I'm pulling up to his house so he doesn't come out swinging," Con said. "You have his address?"

"Yeah…. Wait, you mean *you're* going?"

"I said I would, didn't I? It'll take me, what, a day, maybe two, to find Max and talk to him. I can consult with John about Ciara's case over the phone until I get back." Con leaned forward, fixing him with a heavy gaze. "She needs you here. Let me do this for you."

He could see Eamonn was considering. Con was counting on his brother's desire to be near Ciara in her time of need overriding the desire to inflict pain on Max.

"Tell you what," he said to buy more time. "Let's call that friend I told you about and see if he's made any progress digging up dirt on this character. It might be useful when I interview him."

"I hope you'll interview him with your fists," Eamonn grumbled.

"I'll do what's necessary to help Ciara," Con said carefully.

"Fine. Let's call your guy."

With a nod, Con dialed Eric, then breathed a prayer of thanks when he picked up on the third ring.

"Yo, Conman."

"Eric, howya? I'm here with my brother, Eamonn. Can I put you on speaker?"

"Sure thing."

Con placed the phone down on the coffee table, and both he and Eamonn leaned in. "So, did you find anything?"

"Yeah, so…." They heard Eric blow out a puff of air. "This guy's a piece of work."

"What kind of piece of work?" Eamonn asked, visibly agitated.

"That's Eamonn," Con said.

"Hey, man, nice to meet you," Eric replied. "So, this

Max guy is pretty sophisticated when it comes to covering his tracks, but I did manage to trace him to some fairly shady discussion boards. Dark web stuff. I'm warning you, it's weird."

"We already knew he was shady," Con said. "What kind of weird?"

"Creepy weird," Eric said. "I'll tell ya, I learn something new every day. He's part of this online community, people who invent and lead obscure religious groups. Like *really* obscure. Like 'I made up this religion while living in my mother's basement' obscure. They refer to their groups as 'exclusive' and 'niche,' though."

"Sounds like our man," Eamonn said.

"All right," Con said, "what else?"

"Well, from what I read, they compare notes on how to run these groups in ways that maximize their control over members, with a focus on financial exploitation."

"Neve was right," Eamonn murmured to Con. "His father taught him well."

Eric continued, "They compare notes on how to manipulate people in different ways, like through rituals that make people feel like they belong to something powerful and ceremonies where they commit hard. Nothing too crazy—no blood sacrifices or anything—but the folks on this discussion board talk in code a lot, so it was hard to understand everything they were saying."

Con scowled. "What kind of code?"

"Well, not code, exactly. They just give regular words alternative meanings that only people on the board understand. Kind of like in those culty motivational seminars."

Con could see Eamonn's face reddening with rage. His imagination must have been running into dark territory. "Do you have any more specifics about what Max was saying? We don't care about those other nutters."

"Yeah, so Max is a strange cat. On the one hand, he seems really cold and businesslike about the financial control aspects," Eric said. "He talked about having some kind of insurance policies on his followers, but I haven't found any details yet. On the other hand, he's pretty hardcore when it comes to his own made-up religion. It's like he's a true believer."

"True believer in what?" Con asked.

"In his own BS. I'm thin on the details, but Max seems to believe what he's doing to people is 100 percent justified because he really sees himself as some sort of spiritual authority. He talks like it's his right for people to give him their money and loyalty, because he's got some kind of special connection to this ancient god. He even said they hold rituals in an island sea cave under a tenth-century stone church."

"Near Galway, no doubt," Con murmured to Eamonn, recalling Ciara's words.

"It's pretty elaborate stuff," Eric added, "and there's definitely a vibe that he and his partner believe their homegrown religion is based on something real."

"What partner?" Eamonn asked.

"There was another person on the board who runs

the cult with Max. At least, *I* would call it a cult," Eric said. "On the boards, Max goes by POT, all caps. The other one goes by TOT. The two of them used some of their own terminology, too, that was different from the rest of the board—like they'd done their own world-building."

"World-building, like in a video game?" Con suggested.

"Yeah, maybe. That could make sense. Is that what this is? Tied to a game?"

"We think so." Con and Eamonn exchanged a knowing look.

"Well, if that's the case, these two seem to take it pretty damn seriously."

"Yeah," Eamonn said, "sounds like they drank their own Kool-Aid."

"They sound like fecking delusional narcissists to me," Con said.

"Truth." Eric cleared his throat. "Listen, I'm really sorry your girl got mixed up with this guy, Eamonn."

"It's in the past," Eamonn said, "but thanks."

"Uh, sorry, you guys, but I have to run," Eric said. "We're headed out the door. Con, you want me to shoot you what I have?"

"Yes, do that," Con said.

"Okay. I'll send it to the secure account. If I come up with anything else, I'll let you know, but as of Monday, I'll be off the grid for a couple weeks. Camping in Colorado."

"Not a bad idea, all things considered," Con said.

No doubt Eric would be glad to get far away from Brickhaven's potential threats for a while, not to mention the Secret Service's prying eyes. "Thanks again for this. It helps a lot. Give Katie our best and enjoy yourself."

"Yeah, thank you," Eamonn added.

"No problem. Good luck," Eric said, then clicked off the line.

Toward the end of the conversation, Con had heard in Eric's voice that he was holding something back, no doubt because Eamonn was there. But it had been crucial to have Eamonn on the phone call so he'd feel he was a part of Con's efforts and not being left out of the loop. He would follow up with Eric later.

"Sicko," Eamonn snarled.

"Yeah." With a heavy sigh, Con leaned back. "I wish I could say I'm surprised to hear there's an underground group of cult leaders swapping secrets."

His brother's face twisted with disgust. "Almost as bad as Catholic priests."

"Huh." Con didn't argue. Although their parents remained devout, like himself, Eamonn had left the Catholic Church behind years ago. In his brother's case, it was after learning a friend had been abused by their local priest for years while they were in school together. Understandably, Eamonn's feelings about religion were still powerful and raw. "What was it Eric said? 'Nothing too crazy, like blood sacrifices'? At least that's something to be thankful for."

"Max is the one who should be thankful. It doesn't

sound like he's doing anything nasty enough for me to kill him over."

So far. "You'll let me do this, then? Interrogate this gobshite for you?"

Eamonn considered for a few moments, then acquiesced. "Okay. You win." He rubbed his eyes, and Con saw the deep fatigue lining his face. "You're right. My place is with Ciara. I want to see what your friend sends you on this guy, though."

"Of course," Con said, comfortable in the knowledge that he'd be carefully selecting what he forwarded to his brother.

"Hey, though. What about Neve?"

"What about her?"

"You going to take her with you? You're still on a date, aren't you?"

"I don't imagine my conversation with Max is going to be a very romantic activity. Besides, I'm sure Neve will prefer to stay here and help with Ciara."

But he knew that wasn't true as soon as he said it. There was a much stronger chance that Neve would want to go with him, especially since he was fairly thin on reasons why she shouldn't. He could hardly say, "Stay here because I have to go see this creepy fecker and possibly beat him to a pulp."

When he'd first offered to take care of Max for his brother, it had been a stalling tactic and purely theoretical. Now he had to work through the logistics, and Neve was a sticking point. The love of his life, yes, but in this case, also a problem that required managing. He wondered how much of a fight he was in for.

"Won't she be angry, though?" Eamonn looked concerned now. "I wouldn't want our situation causing problems between you two. Neither would Ciara. If this is going to screw things up—"

"Ah, don't worry," Con interjected. "Neve's well practiced at being angry with me—and I at talking her down." He forced a reassuring smile for his brother's sake.

Eamonn gave a hint of a smile in response. "Talking her down? I bet that sounds a lot like groveling."

"You're not wrong. Try to get some sleep, will you? You look like hell, and Ciara needs you to be at your best."

"I'll try. You too. You're the one who needs to rest up. You know, just in case."

"Right. Just in case." Con hoped words were all he would need to exchange with Max. After all, if he came back with swollen knuckles, Neve might just see him for the brute he really was, pack up, and head home without him.

CHAPTER 10

CON

The next morning, as he tossed his overnight bag onto the back seat of the SUV, Con heard Neve's footsteps on the gravel, coming fast and hard. She must have already spoken to his parents.

"Were you even going to wake me up before you skulked off?" Neve called out as she approached.

He shut the door and turned. Neve came to an abrupt stop a few feet in front of him, a flush-faced, resplendent goddess of fury. Her long brown hair was wild, and while her eyes were soft green, they were wide with outrage.

She was a slightly rumpled goddess, granted. Neve must have just rolled out of bed, judging by her slippers, yoga pants, and faded REO Speedwagon T-shirt. She'd wrapped a black cardigan around herself, but too quickly, and now it was falling off one shoulder. Never had she looked more beautiful.

"Well?" Neve punctuated her question with a foot

stomp, which was immediately followed by a wince. Clearly her thin-soled slippers were not designed for gravel driveways.

"Don't your feet hurt?"

"*That's* what you have to say to me?" She tossed her head, sending her hair flying back.

Con wanted nothing more than to close the distance between them, slide his fingers into that hair, tilt her head back, and—

"For God's sake, Con, your parents just told me you're going to Galway to see Max! *By yourself!* Is that true?"

She was shouting in earnest now. He needed to pull himself out of his passionate fantasy.

"I can hear you, Neve," he said, tilting his head at the house by way of reminding her they could be overheard.

"I don't give a good goddamn who hears me," she exclaimed, but her voice was lowered.

"Of course I was going to wake you before I left and explain everything."

"Perfect. Well, now's your chance." She formed a gun with her fingers, pointed it at him, and pulled the imaginary trigger. "*Go.*"

"All right." He held his hands up in surrender. "Look, Eamonn came over last night. Ever since the hypnosis, Ciara's arm feels like it's burning all the time."

Con fell just a little bit more in love with Neve as her

expression instantly softened from anger into compassion.

"Oh my God, how awful! Is there something wrong with her arm, or…?"

"Not that they can tell so far. They're running tests. Most likely, it's a somatoform pain response."

Neve's shoulders collapsed. "Oh dear."

"They had to sedate her." Neve shared Con's experience with such disorders, so she knew how hard they could be to treat. "Eamonn has it in his head that Max knows something that could help her situation. He's tried reaching out, but the prick's not responding. No surprises there, and personally, I doubt he'll be of any use to us. But I offered to go talk to him to prevent Eamonn going. With his state of mind right now, I don't know what he'd do if he met Max face-to-face."

He watched as she stared at a point on the ground between them, processing this new information. Finally, she looked up, eyes narrowed. "What'll *you* do?"

"What do you mean, what'll I do? I'll find the bastard and ask him what he knows about Ciara's arm, her nightmare, or both."

"Find him how?"

"Eamonn already had his home address from Ciara. If he's not there, I can always go to Wicked Games and find him there."

"And because he's such a nice guy and has shown nothing but kindness toward Ciara, of course he'll talk to you." She folded her arms across her chest like they were plates of armor, and she was girding herself for battle. "What if he knows something but refuses to tell you?"

Con pressed his lips together in a hard line. The temptation to lie was strong, but not as strong as his aversion to making Neve as furious as she'd been the last time he'd lied to her outright. He decided to treat her question as rhetorical and change the subject instead. "I gave Eamonn your number. He'll call you later with an update. We don't know yet if they'll allow Ciara visitors today."

Frowning, she jabbed at the gravel with the toe of her slipper. "You do know what I do for a living, right? Ask people questions? Encourage people to talk, even when they don't want to, and about sensitive topics? Fill in blanks?"

Con sighed and closed his eyes. "And I know you're excellent at it. That's not in question."

"Then why not bring me along?" She took another step toward him and laid her hand on his chest. "Unless you're planning on handing out some... what did you call it? Extralegal justice?"

Christ. So she'd only been pretending to be asleep when he was talking to Eamonn in the car. He wrapped his hand around her fingers. "You were eavesdropping!" With urgency, he searched his memory. "What did you hear?"

But his accusatory tone failed to throw Neve off her line of questioning. She pulled her hand from his. "Tell me the truth! Is that why you don't want to bring me along? In case you decide to beat up Max?"

Con ran his hand through his hair. "Jaysus, Neve. I'm not planning to hurt the man."

"But you might."

If he opened his mouth, he would have to either lie or horrify her. Helplessly, he shrugged.

"Oh, great!" She began to pace back and forth in front of him. "Wonderful. So you end up in jail, and I end up having to go back to the States alone, and we don't help Ciara at all. In fact, we might make things worse."

Con was somewhat relieved that Neve didn't appear as alarmed by the idea of his perpetrating violence as she was by the potential consequences for him, Ciara, and herself. "Neve, just stop for a minute, please." She ceased pacing and turned to face him. Gingerly, he reached out and took her hands in his. "Look, I promise you I'll do everything humanly possible to make sure things don't go south with Max. But I've got to go and try to help sort this out for Eamonn. Otherwise, you know as well as I do there's a chance Ciara won't get better—not for a long time, anyway."

"Of course you have to help. That's what we came here to do. It's just…." Neve wove her fingers between his. "That night we spent in cells in the West Wing, I thought about what it would be like if Brickhaven succeeded in framing us for something and one or both of us ended up in jail. What my life would be, without being able to see you, touch you…." Her eyes, the color of sea glass, sparkled as tears gathered.

If any other woman talked to him like this, he would

assume she was trying to manipulate him. But not Neve. She was pure sincerity. His heart swelled so much it felt like it was pushing against his rib cage.

Christ, this woman is going to be the death of me.

"So, to be clear," Con asked carefully, "it's not me hurting Max you object to, it's me risking arrest?"

"It's both!" She yanked her hands away from his. "I mean, you're a doctor, Con. You heal people, not harm them. You took an oath."

"*Patients.*" He tilted his head to one side. "I took an oath not to harm any *patients.*"

"Good grief!" Neve dropped her head into her hands for a moment. "So, you're telling me my boyfriend is a hairsplitting sociopath. Okay, well, that's a new piece of information that I'll have to process later. But for now, there's no way I'm letting you go to Galway by yourself!"

He almost smiled at the captivating mixture of love, worry, and indignation skittering across her face. But he knew that would set her off, so he forced himself to look sober. "I appreciate that, Neve, and everything that's behind it. But the fact remains, I'm going, and you're staying."

"What? Who the…? I can't believe…." She huffed and threw her hands in the air. "Well, you may not be aware of this, but tourists have freedom of movement in Ireland!"

"I'm leaving in a few minutes," Con said, hoping cold, hard logic might get through to her. "By the time you rent a car, I'll be well gone. You don't know your way around here, and even Google Maps is only about 70, 75 percent reliable in Ireland. So if you try to follow me, you'll end up at a B&B in Nad."

Nad was just down the road, of course, and Eamonn assured him the GPS had improved and was nearly pinpoint perfect. True or not, though, his words had their intended effect. Doubt crept into Neve'e expression.

"You seem excessively *un*concerned about ending up in jail!"

"And you seem excessively concerned for the well-being of someone we know to be a right bollocks." Their conversation was going in circles. He needed to bring it to a close. "I didn't bring you home with me to put you in yet another potentially dangerous situation. You're not going with me, and that's it."

"So you admit it's potentially dangerous."

"For you, yes."

"But not for you."

"I can handle myself."

"And I can handle an interview, even with a 'right bollocks'!"

Con marveled at her confidence—justified in the mental health realm but totally misplaced in this instance. What if, God forbid, things did get dicey in Galway? Neve wasn't long out of recovery after getting stabbed by her patient, she was still tender from her recent surgery, and her body's delicious softness, while incredibly appealing, wouldn't exactly work to her advantage in a fight.

"Look, the best insurance I have against things going skew-ways with Max is my physical... presence," he said, unsure how else to describe the impact his size had. "No offense, but your being there would instantly deflate the all-important implied threat in the room."

At least she had the sense not to argue with that. "Okay. But I can wait in the car, be your getaway driver. I'd feel much more comfortable being close by, with you knowing you'd have to explain yourself to me afterward."

And he would feel *less* comfortable. Not to mention distracted, preoccupied, and unable to focus on the task at hand. "It's not going to happen, Neve. I need you here supporting Ciara and Eamonn and acting as my eyes and ears at Laoch Garr. I only feel comfortable going away because I know you'll be here, managing things."

When the spark in her eyes dulled the slightest bit, Con knew she'd finally realized he wasn't going to budge. It was all he could do to stop himself from changing his mind, just to see that spark brighten up again. Instead, he stepped forward and squeezed her shoulders. "Is it so bad, staying with my family?" he asked, knowing the question was unfair even as he posed it. "They love you. You'll get the chance to talk about me behind my back, look at baby pictures. Isn't that what you said you wanted to do on this trip?"

"Yeah," she admitted, "but I was hoping to do those things between long kissing interludes." Tears once again gathered in her eyes.

He pulled her against him, wrapping her in his arms and holding on tight. Tucking his face down into her hair, he inhaled the exquisite scent of her, hoping the memory of it would sustain him while he was away. "I don't want to be apart from you either. I can hardly stand the idea, in fact." He placed a soft kiss on the top of her head and pulled away, meeting her upward gaze. "But I've got to go."

"No wonder they call you Tarbh." Although her words were cross, when she blinked, a single tear fell down her cheek.

Con cleared his throat to keep his voice from cracking. "I'll have my mobile with me. You can call me anytime, and I'll ring you regularly."

"How regularly?"

"Every time I stop for petrol, at least. And whenever I get to where I'm going. And when I find Max, and after I talk to him. And again when I'm on my way home. Every time I sit down for a meal." He gave her a gentle smile. "Any other times you'd like me to call?"

She pulled her phone out from the pocket of her cardigan and looked down at the screen. He waited for a snappy comeback, but none came. Instead, with a sigh, she leaned into him, sliding her arms around his waist. "That should do it. My phone's charged up. I'll be waiting. Just come back safe. And not in handcuffs."

In that moment, Con feared he might be crushed under the weight of the love-induced guilt he was feeling. If he stayed a moment longer, he wouldn't be able to bring himself to leave. Pulling away, he squeezed her hand. "I'm going to go say goodbye to the folks now. Come with me?"

But she shook her head. "I don't want to be here when you drive off. I'd end up crying in front of your parents, and I don't want them thinking I hate the idea of staying here with them." She squeezed his hand back, and while she couldn't bring herself to smile, he could tell she was trying. "I'm just going to go for a walk, okay? Drive safe, and call me like you said, the first time you stop for gas."

"I promise." He cupped her chin, holding her gaze with his. "I love you."

"I love you too." She took his hand away, kissed his palm, and turned on her heel. With a quick wave, she walked past the SUV in the direction of the garden.

The pull to go after her was impossibly strong. Thinking of his brother, Con had to marshal every bit of willpower he could to walk back toward the house. The confrontation with Neve had been even more taxing than he'd imagined. All the more reason to do what he needed to do as quickly as possible and get back home to her.

CHAPTER 11
NEVE

This was a really stupid thing to do. Really, really stupid.

That was the one thought that kept running through my mind on repeat as I was tossed around like dice in a box. Every time Con took a turn—and there seemed to be hardly any straight roads on the way to Galway—I had to brace myself to keep from banging into the sides of the SUV, or slamming into the back seat, which would no doubt lead to my instant discovery. And I couldn't risk that, not until we were far enough away from Kilshannig that Con wouldn't see the sense in turning back.

What the hell were you thinking? Right at that moment, I could have been back at Con's parents' house having a lovely breakfast and a hot shower in preparation for accompanying Eamonn to Laoch Garr. Instead, I was breathing through impending motion sickness and fighting to keep my slippers from falling off. Very dignified.

How old are you? Five? It was true; I had acted on a mad impulse. While Con and I were talking by the SUV, I just kept thinking about what I'd learned through my internet search the night before. In Ireland, the sentence was up to five years in jail for assault causing harm. And now Con was going after Max.

I didn't think I could stand being away from him for five days. But five years? Not to mention that a conviction could spell the end of his medical career and impact the rest of his life. There was no way in hell I was going to let that happen.

Not that I didn't believe Con when he said he wasn't planning to hurt Max. But what if that man was as diabolical as we suspected? If Con showed up at his house without an invitation, might Max attack him, forcing him to defend himself, and then make it look like Max was the victim? And then there was the real risk that Con could get hurt, no matter what reassurances he gave me.

Those thoughts had preyed on my mind while he and I were arguing. My anxiety built up and up, and when he said he was going back to the house, it was as though my brain went haywire. I'd seen that the SUV had a parcel shelf in the back that concealed the trunk's contents from sight. When I turned back to the house, an uncontrollable urge sent me doubling back to the car. I opened the hatch, climbed inside, and pushed the

Close Door button. The hatch shut with a light click, and I was in near-perfect darkness.

Rational thought had abandoned me completely. All I could do was lie there, shaking and trying to breathe. After a few minutes, I heard Con open the car door. I felt the vehicle shift as he sat down, and the next thing I knew, we were moving. The only other objects in the back with me were some empty shopping bags and a scratchy wool blanket, which I was currently using as a makeshift pillow.

It felt like we'd been driving for hours, but it may have only been fifteen minutes for all I knew. I was afraid to take my cell phone out and look at it for fear that just as I did so, Con would lurch to the right or left, sending it flying. It could get lost in there, or worse, broken.

It occurred to me multiple times to just call out to Con, get him to stop the car, and risk having him turn around and take me back. At least that would put an end to this foolishness. But each time I thought about it, I pictured him being so startled by a voice coming from the back of the car that he might drive off the road, or brake suddenly and cause an accident. So I just dug my nails into the blanket beneath my head and reassured myself that he would have to stop for gas sooner or later. When he did, if enough time had passed that it would be impractical to turn back, I would present myself as a *fait accompli* and ride in comfort the rest of the way to Galway. A small part of me hoped he would be pleasantly surprised to find me there. But every time that hope raised its hand, it was shouted down by more sensible emotions.

In the meantime, I tried to pretend I was on the Space Mountain ride at Disney World and this was supposed to be fun. At least his parents wouldn't be worried, since Con had no doubt explained that I needed some time to myself and had gone for a walk.

My stomach lurched as the car slowed yet again, but this time after he turned, he kept slowing down until we came to a stop. *Thank God,* I thought when I heard the engine turn off. We were stopping for real.

I pulled my phone out of my pocket and checked the time. We'd been on the road for well over an hour. Surely Con wouldn't turn back at this stage. I turned on the flashlight app and looked around for a button to open the back hatch, but there was none. Not too surprising, I guessed, given that it wasn't a passenger compartment. But I couldn't find a latch, a handle, or any other way to open the hatch from the inside either. Next, I tried to remove the parcel shelf, but it was attached in such a way that it locked into place while the hatch was shut.

Don't panic, I ordered myself as I set to work on the back row of seats. I knew there must be a way to put those seats down and lay them flat to create more storage space. Again using the flashlight, I searched, but there were no visible buttons or latches. I tried bracing myself against the back hatch and pushing on the seats with my feet, but they wouldn't budge. Patience gave way to frustration, and my pushing turned into kicking. Nothing.

I began to feel nauseated. Anxiety was creeping in. My face flushed with heat, and my skin was starting to feel clammy. It felt like Con was taking forever to come back to the car. Who knew where he'd gone? Were we even at a gas station, or was he making a longer stop somewhere else?

When my heart began to bang against my chest, I knew I had to get out of there, and quickly. Knowing it was a lunatic move but out of better ideas, I turned around and started kicking the door to the hatch. Someone would hear me, wouldn't they? Someone had to come and help. Just in case, though, I added shouting to the mix.

"Help!" I called out. *Boom, boom, boom.* "I'm in here! Help me!"

I kept that up for a few minutes until finally, I heard voices outside—women's voices. Then the blessed click of the hatch being opened.

Thank God.

I covered my eyes against the daylight and burst out the back of the SUV. There were two pairs of steadying arms waiting to help me. Once I was able to focus, I saw I'd been rescued by two petite older women. With the sun behind them, their striking white hair glowed like halos.

"Oh my dear, are you all right?" The woman on my right wore a bright pink raincoat. She appeared genuinely worried.

"Yes, I'm okay," I said, forcing a smile. "Thank you so much for opening the door."

"Of course," the woman on my left said, adjusting her floral scarf. "But who locked you in there? Was it that big man in the shop? You should come with us, pet. The gardaí—"

"Oh no, there's no need for that!" I found my footing and straightened up, laughing lightly. "I'm with… the big man, I guess, in the shop, but he didn't know I was in the back there. I closed myself in by accident."

The women exchanged skeptical looks. The one on my right rested her hand on my arm. "We'll stay with you until he comes back, just to make sure you're all right."

"I am, really." I patted her hand. "I know what you're thinking, but this isn't… *that*. I mean, this isn't a kidnapping situation or domestic violence or anything. Honestly, it was a silly accident."

"You're an American?" asked the woman with the scarf.

"Well, yes."

"You're a long way from home, then. Really, we're very happy to help you."

The next thing I knew, a yellow-and-blue police vehicle was pulling up next to us.

"That's what I was saying," she explained, "that we called the gardaí, and they were on their way here."

Oh, good grief. I tried to smooth down my hair and clothes as two officers climbed out of their car and joined us. "Thanks so much for coming," I said, "but there's been a misunderstanding."

The officers looked the three of us over. "Who was it who called us?"

"We did," the woman in pink said. "This American woman was locked in the back of this car. We heard her kicking and screaming, and we opened the door for her. She says that tall gentleman in the shop is the driver."

"That man?" One of the officers pointed at Con, who was coming out through the door into the parking lot.

"Yes!" She stepped in front of me, placing herself between Con and me. The other woman followed suit. Their expressions were flinty, and despite their smaller stature, I had no doubt they were fully prepared to protect me from "the tall man" if the guards failed.

While I was both impressed and deeply moved by the women's courage, the situation was getting out of hand. "He's my boyfriend. There's been a misunderstanding…."

But the officers were already on their way to intercept Con. "Is this your vehicle, sir?"

"Yes it is. Is there a—" Con stopped midsentence when he spotted me standing behind my self-appointed protectors. "Neve?"

"You know this woman?" one of the officers asked.

"Yes he does," I said loudly. "Like I said, he's my boyfriend. He didn't know I was in there. Hi, Con! Surprise!" I tried to sound cheerful in the hopes that everyone involved would realize I wasn't on the receiving end of any nefarious treatment.

"Are you all right?" But Con's effort to approach me was thwarted by the gardaí, who placed themselves in his way. Instantly, his face transformed into a dark cloud.

To prevent some sort of incident, I darted around my lovely rescuers and walked up to the officers. "Again, I really appreciate you coming, but this has all been one big misunderstanding. He didn't know I was in the back of the car. I had shut myself in by accident."

The officers exchanged the same skeptical look the women had earlier.

Con nearly leveled me with his own glare. "By accident?"

"How did that happen, exactly?" one of the officers asked.

I truly hated lying, and to make matters worse, I was really bad at it. This was compounded by the fact that I hadn't even had my morning cup of coffee yet. But with the officers there, I knew things could get very serious, very quickly if I didn't think fast and come up with something plausible.

"Yeah, so, hah! Funny story," I began, smiling broadly. "He was leaving on a trip this morning, and I wanted to surprise him. I was going to hide in the back of the SUV here, then jump out and give him a goodbye kiss. So I climbed in there and pushed the button to close the door, not realizing that the same button didn't open the door too. I was just curled up in there, waiting for him. But then he took so long coming out to the car, I guess I must have fallen asleep!" I threw my hands in the air and laughed. "I didn't wake up until just a few minutes ago. When I realized the car had stopped and I couldn't open the hatch, I started shouting and kicking the door. Thankfully, these two wonderful ladies heard me and came to my rescue. Thank you so much, by the way."

I turned back to the women and held up prayer hands. They didn't appear at all convinced. When I turned back around, the officers also appeared suspicious. Con's expression, on the other hand, was utterly inscrutable. It was his reaction that concerned me the most.

The officers continued to look me over for a few moments, taking in everything from my flushed face to my slippers. One of them asked Con, "Is that what happened?"

"If that's what she says," he replied, his voice cool and neutral. "That does sound like the type of... *spontaneous* thing she might do." He reached between the officers and took my hand. "Are you all right, love? You look a bit flushed."

"Yes, of course! I'm fine, totally fine."

The combination of Con's show of concern and my crazy tale deflated the tension of the situation. No longer kidnapper and victim, he and I were now the long-suffering boyfriend and the wacky American chick.

With the officers there and the mystery solved, the two women excused themselves, but not before I thanked them profusely. They really were heroes, as far as I was concerned. Con even braved the daggerlike looks they were shooting at him and thanked them, as well. The officers checked Con's license and the car's registration, took down his information, and then asked us both a few more questions. They wanted to know where we were staying, when I arrived in Ireland—general questions that seemed to be geared toward confirming we were neither lunatics nor outlaws. Once they were satisfied, they left as well—but not before writing Con a ticket for carrying a passenger who wasn't wearing a seat belt. I wanted the ground to swallow me whole.

As relieved as I was that the officers were leaving without further incident, their departure meant that now I was alone with Con—normally a welcome circumstance. But in that moment, I had no idea what to expect.

Without saying a word, he went to the pump and began gassing up the car.

Okay, I guess I should have expected that.

"Oh, here," he said, fishing his wallet out of his pocket. "If you like, there are drinks and some snack foods in the shop."

Embarrassed at having to take his wallet to feed myself, I did so anyway, since I was dying of thirst. As I shuffled toward the shop, I wondered if this was some sort of trap. Was Con trying to lull me into thinking he wasn't that angry, only to unleash his rumored volcano of fury later? Or was he making soothing noises to preemptively defuse my anger when he turned around to take me home? These thoughts so absorbed me that I nearly forgot to pay for my soda and trail mix on the way out the door. The shopkeeper eyed me like I was a stray dog that had wandered in and might bite. As quickly as I could, I returned to the car, handed Con his wallet, and slid as far down as possible in the passenger seat.

Finally, he climbed in next to me, moving gingerly. I could tell his leg was bothering him—and no wonder, after a long flight and barely any rest.

"You okay?" I asked, nodding toward his knee.

"What? Yeah, fine." He arched an eyebrow at me. "Buckle up."

"Oh, right," I said, swallowing hard.

Con waited until my seat belt clicked before he eased the car back onto the road.

CHAPTER 12
NEVE

had no idea if we were heading back the way we came or continuing on to Galway. But given the fact that I had just brought officers of the law into our lives, I decided to wait and let Con start that conversation.

After an uncomfortably long period of time, he said, "Right, so."

I braced myself, prepared for a major scold-fest.

Instead, he surprised me by saying, "The next town is Killarney. We'll stop there and get you a proper breakfast, pick up some clothes. And shoes," he added with a dubious glance at my slippers. "If you want to freshen up, we can get a hotel room."

A hotel room? That definitely sounded like he planned to proceed onward. "You're not taking me back to your parents', then?"

There was a pause as Con cast me a sidelong glance.

"What good would that do? I tried leaving you there once, but it didn't work, did it?"

Though his tone was dry, he didn't sound angry. I had no idea what to make of that. But it did occur to me that his parents might be starting to worry. "We should call them, though."

"You have your phone?"

I pulled it out of my pocket. Thankfully, it was unscathed. Con recited the number, and I dialed. "Hello?"

"Hello, Imogen!"

"Put it on speaker," Con murmured. I hit the button. "Hello, Ma!" he said, sounding almost jaunty. "I'm afraid I did something a bit *impulsive*." On the last word, he gave me a pointed look.

"Is it something to do with the fact that we haven't seen Neve in over an hour?"

"Yes, I'm afraid it is," he replied. "I was driving down the road and saw her walking there. I simply couldn't imagine being apart from her for days, so I talked her into getting in the car."

"Well, that's very romantic," Imogen said, "but why didn't you come back for her things? The last time we saw you, Neve, you were wearing slippers!"

"I knew if I brought her back, she would be lured into the house by the smell of rashers. Once you started feeding her, like any reasonable person, she'd refuse to leave."

Less than thrilled at being depicted as so intensely

food motivated, I narrowed my eyes at him. The corners of Con's mouth quirked upward.

"Well, all right, then." She sounded delighted. "You two have a nice trip!"

"Don't worry, I'll take care of her."

Another sideways glance from Con had me wondering what exactly he meant by that. But that concern was blotted out by my utter relief that he'd not only handled the conversation but also managed to come up with a story that preserved his parents' opinion of me. Matching his cheerful tone, I said, "Bye, Imogen!"

"Bye, bye bye bye!" she said rapidly before clicking off.

As soon as I put my phone away, Con's face once again became a mask of neutrality, his eyes focused on the road. So his bright mood had only been an act. I closed my eyes and swallowed hard. "Thank you for doing that."

"No bother."

I waited a while, but he was in no apparent hurry to start up a conversation. I cleared my throat and asked, "So… are you mad at me?"

Keeping his eyes on the road, he replied, "I'm still working that out."

"Oh." So he *was* mad, but I wouldn't have to hear about it until later. At least that gave me time to put together my own thoughts. He wasn't the only one with a bone to pick, after all.

"I *can* tell you," he continued, "that when I saw you

at the petrol station, the first thing I felt was sheer joy. I hated every moment I was away from you—or thought I was."

"Oh!" And just like that, Con made my heart skip a beat, something for which he seemed to have an infinite capacity.

Just as I began to feel some sense of relief, however, his tone grew stern again. "That said, we do need to have a conversation about what happened."

"Um…." I bit my lip in disappointment. "Now?"

"Works for me. Quick question."

Oh Lord, clipped sentences. Not a good sign.

I took in a slow, deep breath and released it. "Yes?"

"So, it was your lieutenants, not you, who called the gardaí?" he asked.

"My *what*?"

"Those two women," Con mumbled, as though afraid they might overhear. "They were quite intimidating."

I proved unable to keep my eyes from rolling. "Yes, those two *very* kind ladies called the gardaí. Of course it wasn't me!"

"Ah." He drove on for a few moments, considering. "That makes sense—kick and scream so someone else called the guards on your behalf. Always more convincing with witnesses. But if your plan was to preempt my potential arrest for assaulting Max with an arrest for kidnapping you, why did you then tell the guards I was innocent?"

"Oh, for the love…." With an exasperated sigh, I

turned to face him as far as the seat belt allowed. "You can't possibly think I wanted you to get arrested!"

He gave me a quick look of genuine confusion. Turning back to the road, he said, "I don't understand your strategy, then. You'll have to explain it to me."

"Good grief, Con!" I barked out a laugh at the absurdity. "Look, I didn't…. I wasn't…." I threw my hands up. "I didn't have a strategy, or even a plan. I just wanted to come *with* you!"

"So I was right." A knowing smirk made the corners of his eyes crinkle. "It *was* an impulsive decision."

Now he was irritating me. "Yes! Totally impulsive, okay? And I never would have done it if I'd known there would be trouble with the freaking *law*! I thought it would be *you* who let me out of the back eventually."

"Eventually?" His smile disappeared again. "When, exactly?"

This wasn't a conversational rabbit hole I wanted to go down, but Con seemed determined. "I figured when you stopped for gas. But then you walked away, and…."

His eyebrows lifted. "And?"

"And I just…." I flopped back against the seat. "I don't know. I freaked out a little bit, okay? I wasn't sure how long you would be, and I was getting really uncomfortable…."

"You had a panic attack."

I didn't like the certainty with which he made that pronouncement. "I did *not* have a panic attack," I said, even though I knew he wouldn't believe me. "It was more of an... anxiety surge."

But he continued as though he hadn't heard me. "An entirely predictable event, based on the fact that you have a history of panic attacks, you were trapped in a small, confined space, and, given the roads I took, you were likely being tossed about quite a bit."

I pressed my lips together and looked out the window. Tall trees thick with vines lined both sides of the road, blocking out the sun. It looked like we were traveling through a dark green tunnel. *Trapped again*, I thought as a hot blush crept up my neck.

"And so, having reached a point of crisis, you began screaming and kicking, not thinking at all about the dire conclusions someone might reach upon opening the hatchback and finding you there. Is that it, or thereabouts?"

"I told you I didn't want you to go without me," I exclaimed. "You didn't *listen*!"

"I listened. I just disagreed," he said, maintaining an infuriating level of composure. "I didn't want to take you with me into a situation with unpredictable risks. Still don't. But here we are." Shaking his head, Con added, "It's the White House all over again."

I gaped at him. "What?" I couldn't believe he brought that up.

"I'm realizing you have a surprising propensity for putting yourself in harm's way."

"Are you kidding me?" My leg started bouncing up and down as annoyance flowed through me. Yes, it had been risky, using my invitation to a White House event to gain access to the president. And yes, we'd ended up spending the night in Secret Service jail while we waited for them to clear us. But if we hadn't taken that risk, Brickhaven might have succeeded in killing the president. "This car is not the White House. Plus, we *all* agreed that was a risk worth taking!"

"You and Eric agreed. I went along to watch your back."

Now he was rewriting history. "That's not how I remember it!"

But Con just stared straight ahead, infuriating me further.

"Fine!" I huffed. "Even if that *were* true, what are you saying, exactly? That you can watch my back, but I can't watch yours?"

"It's situational," he said as though stating the obvious. "If this were a mental health emergency—" After a pause, he corrected himself. "Scratch that. Even then, if I was there, I'd still be watching your back, since we never know how those things will go."

My stomach dropped a bit, just as it always did when something reminded me of the stabbing nearly two months ago. In a session on the psychiatry unit, my clinical instincts had failed me, leaving me caught off guard and vulnerable to my patient's violent outburst. I had taken a month off work due to my injuries, but I still wasn't fully recovered mentally or emotionally. Although no one else held me responsible for what happened, insecurity and self-blame still plagued me.

"But in Max's case," he continued, "the situation requires a specific combination of skills and qualities that I have and, fortunately, you do not share."

I tried to imagine Con adding "massive, muscular ex-rugby player with the moral flexibility to be violent when required" to the Skills and Qualities section of his résumé. "You may be better equipped than I am to handle Max, but you still need backup. You're not invincible! Not bulletproof, knife-proof, immune to poison...."

"And you are?" Con tapped his finger on his bad knee. "You'll be pleased to know I am well aware of my physical vulnerabilities. And I promise, if in the process of confronting this arsehole he produces a gun, a knife, or a... goblet of hemlock, I'll get out of there immediately and call the guards."

It became evident that Con wasn't going to budge on that point—not at the moment, anyway. I pushed down on my still-bouncing leg, which was nearly launching itself into space. "Okay, fine. But you still haven't addressed the fact that I told you I didn't want you to go without me, and you went anyway."

"I *tried* to go without you." He began to smile but stopped when he caught the look I was giving him. "All right, look. If I had done a more thorough job of listening to you back there, I might have realized...." I could tell he was searching for the combination of words least likely to offend me. "I'd have understood the depth of your conviction on the matter. I'm sorry I didn't." He reached over and put his hand on top of mine. "Tell you what. Let's make a pact."

The sun began to break through the canopy of leaves outside, speckling Con with flashes of light. Equally curious and wary, I asked, "What kind of pact?"

"From now on, if one of us tries to put their foot down like you did back at the house, the other will stop and listen. No exceptions. We'll push pause on whatever the disagreement is about and keep talking until we find an answer we can both live with. Fair?"

I was pleasantly surprised. That actually *did* sound fair. In fact, had that pact been in place before, all this craziness might have been avoided. "A listening pact? I like that."

"Good," he said, putting his hand back on the wheel. "Now that's settled, I'll ask you again, and please tell me the truth this time. Are you all right? How are you feeling?"

I wasn't sure where they came from, but tears burned behind my eyes. I pushed them away with a few strong blinks. "Yes, I'm fine."

"Do you have your anxiety meds with you?" Now his voice was edged with worry.

"Obviously not," I said, gesturing at my lack of anything but the clothes on my back. "Like I said, I didn't plan for any of this. But I don't need them. I'm fine, I swear. There's no need—"

"To worry?" Con took one hand off the wheel and pinched the bridge of his nose. I had seen that gesture before. He was fighting off a headache, this time courtesy of *me*. I decided to just stay silent and let him say whatever it was he needed to get off his chest.

He paused to rub his hand across his forehead, as though trying to soften a band of tension. "No need for *me*, the man who is in love with you, to worry about *you*, the woman who locked herself in the back of my vehicle? Thank God you only had a panic—*anxiety surge*. You could easily have been injured, or worse."

The pain that scraped his voice once again triggered the threat of tears, but I fought them back again. "I'm sorry. I wasn't thinking."

"It's good of you to say that, but I don't want an apology," he said adamantly. "What I want is for you to live a long and healthy life—with me, if I can manage to talk you into it!"

Wait, did he just say…? Now there was no holding back the tears. They began to fall, wetting my cheeks.

"But if you persist in 'not thinking,'" he went on, "I'll have to start doing the thinking for both of us. And I know I'm on solid ground when I say you wouldn't like that." Con only looked over when I started sniffling. "Are you crying? Christ, I'm sorry. Come on, love, there's no need for that. There should be tissues in the glove box."

"Thanks," I whispered. I found the tissues and tried to clean myself up, but the tears kept coming.

"Dammit, was that too harsh?" Con asked. "I know I can get carried away—"

"No," I squeaked out. "It's not that!"

He blinked in confusion. "What is it, then?"

"Did you…?" I paused to blow my nose. "Did you mean what you just said? About wanting me to live a long life with you?"

"Jaysus!" He tossed his head back, looking heavenward. "Of *course* I did! What did you think this was about, all of this?"

"All… all of what?"

Con rubbed his forehead again, harder this time. "Me being in love with you. Pining for you since the day we met. Waiting two full years for you to break up with that Stephan gobshite. Bringing you to Ireland to meet my family. Having a coronary after finding you stashed in the back of the car. My God, Neve, everything we've been through together over the past few weeks. Of course I meant what I said!"

"But I thought you didn't want to get married!"

"Hang on now, that wasn't a marriage proposal," he warned. "That's going to be much grander, with the ring bought and everything. Otherwise, Una will skin me alive, to say nothing of Ma. Not to mention I have to ask your father first, don't I?"

I managed to pull my jaw off the floor and answer, "Well, you don't *have* to, of course, but I'm sure he would appreciate it—but not when we've only been dating for a few weeks!"

Con huffed. "But I've been in love with you for two years! Doesn't that count?" When I shrugged, he continued, "Right, so. I'll ask him first. Of all things, I want to make sure I do this properly. But wait, hang on." His eyes squinched up in confusion. "Why did you think I didn't want to get married?"

"Because of what you said to Eamonn in the car!"

"Fecking hell," he muttered, gripping the wheel. "I'm going to hang for all the things I said to Eamonn in that goddamn car! Can we just agree, right now, that if you're wondering about anything I said to him in the bloody car, or anything else I say, ever, you'll just ask me instead of jumping to conclusions?"

The flood of emotions I was feeling bubbled over into nervous laughter. "Okay, agreed."

"Thank Christ for that." His face relaxed into a relieved smile as he reached over and squeezed my knee. "First you're not thinking at all, then you're over-thinking. I don't know what to do with you sometimes. Fortunately...."

Con nodded at the window. The road had opened up. A patchwork of fields in various shades of green spread out in every direction. He pointed at a large road sign.

"Killarney?"

"Yes, Killarney. And not a moment too soon." He smiled. "I know you're not much for shopping, but according to Ma, all women love doing it here. First, though, we should get some proper food into you."

"I don't know." I looked down at my rumpled clothes. I was running around braless, for goodness' sake. "Maybe we should go shopping first. I could use some coffee, but I'm afraid I'd scandalize everyone in this getup."

"Not at all. You look gorgeous, as always, and you can wear my coat. Besides, once you open your mouth, everyone will know you're a Yank," he added with a wink. "They'll just assume wearing night attire in public is the latest fashion over there."

As we entered the picturesque town, Con scanned the streets. "There's an American-style diner down here. You'll fit right in, and we can plan out what to do next."

"Okay," I said, unable to keep the grin off my face. After what he'd just confessed, I was *happy* to let Con do the thinking for both of us—for the moment, at least.

CHAPTER 13

NEVE

I t was nearly noon by the time we were settled into the snug of Lenahans Public House. A snug, Con informed me, was the word for a small room in the front of the pub. In this case, we were separated from the rest of the venue by dark wood walls with frosted glass windows along the top half, giving us privacy and room to spread out a bit—room I needed after our shopping spree. I clipped tags off my purchases and folded them neatly into my new carry-on suitcase. After the comforting familiarity of a good diner breakfast, Con had taken me to Dunnes, a department store where his mother regularly shopped. After wading through the confusion over what sizes I wore in Ireland—bigger for clothing, smaller for shoes —I pulled together the least expensive three-day wardrobe I could find, since Con thought it unlikely we would be away any longer than that. One exception was the underwear I found—a seven-pair pack of panties, with the days of the week printed on the waistbands. On sale, they cost less than any other three pairs purchased separately. Plus, they were in the seven colors of the rainbow—way too much fun to resist.

It had been entertaining, watching Con try to avoid looking at the bra I chose as the cashier rang it up. I'd picked out the most comfortable one I could find, but it happened to be black with lace on it, and he couldn't quite tear his eyes away.

Yet again, it felt weird to let him pay for everything, but unless I wanted to wander around in my pajamas for the rest of the trip, there was no other choice. He kept saying he enjoyed treating me, though, and I got the aggravating impression that he was only humoring me when he agreed to let me pay him back later.

After I picked up a few toiletries at a nearby pharmacy, we went to the pub, which was quiet at present. I turned down Con's offer of getting a hotel room for the afternoon just so I could freshen up. That seemed much too extravagant, especially since I'd showered the night before and could easily brush my teeth in the pub's ladies' room.

While I packed my bag, Con squinted at his phone and waited for his pint of lager to settle.

"Eamonn hasn't called yet?"

"No, but he texted." He read, "Ma told me N went with you. Glad you took my advice."

"He told you to bring me to Galway?"

He arched a teasing eyebrow in my direction. I

smiled, relieved that the tension between us over my stowing away appeared to have dissipated.

"C is the same, still sedated," he read on. "Only one visitor allowed. N would have been bored here anyway. Will call you with any updates. Did you get the info from E? Travel safe."

"What info? Who's E?"

"Eric. He agreed to do some digging for us on Max."

I moaned aloud. Eric had already done way too much for us recently. "You got Eric involved in this?"

"Only tangentially," Con said defensively. "And don't worry. I promised we'd pay him back."

"*We?*"

Looking a bit sheepish, he muttered, "I told him we'd help out at a charity dinner at Katie's church."

"Hmm." That actually sounded like fun. "Okay. Continue."

Looking relieved, Con said, "Eric told Eamonn and me last night that Max is a member of some dark web hobby board for con artists who invent their own cults."

Good Lord. My mouth fell open. "That's a *thing*?"

He nodded. "These langers compare notes on how best to manipulate their followers and take their money, that sort of thing. Eric didn't find any evidence of overt illegal activity or anything else too bizarre going on, which was some comfort. But he did confirm Ciara's suspicions that Max takes the whole cult thing very seriously and appears to believe his own bullshit. I'm not sure if that makes him more dangerous or less."

"More, I'd guess. It's easier to reason with a cynic than a zealot."

"Fair point." Con examined his pint, then took a long swallow. "Ah. God, I missed that. I've yet to find a pint like this anywhere in DC."

I loved watching him enjoy something so intensely. I made a mental note to research where to find the best pint of Irish lager in Washington and to take him there on a date sometime. "So what other information was Eamonn asking about?"

"Eric said he would send me what he'd found. I was just reading over his email. He copied and pasted a few chats in there that Max was involved in, talking about *TOT*'s rituals, describing their ceremonies, that sort of thing. He also told Eamonn and me that Max holds his rituals in an island sea cave under a tenth-century stone church. I did some internet searching, and there's only one island near Galway with a church like that—Saint Cillian's Island. I'm betting that's the same sea cave Ciara mentioned."

A chill slid down my spine. "The one from her nightmare?"

Con nodded. "But Eric also attached a couple of video files to his email, which he didn't mention on the phone call with Eamonn. I'm guessing he meant for me to have a look and decide whether to share."

Secret videos? That sounded ominous. "Videos of what?"

"I haven't had a chance to look yet, but I found an

Airbnb in Galway that offers a secure internet connection. I brought my laptop so I can view it tonight."

I couldn't help grimacing. "I almost don't want to know what's on there."

"Same. I'm only watching them myself to find any leverage we can use on Max."

We sat with our own thoughts for a while. Con savored his beer while I finished packing. I picked out a comfortable outfit for the next leg of the journey. "I'm going to go get changed and call my folks."

"They'll be awake at this hour?"

"Yeah, it's seven thirty in the morning, there. They're usually up with the birds—literally. They get up early to feed them."

"I'm sure the birds appreciate that. Tell them I said hello."

Later, I emerged from the ladies' room, feeling fresh and wearing new khaki jeggings, a white turtleneck sweater, and black slip-on sneakers. I took my phone to an empty nook in the back of the pub. I felt a little silly for calling my parents so early in the journey, but I already missed them. Plus, it had been a harrowing trip in some ways, and hearing their voices always made me feel normal again, regardless of what was happening around me.

My mother answered. "Honey, is that you?"

The sound of her voice sparked a surge of tender emotions. "Hi, Mom."

"Jim, it's Neve," she called out to my dad. "I'll put you on speaker."

"Okay."

"Hi, honey," my father said. They sounded so close by, I almost wanted to cry.

"Hi, Dad. How are things with you guys?"

"We're fine," he said. "Just got finished feeding the birds. But forget about us!"

"Yeah," my mom chimed in. "Everything's the same here. What's happening with *you*? How's it going so far?"

"Is Con behaving himself?"

"Of course." I grinned and shook my head—such a "Dad" question. My parents knew Con well enough that they already thought the world of him.

I proceeded to give them the warts-free version of our trip so far. Yes, the flight was smooth. Yes, Con and I were enjoying ourselves, and his family was wonderful. Yes, we were helping his brother with Ciara. Ireland was as beautiful as it looked in the pictures, and it really *was* that green, even in September.

My parents and I had always been very close, and I wished I could tell them the whole truth of what was going on. It was an old source of discontent. As a therapist, I was bound by confidentiality and therefore unable to talk to them about work. And since work was my life, that meant there were large chunks of my experiences they knew nothing about. That was one of the reasons why those of us like Con and me who worked on the psychiatry unit got to be such good friends. We were the only ones who really understood each other's professional lives.

I wasn't at work now, though, and my parents were the smartest, wisest people I knew. I was certain they'd have great insights to share about what I should do with Con's admission that he planned to propose some-time, as well as practical tips about how to handle a character like Max. But now that Con and I were becoming a real couple, it felt like it would be a viola-tion of his privacy to talk about "us" outside of us. And although I wasn't officially bound by patient-therapist confidentiality with Ciara, it would be wrong of me to discuss anything related to her case or her personal life without her consent. So I kept the conversation confined to simpler topics.

"It sounds like you're having a wonderful time," my mother said. "But you sound a little off. Are you sure everything's okay?"

It took everything in me to swallow my emotions and say, "Yeah, of course. I'm just tired. Jet lag."

"I've heard it can take a while to adjust," my father replied. "Make sure you're getting enough rest, young lady."

I couldn't help smiling. "Okay, Dad, I will."

"Tell Con we said to let you take a nap. You can't enjoy yourself if you're worn out."

"Got it, Mom. I'll tell him."

With that, the conversation trundled to a halt, and we signed off. When the line dropped, my heart dropped a little bit too. At least I was with Con, the only person on Earth whose presence could comfort me in that moment.

On my way back to the snug, I ran into him at the bar, settling up.

"Anything for you before we go?"

I walked right up to him, snaked my arm around his back, and rested my head against his chest. "No, I'm good."

The bartender smiled at us, then walked off.

Con turned toward me and wrapped me in his bear-like embrace. "Missing your parents?"

"Yeah," I murmured into his shirt.

"They're pure class," he said with reverence, then kissed the top of my head. "I'm sure they were happy to hear your voice."

"It was good hearing theirs too."

"We'll be back having dinner at their house again before you know it."

Guilt pricked at me. I pulled away and looked up at him. "I'm sorry, Con. I don't want you to think I'm not happy to be here, because I am. Ecstatic, in fact."

The sound and feel of him chuckling instantly raised my spirits. "It's all right. You can be happy to be here and miss them too. Hell, I miss them."

"Really?"

"Of course," he said, pulling me back against his body. "I especially missed them earlier this morning when you jumped from the back of my car, sweating and screaming."

"You jerk!" I laughed and tried to escape his embrace, but it was like trying to free myself from a vise.

"It's a shame they weren't there to advise me on how to handle that situation," he continued. "I'm sure they would have had a few good ideas, and I know Leigh would have loved to film the whole scene on her phone. Talk about going viral."

Finally, I managed to escape his grasp by bending my knees and wriggling downward. Once free, I poked him in the arm. "If you ever say a *word* to them about that...."

"Ah, blackmail material at last!" He grinned, and I got the uneasy feeling that he was only half joking.

Altogether unable to think of a comeback, I headed for the snug to retrieve my bag and called over my shoulder, "Aren't we needed in Galway?"

"We are indeed." Con jingled his keys behind me. "Better buckle up, love. We might be in for a rough ride."

CHAPTER 14

CON

I t was a clear night in Galway. The apartment Con had rented through Airbnb turned out to be much nicer than it appeared online. It was clean and modern with a wall of windows overlooking Galway Bay. Unfortunately, there was only one bedroom with a short double bed—perfect for someone his size to lie on diagonally but too small for him plus Neve. After they'd gone out to dinner and picked up a few groceries, he'd suggested she rest on the bed for a while, knowing she would likely fall asleep and not wake until morning. Fortunately, that was exactly what happened. The couch would do him fine.

Tomorrow would be Saturday, so Con planned to track down Max at home. If he wasn't there, he'd try the office, and if that failed, he would go to Saint Cillian's Island and search for this sea cave. If that was his secret lair, maybe Con could find something there that would incriminate him.

A bit of internet research uncovered that Saint Cillian was one of the patron saints of sailors, and the island was accessible only by boat one day every summer for Saint Cillian's Festival. On that day, local fishermen would ferry pilgrims to the old stone church for a celebratory Mass, but there was no mention of a sea cave. Con had found no clear direction on how to reach the island at other times, but he would find a way. Perhaps he could convince some sympathetic fisherman that he was a devotee making a pilgrimage.

First, though, there were the videos Eric sent. Con was glad Neve was sleeping through this. It was one thing to hear about something but quite another to see it. Whatever shenanigans Max and his *TOT*s had gotten up to, they were sure to be disturbing, and Neve had dealt with far too much that was "disturbing" of late.

He also feared that Eric might not have spoken about the video on the phone call with Eamonn because Ciara appeared in it somewhere. Although Eric didn't know what she looked like, he might have spotted a woman and decided it was best to show Con first, just in case. He hoped to God Ciara wasn't on there, but if she was... well, he'd cross that bridge when he came to it.

As promised, the Airbnb owner had an ethernet cable plugged into the modem on his desk—a more secure method of connecting to the internet than Wi-Fi. As a hacker, Eric prioritized keeping their communications as protected as possible, and he had drilled that caution into Con. He logged onto their shared server.

Eric had written of the video file, **FYI, THESE WERE POSTED ON THE DISCUSSION BOARD ONLY. I FOUND NO TRACE OF THEM ANYWHERE ELSE ONLINE.** That bit of information was reassuring but also ominous: Why had Eric felt the need to do such a thorough search?

It was time to stop putting off the inevitable.

Con double-clicked on the first video file. It opened with a still shot, a close-up of a detailed carving on a stone wall. He pressed Pause and examined it. The carving appeared modern, with clean lines depicting a lightning bolt over a wheel with eight spokes. The wheel was embellished with Celtic swirl designs. He grabbed a screenshot of the image so he could research it later.

When he hit Play again, Con found himself looking at what must be the inside of the sea cave. *Impressive editing,* he thought as the video switched seamlessly between multiple camera angles. Meanwhile, gloomy ambient music played in the background.

The cave was an irregular shape, carved from the light gray stone by nature rather than by human hands. While the walls and roof were jagged, the floor appeared fairly smooth. Ridges in the rock formed a few steps that led down to a narrow beach. The mouth of the cave was very narrow, with barely enough of an opening to let the water in. He imagined the cave would be nearly impossible to spot from the sea; you'd have to know exactly where it was and what to look for. Aside from a bit of white foam atop the small waves, the water appeared black, so the video must have been shot at night. Artificial lights on the ceiling illuminated the cave, creating dramatic shadows and highlighting a raised stone slab in the center of the floor. It was an unexpectedly professional production.

Max must take his contributions to the cult hobby board very seriously indeed.

Next, the deep, round sounds of a bodhrán echoed through the cave. The drummer entered through a gap in one of the walls, dressed in a hooded black robe with a white rope tied around the waist, beating out a rapid rhythm. Other people in the same garb filed in behind the drummer, about twenty in total. They formed a circle around the stone slab, leaving an opening near the gap in the wall.

With the people there for reference, Con estimated that the floor of the cave was about a thousand square feet in size, with the ceiling around twenty feet at its highest point. He was surprised he hadn't heard of such a striking geological structure, and that it hadn't become a tourist attraction. Saint Cillian's followers must have been quite dedicated to keeping the island protected.

If they only knew it was cult central.

The beat of the bodhrán slowed. From the gap emerged four more figures carrying something that looked like a stretcher with a person lying on it. He slowed the video's speed and squinted, trying to make out what was happening, but he didn't have to wait long. The stretcher-bearers entered slowly, and those gathered stood in reverent stillness as they brought the stretcher in and gently laid it on the stone slab. Then the drum fell silent.

Christ on high, that's Ciara! Con stared wide-eyed at his soon-to-be sister-in-law as she lay there on the slab, cloaked in a long, sleeveless black dress, hands folded on her chest. He took some comfort in noting that anyone who didn't know Ciara already wouldn't be able to identify her from the video. Her whole face was painted white, and blue triskele symbols adorned her forehead and cheeks. With the makeup, her crown of red flowers, and the distorted, shadowy lighting, at least she had some degree of anonymity in this twisted charade.

Ciara's eyes were closed, and she wasn't moving. *Maybe it's part of a performance,* he reassured himself, but the sick feeling in the pit of his stomach told him otherwise.

One of the stretcher-bearers joined the circle. The other three positioned themselves around the stone slab, one at the head, one on the side, and one at the foot. The person at the head raised their arms in the air as the drum played louder and faster.

Although Con couldn't see their faces clearly, he could make out their shapes. The two standing at the head and on the side had broad shoulders tapering down into lean, straight figures. Two men, he guessed, with the one at the head of average height and the one at the side half a foot taller. The figure standing at the foot was quite a bit shorter with visible curves—most likely a woman.

The man at the head of the slab called out in an urgent tenor voice, "Taranis, hear us!"

The rest of the attendees repeated his chant.

Since he appeared to be leading the ceremony, Con guessed that must be Max. *I could take him,* he thought after a quick evaluation of the man's size and bearing. Perhaps the other man or the woman was the partner going by "TOT" on the cult discussion board.

The man continued, "God of the sun, source of all life, bring us your thunder!" An American accent— almost certainly Max, then.

The drumming started up again, and the chanters repeated his words.

Max's hands abruptly closed into fists, and the drum stopped. "Tonight, we gather here for a celebration. Tonight, we complete the wheel of life! Man, woman, and Taranis: three in one, each element essential to the turning of the wheel of time, the wheel of history. Today, under the light of the sun, you witnessed the taking of our vows. Tonight, in the dark of the new moon, we thank you, Taranis the Great, for bringing to your humble priest his sacred mate!"

Cold horror shot through Con's core, and he quickly clicked Pause. He didn't want to watch any more of this. The more he saw, the more he was convinced Ciara was lying there unconscious. And if Max was calling her his mate, God only knew what would come next. But he had to keep watching, for Ciara's sake. He had to know what happened if he was to get any leverage over Max.

Leaning back in the chair, he took a deep breath and let it out slowly. *Eric said nothing too crazy, no blood sacrifices,* he reminded himself, gathering his courage. Whatever happened next, he could decide later what to do with the information and with whom to share it.

Con winced as he pressed Play.

"As the high priest of Taranis, I hereby claim this human incarnation of the goddess as my spiritual vessel," Max continued.

"Good God," Con muttered.

"Her fate and mine will now and forever be intertwined as we embark on our mission to complete the circle of life. All hail Taranis!" Max called out, gesturing to the crowd to repeat his words.

They began to chant, "All hail Taranis!" repeatedly as the drummer played a steady beat.

The man to Ciara's left walked out of the circle and back to the gap in the wall. Max held out his hands, palms down, and waved them back and forth about six inches above Ciara's head. Then he walked clockwise around the stone slab, waving his hands over each part of her body as he went. When he returned to his position at her head, he held his hands aloft, and all at once, the cave was plunged into perfect darkness. Some in the crowd gasped, but others kept chanting as the bodhrán continued playing.

Although he was just watching a video of the event, Con could almost feel the pressurized energy Max had managed to build among the crowd. *This bastard picked up quite a few tips from his cult leader club,* he thought ruefully.

The man who had left a few moments before returned through the gap in the wall, carrying a wand glowing with a purplish light. Once again, he took his place at Ciara's left side. The bodhrán stopped, and the chanting with it. There were several moments of silent anticipation. Then the drum boomed back into a rapid, complex rhythm, and the crowd cheered as the man with the purple wand held it over Ciara, then rolled her left arm over to reveal a whitish symbol glowing on the skin of her inner forearm.

I'll be damned. It's a black light tattoo. The purple wand was a UV light, and they had tattooed Ciara with some type of glow-in-the-dark ink.

He squinted at the monitor as the camera zoomed in on her arm. The tattoo was similar in design to the carving shown at the beginning of the video, with an eight-spoked wheel. But instead of a lightning bolt behind it, there were several rows of wavy lines, like a symbol for water.

Eamonn was right after all—Max *had* mutilated her.

Now the camera zoomed out to show Max pulling up his right sleeve and holding his arm next to Ciara's under the black light. An almost identical tattoo glowed on his arm, but with a lightning bolt instead of wavy lines behind the wheel.

The camera slowly zoomed out farther as Max began a call-and-response chant. "Fire and water," he called out.

The crowd responded, "All hail Taranis!"

"Death and birth!"

"All hail Taranis!"

"Dominance and deference!"

"All hail Taranis!"

"Destruction and creation!"

"All hail Taranis!"

The lights gradually came up again, illuminating the cave. Con could see that, unlike Max's forearm, Ciara's was an angry red, particularly around the lines of the design. The tattoo must have been fresh when the video was filmed.

He imagined Max could have knocked Ciara out, tattooed her, and then paraded her out on the stretcher for the benefit of his followers, all in one night. His fellow cult leaders would no doubt be impressed by such ambitious efficiency.

It appeared the ceremony was winding down. The drumming became less frantic. Max put his sleeve back down and stood up while the man on Ciara's left moved her arm back into its original position, with her hands folded over her heart. Max, purple wand man, and the woman were joined by the fourth stretcher-bearer. There was no sign of life from Ciara as they carried her back toward the gap in the wall. The bodhrán player fell in behind them, playing a slow, steady beat, and the rest of the group formed a procession behind him. They all filed out of the cave, and the lights again dimmed to darkness.

Con couldn't help smirking when the final screen

came up: **Copyright: This has been a *Temple of Taranis* production.** What the hell was the purpose of that? Was Max genuinely afraid someone else might steal the credit for this sick piece of theater?

The last thing he wanted to do was watch the second video, but he knew he had no choice. He double-clicked, and an unsteady video appeared, as though it was being recorded on a mobile phone. The focus of the image was Max and Ciara, standing outdoors on what appeared to be the top of a hill. It was a bright day, and they both wore white, flowing robes. Con could see the backs of several heads, so the video was being shot from amid a crowd of people facing the couple. Ciara was beaming and wearing another crown of flowers, this time white and yellow. Max was smiling as well, but his expression was victorious rather than joyful.

Another white-robed figure with a shaved head moved in front of them. He held a red-and-gold braided cord above his head, and a cheer rose up from the crowd. "Ciara, repeat after me," he instructed. "Male and female, wheel of creation."

Concentrating on getting the words right, Ciara repeated, "Male and female, wheel of creation."

"Sacred elements, fire and water," the man said, and once again she said the words after him.

"All hail Taranis!" he said, and the whole group joined Ciara in that response. Then the man turned to Max. "Maximillian, repeat after me," he said, and they went through the whole process again.

After the group once again repeated, "All hail Taranis," the man joined Ciara's hands with Max's and wrapped the red-and-gold cord around them three times. "Max and Ciara, your hands are now bound together, as you are bound together."

This brought a loud cheer from the crowd, who raised their fists in the air. Then the video stopped abruptly.

So Ciara and Max had been handfasted, or something like it. These could be the "vows" Max referred to that he and Ciara had taken, that were witnessed by the crowd in the cave video.

Con didn't remember hearing anything about a handfasting from Ciara, Eamonn, or Neve. Of course, it was possible Ciara was just playing a theatrical part, a role. It certainly hadn't been a typical handfasting ceremony with traditional vows exchanged. But the symbolism was there. And whether or not Ciara had only been performing for the crowd, Max's demeanor had been quite serious. Perhaps he was a great actor, but Con thought it more likely that either Ciara had chosen to be handfasted to Max and failed to mention it to Eamonn, or the fake ceremony she'd participated in to support Max's extracurricular activities wasn't fake at all in Max's mind. Neither possibility comforted him in the least.

Con hoped a stiff drink might help him shake off the dismal, clammy feeling he had after watching the videos, but he also feared anything he put in his stomach would come right back up, so deep was his disgust. He had come across a few malevolent characters in his time, but Max was at an entirely different level. A sound drubbing was way too good for him.

The idea he'd presented to Eamonn initially as a stalling tactic might give them what they needed after all. Eric *had* found something useful on Max. This video could potentially get him put away. But for that to work, Eamonn and Ciara would have to know about it first.

Showing it to them could retraumatize Ciara, not to mention push Eamonn over the edge from outraged into murderous. It had nearly done that to Con, and the woman involved wasn't even Neve. On the other hand, the video did answer some questions that might be important to Ciara's recovery. It wasn't often that Con felt out of his depth, but this was one of those times. Maybe he was too close to the situation. In any case, he was grateful Neve was with him. He could ask her what she thought was the best way to handle it.

And she *was* with him, despite his efforts. He still couldn't quite believe she'd pulled such a dangerous stunt. For a responsible professional, she certainly took a lot of risks. He'd always known Neve felt things more intensely than other people, but only recently had he witnessed how those strong emotions could drive her to make rash decisions. He would definitely be listening to her more carefully, as promised. But he would be doing so with an ear toward understanding why her judgment sometimes took a back seat to her feelings. If he could decipher that, he'd be better able to head off any reckless actions on her part in the future.

At least she didn't get hurt, and she's safe now.

Con eased himself into a standing position. His knee was giving him hell tonight. Not a surprise, after all the cramped sitting and driving he'd done over the past couple of days. He took some anti-inflammatory pills with a glass of water and went to check on Neve.

She'd left the bedroom door open a crack, so he peered in, not wanting to disturb her. Through the narrow opening, he could see her head and shoulders. She was lying on her side facing the door, still collapsed on the bed—and still wearing the same clothes she'd arrived in. She was curled up a little, and the face he loved more than reason was the picture of peaceful repose. Long chestnut-brown waves of hair fell around her head like a beautiful, chaotic storm cloud. Con stood there, his eyes caressing her as he imagined the scent of her hair, the feel of her skin under his fingertips, the explosion of longing and passion inside him whenever his lips met hers.

God, she was bliss. Two years ago, when they met in rounds on the psychiatry unit at Capitol Hill General, if anyone had told him he would one day be lucky enough that Neve would be with him in Ireland, dating him, lying in a bed where he had the luxury of watching her shoulders rise and fall in tiny movements as she breathed, he never would have believed it, not for a second. He didn't know what magic this was, or how long it would last, but he knew a miracle when he saw it, and he was going to hang on to her with every bit of strength he had for as long as he could.

Neve was everything bright and good and kind. The irony was it was that goodness that led her to want to help people and become a psychotherapist, thereby exposing her to the darkest parts of human souls—the parts that drive us mad, play tricks on us, lead us to harm ourselves or other people, or tell us we don't deserve to live any more.

Neve had no fear of the darkness, though. She seemed happy to go there if needed to help her clients find their way out. But as much as Con respected how wonderful she was at her job, he worried about what it might do to her long-term—and what it already *had* done. The scars on her abdomen stood as a testament. Not to mention the panic attacks—or "anxiety surges," if she insisted—which were ongoing, so he'd learned on this trip. Neve continued to downplay them and treat them dismissively. That worried him, not least because they put her out of her right mind and drove her to do things like stow away in the back of his car.

Regardless, he knew he would never be able to talk her into changing jobs. She considered it a calling, and she had too much love for what she did to consider doing anything else. Plus, she would likely never forgive him if he tried to talk her into quitting. The only thing for it was to stay by her side, to be there to help her handle whatever came her way, and to soothe her when the anxiety or self-doubt became too much.

Yes, that was it. He could soothe her. With massage

oil. Naked. Until she was writhing beneath him, panting with want and gasping his name from kiss-swollen lips.

Con took a chance on the hinges creaking and pushed the door open a few more inches so he could see from the top of her head all the way down to where her waist began its sexy slope up to her hip. He was achingly jealous of her formfitting sweater and the blanket half covering her body. He stood there taking in her sumptuous curves as long as his leg would allow, thinking of all the things he wanted to do with Neve. To Neve. Things he *would* do one day soon, God willing. Once she was fully recovered from stab wounds and biopsies, that was. Another week, maybe two.

She'd tried to convince him that they could do more than kissing without straying into medically risky territory, but he knew better. Just kissing, they were combustible. Once clothes were dislodged and hands began to wander, not to mention mouths... well, after years of managing chronic pain, Con knew exactly how much self-control he had, but he had no idea about Neve. And if she ever fully unleashed the bounteous passion he sensed inside her, his own self-control might even prove less reliable than he thought. He wouldn't do anything that might disrupt her healing. The moment it was safe, however, he would whisk her away somewhere luxurious and private—a place where "self-control" wasn't even in the dictionary.

Unless, of course, before that time came, she managed to see inside his head, get a glimpse of his voracious and primal intentions, and run for the hills. Neve was so intuitive, Con wouldn't put mind reading past her. But he didn't have to worry about that tonight. She was out for the count. And watching her sleep had been just the tonic he needed.

Right now, he had other things to worry about. Like how to approach Max tomorrow in a way that would make him most likely to cooperate. And once he had the information he needed, how to convince Max to destroy all copies of the video file. Not to mention he had to figure out who to tell about the damn video, and when.

With those thoughts churning in the background, Con decided to start with something easy. First, he looked Max up online. No social media, just a few interviews with gaming magazines, snapshots from conventions, and an official profile picture on the Wicked Games website. Con studied the photo. Light-colored hair hung down to Max's shoulders. He was lean, with a sort of Neanderthal look about him—an oblong face, prominent brow ridge, and a large nose and mouth protruding forward. There was also something about his expression—the half smile, the taunting eyes—that gave the strong impression of someone who was just begging to be punched.

Next, he read everything he could find online about Taranis. In ancient Celtic mythology, he was the god of thunder as well as the sun and sky, and his symbols were a lightning bolt and a spoked wheel. That explained the stone carving in the video, as well as the tattoos. The ancient cult of Taranis also involved human and animal sacrifices. Con supposed he should be grateful Max hadn't taken it that far—not yet, at least.

Sheer curiosity drove him to watch videos *Temple of Taranis* gamers had uploaded to the internet showing themselves playing. It was a fairly gruesome quest-themed game, and it was showing its age, with graphics that were quite rough compared to the newer games he and Eric played. *TOT* appeared more invested in the narrative aspects, with complex plots, heavy use of—poorly researched—Celtic mythology, and the promise that each new level achieved would bring players one step closer to unlocking spiritual truths and reviving the reign of the ancient gods. Some of the die-hard *TOT* fans confessed to feeling a sense of genuine connection to the mystical aspects of the game, which Con had to admit were well told—for pure fiction, that was.

From that angle, he understood the game's appeal somewhat. The ugly underbellies of many religious groups had been exposed in recent years, leaving many members to leave. But Con knew some people who abandoned the religions of their childhood still longed for a spiritual community that gave them a greater sense of purpose and belonging. He could see, then, why the disaffected might be drawn to a game like *Temple of Taranis*, a sort of substitute religion packaged with their entertainment. It appeared Max was using that angle to draw hard-core players to Galway for his ritual-heavy *TOT* gatherings. All these high-level players came from outside Ireland, which no doubt made it easier for Max to sell them his version of local spiritual practices and legends—and himself as an expert. It seemed plausible that those attending these events might even take Max and his invented sea cave ceremonies seriously.

One thing was certain: Max was a master manipulator. Con didn't know if it was by accident or by design, but this arsehole had hit upon a formula that combined spiritual seeking with the emotional power of in-person role-playing. He was using his gatherings to exploit the desires and vulnerabilities of *TOT*'s most dedicated gamers. And he was also exploiting their pockets. Not only were the gatherings expensive to attend, but the game itself required the purchase of costly upgrades for players to rise through its various levels.

Max must either subscribe to the delusion that he'd been given some special mandate by Taranis or be a certified narcissist and attention seeker of the highest order. The only way to find out was for Con to take the measure of the man himself. Then he could figure out how best to pull information out of the sick bastard.

Finally tired enough to sleep, he took a few more painkillers, stripped down to his boxers and T-shirt, and settled himself as best he could on the couch. Closing his eyes, he had the singular pleasure of falling asleep to the image of Neve resting peacefully in the next room. Truth be told, although he objected to her madcap method of tagging along, he liked it much better having her close at hand.

CHAPTER 15
NEVE

Ugh, *I am so gross.* I'd slept the whole night in my clothes. I couldn't get out of them and into the shower fast enough.

At least I'd slept well, and long. But the other side of the bed was undisturbed. Either Con had slept in a different bedroom I had missed somehow, or he was already up and had remade his side of the bed. I was more than a little disappointed that our first night alone, with both of us healthy and a bed to share, had been spent sleeping soundly. But I had to admit it was a relief to feel well rested.

As I tested out my limbs in the shower, I was glad to find that nothing felt too sore or bruised after the previous day's adventure. Although I was beyond happy to be with Con instead of away from him, in retrospect, I could see that climbing into the back of his car had been a risky move. Whatever impulse had come over me in that moment, it was quite embarrassing. I decided to try to forget about it completely and pretend it never happened. I just hoped he would be equally happy to leave the whole episode in the past.

Damp-haired, barefoot, and dressed in fresh clothes, I arrived in the living room to find Con asleep on the couch. First, my heart fluttered at the sight of him— deliciously rumpled and showing more of his skin than I'd ever had the pleasure of seeing. But then my heart sank at the realization that he'd spent the whole night out there. Knowing him, he probably hadn't wanted to disturb me. But he didn't look at all comfortable on the couch, which wasn't quite as long as he was tall. His six-and-a-half-foot frame had only a small blanket to cover it, and that had become twisted around his limbs. He'd removed his leg brace and leaned it against the coffee table.

The least I could do was make him breakfast. But my feet refused to move toward the kitchen until I stood there for a while longer, taking him in. The warm glow of attraction I'd felt for Con since our very first meeting tingled through me. Even asleep, he radiated the vigorous energy that drew so many people to him. The waves in his brown hair were going every which way, giving him an appealing air of vulnerability that he never showed while he was awake. What a relief it was, not having to repress my feelings for him anymore. Now that our friendship had morphed into more, I could allow that warmth to flow and spread freely into every corner of my body and heart.

His T-shirt had ridden up in places, revealing boulder-like arms with a slight farmer's tan and about six inches of stomach. His belly was slightly rounded, and his heavily muscled frame had a softness to it—no doubt a testimony to our shared love of rich food and eating out. But the legacy of years playing rugby and his ongoing dedication to working out were also evident, standing in stark contrast to my own shameful lack of discipline in the fitness department.

But I was too drawn to the sight of his legs to dwell too much on my own physical insecurities. They were so beautifully formed, they brought to mind sculptures of gladiators from ancient Greece. My chest ached as I saw through gaps in the blanket that the skin of his left leg, the one so badly injured in the accident, was jagged with scars. Multiple operations, he'd said. I could only imagine how much agony each of those lines represented, and how much strength and patience it must have taken to recover.

Although he didn't like to talk about it, Con had told me before that it was unlikely he would ever recover fully. All these years later, his leg still pained him, along with other parts of his body at times. Seeing those scars, a visible reminder of the fortitude and grace with which he carried all he'd been through—and continued to go through—well, I couldn't help falling in love with him all over again. Every day, it seemed, I discovered a new layer of him to adore.

I knew it would make Con uncomfortable if he knew I'd spent so long looking at his leg, though, so I forced my eyes back upward. His large, rough-hewn features were more relaxed and completely free of tension than I ever remembered seeing them before. He almost looked like his own strikingly handsome doppelgänger. Then I spotted a soft line of hair growing down the center of his stomach. It started somewhere beneath his T-shirt and extended down under the waistband of his boxers. I leaned forward a bit to get a better look. There was something about that line that was just so… intriguing.

Oh my God, behave yourself! Heat flared in my cheeks. If I didn't stop staring at him soon, my thoughts would cross over from admiring into indecent.

Turning on my heel, I went to the kitchen and focused on the breakfast fixings we'd brought in the night before, figuring omelets shouldn't be too hard to make, or too noisy.

First things first: I put a pot of coffee on to brew.

Chopping vegetables and whisking eggs helped pull my brain out of the haze of attraction. Before I went to bed, Con had planned to watch the video file Eric sent him. Just thinking about *that* brought cold reality racing back.

The egg mixture popped and crackled as I poured it into the frying pan. I turned the heat down a bit and gave the omelet sprinkles of turmeric, chili powder, and paprika from our host's spice cabinet. As I watched the eggs cook, I thought about our plan for the day: find and talk to Max. Of course, the plan may have changed, depending on what was in the video.

Poor Ciara. I wondered how she was feeling, and

how she fared last night. *As soon as Con's awake, calling Eamonn should be at the top of our to-do list. I can't imagine how impossibly hard it must be for the two of them, going through all this.*

From the kitchen, I could see Con shifting on the couch. No doubt smells from the kitchen were rousing him. Just as I took the eggs off the stove, the coffee maker gasped and sputtered, its brewing cycle complete. Watching Con out of the corner of my eye, I cut the omelet in two and slid it onto plates.

He rubbed his head vigorously and sat up slowly with his back to me, stretching. Then he turned and flashed me the sexiest crooked morning smile I'd ever seen.

A quiet knowing settled in my heart, softly but certainly, like a butterfly coming to land on a leaf: I wanted to see that smile and no other every morning for the rest of my life. If he'd meant what he said the day before, there was even a chance that could happen.

"Morning, beautiful." Con only cemented my desire with those words, his voice rough and extra deep from sleeping.

"Hi, handsome."

He turned to one side, then the other. "Where's this 'handsome' fella? I'll be having words with *him*!"

God, I love this man, I thought as I laughed, wondering what on earth I had done to get so lucky.

———

An hour later, I sat next to Con on the couch in stunned silence. Fast-moving clouds blew by outside, casting shadows of light and dark across the room, his face, and our empty plates on the coffee table. Devastation chilled me to the bone as I tried to process the videos he'd just shown me.

Max had committed sickening, heinous crimes against Ciara. He'd rendered her unconscious somehow, tattooed her, and used her as a puppet in one of his ceremonies. Not to mention he lied to her about the tattoo and filmed her without her consent—although the latter crime, at least, gave us some evidence to use against him from a legal perspective. And those were just the crimes we knew about.

No wonder she was suffering. Now we could finally make sense of her symptoms as part of a traumatic response to the violations she'd endured.

Then there was the handfasting. I was sure Ciara would have mentioned it to me if it had been anything more than role-playing, but even something like that done innocently and for show could get twisted by someone as delusional as Max appeared to be.

Ciara's health being the priority, we decided Con should call Dr. Boyle and give him a brief description of the video, explaining why we had reason to believe a black light tattoo may have been inked on Ciara's arm without her knowledge or consent. They discussed the possibility that her current symptoms might be either a somatic pain response to that traumatic event or a physical reaction to the ink—possibly a combination of both.

Con had done a bit of research and learned that some fluorescent tattoo inks contain phosphorous, which could cause pain and burning. Although it would be highly unusual for such symptoms to appear so long after the tattoo was created, he didn't know enough to say whether it was a possibility in her case. In any event, if Ciara had a bad reaction to the tattoo initially, her body might be reliving that trauma. Dr. Boyle said he would look into it immediately.

They both agreed it was best to let Dr. Boyle decide when to tell Ciara about the video and the tattoo. After all, he was *in situ* and best placed to know what was needed for her recovery. Dr. Boyle pointed out that he couldn't share any of this new information with Eamonn without Ciara's consent, and Con promised to keep it confidential as well.

After the call ended, I asked, "Shouldn't law enforcement be involved at some point? I mean, these are criminal acts we're talking about. How does that work here?"

"More or less the same as it does in the States," Con said. "It would be up to Ciara to bring a case against Max, especially since we have no video evidence of any illegal activities. Max could say Ciara was pretending to be asleep or unconscious in the video. She could testify otherwise, but first she told everyone the tattoo incident was a dream, then changed her story during a stay in a psychiatric hospital. You can imagine her case isn't as strong as it could be."

"So it could turn into a question of 'he said, she

said.'" I hated that he was right. "We could try to find other witnesses to the tattooing itself."

"If there are any. Ciara says she remembers other people being there, but as you said before, her nightmare could be a mixture of dream and memory. Max could have inked the tattoo by himself, in which case he could just deny it."

That grotesque image sent a shudder through me. "I wouldn't put it past him. What about the stretcher-bearers from the video? They could confirm that Ciara was unconscious."

"Perhaps, but from their actions, I'm guessing they're Max's followers. If they could even be identified or found, they might just say what he tells them to say." Con rubbed his face. "It would come down to whether Ciara wanted to put herself through a court case that she might well lose."

"Good Lord." It was the same issue we ran into often with patients on our adult psychiatry unit who were victims of abuse. Was there enough proof, or would contradicting accounts be given equal weight? Would the victim be considered a less-than-reliable witness because of their psychiatric diagnosis? I had appeared in court more than once to advocate for patients in such cases, and it always enraged me to see how stigma against those with mental health disorders was wielded as a weapon by the perpetrators of their abuse. It seemed mind-boggling to me that such tactics still had an effect in the twenty-first century. Add to that the risk of having one's private life dissected in public by an adversarial opponent, and it was no wonder victims like Ciara so often opted against pressing charges. As disgusted as I was by the idea of people like Max getting away with their crimes, I couldn't even say for certain whether I would choose to pursue legal action if I were in Ciara's position.

I was a little surprised that Con had agreed to keep the video a secret even from Eamonn, but he pointed out that Ciara's team was already handling a complex and delicate situation. Not to mention if he told Eamonn about the video, his brother might go off half-cocked. Con believed we had a better chance of keeping the situation under control if we let Dr. Boyle handle the flow of information—for now, at least.

"And besides," he said, "this is her story to tell, not mine. It should be up to her whether to share this with my brother. Not that I endorse secrets between couples, mind you," he added with a freighted look in my direction.

"You're one to talk, Mr. Closed Book!"

"If I keep any part of my book closed, it's only to keep you from running away," he said, spreading his arms out as if he'd just presented a winning argument. "Such exceptions are justified—for me, that is."

"Not for me?"

"You've got nothing to hide."

"As far as you know."

Con shook his head at my exaggerated wink. I was grateful for the brief moment of levity, a reminder that as dark as things seemed at the moment, beyond the clouds, the sun still shone.

Eamonn called not long after, and he sounded despondent. Ciara's condition was unchanged. No further self-injury, thankfully, but the burning pain persisted, and they were still keeping her sedated.

When Eamonn asked what information Eric had sent, Con told him it was nothing new, just transcripts from Max's discussion board further illustrating what Eric told them on the phone. I took it as a sign of Eamonn's exhaustion that he didn't press for more details. Con reassured his brother that we wouldn't rest until we found Max and got as much information as we could out of him.

Eamonn asked Con to put him on speakerphone, then told us both he was pleased I had accompanied Con to Galway. "It's been hard enough for Ciara and me to be separated," he said. "I wouldn't wish the same on you two."

"Oh, Eamonn." Guilt pricked me as I heard the suffering in his voice. "It was an *impulsive* decision," I said, giving Con a side-eye, "but afterward, I was worried it was the wrong one, leaving you and Ciara alone with everything that's happening there."

"Don't be silly! I'm not alone. We have John and the rest of Ciara's team, and my parents. Don't worry, we're well looked after. Believe me, you'll be of more help to me keeping an eye on Deadeye there."

"Oh?" I teased as Con rolled his eyes. "So he needs looking after?"

"He does, God knows!"

"All right," Con declared, "conversation over. You two can resume smearing my good name when we get back home. Eamonn, look after yourself. Give our best to Ciara."

"I will. Thanks again, both of you."

"Stop saying 'thanks,' for God's sake. We'll call you when we know something more."

"All right, so. Bye."

"Bye."

As Con put down the phone, I scooted closer to him until our arms were touching. "So, according to a very knowledgeable source," I said with a sly smile, "*you're* the one who needs looking after."

With a glint in his eye, he said, "No better woman." Then he leaned in, and for a thrilling moment, I thought he would kiss me. Instead, his cheek slid past mine, and with his mouth next to my ear, he murmured, "Be grateful you're an only child."

I leaned back, laughing. "I'm telling Eamonn you said that."

"Ah, so you're a snitch." He nodded as though taking note. "Then whatever souls who were spared being your siblings should be the grateful ones."

Before I could launch an objection, he put his hands on either side of my head, sliding his fingers into my hair. His eyes met mine with a powerful surge of affection. Then he tilted my head down and placed a tender kiss on my forehead. A sigh of pleasure escaped my lips.

"Don't start making those sorts of noises now," he warned. "We have work to do today, and it would take less than a second for you to derail me completely."

Knowing the same was true for me, I pulled away, straightened up, and took a quick cleansing breath. "You're right," I said as I rubbed my face, careful to avoid the spot he'd just kissed. "Work to do. Okay, so what's next?"

"Well, the plan I *had* was a one-person operation, so…." He raised a hopeful eyebrow. "I don't suppose you'd consider…."

"Staying here?" I asked dryly. "For real? Are you seriously asking me that?"

"Asked and answered. Right, so." Con clapped his hands onto his thighs. "Next, then, I suppose we come up with a *two*-person plan. Right after I take a shower, that is." He tilted his head, his eyes flashing with devilment. "I'd invite you to join me, but it might well render me constitutionally incapable of letting you leave the apartment for the rest of the day. And the entire night. And tomorrow, for that matter."

I dug my fingers into my knees and tried to reel in the lust that suggestion unfurled inside me. Con was trying to kill me. That was the only explanation I could come up with for his decision to dangle such a tantalizing suggestion out there, then pull it back so quickly. He was right, of course; time was of the essence, and if we wasted any by fooling around, we'd be letting Ciara and Eamonn down.

"Make it a cold shower, you fiend." I stood up. "I'll go finish getting ready."

I felt his eyes following me down the hallway. I hoped the extra sway I pushed into my hips would make him regret putting impossible ideas in my head.

CHAPTER 16

NEVE

I sat at Con's computer, determined to do something useful—and distract myself from picturing him in the shower.

A search for Max Hinsen called up Max's professional page on the Wicked Games website—a minimal bio with a picture. He had a striking appearance and looked affable at first. But the longer I examined his eyes, the more I sensed a thread of cool and calculating menace behind them. There wasn't much else out there about him. Max must have kept his online activities confined to the dark web, which I had no idea how to access.

I also did a search for Deirdre. She seemed like the person who might be able to help us most if Max wasn't willing. Eamonn had given Con her number, so I tried that. She still wasn't answering her phone, but I left a message. Then, through Ciara's social media, I was able to find Deirdre on a couple of sites. She had a friendly looking face, striking blue eyes, and long, fiery red hair. I sent her messages explaining who I was, telling her we needed her help with Ciara, and giving her my email and cell phone number, should she decide to get in touch. It didn't look like she'd posted anything recently, so I knew it was probably a long shot. However, if Max proved to be as uncooperative as I suspected he would, she might be our *only* shot.

—————

It was nearly an hour's winding drive west from downtown Galway to reach the town where Max lived. I didn't know what I was expecting his house to look like, but I was surprised when it turned out to be a beautiful stone cottage sitting at the top of a U-shaped hillside drive. Con said it was probably of nineteenth-century construction, but a modern-looking extension had been added on the back. The front door was wooden and ornately carved, with a shiny new bronze plaque above it that read "An Caisleán Mór."

"The Big Castle?" Con translated. "It's not a kip, I'll give him that, but talk about delusions of grandeur."

We walked around the house, and I was surprised that in a building that old, there was no external access to the basement. Con explained that basements weren't common features in Irish homes due to problems with damp. Instead, large stone outbuildings like the one we saw near the house were favored for extra storage space.

The hill in front of the house sloped down to a body of water the map on my phone identified as Clynagh Bay, where a speedboat was docked at a small pier. No cars were visible on the drive or in the paved area in front of the outbuilding, so we weren't too surprised when no one answered the front door.

Since Max didn't know us from Adam, we decided to introduce ourselves as community liaisons for a local crisis intervention unit. We'd speak in vague terms about a health problem someone he knew was having. Then we would tell Max we'd been contacted by Ciara's family because they thought he might be able to help fill in some gaps about her health history during the period of time she was living in Galway, and because they'd been unable to reach him, we'd been asked to come out.

But since he wasn't home, Con declared it incumbent upon us as "community liaisons" to explore a bit. Walking around the house, I observed that Max didn't seem to have much time for gardening. There were none of the usual shrubs, trees, and bushes that adorned most of the houses I'd seen in Ireland so far, just lawns, although those appeared well maintained. Con noticed a white satellite dish about two feet in diameter sitting on a raised concrete platform between the house and the outbuilding. Max must've prioritized having a reliable internet connection.

We walked down to the waterfront. In the distance, we could see the point where the inlet widened and opened into the ocean. The speedboat docked there was about twenty feet long, gray and white with a sleek, low-profile body.

"Perfect for sneaking out to one's cult island under cover of night," Con said, climbing onto the boat to have a look around.

I walked to the back so I could see the boat's name. "*Wicker Man*?" I called out.

"What?" Con's head popped up from where he was searching the interior.

"That's the name of the boat."

Several under-the-breath curses later, he joined me. "That sick bastard."

"What does it mean?"

Con pinched his nose and squinted for a moment before answering, "A wicker man is a hollow wicker statue used to make human sacrifices. In ancient times, they would put people inside and burn them. There was a horror movie about it in the seventies, but I also came across it last night while doing some research. Although there's precious little evidence, some scholars speculate that wicker men were used in the worship of Taranis."

"Oh God." I swallowed the bile rising in my throat. "Taranis worshippers practiced human sacrifice?"

"Human and animal, I believe it was. At the same time, sometimes."

We stared at the name prominently displayed on the back of the boat. I knew Con must have been thinking the same thing I was. "So, not a good sign that Max named his boat after a murder mechanism."

"No, not a good sign at all."

He completed his search of the boat but found nothing of interest. There were several other piers nearby and houses with lines of sight to the water, so Con decided it would be too risky to break into the locked compartment below the console. Disappointed to be leaving with no new useful information, we headed back to the car.

The Wicked Games Corporation had its offices in a three-story building near a busy park in the center of the city called Eyre Square. Although the website said the building was open on Saturdays, the lobby was almost empty—not surprising on a weekend. Still, we approached the receptionist.

She was in close conversation with a tall man sitting on her desk. They were dressed in business casual attire and appeared to be in their late twenties or early thirties. The man got up and stood to one side as we approached.

The receptionist gave us a tight, professional smile, and I got the feeling we had interrupted something—a flirtation, perhaps. "May I help you?" she asked in an American accent.

"Yes," Con said. "We're visiting Galway and hoped to drop in on a friend of a friend. Max Hinsen?"

"Can I see some ID?"

We handed her our drivers' licenses, which she examined for a tick longer than seemed necessary. She slid the IDs onto a scanner and returned them to us.

"Thanks. I'll be happy to check and see if he's in today. Who's your friend?"

"My friend?" Con asked.

"You said Mr. Hinsen is the friend of a friend?" Her smile grew tight with impatience.

We had discussed how to answer that question and decided to stick as close to the truth as possible without giving away too much information. This time, I piped up. "Her name's Ciara." I gave her my warmest smile. "We're friends from college."

"Oh, Ciara!" The receptionist's expression relaxed, and she exchanged a glance with her companion. "Why didn't you say? Everyone here loves her." The man nodded and almost smiled. "She's looking after her mom in Cork now, right?"

"That's right. She told us she used to work here with Max, so while we're in Galway, we just thought we'd drop in."

"That's so nice!" The receptionist flipped her long black braid over her shoulder, picked up the phone, and dialed an extension, but after a few rings, we heard the voice mail come on. "It appears he's not in today, I'm sorry to say."

"How about Deirdre?" Con asked. "Ciara mentioned her as well."

I thought I saw the barest flicker of irritation on the receptionist's face as she replied, "Unfortunately, Deirdre's on vacation at the moment." She tapped her finger on the desk. "Sorry, bad luck!"

"No, it's our fault. We should have called ahead." I tried to look apologetic. "Thanks for checking."

"No problem! Hey, when you see Ciara, tell her we all hope she's feeling better."

Con and I froze in place, but only for a second. I hoped it went undetected. "Feeling better?" I asked.

"Yeah. Max said she was under the weather?" The receptionist sighed and began playing with a sparkly diamond ring on her left hand. "I know from experience how inconvenient it is to get sick while you're trying to plan a wedding."

"Oh, well, congratulations to you!" It seemed odd that a jilted and bitter Max would be talking to people about Ciara's upcoming nuptials. "So, have you and Ciara been sharing wedding ideas?"

"Oh no," she said with a light laugh. "I've been married almost a year. Plus, I haven't talked to her since she moved back to Cork, but Max told me about their plans. I'm so glad they're finally getting hitched. This long-distance relationship thing has been so hard on him—and her, too, I'm sure."

What on earth…? I felt Con shift uncomfortably next to me as it sank in that Max was telling people he and Ciara were getting married.

"Of course," I said, putting my hand on my heart.

"So, where are you going next?" she asked. "If you need any tips on what to see while you're in the city…."

"Do you know anything about Saint Cillian's Island?" Con asked, going completely off script.

"There's a religious shrine Neve would love to visit, but we'd have to see it today. She flies out tomorrow."

"Oh, it's a shame you're not staying longer! I've never heard of that island." The receptionist turned to the man. "Have you?"

"I have, but I'm no expert," he said, running a hand briskly over his shaved head. "I believe you can only reach the island in the summer, during a feast day." The man spoke softly, his vowels broad and flat. It was an Irish accent, but different from Con's.

Could this be the same guy from the video who'd officiated the handfasting? It was hard to tell. Shaved heads were growing more popular, and the man in the video had been nearly shouting, so it was difficult to compare their voices.

"That's what we heard. That is a shame."

"Yeah." I went along with Con's story, nodding slowly. "I'm sorry I missed that. I wish there was some other way to visit. My grandparents are from this area, and Saint Cillian was very important to them when they were alive. I wanted to go there and pay my respects."

"Hmm." The man rubbed his neck, looking thoughtful. "If there is a way to get there, they would know at the Galway City Museum. It's not far from here, on the river."

"Grand," Con said. "That's a great help. Much appreciated."

"Yes, thank you!" I added. "It was so lovely meeting you both."

"You too," the receptionist chirped. "Good luck, and travel safely tomorrow!"

"Thanks! Have a great weekend," I replied as we headed toward the exit.

We left the building and walked around the corner. I leaned back against a brick wall. "Wow, that was weird."

"Very strange that Max has been telling people he's marrying my future sister-in-law."

"Why did you ask them about the island?"

"They may never tell Max that two people who know Ciara came by asking about Saint Cillian's," he said, "but if they do mention it to him, he might just be curious enough to make himself available the next time we come by."

"So you were just trying to smoke him out? Were you serious about visiting the island?"

"Why not? We've had no luck finding Max so far, but we might get lucky and find some useful information in that sea cave, or the church above—a computer or a notebook, something with clues. There must be some way to access the cave by land. The video showed the mouth of the cave, and it was very narrow. They couldn't have brought in so many people and all of the electronic equipment needed for that production by water."

The idea of visiting the island gave me goose bumps of equal parts excitement and terror—excitement about finding more information that might help us nail Max and terror at the idea of being in the same place where Ciara had suffered such torment.

Con frowned at me. "You don't have to come with, you know. This is much more than we planned for today. I can take you back to the apartment and go on my own. In fact, I would strongly prefer it."

"No way, mister." I touched my fingertips to my lips, then to his. "I go where you go, remember?"

"I do recall something about that," he grumbled, but I saw the effort it was taking him not to smile. "At least the island is uninhabited. For once, we won't have to deal with any unpleasant surprises."

He was right; we did have a way of attracting those. "I'm game. I should just tell you one thing, though, since we can only get there by boat."

"Ah, no. Don't tell me you get seasick!"

"No, it's not that. I just don't know how to swim."

Con's eyes widened. "How?"

"What do you mean, how? I never learned."

"But your parents have a swimming pool in their backyard!"

"It's only four feet deep."

"But I saw pictures of you at the ocean in your parents' house—from every year of your childhood, it looked like!"

His ongoing disbelief made me feel self-conscious. Heat slowly crept up my neck. "You can wade out into the ocean without knowing how to swim. And I did go out on boats and everything, but I always wore a vest.

I'm not afraid of water, I just don't know how to be in it without sinking like a stone."

"All right, no worries," he said, but he definitely looked worried. "We'll make sure you have a safety vest on, then. Everyone on a boat should wear a vest, in truth, but the standard size barely fits around my neck."

I couldn't help smiling at the image of Con wearing a glowing orange vest as a scarf. "It's okay. If we get tossed in, you can use me as a flotation device."

He just shook his head and grumbled, "I'll have to talk to Jim and Leigh about this. Raising their daughter in a house with a swimming pool in back and never teaching her to swim…."

"They tried!" I pressed my fist against his arm in a faux punch. "It's not their fault I was incapable. Leave them alone."

"All right, all right." Finally, he smiled. "We'll be walking back through Eyre Square to reach the museum. I saw an ice cream parlor there if you're interested."

Con knew me well enough to know that was an outstanding peace offering.

We followed a route closed to everything but pedestrian traffic, and I wished we could slow down and take in the city. It was a beautiful scene, bustling with activity despite the cloudy weather. A smattering of meandering, backpack-carrying tourists filled the street, which was lined with colorful storefronts. Flags strung across the road fluttered in the wind. Con said the street musicians in Ireland were called buskers, and they appeared at regular intervals, playing everything from traditional Irish tunes to American blues, giving our journey a lively soundtrack.

There was something magical about ice cream. We stopped at the parlor as promised, where they made their ice cream in-house. It was delicious, and we devoured our cones in silence as we walked through the park and down a street lined with shops. I made mental notes of all the eateries and stores I wanted to visit once we finally had a moment to breathe.

The Galway City Museum was an impressive white-and-gray modern construction built just next to the Spanish Arch, a stone structure that a nearby plaque informed us dated back to the pre-Middle Ages. As we entered the museum, a guide greeted us. We asked about possible ways to get to Saint Cillian's Island. He explained that we'd missed the feast day, but Con told him the same tale we'd spun for the receptionist at Wicked Games.

The guide then led us up to the Claddagh Exhibition, where a display featuring floor-to-ceiling windows looked out over the River Corrib at a section of the city called the Claddagh. He explained that until the Great Hunger in the 1840s, the Claddagh was a mazelike fishing village, home to Gaelic speakers with their own independently elected king. We had a great view of Claddagh Quay, which included a large pier where several boats were docked.

The guide said he had a friend from the Claddagh named Bronagh who worked at a nearby jewelry store.

He offered to call her and ask if she knew anyone who might be willing to ferry us out to the island. Since the Claddagh was a close-knit community, the guide suggested that would give us as good a chance as any at finding a boat. Grateful for the help, we took him up on the offer. He called Bronagh, and after a short conversation, he said she'd agreed to ask around for us.

Con leaned down to me and murmured, "You never know, it might grease the wheels a bit if we went to the jewelry store and thanked his friend in person."

I nodded. "Good plan."

The guide gave us instructions on how to make the short walk to the jewelry store. The wind had picked up while we were inside the museum. I drew nearer to Con, who tucked my hand into the crook of his elbow and pulled me in close.

Walking through the picturesque city with him under dramatic skies created such a romantic scene, I felt a surge of resentment toward Max for intruding on our precious time together and turning this into a day of business rather than pleasure. Only the promise that going to the island and finding the sea cave might help us find answers for Ciara gave me some measure of comfort.

CHAPTER 17

CON

There it was, as promised: a red building with a bright yellow door and a golden claddagh symbol hanging above the entrance. The sign read "T. Dillon & Son," and a plaque on the wall said this was the place where the original claddagh rings were made in 1750.

Inspiration struck Con as Neve stepped up to the window and peered at some rings in a glass case. She had said it was too soon to get engaged after dating for only a few weeks, but there was nothing stopping him from putting another kind of ring on her finger.

"I've seen these," she said. "They're popular in the US. These are claddagh rings?"

"Yes." He pointed out a lovely gold one. "See there? The hands represent friendship, the crown, loyalty, and the heart, love."

"What beautiful symbolism," she murmured, eyes alight.

"The claddagh ring has a lot of significance here. They're used for wedding rings sometimes," Con said, doing his best to imbue the ring he was about to buy with the weight of commitment. "You'd only be given one by a very close friend or someone who truly loves you. Let's go inside, shall we? Meet Bronagh and take a closer look."

He held the door open and then followed Neve into the store. The woman behind the counter had ivory skin and black hair with a straight fringe that almost covered her eyes. Her face brightened when she saw us. "Hi, I'm Bronagh. Con and Neve, I assume?"

"That's us," Neve said warmly, extending a hand. "Thank you so much for your help. I've always wanted to visit Saint Cillian's Island, but I fly out tomorrow. Poor planning, I know, but I really appreciate any help you can give us."

Lying normally took quite a toll on Neve, but if it was bothering her now, she didn't show it. Instead, she came across as a perfectly genuine, if slightly scatter-brained, American tourist. The pink sweatshirt she was wearing with NYC on the front in large black letters enhanced the look.

"It's not me who will be helping you," Bronagh said, "but you're very welcome. I've texted a few friends with fishing boats. We'll see who comes back to me. I can't say how long it will take, so feel free to look around. There's a claddagh museum in the back if you're interested."

"Thank you." Con gently steered Neve into the back

room to give them a moment of privacy. "Very smooth job of lying back there. I'm impressed."

She tensed up immediately. "I'm glad you think so, but I only did that for Ciara's sake. You know I hate lying—*and* being lied to."

Well, that put him in his place. He'd been on the receiving end of Neve's wrath for lying to her before, even though he'd done it for an exceptionally good reason. "Take a compliment when you're given it," he teased. "Let's have a look around."

Con enjoyed watching Neve as she walked slowly around the room, examining the framed photographs, maps, and historical documents hanging on the walls. She took her time looking through the contents of the display cases and reading everything, peppering him with questions about Irish history. Her natural curiosity and wonderment were two of the qualities about her that he'd always adored. Neve's genuine interest in all things Irish further warmed his heart.

After taking in the museum, they went back to the showroom. Neve gravitated back to the counter with the rings.

"We're in the market for one of these today," Con told Bronagh. "Neve, do you know your ring size?"

She looked a little confused, as though trying to figure out whether he truly wanted to buy her a ring for his own reasons or if his motive was to further "grease the wheels" with Bronagh. "Um, no," she said. "I haven't had a reason to get measured."

"Well, you do now."

Bronagh was already holding up a metal loop with sizing rings. "Which finger?"

"I've never really worn rings," Neve said. "I don't know."

"Well, if you don't have a preference...." Con reached over and lifted her left hand. "Third finger."

Bronagh took Neve's hand and squinted at it.

As though whispering about a scandal, Neve said, "But that's the finger for wedding rings!"

"We should measure the same finger on the right hand, too, then. See if they're the same, or at least a close match." Con nodded to Bronagh, who complied. "That way, when you get your engagement ring, you can switch the claddagh ring over."

Now a proper blush brought a charming pink hue to Neve's cheeks—a shade that was quickly becoming his favorite color. Wide-eyed, she turned away from Bronagh and mouthed, "Are you serious?"

Con nodded, giving her a look that would push any doubts from her mind. "Quite," he murmured to her, then asked, "What do you like? Yellow gold? White gold? Rose?"

Her mouth fell open as she turned back to the counter. Having determined her ring size, Bronagh pulled out rings of all three colors and tried them on Neve. After a period of indecision, no doubt lengthened by her surprise at the whole situation, she chose a lovely white gold option.

Con slipped Bronagh his credit card before Neve had a chance to object. He picked up the ring. "Now," he explained, lifting her left hand in his, "if you wear this with the crown pointing toward your hand"—he demonstrated, pushing the ring just as far as her fingertip—"that means you're available. However," he said, turning the ring over and sliding it onto her finger with the crown pointing toward her fingernail, "you'll wear it this way, to show you're taken."

"I see." Neve looked up at him, a smile playing at the corner of her lips. "So *that's* how it is, is it?"

He raised her hand to his lips and placed a gentle kiss where the claddagh ring now sat. "That is indeed how it is."

Her eyes softened with what looked like a mix of joy, gratitude, and affection. He felt like the king of all creation.

"It looks lovely on you," Bronagh said.

"Thanks." Neve held her hand out so both she and Bronagh could get a better look. "It's really beautiful. Thanks so much for helping us, and thank you," she said, turning her gorgeous smile on Con. "I love it."

"The claddagh rules state you can never take it off now," he instructed, pushing his luck as far as he dared. "Not even in the shower."

"There are rules, huh?" Neve grinned. "Okay, got it."

They heard a ding, and Bronagh picked up her mobile. "Ah, good news," she said. "My friend Lorcan says he can take you out to the island. He wants to know how much time you wish to spend out there."

Con and Neve exchanged a look. "An hour, maybe two?" he proposed, and she nodded.

Bronagh texted Lorcan back and got an immediate reply. "That's fine. He says it's a ninety-minute trip each way, so his charge is three hundred euros. Can you meet him at the pier in half an hour?"

"Absolutely." The price seemed steep to Con. Then again, this was a last-minute, private charter, and he was willing to pay whatever was required. "Thanks a million, Bronagh. You've been a great help."

"It's no bother. Just head out to the ramp on Claddagh Quay and look for the fishing boats. Lorcan will find you."

"Thank you so much, Bronagh, for everything," Neve said, pointing at her ring finger.

"Enjoy!" Bronagh called out as they left the shop.

Once outside, Neve stepped in front of Con and wrapped her arms around his waist. He in turn put his arms around her shoulders and pulled her in close. He felt the vibration of her voice against him as she murmured, "That was too generous, but I love my ring. Thank you."

"You're most welcome." He kissed her hair just above her ear. "Thank you for doing me the favor of wearing it. Now everyone will know you're taken, so I'll have to beat off fewer potential suitors."

Neve's body shook with laughter for several seconds before she pulled away. "You're ridiculous, you know that?" Then she grabbed him by the hand and, with an almost childlike expression of glee, began dragging him down the street. "Let's go take a boat to an island!"

Con was all too happy to follow her. In fact, the way he felt about Neve, for as long as he lived, he would follow her anywhere.

————

"Why are you looking at him like that?" Neve asked, her mouth just next to Con's ear so he could hear her over the growl of the boat's outboard motor.

He continued to glare at Lorcan's back from their seats toward the stern. "He's taking advantage, charging too much."

"Please! That's not it. It was that comment he made, wasn't it? What's a 'fastook,' anyway?"

The first thing out of Lorcan's mouth upon meeting them had been "Feck, you're a big fastook, aren't you?"

Normally, Con was happy to have the craic. But on top of the "fastook" jibe about his large size and physical awkwardness, Lorcan then proceeded to refer to Neve as "ya fine thing." Which might have been harmless enough, but judging from the way Lorcan looked at her, he'd been flirting with her right up to, but not quite crossing, the line. Slagging Con was one thing, but hitting on Neve? Con hoped the man was better at boating than he was at social graces.

There was only one lifejacket, and it was so old the

original bright orange color had faded to pink. Con couldn't fault Lorcan for that, though, since he said he fished solo and didn't normally have any passengers. Fortunately, the vest fit Neve well enough once the straps were adjusted. At any rate, she shouldn't need it. There was only a yellow weather warning—or "normal weather" for Ireland—so he felt confident they were safe from capsizing in the thirty-foot boat.

"It's… hard to translate," Con replied.

Neve paused. The brim of her baseball cap dropped as her brow wrinkled. "Could *I* call you a big fastook?"

He couldn't help smiling at her attempt to work out the Irish slang, especially wearing her new tourist-gear cap, black with GALWAY and a shamrock stitched in green. "*You* can call me anything you like," he said, placing his hand atop hers. "Warm enough?"

She nodded, but she was clutching his arm with both hands, her fingers digging in. He didn't blame her for wanting something to hang on to. The water was a bit rough and quickly getting rougher as more clouds rolled in. At least it wasn't raining. There was a canopy over the cockpit, but it was only large enough to protect whoever was steering the boat.

Con did his best to wrap his arm around Neve's life-jacketed shoulders, pulling her closer to him as they moved ahead through Galway Bay toward the ocean. Lorcan told them Saint Cillian's Island was a bit north of the Aran Islands. With the trip out there taking an hour and a half, they would be arriving later in the day than Con would have liked, but at least they'd be able to look around the place while it was still light out. Meanwhile, he was grateful for the pac-a-macs they were wearing, which Neve had insisted on buying in Killarney. The waterproof jackets were doing a decent job protecting them from the wind and spray.

When they met on the pier, Con had asked Lorcan if he knew of any sea caves on the island. He said he hadn't heard of any, but once they got on the boat, he would radio some friends who were more familiar with the island. Lorcan seemed confident he would have the answer before they reached their destination.

It was too loud for much conversation, so Con and Neve sat in silence, enjoying the smell of the salt water, the sensation of cutting through the waves, and the sight of the coastline they were following. The best part of the ride, however, was having Neve next to him, feeling her there, knowing she was safe. The warmth of her, her scrumptious scent, the feel of her side pressed up against his... and then there was the fact that she kept stealing glances at her new ring. He could tell she really did like it, and nothing could have made him happier. Seeing it on her finger and knowing it meant she was his—there was no word to describe the mixture of pride, awe, and gratitude it inspired in him.

Out on the water, they were far from all that troubled them, and a world away from the slings and arrows of Washington, DC. Part of him wished they could stay on that boat forever—after they tossed Lorcan overboard, that was.

About an hour in, boredom must have set in for

Neve, because she pulled out her phone. Lorcan had told them they were unlikely to get a signal on the island, but they could use their phones on his boat, which was equipped with a mobile hotspot.

With her occupied, Con went to Lorcan and asked for a map that showed the island. No harm learning the lay of the land. Lorcan said they used electronic maps for the most part these days, but he did have some old paper maps tucked away in a console compartment.

Con sat next to Neve and studied the map while she scrolled through her phone. The island was roughly an oval shape and appeared to be in the form of an enormous hill that peaked where the church was located. There was also a narrow inlet shaped like a fishhook that curved in near the church, which appeared to sit near the top of a cliff. Con figured the entrance to the cave must be around there somewhere.

He was pulled away from his task when, several minutes later, he felt Neve stiffen and sit up straight. She was looking at her phone, mouth slightly open.

"What is it?"

"Um… I'm not sure. What's a dermoid cyst?"

"What? Why?"

She handed him the phone. On the screen was the operative report from her biopsy. Now Con shared her surprise. Those reports were never released to patients until their follow-up appointments, and Neve's appointment wouldn't happen until after they got home. "Where did this come from?"

"I don't know. I just got an alert that I had new information on the patient portal website, so I checked and found that. I don't understand the medicalese, though."

He had seen such errors happen before. Someone must have clicked the wrong box or typed the wrong name into the wrong field. No matter. He was on hand to interpret the report for her, and there was no reason to think it was anything other than good news.

"Let's have a look." Con scrolled through the report. While the pathology results were still pending, the surgeon confirmed the results of Neve's earlier scans. "It says both ovarian tumors are mature cystic teratomas, also called dermoid cysts. Nothing to worry about at all. They're still waiting on the lab, but the surgeon shares Dr. Mohinder's opinion that they're not cancerous."

"That's good news, right?"

"Yes, definitely good."

"Do I have to have the cysts removed?"

"Let's see." He read on a bit farther. "That's being recommended as a precaution, but it's not urgent. There's no imminent danger."

As he continued to scan the document, however, Con spotted something that stopped him in his tracks: APPARENT DIFFUSE SEEDING OF ENDOMETRIAL TISSUE AND ASSOCIATED FIBROTIC CHANGES NOTED TO FALLOPIAN TUBES AND PROXIMAL OVARIES BILATERALLY, CONSISTENT WITH ADVANCED STAGE IV ENDOMETRIOSIS.

Oh hell. His heart dropped to his stomach. None of that was life-threatening, thank God, but scarring of the fallopian tubes, damage to the ovarian tissue…? Definitely not good news, and he had no idea how Neve would react.

Con swallowed hard. Should he tell her? Or would that kind of news be better coming from Dr. Mohinder? He needed time to think this through. Either way, it would have to wait. As it was, they were nearly shouting at each other over an outboard motor while bouncing across waves. It was no time to have a serious conversation.

Quickly, he scrolled back up to the top of the report and handed her the phone. He hoped she would let it go at that. But even if she kept reading, he was confident she wouldn't understand the alarming bits of "medicalese" he'd just read.

"No imminent danger?" She smiled. "Smooth talker."

He forced himself to smile back. *Immediate crisis averted.*

But Neve returned to scrolling through the report, and after several moments, her expression changed. "Wait, what's this… oh." All emotion drained from her face as she stared at the phone.

He looked over. She had pinch-opened the touchscreen, enlarging the "Surgeon's Note" section at the end of the report.

IMPRESSION: COMPROMISED TUBAL PATENCY EXPECTED

WITH THE DEGREE OF TUBAL FIBROSIS NOTED. INFERTILITY ALMOST CERTAIN IN THIS CASE.

Silently, Con cursed himself. He should have scanned the entire report before giving the phone back to her.

Gently taking it from her outstretched hand, he read through the rest of the note. While follow-up tests were offered, the surgeon expressed a high level of confidence that they would only confirm his initial impression.

Con usually appreciated it when his fellow doctors were forthright in stating their opinions, but under the circumstances, he wished the wording had been a bit more equivocal. Neve knew Con had handpicked her surgeon—highly experienced and with a stellar reputation—so he couldn't even give her a convincing reason to doubt the report's conclusions.

Slowly, he placed his hand over the screen. "Neve—"

But before he could say more, she took the phone back and shoved it into her pocket.

Con had never been at such a complete loss. He wanted to pull her into his arms and comfort her, but now she had such a vacant look on her face. Maybe she would prefer not to be touched. Instead, he searched for words, something he could tell her that she could hold on to. "We'll go through the report together—all of it, in detail— and talk it through. But that's something we should do when we have plenty of time, and we're not on a boat."

Neve nodded once, then turned away from him and looked out over the water.

He hated himself for not knowing what to do, how to take care of her in that moment. In his practice, Con had seen patients who were having trouble conceiving. Since that wasn't his area of expertise, however, he'd always referred them to reproductive endocrinologists or gynecologists. So while he'd given people bad medical news before, he'd never had this particular conversation—and he'd certainly never had it with a woman he loved.

Leaning in close, he asked, "Do you still want to do this?"

"Of course!" she snapped, brows drawn together in irritation. "What kind of question is that?"

So *that* had been the wrong thing to say, evidently. As Con sat there trying to imagine how she might be feeling and what he could do to support her, the note of the engine lowered, and the boat slowed. An island rose up before them, a granite mountain with blankets of green between the boulders.

"We're here," Lorcan called over his shoulder, "and I've got an answer for you. There is a sea cave on the island. You used to be able to reach it by climbing from the surface down a passageway. There was an entrance somewhere near the church. Can't say for sure now, though, because the cave is closed to the public."

With great effort, Con forced his attention away from Neve's predicament and back to the task at hand. "Why's that?"

"Not safe. The tide rises quickly around here, and when it does, the mouth of the cave gets submerged and the whole thing floods. The cave was either a secret or forgotten for centuries, but it was rediscovered back in the 1950s. After they opened it up, a few people got trapped in there and drowned, so they closed it off for good."

"Oh, how awful," Neve said.

Con wondered if the sadness in her voice was only for the drowning victims or if it was also emotional residue from reading her medical report. "Thanks for finding that out for us."

"No bother." Lorcan slowed down and steered around the rocky shoreline as they all looked for the church. The island was only about one square kilometer in size, so it shouldn't take long to find it.

Con didn't want to leave his medical conversation with Neve where it was, raw and open. At the same time, he didn't want to say anything that might upset her further. Nor did he want to give her what could only be empty words of comfort; it wouldn't work, and besides, she deserved better than that.

Gently, he placed his hand on her knee. She didn't respond, so he said, "Neve."

This time, she turned to look at him. He smoothed from her face a few pieces of hair the wind had pulled out from under her cap. Holding her gaze, he said, "We *will* talk this through later, all right? We'll talk about everything."

"Okay. Yeah."

Neve pressed her lips into a smile. But Con could see in her eyes the wound left by the medical report, and it tore at his heart. Best to get whatever information they could find on Max quickly and head back as soon as possible. Then they could talk properly.

He took out his own phone and looked up the tide timetables for Galway.

CHAPTER 18
NEVE

f I were religiously inclined, one look at the stone church at the top of the hill might convince me to follow Saint Cillian. It was stunning, and whole, which was unexpected. After hundreds of years, I thought we'd see the remains of a few walls with stones piled around them. But Saint Cillian's church had been built out of large granite stones all the way to its roof, and it was still standing. A narrow, tall structure, it seemed to slice the sky.

The sight of it was so striking, it even took my mind off the medical report for a moment.

It seemed to me that seeing the word "infertility" should have upset me more than it did. Aside from some numbness, my predominant feeling was relief that I almost certainly didn't have cancer, and that there wasn't any "imminent danger," as Con put it.

I couldn't tell if I was still in shock from the news or if it just wasn't affecting me in the way I expected.

After all, I had never been one of those women who had always wanted to be a mother. So far, my focus in life had been on learning to be a good psychotherapist, and that had been a pretty all-encompassing task. My ex, Stephan, had been my first serious relationship, and I figured out early on that I didn't want to be a parent with him. He was an overgrown child himself. Plus, he always expressed concern that having children would interfere too much with his career—and with mine, since he never missed an opportunity to tell me what I should do and how I should feel.

Now Stephan was firmly in the rearview mirror, thank God, and I was with Con. But our relationship was so new, I hadn't even had a chance to think that far into our future—not until I overheard the conversation between him and Eamonn in the car, that was. It seemed Con was in the "no kids" camp, although I had promised not to jump to any more conclusions about that car conversation without talking to him first.

As Lorcan steered the boat toward a stone-built pier, I tried out the idea in my head: *Con doesn't want kids.* I waited for some emotion to kick in, but none came. Next, I experimented with the thought *I can't have kids.* I felt something that time. It was like a stone appeared in the pit of my stomach. But it was a small stone, more like a pebble, and I couldn't put my finger on what emotion it represented. That would require introspection, something I didn't have the time or mental space for at the moment. Lorcan was nosing the boat up to the pier, and Con was standing in front of me, holding out his hand.

I needed to focus. *Max. Ciara. Sea cave.* I took Con's hand and let him steady me as we walked over and climbed onto the pier. He helped me unbuckle my life-jacket, and I tossed it back onto the boat.

Lorcan was rooting around in the cabin. He emerged with a flashlight, a protein bar, and a bottle of water for each of us. "You might need torches," he said, gesturing toward the darkening sky.

"We're not taking your only flashlights, are we? We do have them on our phones," I mentioned.

"Ah, don't worry, ya fine thing! I've lights on the boat," he replied, grinning as Con flinched at his repeated flirtation. "Watch those phone flashlights. They suck the life right out of the battery. I'll leave you to it, then. It's a quarter past six now. What time should we meet back here?"

"You're not waiting for us, then?" Con asked, echoing my thought.

"Not when there's fish out there calling to me" was Lorcan's jovial reply.

"What do you think, Neve? Eight o'clock?"

I didn't love the idea of being on the island after dark, but we probably weren't going to get another chance like this. We should take full advantage of it. "Sure. Sounds good."

"Grand. I'll set an alarm on my phone."

"Eight o'clock, then." Lorcan started the engine. "Good luck with your saint!"

"Good luck with the fish!" I called back as he pulled away from the pier.

Con drew me to him and held me in his embrace for several long moments. I slid my hands under his jacket and around his waist, holding on tight. I imagined myself as a boat, my arms as ropes lashing me to a dock piling. No matter how rough the waters, I knew Con would always be there for me, stable and stationary, keeping me from being carried out to sea.

He placed one hand on top of my baseball cap. "You sure you're all right?"

He's worried about me. I didn't want that, especially when we had a job to do and a limited amount of time in which to do it. Through sheer will, I pulled away from him and forced myself to smile. "Yeah, I'm good. Let's get this done."

Con examined my face for a moment longer, then tapped the brim of my cap. "I'm glad one of us is wearing a good luck symbol."

"Oh, right—the shamrock." I smiled. "I thought it was going to fly off a couple times on the way over."

"I, for one, am glad it's still with us."

We walked down the pier and stepped onto the island itself. The hard gray rock where we were standing softened into patches of grass on the hill above us. I turned to look back across the water, and although the sun was setting, I could still see the mainland. Houses were visible, though tiny from where we stood.

"You go first," Con said, pointing up the hill.

"Why?"

"If you lose your footing, I can catch you. I'm not sure you could do the same."

"Gotcha." I began to pick my way up the hill, careful to avoid loose stones and places where the granite was covered with moss or mud. It was slower going than I expected but steady.

As we walked, focusing my attention on the ground in front of me put my mind in a meditative state. My thoughts drifted back to the topic of children—specifically, to a Sunday dinner at my parents' house about a year ago. They had taken me aside and told me I shouldn't feel pressure to have children for their sake. My mother revealed for the first time that they had tried and failed for several years before she became pregnant with me. She said they considered me a miracle, and they didn't expect more than one of those in a lifetime—though of course they would adore any grandchildren who came along. My father added that it didn't make any sense to them to mourn the absence of people they'd never met. Still, when I saw the joy with which they talked about their friends' grandchildren, I couldn't help wondering if they had just said those things to take any pressure off me. Although I'd never said it out loud, I was sure they knew I didn't want to have kids with Stephan, who I was dating at the time. I wondered if, now that Con was in the picture, they had new hope.

There it was again, that stone in the pit of my stomach. It had returned, the same emotion I felt when I first tried on the thought, *I can't have kids.* Was it the idea of disappointing my parents that was affecting me so profoundly? I turned that possibility over in my mind like I was examining a shell I'd picked up on the beach. It made sense. After all, I was so close to them, loved them so much. I'd always wanted more than anything to make them happy and proud.

With my next step, I slid on some loose rocks. Jumping to one side, I found solid ground and stopped myself from falling.

"You okay?" Con called out from behind me.

"Yeah, fine," I replied. But the spike of adrenaline reminded me that I really needed to get my mind off the medical report and on the task at hand. *Be in the now. Focus.*

Moments later, my foot landed on a stone pathway around the church. "We're here."

The church rose above us, small but amazing in structure. The rectangular part of the building was about ten feet tall, but the steep roof had to be another twenty feet high. The church had a small footprint, about twenty feet in length and fifteen feet wide, and was entirely constructed of gray stones mottled with white and brown. Con and I both stood with our heads back, looking up and taking in the striking sight.

"Impressive." He released a hard breath and reached down, massaging his thigh.

His leg is bothering him. I laid my hand on his arm. "Maybe there's a place to sit down inside."

With a nod, he began walking around the church. I followed, and when we reached the far end, we found an arch-shaped opening filled by a heavy wooden door. It had an old-looking metal handle with a thumb lever.

Con pushed the lever down and tried to pull the door open, but it didn't budge. "Christ," he muttered.

"He can hear you," I whispered.

That got a half smile out of him, anyway. "He'll understand. It's not locked, at least, but it is stuck." He slammed his shoulder into the door a few times.

"Don't break it!"

"I'm just loosening it up." Con squinted at me, but there was a glint of amusement in his eyes. "If you think I'm strong enough to break this door down, your blood sugar must be crashing. The ice cream was a bad idea."

"The ice cream was *your* idea."

"Never again."

I rolled my eyes. "Trust an endocrinologist to ruin the fun."

"At least you can't say I never took you anywhere." Con flashed me a smile of genuine amusement, then turned his attention to the door. He braced his right foot against the building and leaned on the handle again, wriggling the door as he put his back against it and pushed. Eventually, it scraped open an inch. He kept at it, working the handle and pulling on the door until it finally swung open. "See? Still in one piece!" With a wink, he handed me a flashlight.

I clicked it on and stepped into the church. It was very dark inside, with only three tiny slits of windows built into the walls, high up and close to the roof. We both coughed as we inhaled the stale, musty air. I flashed my beam around and saw that the church looked on the inside much as it had on the outside, but the stonework was of a more consistent gray color, not having been exposed to the elements.

Con shone his light as well. "Nowhere to sit," he observed.

"There's an altar." The church was empty, aside from a stone slab toward the front.

"And spend eternity in purgatory? No, thank you. Breaking in is one thing. Putting my arse on the altar is a step too far."

I squinted up at him. "For an agnostic, you have a very complicated moral code."

"Ah, but it has a strong internal logic," he quipped. "We'll need some energy for this. Let's eat those protein bars, then have a look around."

We made quick work of the bars and downed our water bottles as we scanned the church. Then we pocketed the wrappers and empty bottles and set about exploring.

Con went left, and I went right. Copying his movements, I walked around, tapping my flashlight lightly along the wall, listening for any change in sound that might indicate some kind of opening or a hollow space behind the rocks. After we covered the walls, we stooped down to tap along the floor, working our way inward. Finally, we met back at the altar.

"Solid as a rock, unsurprisingly," Con said.

"On my side too."

We stood there for a few moments longer, admiring the structure. Then we walked back to the door. Con made the sign of the cross as we stepped outside.

"Really?" I asked. "Now you're showing respect? *After* you broke in?"

"*Because* I broke in! Can't be too careful." He pushed the door closed.

We walked around to the far side of the church where, after twenty feet of grass, the ground stopped at a cliff that dropped straight down to the water. It was part of the fishhook-shaped inlet carved into the island. "Did Lorcan bring us around this way?"

"No, but given the shape of the inlet and the narrow opening, this whole area is likely concealed from view," Con said. "That's about a sixty-foot drop. The cave must be down there. Let's look for the entrance to that old passageway, but stick together."

He didn't get any argument from me. Shamrock on my hat or not, I didn't want to be wandering around by myself near the edge of a cliff. We searched around outside the church. Now we had to use the flashlights outside too. Since the sun had fully set, with the clouds overhead, it was a dark twilight.

There was only one other object visible that wasn't part of the natural landscape: a narrow stone slab about my height, set atop a granite pedestal between the church and the cliff. The pillar was large and rounded on top, and there were some curved depressions in it. Con speculated that it may have been a Celtic cross worn down by time. It was surrounded by five-foot wire fencing with a sign on it, in English and Irish, that read "Danger: Loose Stones. Do Not Enter." From the texture and appearance of the pillar, it looked about the same age as the church.

Con walked around it, examining the wire fencing. After the church break-in, I knew it was useless to ask what he was doing or why, so I just watched as he pushed and pulled on the wire, finally wrangling it down until there was a section he could step over. He ran his hands all over the pillar and pedestal and tapped his flashlight everywhere but found nothing unusual.

"Well, I don't know what the sign is about, then," I said. "The stones don't look loose to me."

"Hmm, you're right." Con stepped up onto the pedestal and hugged the pillar, pushing on it to see if it would move.

I bit my lip, picturing it toppling over and taking him with it. After a few minutes of watching him push and shove to no avail, I ventured, "Not to be a backseat driver, but if that's not working, maybe try...."

He looked over at me expectantly, red-faced and out of breath. I held my hand up and made a gesture like I was opening a twist-top bottle. "Something different? Rotating, maybe?"

"Hmm." Con repositioned himself so he was hugging the stone and began applying pressure from different angles. He looked as shocked as I felt when one of his rotating movements managed to twist the pillar about forty-five degrees.

"My God, it actually worked!" Wiping his sleeve across his glistening forehead, he grinned. "Well done, you girly swot, you!"

"What's a girly—wait!" I stopped and closed my eyes, concentrating. Through the rush of the wind, there was another sound, a scraping noise. "I think I heard something inside the church."

Con climbed back over the fencing. "Let's go."

My heart pounded like a struck drum as we once again entered the church. We flashed our beams around, not finding anything until we walked past the altar. Just behind it, the floor had opened up, creating an entrance to a spiral stone staircase.

Con pointed his flashlight down into the opening. "That's incredible. This must have been built into the original church, and it's still functional. Although it does look like it's been maintained recently."

I leaned in and looked. Sure enough, the stairs had multiple visible repairs using what looked like cement. "I can't believe we found it."

"Thank God we did," Con said. "The water's damn cold. I didn't like the idea of swimming out to search for the ocean entrance."

I gaped at him. "I *never* would have let you do that."

"Well, you couldn't have stopped me—not without your life jacket," he teased.

With a smirk, I pointed at the opening in the floor. "We'll never have to find out now, will we?"

We stood there for a moment, smiling and basking in our victory. I stepped forward. "Me first?"

"Not a chance." Raising both eyebrows, he asked, "I don't suppose I could talk you into staying above-ground? Up here, standing guard?"

"You mean leave me here alone to deal with any sociopathic cult leaders who might come by for a visit?"

"That's a no, then." Con looked at me for a moment, considering. "At least promise me you'll let me know if you feel even a *hint* of a panic attack starting."

Although I was embarrassed by the request, it was fair. I had given him enough reasons to worry about my mental health. "I'll let you know, I promise. And if you say the word, I'll hightail it back up here. Okay?"

"And I'll be right behind you."

"Deal. But right now, I feel no anxiety, just impatience. So can we please get on with it already?"

Con shot me a glance that told me he was uncertain whether to be pleased or worried by my enthusiasm. "Just take it slow. It looks dry here, but if this does lead to the cave, the rocks could get slippery farther down. And remember what Lorcan said about the cave being dangerous. It floods with the rising tide. I checked, and high tide isn't until ten forty-five tonight. We'll be gone well before then, but the water will be rising all the time, so let's not take any risks."

"Okay, got it."

"Right, so." He shone his flashlight down the staircase with one hand, held on to the wall with the other, and took his first step downward.

CHAPTER 19

CON

Con stared at the padlock securing the gate at the entrance to the sea cave. The gate appeared to be made of stainless steel with the frame embedded deep into the wall. The padlock went through two loops on a large metal plate that was welded into the gate itself. No weak spots to exploit.

"There might be a key somewhere," Neve said.

"That would make things easier, all right."

They climbed back up the stone steps until they reached the location of the carving in the wall from Max's video, with the wheel and the lightning bolt. Beneath it was a straight line cut into the rock with a date carved beneath it: 17/07/1952. Con thought the notation was most likely a high-water mark.

"Do you feel that?" Neve held her hands near the wall.

"Feel what?"

"It's cool air, like a little bit of a breeze. Coming from up there."

Several steps above the carving, they felt around and discovered a crevice in the wall. It was a tall, narrow opening, hidden from view by a subtle outcropping in the rock. When they leaned in closer, they could see that the edges of the crevice were jagged, the walls several feet thick. It appeared to have been naturally formed, and the shape was too small and irregular for a person to fit through.

When they shone their flashlights inside, they saw a small cave whose floor extended in about four feet, ending abruptly at a ledge that opened into a larger space. Their most interesting discovery was what appeared to be a folding metal ladder stashed just inside the crevice. It was tied to two bolts that had been drilled into the rock, with ropes coiled beside them. Con could reach the ladder easily, so he guessed it was there to provide a way for someone to get from the larger cave up to that ledge. Once they got through the gate, he would come back and push the ladder over the edge so he could climb up and investigate.

"Maybe the key's in here," Neve said, reaching into the crevice and feeling around.

He did the same on the opposite side of the opening. After checking every area they could reach, they stepped back in defeat and leaned against the opposite wall.

"Maybe back in the church?" she suggested.

"I doubt it. I'm fairly certain we would have spotted

it before. It seems Max is too cautious to leave the key in a place where it could be discovered."

Con knew what he had to do next. Raking a hand through his hair, he turned to Neve. "I can't emphasize strongly enough here that I was not going out of my way to look at the undergarments you purchased when we were checking out at Dunnes. But if I'm not mistaken, there was some indication on the packaging that your brassiere has wires in it. Correct?"

She squinted at him. "Uh, yes, it is an underwire bra." As though daring him to look, she moved her hands slowly beneath her breasts. "There's a wire on each side. And you're asking why?"

Now that she'd drawn his attention there, he couldn't stop staring. "So, I'll need those wires."

She crossed her arms over her chest, looking aghast. "Seriously? For what?"

"To pick the padlock. You can keep the rest of the bra," he reassured.

"You know how to pick a padlock? With bra underwire?"

He shrugged. This was getting more awkward by the minute. "I've only done it with paperclips, but I understand bra underwire is an acceptable stand-in."

"Why do you know how to pick locks? Wait, never mind. I'm not sure I want to know," she said, turning her back to Con. He watched her perform intriguing contortions as she somehow managed to remove her brassiere without taking off her sweatshirt. She turned back around and tossed it to him with a grin. "There you go. Merry Christmas early."

He was certain his heart stopped completely for a good ten seconds. There he was, holding the brassiere that just seconds ago had touched Neve so intimately. Knowing it must smell of her skin, he steadfastly resisted the urge to check. "Thank you," he croaked, suddenly parched.

He examined the garment, finding the weakest spot in the satiny fabric where he could work the wire until it poked through. Neve looked on with fascination as he destroyed her new lingerie. Once both wires were freed, he handed the brassiere back to her. "It's all yours."

Turning away from him yet again, she somehow slipped it back on without flashing more than a bit of skin on her lower back.

All at once, it struck him. Con hated Max. He hated all cult leaders. He hated caves and islands. He hated clothing and the people who made it. He hated all people and things that were standing between him and what he wanted in that moment: Neve beneath him, without a stitch of fabric between them.

He allowed himself to indulge in that delicious image until she turned back around. Squeezing his eyes shut to keep himself from staring indecently, he said, "All right, let's see what we can do."

Neve followed him back down to the padlocked gate, where he bent one wire in half to form a tension wrench. Then, using his teeth, he made several smaller bends in the tip of the second wire, forming a rake pick.

Watching carefully, she asked, "So why *do* you know how to pick locks?"

"Another thing I learned growing up in the countryside," he said, closing his eyes in concentration. "Had to rescue a few dogs from bad situations."

"Wait. You're a doctor *and* you rescue dogs? That's a bit of overkill in the heroic department, don't you think?"

"If you consider that heroic, I'll have to do it more often." *Pop.* Con smiled as he pulled the padlock open and removed it from the gate's metal loops. "There we go." He hung the padlock on one of the crossbars and held out the wires. "Would you like these back?"

"Oh, no." She waved them off. "You keep them. Souvenirs."

He tucked the wires into his pocket for safekeeping. He'd treasure them always.

Neve shone her flashlight into the dark of the cave. "It feels creepy going in here, knowing what happened to Ciara."

"It does." Con placed his hand on her cheek, feeling how cool her skin had become while they were underground. "I can go in alone."

She took a deep breath and released it in a slow, measured exhale. "No. I'm coming. And don't worry, I'm not having an anxiety surge."

He reached down and squeezed her hand. "Let's go, then."

Con pointed his own flashlight into the cave and stepped inside. Once illuminated, he could see that it was, in fact, the cave from the video. That was one piece of information confirmed, at least. The layout and dimensions were the same, with the stone slab there in the middle.

The floor of the cave was dry for the moment, but the tide covered all but the top step leading down to the ocean. They searched the cave section by section, but there was nothing else visible, nothing that would tell them anything new about Max and his activities.

Shining their lights around the roof of the cave, they were able to locate the ledge near the very top.

"There's got to be something up there," Con mused. "Otherwise, why the ladder? I'll go push it off the edge. Stand over there so it doesn't hit you on the way down."

"Okay." Neve stood off to one side.

He climbed the stairs to the crevice. With a bit of maneuvering and a good shove, he was able to push the ladder until it fell over the edge. The ropes and bolts held fast. Carefully, he made his way back down to the cave.

Neve was jumping up, trying to grab the ladder, but it was a few inches out of her reach. Con grabbed it and unfolded it, and they worked together to place it in position. At its full length, the ladder was about fourteen feet, just long enough for its purpose. It was made of aluminum and a bit flimsy, but Con only needed it to hold his weight for one trip up and down.

"Hold it for me?"

"I could go," Neve said, but her voice wavered.

It sounded like she was about as comfortable with heights as she was with swimming. That was a relief, because it meant she wouldn't fight him on this. She was safer on the ground. He also didn't know what Max might have stashed up there, and he didn't want her to be exposed to anything too disturbing. Still, she was brave to offer. Neve was always brave. "No, I'll go. Eric told me what to look for."

He was glad she didn't press for any further explanation, just nodded and grabbed the ladder's legs.

"Thanks. And could you hold your flashlight against the side there, pointing up, so I can see where I'm stepping? Perfect. I'll yell down if I find anything."

"Be careful," she said, and he heard a genuine note of worry in her voice.

"I will." But she still looked concerned, so he leaned down and placed a gentle kiss on the corner of her mouth. "Back shortly."

Con dropped his own flashlight into his jacket pocket and began to climb. It was slow going. His leg brace made it tricky to navigate the ladder, and he swore under his breath each time he pushed off with his left foot. With everything else on his mind, he'd nearly forgotten about his damned leg. It hadn't hurt too badly on the climb up to the church, but now he was feeling it.

Painstakingly, he made it to the top. With a grunt, he made one final push up onto the ledge. "Made it," he shouted down.

"What does it look like?"

Con got out his flashlight and shone the beam around the small cave. It was about ten feet long but high enough near the ledge that he could stand up without hitting his head. On one end, he saw a couple of long containers. "There's something here. I'm going to have a look."

"Okay," Neve shouted. "Let me know if you need any more of my undergarments."

He chuckled. If she only knew the plans he had for her undergarments.

Con had to stoop down a bit as he crossed over to the containers. There were two large, dark green storage trunks stacked one atop the other, made of molded plastic with handles on the sides, and they looked heavy-duty. Next to them sat a smaller red-and-black box with dials and openings for various types of cables and plugs on the front. A quick inspection showed him it was a generator. A tray table with wheels was folded up and leaned against the rock wall.

He was relieved to discover the trunks weren't locked, just latched. Max, or whoever put them there, must have thought the location provided security enough.

"There's a generator and a couple of containers," he called down to Neve, not wanting her to worry in the silence. He lifted the top crate and placed it to one side. Unlatching it, he shone his flashlight in.

So this was where Max kept his filming equipment. There were several LED spotlights, electrical cords, computer cables, a large digital camera and several smaller ones, and a few tripods. That made sense—Max could lower the crates down when he needed them or take what he needed bit by bit. That saved him the trouble of lugging all that equipment back and forth to the island, not to mention up and down the hill and the spiral staircase. Each item was stored in a large plastic zip-closure bag, presumably to keep moisture out.

Con wanted to get as much information as he could while still leaving everything looking as untouched as possible. If Max didn't notice anything was off, it would buy them some time to build a case against him—if in fact there was one to build. The easiest thing, for example, would be to take the camera. But if that went missing, it would alert Max to the fact that someone had found his secret stash. If that happened before they had a chance to move against him, Max could remove or destroy whatever was there, cover his tracks, even leave the country.

But Eric had taught Con that small digital devices like phones and cameras had memory cards or SIM cards, which held a lot of information. That was something he could take without it being immediately obvious that anything was missing. He took the camera out of its plastic bag and popped it open. Sure enough, there was a small blue memory card, just an inch wide. He took two plastic bags with cables in them, combined the contents, and put the memory card into the emptied bag. Then he put everything else back where he found it, closed that crate, and turned to the second one.

This crate held some small cans of fuel for the generator and a box of basic tools. There was also a smaller plastic carrying case. Con's stomach dropped as he read the logo: "SYCK INK WIRELESS TATTOO KIT." Swallowing down bile, he opened it to find a tattoo pen machine, needles, a battery, and a charging cable.

Poor Ciara. That sick bastard *had* tattooed her in the cave. Her recurring nightmares were more memories than dreams after all.

There was a duffel bag in the crate, as well. Con unzipped it to find a woolen blanket, a sweatshirt, candles, a box of matches, a half-empty bottle of bourbon, and…

"Jesus wept," he murmured. It was a bottle of prescription pills. He read the label: flunitrazepam, from a pharmacy in Galway, in Max's name.

So the sedative was legal in Ireland, at least via prescription. There were no refills on the bottle, thank God. If he took them away, Max might notice they were gone, but there was no way in hell Con was going to leave roofies behind for use on the cult's next unsuspecting victim.

To keep the memory card from getting lost, he put it into the bottle with the pills, then placed that bottle in the plastic bag, zipped it closed, and shoved the evidence deep into his pants pocket.

"I'm coming down," he called to Neve, then closed up the crates and put them back in their original positions.

"Con!" Neve screamed. The alarm in her voice turned his blood to ice.

He rushed to the edge and looked down. She had let go of the ladder and was rushing toward the cave's gate.

"Hey!" she shouted.

"What is it?" But given her urgency, he didn't wait for a response. He turned and began climbing down the ladder as quickly as physically possible. Just as he saw Neve turn back toward him, he felt the ladder shift to one side. He gripped it hard and looked up just in time to see the top of the ladder sliding to the left, as though it was being pulled.

He continued his climb down as Neve ran toward him. She grabbed the bottom of the ladder, trying to steady it. But he was still five feet above the ground when a quick, sharp yank from the top of the ladder spun it around. Con lost his footing, then his grip. He fell hard, landing on his left knee and hip, his leg brace crashing against the rock floor. A bolt of blinding pain shot through his body. Con looked up and saw Neve coming toward him, the ladder swinging wildly behind her.

"Get down!" he called out, but not in time. The ladder caught her in the back of the head. She pitched forward on top of him. He caught and held her as someone pulled the ladder up quickly toward the ledge.

Pushing through his pain, Con placed his hands on either side of Neve's head and rolled, easing her onto the floor while keeping her head and neck as steady as possible. She was grimacing, her eyes closed.

"Neve!" he said, stroking her cheek. "Are you with me?"

"A man," she moaned as her hand floated up toward the back of her head. "Max, I think. Ow!"

Gently pushing her hand away, Con cursed as he examined the spot where the ladder had struck her. No bleeding, at least, but that didn't put her in the clear. He pulled his jacket off, folded it, and gently slid it beneath her head as a pillow. "Stay still. Don't move!"

Above him, just a few feet of the ladder now hung over the ledge. If it was Max who had pulled it up, he might try to lock them in to stop them from coming after him. Con had only seconds to beat him to the gate.

With a loud grunt, he pushed himself up into a standing position and lurched toward the entrance of the cave. He grabbed the bars and pushed as hard as he could, but it was too late. He couldn't see the padlock, which was behind a metal plate. But the hard jolt he felt and the loud clinking noise told him it was already locked back in place.

He heard the tap of feet coming down the stone staircase. "Oh no," a man's voice called out, taunting. "Too slow!"

But Con didn't have time to play around with this langer. *Feck, my brace is banjaxed*, he realized as he limped back over to Neve. Pain forced him to suck air in through his teeth as he knelt on his good knee. Searching for a light source, he tried his flashlight, but it had been smashed in the fall. He'd landed on his phone, which was now crushed.

Fortunately, Neve's flashlight was intact on the ground next to her hat. He shone the light into her eyes to check her pupils. Their response was normal.

"I'm okay," she said, and he was relieved to hear her voice, clear and strong. "It just hurts, but I'm all right." She shifted, trying to sit up.

"Stay down," Con said. "We're locked in, and he's coming back down."

"I tried to stop him, but he was already locking the gate."

"It's all right. We'll figure a way out of this. Just stay here, okay? Don't move." He reached into her pocket and pulled out her phone. After turning on the flashlight app, he placed the phone on her belly and moved her hands on top of it. "Here. I'm taking your flashlight."

"Okay," Neve said.

He pushed himself back up and returned to the gate just as Max arrived. Con stood back out of reach and shone Neve's flashlight on him. There he was, the man Con remembered from the Wicked Games website, still wearing the same irritating smirk.

"Dr. Cornelius O'Brien, one of my first two human sacrifices. It's an honor to meet you. I'm Max Hinsen— but you knew that already."

So, Max knew who he was. That meant he most likely had some idea what they were doing there. And referring to them as human sacrifices was a solid indi- cator of ill intent.

Jaysus. This day is getting worse by the minute.

CHAPTER 20
CON

"Look, you fecking eejit," Con said. "That stunt you just pulled gave Neve a head injury. Open the gate!"

"You know what?" Max tapped a finger on his chin. "I don't think I will."

"You don't think…?" Con took a step closer. "Open the goddamn gate!"

Max's teeth were so white they nearly glowed in the dark when he smiled. "Or…?"

That settles it. I'm going to kill the fecker. "She needs medical attention! What is wrong with you?"

"Look, I'm just adapting in the moment here," Max said. "I didn't *ask* you two to come snooping around."

"Right, so. You caught us in your little bat cave." Con gripped the bars on the gate. "Well done. Now unlock this fecking thing!"

"Hang on now," Max said, stepping back. "Aren't you wondering how I found you?"

"I couldn't care less!"

Ignoring his response, Max continued, "I got a call earlier from Emma and Sean. You met them at Wicked Games? They told me two friends of Ciara's were looking for me and were trying to come out to the island. Normally, I would have assumed you were just a couple of my gamer fans. But I'd already heard from Deirdre that Eamonn's doctor-brother and his American girlfriend were coming to Ireland to help Ciara. Imagine my surprise when Sean checked into it and confirmed that was you and Neve!"

That caught Con a bit off guard. "*Deirdre* told you we were coming?"

"Ah, yes. 'Ciara's friend' is just one of the many roles our Deirdre plays—or *played*," he said, the last word spoken in a bitter tone. "After that, I listened to marine VHF radio until I overheard your fisherman announcing he was on his way here with you and asking for information about the cave. My house isn't too far from the island by water, so I got here first and waited for you to arrive. Your fisherman's not coming back for quite some time, by the way." Max shrugged. "He responded to a desperate SOS call a ways off the coast. I set up a bit of a wild-goose chase for him. And now here we all are!" He swept his hands around him in a grand gesture. "Me on this side of the gate and you on that side. What an unexpected opportunity. I would be a fool not to think through my options."

The murderous rage building inside Con threatened to reach a tipping point. "I'll tell you your options!"

"Con?"

He stopped at the sound of Neve's voice. Looking over, he saw the waterline creeping up closer to her.

"Don't move," he ordered Max.

Con hated revealing he was hurt, but there was no hope of hiding his limp as he made his way over to Neve. The pain up and down his leg was fierce, but he couldn't stop to think about it.

Once he reached Neve, he checked her over again. "The water's getting close. Is it all right if I lift you?"

"I can stand up," she said.

"We can try that, but if you feel at all dizzy or see spots, stop and I'll carry you."

Con helped her up. She stood for a moment, then tapped around on her phone's screen, turning off the flashlight, and slid it into her pocket. "I'm fine. No dizziness. Can you take me to the gate? I want to talk to him."

"You're sure?"

"Yes, please."

"All right." He had no idea what she wanted to talk to Max about, but he trusted it was important. Besides, the gate was the highest point in the cave and therefore the safest.

They leaned on each other and walked to the gate, where Max was still waiting. Con eased Neve into a sitting position with her back against the wall.

"And you must be Neve," Max said with calm civility, as though he were meeting her at a dinner party. "I'm Max Hinsen. You're not badly injured, I see."

She straightened up and turned to look at Max. "Can we talk about Ciara?"

After considering for a moment, Max said, "Sure. Let's talk about Ciara. Emma told me she told you that Ciara and I are getting married. That must have come as a surprise."

"A bit, yes."

"Well, it's a fact." Max frowned as he inclined his head toward Con. "His brother has only ever been a stand-in."

"A stand-in for *you*? Bollocks!" Con guffawed, but Neve shot him a look that pleaded for patience. She must have some sort of plan. He forced his mouth shut and gritted his teeth.

"As hard as that must be for your fragile fraternal ego to bear, yes," Max said. "I allowed them to date because I think it's healthy for a young woman to... *experience* more than one person before she settles down for good. That way, she won't spend her life wondering if she missed out on something."

"That's very progressive of you," Neve said, her tone inscrutable.

"Thanks." Max seemed to take her words as praise. "I thought so."

Neve shook her head. "I'm confused, though. That approach seems at odds with the way you handled giving her that tattoo."

Now it was Max's turn to look caught off guard. "What are you talking about?"

"Oh, sorry, I thought you knew. Ciara has started

remembering things—things that happened when you most likely thought she was unconscious. Like when you tattooed her. It seems she was in a locked-in state, unable to move or speak, but she was aware of what was happening."

Con didn't know where she was going with this, but he had to admire Neve's creative ad-libbing.

"Personally," she said, "I would *prefer* to be unconscious if I were getting a tattoo. But it seems Ciara didn't even know it was going to happen, let alone consent. That has more of a branding vibe about it, or ownership—the exact opposite of progressive."

"Ah, well." Max appeared to shake off his surprise. "You don't understand the nature of our relationship."

"I'd like to."

Max tilted his head, considering. "You appear genuinely interested, Neve, unlike your blunt instrument of a boyfriend here. So I'll try to explain, but since we don't have much time," he said, gesturing at the rising water, "I'll give you the short version."

Max's reference to the flooding cave turned up the flame on the rage boiling in Con's veins. He had to keep his head about him and figure out how to get them out, on the off chance that whatever Neve was trying to do didn't work and Max made good on his threat to leave them there. He scanned their surroundings.

The mouth of the cave was now completely underwater. With Neve unable to swim, that avenue of escape was closing. And they couldn't use the ledge for shelter. It was much too high to reach from where they were, even if Neve stood on his raised hands, and it was too far away from the stone slab for that to be of any use to them. There was also no chance of letting the water carry them up. Even at its highest, the tide would never rise to that level.

Think, Con, think.

"Ciara and I are meant to be together," Max proclaimed. "It's fate."

"That's very romantic, but are you sure about that?" Neve asked. "Ciara told me she broke up with you, that you wanted more than she did."

Max came closer to the gate, stopping just out of Con's arm length. Annoyance flashed across his face. "Yes, I'm sure. Ciara is the one I want, and *my* desires flow from the divine. Besides, while it appears she didn't tell you this, Ciara and I are already handfasted."

It was clear from his victorious expression that Max expected that revelation to land like a "checkmate."

Con knew he was supposed to keep quiet, but he couldn't quite believe the supreme arrogance of what he was hearing. "You thick eejit! Cosplay weddings aren't legally binding. And are you really trying to tell us that whatever you want is automatically the will of God just because you want it?"

"It wasn't cosplay!" Max sputtered, then quickly regained his composure. "Who you call God, I call Taranis, the ancient god of thunder. And no, not 'automatically,' as you put it. Long before Christianity contaminated these shores, this cave and this island were imbued with his power. When I meditate here, I know whatever desires arise within me are coming from Taranis. And it was here that I first came to know Ciara would be mine, and it would be our destiny to bring the glory of Taranis worship back to this place."

As Con tried to rub the growing tension from his brow, he heard Neve ask, "Why Taranis? Did you grow up worshipping him?"

Max snorted. "Hah! No. There are different gods in the Pacific Northwest."

"So, you're a polytheist?"

"Most people are. What are you, Catholic?" Max nodded at Con. "Three gods in one. But my mother taught me we should honor and respect the gods of whatever land we're living in. Now I live in Galway, and Taranis is indigenous to this land."

"I was very sorry to hear what happened to your parents," Neve said softly. "Ciara told me everything your father did. I can't imagine—"

"My father made some mistakes." Tension tightened Max's voice. "But ending their lives wasn't one of them. He loved living in nature. He would never have survived prison. And my mother would have been lost without him. They were fated to be together too. A lot of people thought he was a monster, but he did the right thing."

"Janey Mac," Con muttered to himself, "he *is* his father's son." But he didn't interrupt as Neve continued.

"Still, it's understandable that you left the commune then."

Max nodded. "Like all of us, I had to take my own spiritual journey. As I built my life, I kept searching, letting my instincts guide me."

"Built your life?" Neve asked. "You mean working for Wicked Games?"

"Wicked Games is a useful tool," Max said indifferently. "A means to an end. A way to hone my belief system and create a spiritual community. I'd been searching for a decade when the company relocated me to Galway. Ireland is charged with ancient, sacred power. I studied the local deities, and Taranis drew me to him and to this island. I could feel that I had found my place at last. Then Taranis brought Ciara to me. I know what she told you." He waved his hand dismissively. "Breaking up with me, falling for the stand-in. But these are just minor obstacles. When we overcome them, our love will have grown strong enough for the task at hand."

"The task?"

"Like I said, bringing the worship of Taranis back to this land, where it belongs. Filling the spiritual gap left as the corrupt Catholic Church limps away from here, mortally wounded. Meeting the true spiritual needs of the people. And with Ciara, as the heads of this new-old religion, we'll finally realize our full potential."

"Filling the spiritual gap of people *here*? You don't even have any Irish followers that I know of—aside from Sean, who I have no doubt is only in this to get his rocks off," Con scoffed. "You think you know more about Ireland than the Irish? Any genuine Irish pagan who knew what you were up to would eat the face off you!"

"Eat the face…?" Max appeared both surprised and intrigued. "They're cannibals?"

"Of course not! It's just an expression, you sick eejit!" Con blew out a hard breath. "Do you really expect us to believe you're doing all this for altruistic reasons? It sounds to me like you just want what you want, and you're willing to use any means to get it."

Although visibly irritated, Max kept his voice smooth and even. "Taranis doesn't care what country his followers are from, only that we worship him in his own territory. And it's a common misconception that we're here to serve the gods when it's the gods who are here to serve us. They *want* us to fulfill our desires, to take what we want."

Con guffawed. "That's one hell of a convenient belief system, if you're a selfish bastard!"

"Does Ciara share your beliefs?" Neve asked softly. "She never said anything to me about believing in Taranis."

"She's at the beginning of her journey." Max stepped closer, eyes gleaming. "Deirdre told me you came here to help Ciara. Is that true?"

Neve nodded.

"Perfect!" Max threw his hands aloft. "Well, then. It's all coming together."

Almost afraid to hear the answer, Con asked, "What is that supposed to mean?"

"This, *this right here*, is how you can help her." Max

gestured toward the gate, holding up his thumbs and forefingers to form a square, then looking through the frame at Con and Neve. "I can see it now. Your deaths, your sacrifice, this will send her to me. She won't be able to stay away. She'll come running to my arms."

With one eye on the tide rising toward them, Con muttered, "If she does, it'll be with blades drawn."

"You may be right," Max said, laughing lightly. "She's spirited, and she might be angry at first, maybe suspect I had something to do with your deaths. But I'll reassure her that I didn't kill you, which I'll be able to say in all honesty. The sea will take you, guided by Taranis in his sacred cave. Ciara will come to understand that you died because you came here trying to thwart my relationship with her, and our destiny."

"Max," Neve said gently, "please don't take offense, but when you talk like that, it sounds like you need some serious help. If you release us, we can all walk out of here together, and we can get you the help you need."

Still smiling, Max drew his hand across his mouth. "You mean that, don't you? You still don't understand, but I can see you're a kind person. Him, though"—Max pointed at Con—"I can tell he's thick enough that he'll stand by his brother no matter what. At least until Eamonn does something rash and lands himself in jail. I'm confident that won't take long. Deirdre tells me he's a hothead. With the two of you dead and her temporary boyfriend in jail, even a skeptic like Ciara won't be able to deny the signs."

"And when the winds of fate don't blow her back into your arms?" Con asked.

"Unlikely, but possible," Max said with a sigh. "We all have free will. If she continues to be stubborn, rest assured, you two aren't the only people she cares about who are under my control at the moment. I can provide her with more motivation. But if Ciara continues to deny our fate and ultimately proves unworthy, I'll sacrifice her as well. I have no doubt her death would be a sufficient offering to convince Taranis to bring me another, more suitable mate."

"Bollocks!" Con curled his fists around the posts of the gate. "This has nothing to do with gods and fate. If a girl decides she doesn't want your pathetic arse, you want to destroy her, simple as. You're nothing but a pathetic, mealymouthed shitehawk who can't take no for an answer!"

That hit a nerve. Max lunged forward, snarling, "You have no idea what I am, and if you did—"

Con's arm shot out to grab him, but not quickly enough. Max pulled back into the shadows. "Hah! Too slow again."

Con still didn't know if Max was serious about leaving them there or if he was just taking the piss. Holding out hope for the latter, he said, "All right, you've had your fun for the night. The water's already up over the steps and climbing. Unless you want two murder charges on your hands, open the fecking gate. You go to your boat, and we'll wait for ours."

"I will open the gate," Max said, his voice now chilled with composure. "Tomorrow."

"The cave is going to flood," Con said slowly, deliberately, on the off chance Max was thick enough not to understand that. "We'll be dead by tomorrow."

"You will." Max gave a firm nod. "But you can take comfort in knowing your deaths will serve a greater purpose. Like the death of the ram God sent Abraham to sacrifice instead of his son, Isaac."

Good God. Max was not only an arsehole, he was a complete and utter madman. There would be no reasoning with him after all.

Neve had gone quiet. He turned back to look at her. Eyes wide, she opened her hands, palms up, as though to indicate she was out of ideas too. Whatever else, he had to get her out of there.

"You're determined, then?" he asked Max. "In that case, one ram." He held up his index finger. "Abraham made one sacrifice. Leave me here and take Neve. Get her medical help."

"Con, no!" She struggled to get up.

"Stay down," Con told her. Thankfully, she listened. He turned back to Max. "You know she's no threat to you, and she has no loyalty to Eamonn or Ciara. First thing she'll do when she gets out of here is hop a plane home. But you know if you let *me* out, I'll fecking thrash you. Let her go and sacrifice *me* to your imaginary god."

"I'm not leaving you here!" Neve insisted, clutching his leg.

"It's not up to you," Con replied gruffly. He returned his attention to Max.

"Huh." Max examined Con as though he was seeing him for the first time. "I misjudged you, Dr. O'Brien. I thought you were soulless. But look at you, offering to give your life to protect hers—and Neve, refusing to let you." As he looked between them, Max's expression became almost reverent. "Now I see *everything*. There's true love between you two. It shines. Neither of you can hide it. And what more appropriate sacrifice to bring Ciara back to me than the lives of two star-crossed lovers?"

The water had risen to the point where it was lapping up against Con's shoes. "Let her go, goddammit!" A loud clang made Neve and Max jump as Con slammed his hands against the gate. "I'll give you everything I have. Get me a piece of paper and a pen. I'll execute a will right here."

"I'll do the same," Neve said, her voice pleading.

Con laid his hand gently atop her head, stroking her hair, trying to comfort her as Max continued his mad rant.

"The more you say, the more you prove my point. A love you'd give your lives for, and everything you have…." He took a few more steps back. "And I'm sorry, but I can't spare you, Neve. Leaving witnesses is a novice mistake. Besides, practically speaking, if Dr. O'Brien is saddled with an injured party, there's an even *less*-than-zero chance he'll make some sort of miraculous escape. And it would take a miracle, believe me."

"I'll kill you," Con promised through his clenched jaw.

"That would be a neat trick." Max smiled, and Con wanted nothing more than to knock out every last one of his idiotic teeth. "There's no other way out of this cave but the ocean, and the riptides are vicious. Between that and the temperature, you'd either freeze or drown before you had a chance of reaching landfall." He shot Neve an apologetic look. "I do like you, Neve, but fate has spoken. On the bright side, you should both feel incredibly honored. You're going to be the very first human sacrifices to Taranis in the modern era."

Max turned and began to walk up the steps. Con gripped the iron rails and shook the gate. "You fecking gobshite! Get back here!"

"I'll put everything back where it was up on the surface, just in case your fisherman shows up later looking for you. Even if he knows you meant to explore the cave, it's been over fifty years since anyone other than Taranis worshippers came down these stairs. Everyone else who knew the way is long gone. Kudos to you two for figuring it out, by the way—another sign that Taranis chose *you* for this sacrifice." Max flashed a ghoulish grin over his shoulder. "Don't worry, you'll be laid to rest soon enough. I'll come back sometime tomorrow and make the 'shocking discovery' of your bodies."

"Goddammit, Max!" Con thundered.

"Enjoy your remaining time together!" Max disappeared up into the dark.

Con rested his head against the gate and took a deep breath. Defeated by that gormless maggot. He could hardly believe it.

Not that he was accepting defeat, of course—not with Neve in need of saving.

He turned around to find her pulling her knees against her chest, trying to stay clear of the rising sea. It was hard to tell in the dark, but she looked like she was trembling—and no wonder. The temperature in the cave was dropping quickly.

Con again laid his hand atop her head. "All right. We're getting out of here," he announced as he shone her flashlight around, scanning the cave once again.

"Can we get my phone out too?"

He peered down at her. "Your phone?"

She took the phone out of her pocket, tapped the screen, and handed it to him. "I recorded everything from the time I reached the gate. He's toast."

"You genius!" An explosion of love and admiration filled his chest. "I was wondering why you were talking him to death."

They heard a scraping sound on the ledge. Looking up, they realized Max was pulling the ladder back so no part of it hung out over the edge.

"Christ above!" Con yelled, but there was no reply. "I *am* going to kill him, just so you know," he told Neve, and it was a sincere confession. He helped her up into a standing position. "How's your head?"

"Sore," she admitted, "but probably not as bad as your leg."

"My leg is always sore. Nothing new there." He looked down to find them both standing in a shallow puddle. "Any nausea, dizziness?"

"No," she said, but he noticed she didn't shake her head, instead holding it very still. "What are we going to do with my phone? I tried to email myself the audio file, but there's no reception down here. Can you throw it up on the ledge? It should stay dry there, right?"

"Dry, yes, but it might break, or that arsehole would find it. There's no need, though." Con pulled the plastic bag from his pocket. "Some things I retrieved from the ledge."

Her eyes widened. "What did you find?"

He shook the pill bottle gently. "Max has a prescription for flunitrazepam. Rohypnol."

"Oh my God! The 'date rape' drug?"

Con nodded. "And I took the memory card from his digital camera. I didn't have time to look and see what was on there. Give me your wallet?" He dropped Neve's phone into the bag, along with both their wallets.

As he carefully zipped the bag closed, her wide smile lit a fire within him, spreading warmth through his aching limbs. "That's perfect!" she declared.

He handed her the bag. "Slip it down the front of your shirt, maybe? Less likely for it to float away if it's between us."

"Between us?" she asked as she tucked it inside. Then she inhaled sharply, lifting one foot off the ground. "Jeez, the water's cold." Neve closed her eyes.

Con knew she was trying to pull herself together for whatever came next. When she opened her eyes again, her gaze met his, determined and full of fight. "Okay, so what's the plan?"

Whenever she turned to him for help, it made him feel like the luckiest man on the face of God's Earth. To have the trust of a woman like this—nothing else could even come close.

He leaned down and captured her mouth in his. It wasn't a very long kiss, not the kind he wanted to give her. But it was long enough that her hands wandered up to his chest. Passionate enough to inject her with some of the warmth from his body, lending her some of the fire she'd lit inside him. And firm enough to let her know without a shadow of a doubt that whatever else happened, he was going to get her out of there.

CHAPTER 21

NEVE

"You're not going to like it." Con's expression was so grave, I knew that must be an understatement.

I inhaled deeply, trying to steady my breathing. That kiss… it reached inside me, finding all the empty spaces I hadn't known existed and filling them with love, with fire. His lips on mine galvanized me. Whatever came next, I was ready. "Well, I don't even *have* a plan, so I'm just grateful you do. Whether I like it or not, we're going with it."

"All right."

Con pulled me closer to him until we were standing at the very highest spot in the cave, leaning against the locked gate. I willed myself not to tremble, concentrating on the reassuring feel of his body against mine. The water was rising so quickly it was touching my ankles.

"I've been examining the cave, and Max was right

about one thing—one thing only, granted. The only way out is through there." He pointed to the far wall of the cave, where the narrow strip of an opening to the sea used to be. Now it was underwater.

"Oh." I shouldn't have been surprised, but I'd hoped maybe we could make it to the ledge somehow. Without the proper equipment, though, even I could see the walls would be impossible to climb, with the rock smooth and slick in some places and sharply jagged and crumbly in others.

Con followed my gaze. "It's twenty feet high. No way to reach it."

I bit my lip in concentration. "What if you kind of, I don't know, *threw* me up there, and I tried to grab the ledge?"

He slowly rubbed his forehead. "Three problems. One, it's still too high. Two, we'd have exactly one shot at that, and failure would mean we'd likely end up with even worse injuries. Three, not to presume, but when's the last time you did a pull-up? Because that's what you'd need to do if you did manage to catch hold of the edge."

"You mean, like, a chin-up?"

He raised an eyebrow. "Can you do either?"

"Well, not usually, but adrenaline can make people do things they couldn't otherwise."

"Okay. We're not doing it, but for the sake of argument, reach up there." He pointed to the top crossbar of the gate. "Try to do a pull-up. Let's see."

I was starting to see the absurdity of the suggestion,

but I was committed to at least trying now. I reached up and grabbed the bar.

"Good. Now lift yourself up. Pull like your life depends on it."

Hearing the amusement in his voice, I shot Con a dry look. Then I swung back and forth a little, gripping and regripping the bar before throwing all my effort into raising myself up. I managed to pull hard enough that my elbows bent slightly. I lifted myself onto the tips of my toes, but I could only hold the position for a few seconds before I dropped back down with a punctuating splash.

"Good girl yourself." He patted me on the back. "Better than I expected. Nowhere near good enough, though."

"Well, I'm sure *you* can do them. Maybe you could stand on *my*...." But before any more words left my mouth, I swallowed them, knowing there was no way in hell I could hold up Con's bulk.

He smiled, leaned down, and placed a kiss on my cheek, just next to my ear. I shivered for the best possible reasons that time.

"Right, so." He folded his arms and stared at the far wall of the cave like it owed him money. "Like I was saying, the ocean is the only way out. Staying here means staying drier longer, which is good from the perspective of delaying hypothermia as long as possible. However, given that Max is returning everything to the way it was on the surface and the cave's sea entrance is now invisible, I don't rate our chances of getting rescued before the tide rises and we drown. That means the only option is to swim out, and soon. The longer we stay here, the farther underwater that opening gets and the more difficult it'll be to swim through it, especially with you on my back."

"On your back?"

"You can't swim."

I had never regretted that fact so much in my entire life. "Right."

"So, we'll get in over there." He pointed toward the steps that led down to the strip of beach, which were now submerged. "You'll climb on my back, put your legs around my waist"—he illustrated by sliding his hands around his front—"and lock your ankles if you can. Then you'll slide your arms up under mine, holding me here." He showed me the trajectory he had in mind for my arms and grabbed the front of his water-proof jacket. "I'd have you wrap your arms around my neck, but both of us have to stay alive for this to work." He tried to smile.

I was grateful for his attempt at humor. It helped keep my anxiety from spiking. "Then what?"

"Then I start counting, and when I get to three, you take a deep breath and close your eyes. We dive. And when we surface, you open your eyes and start breathing again. Will you need to pinch your nose to go under?"

I shook my head. "That was the one part of swim-ming lessons I was able to master."

"Grand. We'll be fine, then," Con said with what

might pass for actual confidence to someone who didn't know him as well as I did. "Give me your water bottle."

I pulled my empty bottle out of my pocket, and he did the same. He tightened the lids. "I don't think it'll make much of a difference, but let's put these down your back. Extra buoyancy." I turned around, and he slid the bottles down the back of my sweatshirt. "Now zip your mac all the way up."

As I did so, Con pulled up his pant leg and began unfastening his brace. "I looked at Lorcan's map of the island, so I have an idea how to get us to a spot where we can come up on shore. Once we're on land, we'll need to take off our wet clothes and shelter somewhere out of the wind while we wait for help." He peered over at me. "To prevent hypothermia. I'm telling you this now so you don't think I'm trying to start something if I rip your clothes off."

"Well, that's disappointing," I said, but my voice was too shaky to joke around convincingly. "I do know about the wet clothes thing, though. Girl Scout, remember? First aid badge."

"First aid?" He smiled, removing his visibly bent brace and flinging it into the water. "This will be a breeze, then. Once we reach land, we'll call for help. If we can't get a signal for some reason, no worries. Lorcan may be annoying, but he's sound enough. He'll either come back for us or send someone else to find us."

"Naked," I added.

"Alive," he corrected.

But Con wasn't considering the *other* option. Max had been right about something else: I was the weak link in this scenario. Con would have a much better chance if he escaped by himself without me weighing him down.

Staving off despair, I took a deep breath, released it, and shook out my arms. "Okay. But you could also swim out on your own, get help, and come back for me."

So quickly I gasped in surprise, Con grabbed me by the shoulders, his eyes boring into mine. "I know what you're thinking, and no, Neve. We both know I wouldn't get back to you in time."

I reached up and clutched his hands. "But if you die because you're trying to save both of us—"

"You'll be dead, too, so you won't feel guilty." He put his arm around my waist and started walking us both deeper into the water.

"Hang on!" I cried out, my heart nearly bursting with an explosive mixture of love and fear. "When Max was here, you offered to risk your life to save mine. Why can't I do the same?"

The look he gave me then made my mouth go dry. As he tugged me along beside him, he said with a growl in his voice, "I'm not listening to any more of this *raiméis*."

"What?" I stumbled forward. "What's 'raw maysh'?"

"Irish for 'nonsense'!"

"That's not an argument!"

As we reached the edge of the steps, he turned to me. "Neve, do you trust me?"

Hearing him ask that question triggered a flood of memories—all the times over the past two years I'd needed to trust Con, and he'd been there for me. We'd had a few disagreements, even fiery ones at times. But no matter what, he always had my back, from bad days at work and panic attacks to supporting me after I was stabbed and rescuing me from my murderous boss. Con had never once let me down. He'd even gone to Secret Service jail with me, for God's sake. I *did* trust him, fully and completely, body and soul.

"Of course."

"Good. Because I'm telling you we're both going to make it. So don't have a panic attack out there, all right?" He forced a wink. "Ordinarily I wouldn't mind talking you down, but I'll be too busy swimming."

"Noted," I said, grateful for his attempt to lighten the tone in the middle of a life-and-death situation. Con must have been as scared as I was, but he managed to conceal it somehow.

He placed the softest whisper of a kiss on my lips. Before I could respond, he kicked off his shoes and descended two steps.

And just like that, the mood shifted. Suddenly, it was all too real. We were going deeper into freezing-cold waters, about to dive in. When and where we could come up, God only knew.

Con hissed at the cold, then reached back and held out his hands. "All right, climb on."

"But are you sure—"

"Climb on!" he roared.

It was decided, then. Con wouldn't be talked into leaving me behind.

Goddammit, if he dies trying to save me....

Equal parts terrified and grateful, I sucked air in through my teeth, moving farther into the icy blackness. The cold temporarily made my lungs freeze as Con guided my legs around him. Then he reached back and slid my arms beneath his. "Grab here and hold on tight. Whatever you do, don't let go. I've got you."

I knew from experience that when he said, "I've got you," he meant it. Still, something unexpected could always happen. There was a chance we would both die out there.

My response came out as a breathy whisper. "Okay, I'm ready."

CHAPTER 22

NEVE

"Count of three, and then we're going under. It's going to be damn cold. Just prepare yourself, and remember, take a deep breath, close off your nose and mouth, and close your eyes. Keep your head down, and don't breathe again or open your eyes until we surface. Got it?"

I nodded. "Got it."

"All right. Here we go. Remember, hang on, no matter what. One."

I gripped him tighter.

"Two."

As instructed, I closed my eyes and mouth.

"Three!"

I took a deep breath and closed my soft palate, blocking my nasal passage. My stomach quailed like we were dropping from the top of a giant roller coaster as all at once, we rushed down into the icy water. Inside, I screamed silently at the shock of the cold, which almost stole my one precious breath.

Concentrating hard, I felt Con's body beneath me, his muscles and limbs moving rapidly, urgently. I was afraid I might be holding on too tightly, but he'd instructed me to, so I had to trust him—especially because all around us were strong currents, pushing and pulling, trying to tear us apart. *If I let go....* But I couldn't even think about that. I tucked my head against his back, squeezing his waist with my legs and clutching his jacket.

There was a brief moment of feeling stuck, not moving. Then I felt Con wriggle and struggle until we were free. He kept swimming. Holding on to him took all my strength as we plunged through the ever-shifting waters. My hands started to go numb, then my feet. I used every ounce of strength within me to hold them in place, since they were all that was keeping me attached to Con.

It felt like an eternity was passing. My lungs began to burn under the increasing pressure, and it started to feel as though they might burst. *Hang on. Just hang on,* I told myself as Con twisted beneath me, changing direction. Maybe we were nearly there—or maybe we were about to drown.

Then a surge of strength from Con's kick sent us shooting somewhere fast. I didn't know if it was up or down, but it gave me new strength. Suddenly, like a cork bursting from a bottle, we broke through the surface. I coughed out the now-stale air in my lungs and gasped in, then blinked my eyes open only to close them again as salt water burned them.

Con breathed heavily beneath me, still swimming with all his might. "Hang on," he shouted into the dark. I felt him doing the crawl, raising alternating arms over his head as his legs scissor-kicked beneath us. I was stunned by the sheer power of him, carrying me on his back as he sliced through the undulating surf, waves beating against us.

The meaning of time—seconds, minutes—numbed along with my body. How Con kept going, I didn't know. I lost track of how long we'd been in the water, with no idea if we were making progress toward land. In my mind, I kept repeating the silent prayer, *Please let us live. Please let us live.* It felt like I prayed those words hundreds of times, maybe thousands.

After what seemed like forever—certainly an impossible amount of time for anyone to swim in that water—I felt a hard *thud* beneath me. Con's body changed position again, this time moving upright—not swimming but kneeling. He was crawling along something solid and pulling us out of the water bit by bit. I rubbed my eyes against his back and opened them just enough to see the play of shadows. Cliffs still rose above us, but we'd reached a narrow beach.

Not wanting to be a burden on Con a second longer than necessary, I tried to release my hold on him, but my body was frozen in place—by the cold or by terror, I didn't know.

"Help me down," I called out to him. But he kept

going until we were free of the water completely and on dry sand. Then he helped me unlock my ankles and pulled his jacket from my hands, cradling me in his arms as he slid me around to the front of his body. Still not letting me go, he pushed himself into a standing position and staggered forward, carrying me to the cliff face. Finally, he lowered me to the ground, then half sat, half fell onto the ground beside me.

We both took several moments to catch our breath, desperately sucking in air. But the cold…. There was a breeze coming off the water, and it felt like a thousand razors cutting into my skin.

I turned to look at Con. It was difficult to see him in the dark. There was only a sliver of a moon that night, which didn't illuminate much. But I could see the shadows of him, the outlines, as I waited for my eyes to adjust. He looked like Sisyphus just after the boulder had rolled back down the hill—a colossus in defeat, head lolling back against the cliff wall as his chest heaved.

"Clothes," I managed to say, remembering what we'd discussed back in the cave.

He coughed a few times and spit out some water, then turned his head to take in our surroundings. "There," he grunted, pointing over my shoulder.

I turned to look. Part of the beach was protected behind a curve in the rock. It would be a good place to get at least some shelter from the wind. I nodded.

Con tried to pull himself up again but collapsed back onto the ground. As hard as he'd been swimming, in that moment, I knew I was the one who likely had more strength. Stiff with cold, I stood up and reached down to him.

He shook his head, and I knew he was worried about pulling me down. "Go," he said, again pointing to the sheltered part of the beach.

"Come. *On!*" I grabbed him by the front of his jacket and yanked. It was about as effective as yanking on the leash of a thousand-pound dog, but he got the message: I wasn't going anywhere without him.

Despite his exhaustion, Con managed to shoot me a deadly glare as he took my hand. Leaning against the cliff with his other hand, and with me pulling and tugging, he finally got back into a standing position. I could see what it cost him when he put weight on his left leg and it faltered, his face twisting in pain. I positioned myself on his left side and put his arm around me so he could use me as a crutch. Making slow progress, we finally managed to reach the curve in the rock. We lowered ourselves back down to the ground, huddling in the spot most shielded from the wind.

Once again, Con dropped his head back against the rock and closed his eyes. He wasn't making any moves to disrobe.

"Clothes," I repeated, tugging at his soaked jacket.

He grabbed my hand. "In a minute."

Oh hell no. If there was one thing I remembered from my first aid badge, it was that minutes could make all the difference. I felt some of my energy returning. "You'll become hypothermic," I shouted.

"No I won't," he murmured. "I'm a doctor."

I had no idea what kind of argument that was supposed to be. "Congratulations! Now take your clothes off!"

Releasing my hand, he reached up and grabbed the hem of my shirt. "You first."

Good grief! I felt like I was dealing with a cold, wet, recalcitrant bull. "Fine. Okay." *If that's what it takes to motivate him....*

As quickly as I could, I peeled off my jacket and pulled my sweatshirt over my head. "Ah!" I cried out as the night wind hit my bare skin.

My sound of distress jolted him into motion, but his fingers must have been frozen, as he couldn't manage the zipper on his jacket. I knelt to help, and after what seemed like ages, we managed to get his top half uncovered. There was a jagged, dark line across the front of his right shoulder that looked like a cut. I pointed at it, but Con shrugged it off and kept undressing. The pain in his leg made it hard for him to shift enough so I could tug his pants off, but fortunately, his boxers came off with them, so we only had to do that once. I averted my eyes, my curiosity suppressed by intense worry.

Once he was completely disrobed, I stepped away and took off the rest of my own clothes. For the sake of modesty, I debated about the bra and panties, then remembered my Girl Scout training: remove *all* wet clothing as soon as possible. I pulled the plastic bag from where I'd tucked it into my bra and stripped down.

Con's eyes had closed again, which worried me, especially given that I was standing there with no clothes on. The plastic bag's zip closure had remained tightly shut, and my phone and the pill bottle were bone-dry. I was amazed the touchscreen responded to my icy fingers. The phone still had some juice but no cell signal. *Dammit.* I turned on the flashlight app, sealed the phone back in the bag, and propped it up in the sand so the flashlight pointed out to sea, hoping that would help someone find us sooner rather than later.

Then I curled up next to Con, trying to protect him from the wind. Up close, I could see he did have a fresh cut on his shoulder, but it appeared shallow enough and wasn't bleeding badly. I tried to warm him up by making as much skin-to-skin contact as possible, even though at that moment, we both felt more like fish on ice than warm-blooded mammals. Still, my touch must have had a reviving effect on him, because a moment later, he pulled away.

"Lie down," Con said, helping me onto my back.

He was right—we should get horizontal. That was the best way to shelter ourselves from the wind, and it was the safest position to be in from a medical perspective, should we start to become hypothermic.

But as soon as I lay on the sand, he climbed on top of me, stretching out so his body covered mine. He rested on his elbows and forearms to avoid putting his full weight on my chest, then dropped his head next to mine, his forehead pressed against the sand. "Better," he whispered.

"Better?" I asked. "You're getting all the wind now!"

"My point."

"Argh!" I tried to shift out from under him, but between his weight and his arms and head caging me in, I couldn't make him budge. Besides, even though I knew the effort to survive was taking all our strength and concentration at the moment, wriggling around beneath him when we were both stark naked felt somehow... *indecent*.

"Stop," he grunted, then began muttering something repetitive that I couldn't quite make out.

Even as I felt the beginnings of warmth build up between our bodies, an arrow of fear shot through my chest. *Is Con praying?* He'd always been very clear with me that he and God weren't on speaking terms. If he was praying for help now, we must be in truly dire straits.

"What are you saying?" I whispered, half afraid to hear the answer.

"Nothing."

"Are you praying?"

"What? No!"

"Then what are you saying?"

Con lifted his head and moved it just enough so his left eye was staring straight into my right one. "Cork 1991 All-Ireland championship rugby team."

I blinked. I blinked again. "What?"

He dropped his head down again. "Listing the players."

Oh Lord. He'd spent too much time submerged in the water; it was affecting his brain. "Con, listen to me. You're too cold, and you're getting confused. We have to switch places."

"I'm not confused," he grumbled.

And now his mood was tanking. Another warning sign. "Just listen to me—"

"Neve, stop."

He spoke clearly enough, like he was issuing an order, so I decided to hear him out. I stopped moving, speaking—nearly stopped breathing.

"I'm listing the players to distract myself from the fact that you're under me, naked. But if you keep moving around, I'm going to embarrass myself."

"Oh! *Oooh,*" I sighed as his meaning finally dawned on me. I would have thought the sea had sucked all the heat from my body, but apparently there was enough left to make me blush. "Ow!" I exclaimed as the heat hit my cheeks, making my skin feel like it was thawing and burning at the same time.

"You're warming up." Con pressed his cheek against mine, which soothed the pain a bit. Then he shifted to the other cheek. "We should try the phone."

"No signal."

He raised his head and looked at me. "You already tried?"

"You were out of it for a minute."

"Oh. Sorry. I see the flashlight. Good idea."

My eyes had adjusted to the dark, so I could see every twist in his expression, every crease of self-recrimination. Although my arms were still pinned to my sides, I stretched my fingers out until they found whatever part of Con's flesh was closest and gave him a light pinch.

He flinched, and his expression changed to annoyance, which I much preferred. "What was that for?"

"Apologizing for being out of it. You just saved my life!"

"And you saved mine," he countered. "You got me out of the wind, woke me up, ordered me to strip naked —which I hope will be oft-repeated—"

I knew we were still in a life-and-death situation, maybe even leaning more toward death with each passing minute, but I couldn't help it. I started to laugh.

"Stop," Con said through gritted teeth, but he sounded so stern it just made things worse. I started laughing harder, acutely aware of each and every point at which my body shook against his.

"Sorry," I said on an exhale, helpless to stop the waves of amusement rolling over me.

"Shhh." His whole body tensed, and he moved his arm, placing a finger over his lips.

"Can't... stop...."

"No, I mean I hear something." He did a push-up and angled his head toward the sea.

Instantly sober, I held my breath and listened. Somewhere beyond the sounds of the waves, I heard it too. A low hum, soft and distant.

"A motor." Con rolled off me, then sat with his back against my waist. "Curl up around me to hold in the heat," he directed as he reached for the plastic bag. He pulled out my phone and shone the flashlight out across the water in the direction of the sound, moving it back and forth.

I knelt behind him and wrapped my arms around his chest. *Could it be a boat?* Hope fluttered inside me like a trapped moth, helpless but trying nonetheless.

We sat there frozen in time, in silence. Ever so slowly, a horrible thought crept into my mind like an icy tendril. "It wouldn't be Max, would it?"

Con rubbed my arm with his free hand. "Not a chance. He was sure we wouldn't make it out, and he'd want to be well away from here before someone comes looking for us. But if it is him, and he's enough of an eejit to come over here"—he squeezed my wrist—"I'll kill him. Don't worry."

His repeated promise to kill Max was whispered but filled with such vitriol that I had no reason to doubt his conviction on the matter. I swallowed hard, unsure how I felt about the fact that he was ready and willing to murder someone. But if it was as Con predicted, and Max hadn't come back for us, I'd never have to find out. That, I could live with. "Okay."

The humming noise faded at one point, and my stomach dropped. But Con didn't move, so neither did I. Eventually, the sound grew louder again.

"Look!" He pointed as he shouted, voice hoarse from the cold. Now, the sound of the motor was growing louder by the second, and a bright light flashed across the water.

"Dammit!" He turned my phone around, and we saw the flashlight was off. He shook it, tapped the screen a few times, and pushed the buttons on the side, but to no avail. "Battery's dead."

I shot up and helped Con to his feet. He leaned on me as we stumbled toward the water, waving our hands in the air. We synced our voices and yelled as loudly as we could, "Over here! Over here!"

The air seemed to freeze in my lungs as the searchlight hit us, then flashed away.

Did they see us? We'd shouted with all our might, but the light didn't return.

This can't be happening. My shouts turned into screams. Our rescue couldn't be that close only to disappear. I could still hear the motor, though it was hard to tell over the sound of the waves if the boat was getting closer or moving farther away.

After several tense moments, the searchlight hit us again, and this time, it stopped. Con stepped in front of me, shielding me from the beam as it illuminated us like a light from the heavens. We heard a loud crackling noise, followed by an ear-splitting whine. Then a high, jovial voice exclaimed over a megaphone, "Lorcan didn't tell me you lads would be in the nip!"

I collapsed against Con's back, shaking with laughter and relief.

CHAPTER 23

CON

Con was grateful that he was right and Lorcan had turned out to be a basically sound character, however lacking he was in people skills.

The false SOS call Max sent him on had indeed turned out to be a wild-goose chase, and a lengthy one. So Lorcan had convinced a friend of his to come pick them up, even though it was around 10:00 p.m. and high tide by the time the boat found them. If they had stayed in the cave, they would have been dead by then.

Lorcan's friend Fiona took her bowrider on a full journey around the island without spotting them. However, she saw a few flashes of light from Neve's phone coming from the curved inlet where they'd made landfall. Thinking that odd, given what a dark night it was, she decided to investigate—fortunately for them.

Once they were safely on Fiona's boat and wrapped

in foil sheets and fire blankets, Con and Neve warmed up enough that he could assess them both.

Thankfully, neither of them appeared to be in shock. Neve had a small knot forming on the back of her head where the ladder had hit her, but she didn't appear to have any signs of concussion or other bleeding. As for Con, there was some damage to his leg, for certain, but nothing appeared to be broken or properly torn. He'd have to get a replacement brace eventually, and he expected significant pain and bruising, but he'd been through worse. At least he'd be mobile, which was the main priority until Max was either in jail or dead.

The cave's sea opening had been so narrow that they nearly hadn't fit through. Con had swum as close as he could to the bottom so he, and not Neve, would absorb any contact with the rock. His mac had gotten caught on a jagged piece, and in his struggle to free himself, he'd cut his shoulder. But the wound was shallow enough, easily dressed using Fiona's onboard first aid kit.

While the water had felt freezing, the temperature was high enough—and the swim short enough—that both he and Neve had avoided any serious symptoms of hypothermia. Their hands and feet hurt like hell as heat packs warmed them up, and she experienced a bout of shivering, but as they flew through the water at top speed, Fiona assured them it would be no time at all before they reached the harbor at Rosaveel, where her trawler was docked.

Fiona began to radio Lorcan that she'd found them

safe and sound, but Con stopped her. Bearing in mind what Max had said about tuning in to marine radio, he asked her to contact Lorcan on her mobile instead and to keep their rescue a secret, just between the four of them for the time being. Fiona gave him a strange look but agreed to his request without asking any questions.

Once they reached Rosaveel, Fiona raided her larger boat for clothes. Soon, Con and Neve were kitted out in waders, boots, knit pullovers, hi-vis jackets, and wool beanies. They were warm, dry, and, most importantly, alive.

Fiona bundled them into her truck and stopped off at a petrol station for hot cups of tea. By the time she dropped them at the nearest garda station at Inveran, they were feeling almost back to normal. Unfortunately, that also meant the pain was starting to set in, but it was after eleven o'clock at night now, so there was nowhere to purchase painkillers. They would have to tough it out.

The garda station was a block-shaped, two-story gray building. Fiona came in with them and gave the young guard at the front desk a brief explanation of her involvement, starting with Lorcan's call. Once they had taken down all her information, she left for home.

Con and Neve were ushered into a room in the back of the station with a small table and some chairs. The young guard took the plastic bag with the phone, pill bottle, and HD card from Max's camera, as well as their IDs. Fresh cups of tea were provided. Con asked to place a call to Eamonn but was told he needed to wait until a more senior guard arrived to talk to them. That seemed arbitrary, but he didn't want to alienate the people he was about to ask for help, so he kept his thoughts to himself.

Con and Neve talked over the situation while they waited. As far as they knew, Max thought they were dead. Between Fiona maintaining radio silence about their rescue and the fact that they'd taken every item from the beach away with them, there was no way he would know yet that they made it out alive. However, he would find out if he went back the next day to look for their bodies.

"Once he knows we got away, I'm worried he'll go after someone else next," Neve said, echoing Con's own concerns. "Didn't he say something about someone else Ciara cared about being in his orbit, or something like that?"

"Under his control," Con corrected. He remembered that sinister statement vividly. "Well, it won't be Eamonn. He can't be controlled, believe me. And he and Max have never even met."

"And Max has never met the rest of your family?"

Con shook his head. "They wouldn't know him from Adam. Eamonn told me Max never met Ciara's family either. Deirdre, on the other hand…."

Neve frowned. "Yeah, Deirdre. Those two people at Wicked Games said she was on vacation, but there was something…." She tapped her finger on the table.

"There was. In the cave. He said something about her."

"Right, that she was just 'playing a role' as Ciara's friend. But then he put it in the past tense—'played.'"

"And he seemed angry about it." Con rubbed his chin. "Max and Deirdre might have had a falling-out—which is a good sign of her, if you ask me."

"God, I wish my phone hadn't died," Neve moaned. "I could have checked to see if she emailed or messaged me back yet. When I talked to Ciara, she didn't say anything about Deirdre going on vacation. Is that strange?"

"Not necessarily. Ciara's stuck in hospital. Deirdre might not have told her, not wanting to rub a nice holiday in her face at a difficult time."

"That's true." Neve's hand drifted up to the back of her head. She touched the growing knot there and winced.

"I'm sorry, love." Con reached out and squeezed her other hand where it lay on the table. "I'll ask the guard if they have anything you can take, or some ice, at least."

"Not ice, please! Nothing cold. I'll go."

Although her smile was quick and easy, the concern in her eyes raked his heart. Since his fall in the cave, he'd caught her casting worried glances in his direction every time he limped or grimaced from the fresh pain in his leg. "You have a head injury. I just have a limp."

"A limp and no leg brace!"

"The brace is for backup, extra stability. It's not a necessity." He held her hand against the table, preventing her from getting up. "I'll go."

Bemused, she tilted her head and looked at his hand atop hers. "Seriously?"

"Doctor's orders," he quipped, forcing himself to smile through the pain as he pushed himself out of the chair. She didn't argue for once, and he was relieved. It might not be logical, but Con felt that when it came to his leg and the accident, they'd robbed him of enough already. Whatever physical functioning remained, he was determined to use it whenever needed.

He returned to the front of the station. The young guard was showing the contents of a folder to an older uniformed man who was gray-haired and solidly built. The young guard startled when he saw Con. The older man looked him up and down, then stuck out his hand. "Sergeant O'Leary. You're Dr. O'Brien?"

"Nice to meet you, Sergeant." Con shook his hand, then spoke to both men. "I came out to ask if you have any paracetamol or ice. Neve got a knock on the head. Nothing serious—I checked her out on the way here—but she's feeling it now."

"Will you see to it, Garda Foley?" Sergeant O'Leary had a no-nonsense air about him that Con appreciated.

"Yes, sir." Garda Foley closed the folder and handed it to the sergeant, then turned in the other direction.

"Will you come with me, Dr. O'Brien?" Sergeant O'Leary gestured down another hallway. "We can talk while Garda Foley looks after Miss Keane."

Con hesitated, not wanting to leave Neve alone. "I'd like to keep an eye on her."

"Don't worry, she's in good hands."

"Of course." He realized he was still tense from the evening's events, but he should try to relax a bit now. After all, they were in the garda station and had handed over all the evidence against Max. "Certainly, let's talk."

"This way."

Con followed the sergeant to a smaller office with a desk and a chair on either side. As he took a seat, Sergeant O'Leary closed the door behind them, then settled in behind the desk. He opened the folder Garda Foley had given him and slowly scanned the first page. Then he flipped it over and began to scan the second page.

It seemed to Con that it was taking quite a long time for the talking part of their meeting to commence. He decided to jump-start it. "Sergeant O'Leary, apologies for the interruption, but someone tried to kill us tonight, and they very nearly succeeded. A man named Max Hinsen. He's still out there, and he's very dangerous."

Sergeant O'Leary looked up, eyebrow raised. "Max Hinsen, you said?"

"Yes. You know him?"

The sergeant scowled as he flipped through a few more pages, then held one up, examining it. "I don't, but coincidentally, we have a complaint here filed just this afternoon by a Max Hinsen."

Con shoved his hand through his hair, his patience fraying. "What does it say?"

"It's a complaint of harassment," the sergeant said

as he leaned back in his chair, "against you, Dr. O'Brien."

He wasn't sure if it was due to fatigue or adrenaline overload, but Con couldn't process that piece of information at all. "Come again?"

"The complaint claims you have been harassing Mr. Hinsen, visiting his home and place of business and issuing threats. There are two witnesses."

Con closed his eyes and pinched the bridge of his nose. This Max was a clever fecker. He must have called in the complaint after he got the call from Emma and Sean at Wicked Games. Somehow he'd found out they'd gone to his house, as well. Then he'd laid the groundwork early so that whatever happened, Con would look like the bad guy and Max the victim. "With respect, Sergeant, that is a false complaint."

"Hmm." He pulled out a notebook and pen and began jotting things down. "So you and Miss Keane didn't visit his home and his place of business yesterday?"

Con's outrage spiked. "He made a complaint against Neve too?"

"No. The complaint mentions she was with you but does not implicate her."

That was a relief—and it made sense. It would be hard for Max to invent a realistic motive explaining why an American social worker he'd never met who was visiting Ireland for the first time would harass him. Besides, anyone who met Neve could tell she was an angel who would never harm anyone, or even threaten to. Con, on the other hand….

The sergeant tapped his pen on the desk. "I'll ask again. Did you go to Mr. Hinsen's home and office?"

"Why do I get the feeling you already know the answer to that question?"

"Because I do. We have security camera footage from both places and two witnesses from your workplace visit."

Con reminded himself to keep a lid on his anger at Max so it wouldn't be misinterpreted as irritation with the sergeant. As calmly as possible, he replied, "I was trying to find him so we could ask for his help with my brother's fiancée."

"Your brother…." After more rustling through the folder, the sergeant pulled another paper out. "Eamonn?"

Con nodded slowly.

"I see. We have another harassment complaint against your brother here from Mr. Hinsen, submitted a couple of months ago. It seems no one saw a reason to follow it up—before now, that is."

"Max was harassing Eamonn's fiancée. My brother spoke to the guards—"

But Sergeant O'Leary raised his voice a bit, talking over him. "We also called over to the district headquarters in North Cork and asked them if they were familiar with you. That's right," he said as Con rubbed his forehead. "It seems that as a young man, you made quite a reputation for yourself." The sergeant consulted another sheet of paper. "A fighter, were you?"

There was no use denying it, especially if that sheet of paper was a record of his criminal offense. "That was years ago, Sergeant, when, as you pointed out, I was a much younger man." He leaned forward, resting his hands on the edge of the desk and looking straight into Sergeant O'Leary's skeptical eyes. "We should be discussing the fact that Max Hinsen tried to kill Neve and me tonight. He trapped us in a sea cave on Saint Cillian's Island and left us for dead. He's planning to go back there tomorrow to pretend shock when he finds our bodies. But when he discovers we escaped, he may well try to harm us again, or someone else. He confesses to all of this in a sound recording Neve made on her phone. And there's something more on the HD card I gave you, but I'm not sure what it is. I took it from a video camera he had hidden in the cave. *That's* the matter of urgent concern here, not the sins of my youth!"

The sergeant gave Con's now-white knuckles a pointed look. Once Con let go of the desk and leaned back in his chair, the sergeant began twirling his pen between his fingers. "Dr. O'Brien, *with respect*, it's my job to decide what are the matters of urgent concern."

Christ Almighty. Con had to rein in his emotions and keep this man onside. "Of course."

"For example, Miss Keane has a head injury."

"Yes. Max hit her with a ladder."

"A ladder? In a cave? On Saint Cillian's Island."

It was all Con could do not to reach over, grab the man by the jacket, and shake him hard. "That's correct."

"And where were you when that happened?"

"I was *on* the ladder," Con said, wondering where this line of questioning was headed. "Max yanked it up from above, I fell to the ground, and the ladder swung over and hit Neve."

"You fell." The sergeant nodded at his leg. "Is that why you're limping?"

"I have an old injury, so I always have a bit of a limp, but the fall made it worse."

"Do you require medical attention?"

Con shook his head. "However, I would like to keep an eye on Miss Keane's injury and make sure no problems are developing there."

"We'll keep an eye on her. You allege Max Hinsen tried to kill you. Why would he do that?"

All right, now they were getting to motive. That was a fair question, and an important one. "It's a long story, but the short version is he's a delusional cult leader who thought killing Neve and me would convince my brother's fiancée to come back to him."

"Come back to him? So he was in a relationship with your brother's fiancée?"

"A few years ago, yes. She broke things off, and he didn't take it well, to say the least."

"A domestic dispute," the sergeant murmured, glancing back down at the folder. "For the record, you're saying you did not cause Miss Keane's head injury?"

Once again, Con got the feeling he was missing something important, something just outside his awareness. "What?"

"You did not strike her?"

Fecking hell. What kind of question was that? Con nearly roared, "Of course I didn't!"

"All right, calm down," the sergeant said as though he hadn't just spent the past several minutes trying to draw a reaction out of him. "Just dotting our i's and crossing our t's."

Con didn't know what the sergeant was thinking, but precious time was being wasted. "I would die before I would harm Miss Keane. If you'll just listen to the recording—"

"You may be aware, Dr. O'Brien, that her phone is dead." The sergeant slowly rose to his feet. "We don't have a suitable charger, and it's the middle of the night. We'll contact the Cyber Crime Bureau first thing tomorrow for assistance. At the moment, we don't have any proof of imminent threats. In the meantime, we have our own investigation to complete—in aid of which, I'll need you to come with me while I talk to Miss Keane." He slammed the folder shut.

The sergeant was not going to be rushed, that much was clear. To make the investigation go as quickly as possible, Con decided compliance was the best strategy —for the moment, at least. "I'll be happy to. However, I'm concerned about the safety of my family. Would it be possible for me to place a phone call?"

"After I talk to Miss Keane, yes, I can arrange that,"

Sergeant O'Leary replied as Con got to his feet. "You understand, we're a bit short-staffed at this hour."

"Of course."

Con forced himself to remain calm as he followed the sergeant down the hallway and through a series of turns. Garda Foley fell in behind him at some point, following them both. Con didn't think anything of it until Sergeant O'Leary led them through a set of double doors Con knew they hadn't encountered on the way to his office. They came to a stop in front of a counter, which Garda Foley slipped behind, looking as nervous as a kitten.

Wait a minute… this feels familiar. All at once, Con's stomach dropped to his shoes, and the heat of anger rushed up his spine to the back of his neck. He felt his face reddening as he turned back to face the sergeant. "What's this, then?"

"Dr. O'Brien, you are under arrest for harassment under Section 10 of the Non-Fatal Offenses Against the Person Act. The Criminal Justice Act, 1984, allows for your detention in a garda station for an initial period of six hours to assist with our investigation." Tilting his head to one side, the sergeant asked, "Are you going to take a swing at *me* now?"

Con's impulse in the moment was exactly that. Sergeant O'Leary was a good judge of character, at least.

"Do we need these?" The sergeant held up a pair of handcuffs.

Biting back a reply, Con shook his head.

"Right, so." With a nod to Garda Foley, he began, "You have a right to a solicitor…"

Pushing hard against every instinct to the contrary, Con didn't resist as the sergeant explained his rights. He tried not to seethe openly as Garda Foley photographed and fingerprinted him, then asked him a number of medical and risk assessment questions.

Once he'd been processed, Con was taken down another corridor to a holding cell whose door hung open, its thick steel profile and substantial locking mechanism assuring him there was no chance of escape. Once he stepped inside, Garda Foley had the door shut and locked behind him before Con could even turn around. Then both of the guards turned and began to walk away.

"Look after Neve!" Con called after them with what he hoped was a sufficient amount of threat in his tone.

Point to Max.

But now, Con was more determined than ever to deliver Max a shattering defeat.

CHAPTER 24

NEVE

God, my head is throbbing. And why has Con been gone so long?

It had already been a hellish day, but between the waiting and the pain, it was going even further downhill. I soothed myself by twisting my claddagh ring around my finger.

Finally, Garda Foley returned, this time with a female guard standing behind him. "I have your ice and paracetamol."

"Oh, thank you." I immediately downed two pills, then hissed as I pressed the plastic bag filled with ice against the tender spot on the back of my head. "I'm okay," I reassured him. "It'll feel better in a minute."

"I hope so. This is Garda Jensen. She's going to wait with you."

"Hi, Miss Keane," she said, sitting at the table next to me as Garda Foley left, shutting the door behind him.

"Hi, Garda Jensen. It's just Neve." I shook her

extended hand. She had a pleasant, kind face and wore her blonde hair in a bun at the nape of her neck. "Do you know where Con is?"

"He's talking to Sergeant O'Leary. The sergeant will come back to talk to you, too, when they're done."

It seemed to me like a waste of time not to speak to us together, but I guessed that must be their procedure. I could be patient if it meant Max was brought to justice.

"There's a recording on my phone," I volunteered. "Have you been able to charge it?"

Garda Jensen shook her head. "We don't have a charger that fits."

"I can go back to Galway and get mine," I offered. "I'll just need a taxi or something."

"You're staying in Galway?"

"We have an Airbnb. We're going home tomorrow."

"Well, we'll need to use our own charger, for security purposes. As for returning to Galway, taxis won't be operating at this hour. I can take you home when you're done here."

More delays. I forced a smile. "Okay, thanks. That's very kind of you."

"How's your head feeling?"

I paused and took stock. With relief, I reported, "It's much better. Thank you."

"That's good." She pulled out a notebook and pen. "Do you mind if I ask you a few questions?"

If it'll speed things along.... "Sure, go ahead."

She gave me an odd look—sympathetic but tense.

"Neve, have you ever been a victim of domestic violence?"

That seemed like an odd question. Maybe it was a routine screening. I opened my mouth to say no, then hesitated. *Damn my ex, Stephan.* Before him, I could have answered no without even thinking. But a few months ago, in mere seconds, he'd moved me into the yes column, where I would remain for the rest of my life.

Garda Jensen observed my hesitation, then placed her hand on mine. "It's okay, Neve. You can tell me. Your privacy will be fully protected in this matter."

Now I was wary. "I don't understand. Why are you asking me this?"

"You came in with your partner, and you have an injury," she explained. "Also, we have a report here stating that you were found trapped in the boot of Dr. O'Brien's vehicle the day before yesterday."

"Oh no." I covered my face with my hands. For anyone to think, even for a moment, that Con could hurt me shook me so badly that tears burned in my eyes. But if I let them fall, it could cast doubt on what I said next. "No, no. That wasn't what you think."

"What was it, then?" Her world-weary tone told me she was bracing herself to hear excuses.

I struggled to steady my breathing as a sudden flush of heat rose in my cheeks. "That whole incident resulted from a bad idea—*my* bad idea," I began, searching for a plausible lie. If I told her I stowed away because I was afraid that without me present, Con might hurt Max, that would only fuel her "Con is violent" narrative. "It was supposed to be a surprise. Con was going on a trip, and I got in the back without him knowing about it. I had no idea it would take him so long to stop for gas. Petrol." I smiled and shrugged, hoping I sounded light-hearted enough. "When he finally did stop, he went immediately into the shop at the petrol station, so some kind bystanders helped me out of the car. I know I must have looked a mess, but it was just a stupid stunt. Impulsive," I concluded, using Con's word. "It was fine, though. Everything worked out fine. Speaking of Con, do you know how much longer he'll be?"

"How much longer he'll be what?"

Now it was my turn to blink a few times. "How much longer it'll be before he comes back."

"Several hours, at least, I'm afraid."

"Hours? What… why?"

"Dr. O'Brien has been arrested and detained."

I flew to my feet. The plastic ice bag crashed to the floor. "What did you say?"

Garda Jensen rose and took a step back. "Please calm down."

Don't make things worse, I told myself as I sat back down, very slowly. "What do you mean, he's been arrested? On what charges?"

"Based on a harassment complaint, he's being detained here in the station."

"A *harassment* complaint? By whom—oh my God." I slapped my hand on the table, but too hard. Shaking the pain from my fingers, I glared at Garda Jensen. "Don't tell me. Max Hinsen." *Who else could it be?*

"I'm not at liberty to disclose the name of the complainant," she said. But the way she'd cut her eyes to the side at the sound of his name confirmed it.

"Okay, but on the off chance I'm right, let me tell you about Mr. Hinsen and harassment." I pulled on every bit of self-control I still had to keep calm. "I work in mental health, and while I have never assessed Mr. Hinsen, unofficially, my best guess is he suffers from a very serious case of antisocial personality disorder. Whatever complaint he made against Con, he would have done it to manipulate law enforcement and to deflect responsibility from his own attempts to harass, control, and intimidate Con's brother's fiancée, Ciara. At this moment, she's receiving medical treatment for an illness triggered by the harm Mr. Hinsen has caused her. He has expressed no empathy and no sense of guilt over the trauma he's caused. Not to mention, a few hours ago, he tried to kill Con and me, and I have every reason to believe he'll harm others in the future."

Garda Jensen blinked rapidly. "As I said, I can't disclose the name of the complainant. But even if all that is true—"

"It *is* true."

She nodded. "Even so, we'll have to confirm and verify that information."

I was starting to feel like I was trapped in a police procedural TV show. "It's all on the recording, but we can call Con's brother, Eamonn, *right now*, and he can tell you all about it. Con knows his number."

"Dr. O'Brien has already asked to call his brother. If

you'd like to be present when that call is made, we can arrange that."

"Yes, I would like that, thank you. But may I please talk to the sergeant? Con and I have to get out of here so we can—"

I stopped when I saw the suspicious look on Garda Jensen's face. "So you can what?"

Struggling to find a response that wouldn't add weight to the harassment charges, I settled on "Return to Kilshannig and warn Ciara. Max said he's going back to the cave tomorrow to 'find' our bodies. I'm worried that when he realizes we escaped, he'll try to go after her somehow." I breathed through the panic that was trying to push its way to the surface. "I swear, we'll leave Galway. Just let me talk to Con, please!"

"I'll check and see if that's possible." Garda Jensen got up and stepped toward the door but held up a hand when I moved to follow her. "Wait here, please."

Not what I wanted to hear, and definitely not what my anxiety disorder wanted to hear. I took a long, deep breath in and let it out slowly while the guard's eyes widened with concern.

Normally, a crisis on this level combined with the threat of a panic attack would paralyze my brain. But this time, possibly due to a healthy injection of rage, my creativity was sparked instead. I began to form an idea that might get us out of this mess. "In the meantime, may I make a phone call, at least?"

She paused at the door. "Yes, of course."

"It'll be an international call. Is that okay? And I'll need my wallet back."

"That shouldn't be a problem under the circumstances."

The circumstances being they suspected Con was harassing Max and abusing me. But I was getting my phone call, so I just said, "Thanks very much."

"I'll bring the phone to you." Then she left me alone in the room again, closing the door behind her.

"Oh, Con," I moaned as I pictured him sitting in a cramped cell, his leg most likely in terrible pain.

Does he *have paracetamol and ice? He must be so angry, worried, and God knows what else. Is he holding it together?*

"He's probably fine," I told myself. I was the one who usually had trouble holding it together, not him.

Please, please make sure he's okay, I begged, hoping someone, somewhere heard me, and that whoever it was had the power to answer my prayer.

CHAPTER 25
CON

He'd been here before.

Not here in the cell at Inveran station. But it wasn't the first time he'd been arrested by the gardaí.

Most of the fights he'd gotten into in the past were situations where Eamonn had instigated an argument with someone—or a group of someones—and Con had backed him up. But those incidents were generally written off by teachers, parents, and even the guards as "a few young fellas acting the maggot." There were no consequences, other than the warring parties being ordered to stay away from each other.

However, there was one exception—the one that led to a conviction for assault—and it had followed him around, causing all kinds of trouble. Any time he applied for something—a degree program, a job, his US visa—he had to disclose his criminal conviction, explain the circumstances, obtain character references, and generally jump through several hoops. Fortunately, his record hadn't yet created any obstacles he couldn't overcome. And the truth was, in spite of the trouble it caused him, Con had no regrets. If he were sent back in time, knowing how much grief that one fight would cause him later, he would still make the same exact choices.

With this new arrest, though, he feared his life was about to get much more complicated. Max was quite thorough, it seemed. Getting Emma and Sean to say Con went over to Wicked Games issuing threats put a cat among the pigeons. It would be his word and Neve's against theirs, and that could take a while to get sorted out.

Neve. His heart caught at the thought of her, alone in that dreary room, wondering what was happening. He hoped to God they were keeping a proper eye on her injury. If not, heads would roll—and he would be the one to roll them.

Con shifted again, trying in vain to get comfortable. At least the mattress was long enough that he was able to stretch out. Covered in a blue waterproof fabric with a pillow-shaped swell at one end, the mattress lay along a wide ledge at the back of the cell. It was an adequate place to rest, but his injured leg gave him no peace. Along with a sandwich and a packet of crisps, they had provided him with ice and paracetamol. It helped somewhat but didn't really touch the deep ache. It would take months in physical therapy to get back to where he was before Max tossed him off that damn ladder.

At the sound of footsteps in the corridor, he pulled himself up, slowly swinging his feet over the ledge. The cover over the rectangular opening in the door slid down. At first, he saw Sergeant O'Leary. But his heart jolted when he spotted Neve there, too, still in her fishing gear, her face lit with a victorious smile.

The sergeant stepped back, and Neve's face filled the opening. Con stood and did his best not to show how much discomfort he was in as he approached the cell door. To reassure himself she was really there, he reached out and touched her cheek. "How are you feeling?"

"Okay. I'm fine." The corners of her mouth dropped as she grasped his hand. He felt her press something against his palm—a piece of paper? "What about you?" she asked.

"I'm all right." Whatever she'd slipped him, it must be a secret, so he pulled his hand back quickly, taking the piece of paper and closing it into his fist. With narrowed eyes, he asked, "And what has you grinning like the Cheshire cat?"

To his relief, that brought the smile back to her face. "Sergeant O'Leary has some good news for you." Neve wasn't the preening type, but she nearly did so as she stepped aside.

With his eyebrows raised to points, the sergeant gestured sharply for Con to back away from the door. "Come on, let's go."

Con took a step back. "Go where?"

"You know, as a courtesy, either one of you could have mentioned why you're here. Would have saved us all a lot of time and trouble," Sergeant O'Leary huffed as he unlocked the door and swung it open. "But don't go thinking you're off the hook, Dr. O'Brien. Neve here has diplomatic immunity, but you're one of ours. The superintendent has agreed to release you as a favor and in the spirit of international cooperation," the sergeant said dryly. "But your boss has assured us he'll bring you back here himself to face charges if we decide to pursue them."

Con's head was spinning with questions as he left the cell. *What the hell is he going on about? Diplomatic immunity?*

When the sergeant turned to close the door behind him, Con glanced down, unfolding the paper in his hand. It had one word: **BANAI**.

Well done, Neve! She must have called Agent Banai, their contact in the Secret Service. But they were only supposed to call him if they thought the thugs at Brickhaven were coming after them, not if they got caught up in something unrelated, like a family drama—and overseas, no less. Not that Con was complaining. He just wondered what on earth Neve had said to the stern agent that convinced him to tell the guards what he could only guess was a flat-out lie about the two of them working for the US government.

Con moved quickly to Neve's side, wrapping his arm around her shoulders. She appeared to be sucking on an imaginary lemon to stop herself from smiling so she'd look more somber. He certainly didn't want to ask any questions that might change the sergeant's mind. "Understood."

"The superintendent also agreed to your boss's request that we keep your visit here confidential, but the items you brought in to aid our investigation are staying here. We'll be sharing any evidence against you with your boss, and he doesn't seem like the soft type. So while I understand you have work to do, while you're about it, I'd strongly advise you to keep your heads down and stay out of trouble for the remainder of your stay," the sergeant added. "Got it?"

"You have my word," Con said. "You won't see us again."

That appeared to placate Sergeant O'Leary, who walked ahead of them down the hallway. "I'll get you your things, and Garda Jensen will drive you back to Galway."

Con stole a glance at Neve, who he'd never seen looking more pleased with herself. Still, he was certain he was even prouder of her than she was. "You're some operator," he murmured with frank admiration.

"I have my moments," she whispered.

Minutes later, they were in the back of Garda Jensen's car on the way to Galway. The guard kept cutting them dark looks in the rearview mirror. He understood why she and the other guards would be irritated, of course. In their eyes, two people with diplomatic immunity showed up in the dead of night making wild accusations, not bothering to mention their status when one of them got arrested. Once they heard the evidence, though, Con was confident the guards would realize the threat from Max was real and they were all on the same side.

Back at the Airbnb, Con and Neve kicked off their boots and, still in their fishing garb, collapsed on the couch—Con after assessing her head injury once again and Neve after bringing him some ice, pain meds, and a glass of water.

Both of them had an acute longing for sleep, but it would be just a few short hours before Max would return to the island looking for their bodies, only to be sorely disappointed.

"Right, so," Con said. "Before anything else happens, I have to know. What did you promise Banai to get him to pull those strings?" He couldn't imagine the Secret Service doing them such an enormous favor without expecting some quid pro quo.

Neve reached back and lifted her long brown waves of hair, laying them across the back of the couch. "He was really nice about it. He didn't ask for anything."

Something about that response plucked at his worry strings. "What did you say to him, then?"

Frowning, she said, "Well, you're welcome, first of all."

Con rubbed a hand across his eyes. "Sorry." He reached over, took her hand, and placed a soft kiss on her palm, not removing his lips until he spotted one of her tells: toes curling in pleasure. Then he held her hand and squeezed it lightly. "Thank you for the jailbreak."

After their night freezing on the island, he'd never been so relieved to see her cheeks pinken as she blushed. "Anytime. You did break me out of the hospital once, not to mention swim me out of a flooding cave, so I kind of owed you."

Even if there weren't a mischievous slant to her smile, Con would have known she'd acted out of love, not a calculating sense of transactional justice. Neve was a deeply emotional person, much more so than even she realized. He'd watched her over the years, and when her mind and heart battled each other, her heart always won. She used her intellect and professional skills in the service of her emotions, never the other way around.

That worked perfectly in her case, because no matter what the circumstance, Neve's heart was always in the right place. It was one of the many things he admired about her, and one of the things that proved she was a better person than he was. Her generosity, compassion, and kindness were oceanic; she would embrace the whole world if she could. His care, on the other hand, was reserved for a few chosen individuals: his patients, family, close friends, and Neve. Not that he was cold or untouched by stories of human suffering outside of those few people, but where Neve's empathy seemed limitless, his was definitely finite. He couldn't imagine shedding a tear for anyone outside his own small circle.

For example, he was confident he could end Max and feel nothing.

"Like I told you before," he replied, "I will always save you. In truth, I never expected to find myself in a position where you'd have to save me, but I'm very grateful you did."

"My pleasure." As the blush in her cheeks deepened, she looked away and cleared her throat. "As for Agent Banai, I just explained to him that while we were over here on vacation, you'd been falsely accused of harassment by someone who tried to kill us and would surely try again." Shrugging, she added, "What can I say? He agreed the situation was, as he put it, 'concerning.'"

Concerning, indeed. "So what did he do?"

"He said he would tell the guards we were in Ireland doing some covert intelligence gathering for the US government, and to do whatever the guards said after that. Then he told me to hand the phone over to the person in charge. Sergeant O'Leary took the phone back to his office, so I didn't hear what was said after that, but it was a long conversation. Then he came out and told me once he received official documents verifying who we were and got approval from his superintendent, he would release you. Lord knows how Agent Banai put that paperwork together so quickly, but apparently everything checked out. You know the rest. Oh, and Agent Banai told me to ask you to call him sometime in the next couple of days."

That's the sound of the other shoe dropping. "Did he say why?"

"No. He probably just wants to check in."

Agent Banai had bigger and better things to do than "check in" on Con. No doubt he had some way in mind for Con to pay back the US government for their assistance, though he couldn't imagine what that might be. But since Banai spoke for White House Chief of Staff Liu, he knew whatever it was, it would be a request he couldn't ignore.

Still, he couldn't help smiling back at Neve. She'd done it again: achieved something he thought was impossible, proving once again that anyone who failed to bet on her was bound to lose. "It never would have occurred to me to ask Agent Banai for help. You, on the other hand, didn't hesitate to call in the big guns."

"It took me a while to think of it, but once I did, of course I didn't hesitate." She leaned down and brushed a kiss across the back of his hand. "It was for *you*."

With that, she banished all the pain from his body just long enough for him to reach over, slide his arms under her, and pull her onto his lap where he could ravage her mouth with a proper kiss. He swallowed her delighted exclamation of surprise, determined to push the last several hours from her mind. Throwing petrol on lit coals, Neve curled into him, wrapping her arms around his neck and opening herself up to everything he had to give like she was starving for it—his bruising kiss, his wild hands roaming across the back of her, his resolute arms cinching her body against his.

There they remained, submerged in their own ocean of passion, waves of desire rendering them oblivious to the outside world. The cold temperatures they'd endured during their long swim were a distant memory. Now Con's whole body was ablaze, and Neve was hot to the touch.

The fire within him leapt again as she reached up and clawed at the buckles on his waders, trying to release the straps. She wanted more. Christ knew he did too. It would take every ounce of strength he had to stop himself from going there with her, skin to skin. But he knew he had to use that strength, had to pull them back from the ledge. Because if they went where they both wanted to go, he would want to keep her there forever. And if they reached that point, his desire to do so might be so strong, it would overpower everything else.

I can't believe I'm doing this, he thought as he slid his hand out from under her deliciously round backside, pulled his lips away from hers, and covered her hand on his chest with his. "Neve," he said in a hoarse whisper, "we have to stop."

Her brow crinkled, eyes pressed shut. Her mouth sought his out again as she murmured, "No we don't."

This wasn't going to work if they remained so close. "We do." Con pulled his head back, putting his mouth out of her reach, and shifted her onto the couch next to him.

But she'd turned into a languid octopus who immediately began sliding her tentacles around him again. "Come back" came her breathy whisper.

My God, this woman.... His mouth watered, imagining what her skin felt like beneath the waders and thick jumper she had on, and what it would taste like to feast on every delectable part of her.

But the rational part of his mind knew time was of the essence, people were in danger—not least themselves—and there were things that needed to be done. One of them had to stop this, and it appeared it wasn't going to be Neve.

Marshaling every ounce of self-discipline he'd honed over the years, Con pushed himself off the couch and backed away. His heart nearly failed at the loss of Neve's touch, and then again at the sight of her alone there, arms falling into her lap, expression bereft.

"What...?" Now there was worry in her eyes. "Are you okay?"

"Ah, no," he rasped, jamming his hand into his hair and grabbing it brutally. "There's one thing on this earth I want more than I've ever wanted anything, and I just stopped it from happening. So no, I'm not okay at all. Gutted, in fact."

Neve flopped back against the couch, frowning. "Why did you...?"

The way he wanted to run to her, kiss that swollen lower lip.... "Because once we cross that line, I can't guarantee I'll ever let you out of the bed. Forget going back to work—you won't be leaving the room. We're talking days. Weeks. Months, even."

As his words sank in, her frown softened into a smile. She picked up a throw pillow and hugged it to her lap. With a wicked gleam in her eye, she replied, "Promises, promises."

"Neve," Con moaned. His body nearly trembled with the energy it was taking to hold himself back from her. "As you well know, we have important things to do. But you say the word, and I'll call Max and tell him I'm handcuffing you to the bed indefinitely, so he's free to do as he likes without our interference."

He nearly lost his resolve when her eyes widened, then narrowed, as though she was trying to work out whether he was serious. How he looked forward to surprising her six ways to Sunday when he finally got her into his bed.

Neve's expression began to change and morph, a moving map of the effort it was taking for her to pull herself out of the cloud of pleasure they'd created and back into the reality of the situation. Once she'd managed to get hold of herself, she cleared her throat. "Okay, well." Slowly, she stood up and patted the throw pillow back into its place. "Since you're finding it *so impossible* to control yourself around me—ow!"

Con had lunged forward and grabbed her around the waist. He rotated her until she was facing the hallway to the bedroom, then clamped his hands down on her shoulders. "Enough, siren," he commanded, walking her forward. "Go take a shower before I do something we'll both regret."

"Okay, okay!" she said, grinning. He released his

hold on her only when she began putting one foot in front of the other of her own accord. "But you better cool off while I'm gone, mister."

He lunged forward as though to grab her again. Neve's squeal turned into laughter as she ran to the bedroom and slammed the door shut behind her.

Con rubbed both hands up and down his face as he smiled. He was certain now—one day, Neve *would* be the death of him.

But God in heaven, he would die a happy man.

CHAPTER 26

CON

One hour, two long showers, and four cups of coffee later, Con and Neve had both shifted —albeit reluctantly—back into work mode. Something was off, though. He sensed her mood had taken a downturn, and a much steeper one than was dictated by the circumstances. She seemed preoccupied, frowning and lost in thought. When he asked what was wrong, she said she was just worried about Ciara and what Max would do next. But in stark contrast to their earlier moments on the couch, he could feel that she'd closed off a part of herself and was holding something back.

They hadn't talked about her medical report yet. He knew that might be what was weighing on her. But given the potential urgency and danger of the Max situation, he felt it would be thoughtless of him to raise the topic. It might lead to a very long conversation, and a sensitive one he wouldn't want to be cut short or interrupted. He hoped that once the Max crisis had passed, Neve would bring it up herself. If she didn't, though, he would.

They sat a safe distance apart on opposite sides of the living room, eating the ham and cheese croissants Con picked up at a nearby bakery when he went out to buy burner phones. The phones came charged up a small bit, so they each called their US phones' voice mailboxes. Neve had a message from her parents saying they hoped she was enjoying her trip. Con had two messages from Eamonn, one checking in and one sharing the reassuring news that the burning pain in Ciara's arm was manageable enough that she was awake and no longer needed to be sedated. He also had a message only an hour old from Eric, telling him to check his email account.

They each made brief calls to their parents, explaining that their phones had been "stolen" and giving them their new numbers in case of emergency. They also texted the new numbers to Sergeant O'Leary and Agent Banai, the two other people who might need to reach them urgently. Finally, they called their cell phone carriers in the US and had their respective Contacts lists downloaded from the cloud and emailed to them.

Con plugged the burner phones in to charge and called Eamonn back from the landline. Neve stood behind him as his brother's voice came over the speakerphone. "You were right about the tattoo. We saw it under a UV light. It's like you said, a wheel with eight spokes and wavy lines behind it, although it's kind of mangled now. It's got to be eight inches long. At least it was a relief to have an explanation—for Ciara most of all, although it was pretty rough when she first saw it. Took a while to calm her down." The emotional strain he'd been under was evident in Eamonn's tense sigh. "They're running tests, but the doctors don't think she's having any kind of serious reaction to the ink. They still think that part is in her head, but it's also real, like it's physical. Con, what's the word for that again?"

"Psychosomatic."

"Right. At least now she's up and talking. The burning sensation ebbs and flows, and they have her on some meds for that, but overall, it's getting better. She's finally improving. The doctors hope that now that she's conscious of the reason she was self-harming, she won't have those nightmares anymore and will stop attacking herself in her sleep. She slept peacefully last night, so that's a good sign."

"It certainly is." Con hoped the worst was over for her.

"She's already asking about tattoo removal, although the doctor said there are risks with that too."

"It's all right," Con reassured. "She'll have plenty of time to think about that and decide what to do. The important thing is the psychological boil has been lanced, so to speak, and now she can start to heal."

Eamonn sounded a bit more hopeful as they talked. With everything he had on his mind, Con and Neve had decided ahead of time not to tell him about Max's attempt on their lives or the handfasting. However, they did need to warn him to be cautious.

"Listen, Eamonn," Con began. "We did manage to track down Max yesterday, but he didn't have anything to say that could help with Ciara."

There was a long silence on the other end of the phone. Finally, Eamonn said, "I'm trying to decide whether I want to hear every bloody detail, or if, now that Ciara's on the mend, I just want to forget that bastard exists."

"I'd go with the latter," Con said as he and Neve exchanged relieved looks. "Believe me, any time spent thinking about him is time wasted. That said, he's a bit unstable, putting it mildly, and we may have poked the bear a bit."

"What are you saying? Should I be worried?"

"Feck no," Con said sternly. "I'm taking care of it. But since we reached out to him and to Deirdre before, asking for help with Ciara, I'm saying if either of them calls or emails you back, don't answer. Don't reply. Just ignore."

"Wait, Deirdre too? She's Ciara's best friend."

"Right, but she works with Max…." Con didn't know where to go from there. He turned to Neve with a helpless shrug.

"Yeah," she said, jumping in. "And with the state he's in, it's possible he might try to use her to get to Ciara somehow, without Deirdre even realizing what's going on."

"That bastard." Eamonn muttered a string of curses. "So, what do I tell Ciara?"

"Well, we were told Deirdre's gone on vacation," Neve said. "That's probably why Ciara hasn't been getting any calls from her."

"Oh, that makes sense," Eamonn murmured. "What a relief. Ciara was starting to get worried."

"Block Deirdre's number on Ciara's phone, just to be safe," Con added. "You can unblock it when this is all sorted and Deirdre gets home, and Ciara will be none the wiser." This bit of advice earned an eye roll from Neve, but when Con mouthed, "What?" she just turned away.

"All right," Eamonn said, once again sounding exhausted. "Anything else?"

"Yeah," Con said. "Get some sleep. Do you need something to help?"

"You can't write scripts in Ireland, can you?"

"No, but I can ask John to write you one."

Eamonn scoffed. "He's got his hands full with Ciara. Besides, I might sleep better tonight knowing she's on the mend."

Con knew how tightly strung his brother was when it came to Ciara, so that was highly unlikely. He would call John later. That would also give him a chance to tell John about the tattoo gun in the cave, giving him more insight into Ciara's nightmares. "Do that, and call us with any news."

"I will. When should we expect you back? I mean, don't take that the wrong way—I'm not rushing you home or anything. God knows you two deserve a vacation too."

Her sympathy for Eamonn was written on Neve's face. In order to reassure both of them, Con said, "It won't be long. I'd say tomorrow at the latest. And you're not rushing us home. We want to be there, for you and for Ciara. We can all take a long vacation when this whole situation is wrapped up."

"Great, Con. Thanks. And thanks, Neve. See you soon, then."

After they hung up, Con asked, "So, should I ask what that eye roll was about or leave it alone?"

Smirking, she said, "'Block her phone, she'll never be the wiser?' You're encouraging your brother to lie to his fiancée, first of all. But also, when you say things like that, I can't help but wonder what interventions from Con's School of Subterfuge *I* have to look forward to."

"Oh, I see." He rubbed his jaw. "Well, I can't promise I'll never do something like that in the heat of the moment—for example, if I have reason to be worried about you. But I can promise, if ever I do something like that, I *will* tell you about it." He waited until Neve began to look somewhat placated, then added with a wry smile, "Quite some time after the fact, of course, and when you're handcuffed to my bed. Hey, watch the laptop," he exclaimed as she grabbed a throw pillow and aimed it at him.

"We've talked about you lying to me," she reminded

him, holding the pillow aloft, "including lies of omission."

They had, indeed. Con had committed that night at the diner to memory. They'd had a major argument in the restaurant when he'd kept something important from her, even though it had been for her own protection. Still, she'd been outraged and ran away from him. The twenty-four hours between that moment and when he'd spoken to her again had been the longest and most miserable of his life so far, including the day that damn tractor crushed his leg. It would have been easier to tell her what she wanted to hear, that he'd never do anything that affected her without her knowledge and approval. But then if he ever *had* to—and knowing how both of them were, it seemed inevitable—he'd get in trouble for lying twice.

Con decided to ask the question he was discovering worked like a charm to calm Neve down, and to bring her focus back to all that was right between them. He stood and began walking over to her. As soon as he was safely away from the desk, Neve launched the pillow at his head. He grabbed it out of the air and kept walking. When he reached her, he placed the pillow gently back into her hands and asked, "Do you trust me?"

He drank in her response: eyes closed, breathing slowed, body relaxed. "You know I do."

Con leaned in and kissed her earlobe, eliciting a barely audible sigh—such a sweet reward. "Then let's argue about this after we nail that Max bastard to the wall, shall we?"

"Mm-hmm," Neve said, biting her lip. One last earlobe kiss to seal the moment had her smiling. "See? You *are* a smooth talker."

"So you keep telling me." He winked. "I need to check my email. Eric sent something."

Neve stood behind him as he sat down at the desk and pulled up his encrypted account. There it was, an email from Eric with the subject "Red flag."

"That can't be good," Con muttered as the message loaded. They both leaned in to read it.

Hey Conman,

Heads up: there's been an uptick in chatter over the past half hour on the *Temple of Taranis* forums. It's just a rumor, but some players are saying the game is running an invitation-only, time-limited competition. Over a twelve-hour period, a hand-picked group must complete a series of quests that are already part of the game, but it's timed. The fastest players get access to an online event at sunrise, Irish time. I don't know what the event is, but they're supposedly calling it "Taranis is Owed a Life: The Sacrifice of the Sorceress," and it's being livestreamed from a location called the "Dungeon beneath the Grand Castle." Again, just a rumor, but given everything that's been going on, it gave me the creeps. Thought you should know.

Also, the numbers below are bank codes and account numbers. Your friend is partial to the Isle of Man. He gets regular deposits from a large but

DISCRETE GROUP OF PLAYER ACCOUNTS. SHADIER AND
SHADIER.

I'M AROUND FOR A FEW MORE HOURS IF YOU NEED ME,
BUT AFTER THAT, IF YOU NEED ANYONE TO WORK SOME
HACKER MAGIC FOR YOU, YOU CAN CONTACT MY FRIEND
BANSHEE, WHO'S BASED IN IRELAND. SHE'S GOOD PEOPLE,
AND YOU CAN TRUST HER. WE GO WAY BACK AND HAVE
BURIED SOME METAPHORICAL BODIES TOGETHER. I EXPLAINED
YOUR SITUATION AND THAT YOU MIGHT BE CALLING, AND
BANSHEE SAID SHE'LL HELP YOU WITHOUT ASKING ANY MORE
QUESTIONS THAN SHE NEEDS TO. SORRY I CAN'T BE THERE TO
HELP YOU MYSELF. GOOD LUCK, AND DON'T GET KILLED.

VIKING OUT

Below the text of his email was Banshee's mobile
number, followed by two columns of numbers, about
fifty rows.

"Eric's been busy," Con said, leaning back in his
chair. "Taranis is owed a life." He pressed his fingertips
into his forehead, trying to ease the band of tension that
just snapped into place. "Max must have returned to
the island already and found out we escaped."

"Oh God." Neve jumped back as though scorched.
"Is there any chance he thinks our bodies were carried
out to sea?"

"He seemed to think it would be impossible for us
to swim out of there," Con said, moving his hand to his
wounded shoulder. "For two dead bodies to float out of
that narrow, jagged opening of their own accord—no,
too unlikely."

"But he wouldn't… I mean, do you think he would actually *kill* somebody? I mean, obviously we know he would, but on *livestream*?"

"What do you think?"

She pressed her eyes shut. "Well, he was already dangerous last night, due to feeling rejected, betrayed, and angry. Then we uncovered some of his secrets, and now he knows we got away—yet another blow. Plus, he must be feeling desperate. He has to assume we went to the gardaí."

"True," Con said. "On the other hand, he doesn't know you made that audio recording. There's a chance he might have discovered we have the pills and also the HD card, but we don't even know what's on there yet. It could be unimportant. And with his harassment complaint already pending against me, as far as he knows, it's still our word against his, Sean's, and Emma's. I doubt he's worried about the guards taking any immediate action."

Neve winced. "Which will only add to his delusional level of arrogant confidence, further fueled by his sense of entitlement to the good favor of the gods. So yeah, I think there's a chance he'd hurt someone."

"Who, then?"

They pondered in silence. Neve took the thumb and index finger of her right hand and began squeezing each joint on the fingers of her left. Then she switched hands. It was something Con had seen her do to soothe herself when she was feeling an unpleasant emotion.

She must have some idea of who Max had in his clutches, an idea she didn't like.

"What are you thinking?" he asked.

She shrugged. "We can't know for sure, of course, but lately, I've been getting an uneasy feeling every time we hear something about Deirdre. I know she's supposedly on vacation, but we heard that from Sean and Emma, who lied about us to the police on Max's behalf, so they could easily have been lying about that too. And I know there's a possibility that she was working with Max and betrayed Ciara's trust, but he didn't exactly speak about her with affection down in the cave."

As she spoke, Con began to share the sinking feeling she had about Deirdre. "And Ciara still hasn't heard from her. Even if she was on vacation...."

"She could have responded to messages, or at least called to check in on her best friend," Neve said, completing his thought. "Even if she were working with Max, she would have done that much just to keep up the facade."

"So, we have an idea of who. And we know where."

"We do?"

"The Grand Castle," he mused. "That's another translation of 'An Caisleán Mór.'"

"His house?" She shook her head. "Would he be that stupid, though, to do something like that where he lives?"

"Well, Ireland, Galway—this isn't his native environment. He can't know it inside out, so his options will be limited. And he can't use the cave now, since he knows we might have told the guards about it," Con pointed out. "His house might be the only place he feels safe, where he has full control. I know from Sergeant O'Leary that he's got home security cameras. Knowing him, they probably aren't the only hi-tech surveillance gadgets he has around either."

"Oh, geez." Neve walked over and flopped onto one end of the couch. Holding her head, she sighed heavily. "Have we heard anything more from the gardaí yet?"

Con walked over and sat on the other end. "No. But we should call Sergeant O'Leary, share our suspicions about this 'Sacrifice of the Sorceress' business, and find out where things stand with the evidence we gave them."

"Garda Jensen said they were going to get help from the Cyber Crime Bureau, but I got the feeling that might take a while."

"I got the same feeling, but that might change now."

"Where are we going to tell them we got this new information?"

"I don't know. We can't bring Eric into this." While helping Con and Neve with the Brickhaven threat, Eric had exercised a highly flexible definition of the term "law-abiding citizen." Chief of Staff Liu had absolved him at the time, but only with a stern warning to stay out of trouble. "After all he's done, I won't repay him by putting him in Big Brother's crosshairs again—or Max's, for that matter."

Her eyes widened. "Do you really think Max would go after Eric if he found out about him somehow?"

"Not really, no," Con admitted. "And he wouldn't have any luck if he tried. A hacker like Eric would see him coming a mile away and eat him for lunch before Max even knew what was happening." After pausing for effect, he continued, "Still, there is a very, very slim possibility Max might *make* such a doomed attempt, so if we tell the gardaí our source must remain anonymous for their own safety, it wouldn't be an outright lie. I know how those make you uncomfortable."

He matched Neve's piercing look with a teasing smile. That disarmed her. She pursed her lips but didn't argue.

"Under the circumstances, it seems we need to do something to light a fire under the guards." He leaned forward, resting his elbows on his knees as he thought. Even with this new information, calling Sergeant O'Leary wouldn't guarantee immediate action on the part of the gardaí. But Con agreed with Neve and Eric that the situation seemed urgent.

"Maybe we could ask Agent Banai to call them?" she suggested. "I mean, it would be a little tricky for him to explain why he was getting involved in your family matter, but the Secret Service, they seem pretty… creative."

Con moaned inwardly. "That they are. I'm already dreading whatever Agent Banai is going to ask me to do in return for getting me out of jail."

"I don't understand why you're so convinced that

was a quid pro quo for some future request and not just part of his promise to keep us off Brickhaven's radar," Neve said with charming naivete.

Her point of view was understandable; she was a US citizen, so of course Agent Banai had a duty toward her. However, the US government had no such duty toward Con, and while he knew they were grateful for the help he'd rendered, he doubted they would go out of their way for him without expecting something in return. What that was, he didn't know yet, but he envied her innocence, and he wasn't anxious to strip it from her.

"You're so right," he said with a wry smile. "I'm just a grizzled old cynic. If we make it clear that your life is at risk as long as Max is at large, Agent Banai may very well make a phone call, but I'm not sure how much weight it'll carry. As of right now, there are no criminal charges against Max that we know of on either side of the Atlantic, let alone a case for international cooperation. But you and I have a lot more information about him than either the gardaí or the US government do."

"*Riiight.*" Neve looked out the window, pondering. "Including some information we can't share without Ciara's consent, or without getting Eric in trouble."

"Exactly. And since the guards won't really know what they're walking into or what to look out for, they could miss something crucial and fail to stop whatever Max has cooked up."

In the silence that followed, Con closed his eyes and concentrated. Finally, bit by bit, his thoughts clicked into place, forming a plan. "All right," he said, "I have an idea of how we could get in there first and stop Max hurting anyone, and also have timely backup from the gardaí. But before I share it, I need to know how willing you are to do what I ask without arguing."

Neve's eyebrows rose as she tucked her arms across her chest. "In general, or…?"

"I know the answer to 'in general,'" he replied dryly. "I *mean* over the next few hours, with regard to my plan to nail Max."

"I'll do what you ask," she conceded, "as long as you keep me with you."

"Hmm." That wasn't the plan. Con stroked his jaw. "Does within fifty kilometers constitute 'with'?"

He'd been half serious. Possibly more than half. But given that Neve thought his request was ridiculous, he was relieved that it elicited a burst of laughter instead of bad temper.

Smiling broadly, she said, "Try again."

There would be no leaving her behind, then. He rubbed his eyes and smacked his hand on his forehead a couple of times, even though that method of getting more blood flowing to the brain had no scientific basis. "Together, then. But you'll follow my instructions?" Con knew that last question was complete folly. She might try, but if she changed her mind midstream, there would be no stopping her.

"If you tell me the plan, I can give you a better answer to that question." She gave him a helpless shrug; at least she knew herself well enough not to promise outright.

Which was further proof that she would be the death of him, the absolute end. He might as well write out his last will and testament. But Con could live very happily with that reality, just as long as Neve survived unscathed.

CHAPTER 27
NEVE

an't have children. Can't have children. The unwelcome chant was like a sadistic news ticker running quietly through the back of my mind, matching the rhythm of the car's tires as they crossed the seams in the road.

I tried replacing it with *Don't have cancer. Don't have cancer.* But that only worked for so long before the first version reasserted itself.

Shut. Up! I issued the stern command to my brain. That gave me a few minutes' respite, at least.

I could see from the landscape that we were drawing closer to Max's house, and I seriously needed to focus. It was a little after six o'clock, and the sky was darkening. The whole day had been rainy and overcast, and now the roiling blanket of clouds was barely lit from behind. Over the last hour, the wind had picked up, driving the raindrops every which way. Con called it "upside-down rain," saying it was a regular feature of the Irish climate.

Everything that happened in the cave and the drama at the garda station had pushed my medical report out of my mind completely, but only for a while. Once I got into the shower and had a few moments to myself, the words came rushing back.

Infertility almost certain.

In other words, fundamentally broken.

That grim soundtrack had been playing all afternoon in the background of my mind as Con and I prepared ourselves. First, we'd had another cup of coffee, conscious that neither of us had slept well, or long. But as we sat there sipping, I could *feel* him worrying about me again, and it was putting my neck and shoulders in knots. The last thing I wanted to talk about was my medical report, but to relieve the tension, I showed it to him again so he could look it over and boil it down for me.

Apparently, endometriosis was a condition where tissue similar to the lining of the uterus exists outside the uterus, often involving the ovaries and fallopian tubes, as was the case for me. Con explained it often caused severe pain, but luckily, I hadn't experienced that—not yet, anyway. He did his best to answer my questions: No, they didn't know what caused it. No, it wasn't life-threatening. Yes, it was treatable—to an extent, but upon further probing, he admitted it was also a common cause of infertility.

As far as I was concerned, the main takeaways from

our discussion were that I was almost certainly cancer-free, I probably needed another minor surgery, and I couldn't have children. Con hadn't put it in such stark terms, of course. He'd couched everything in granular medical terminology and phrases like "in all likelihood," "nothing is written in stone," and "they can run more tests." But I knew what he really thought. It was in his eyes and written across his face. He was the smartest person I knew, and the best doctor. If he believed the worst-case scenario, I had no reason to doubt it.

I did my best to focus on the extremely good news that it was almost certain I didn't have to worry about cancer anymore. That was a huge relief, especially since I had seen that monster up close, losing several extended family members to the disease. Still, I felt numb. Maybe the good news and the bad had emotionally canceled each other out.

Con wasn't giving much away in terms of how he felt about the report. He was clearly concerned about me, but other than that, I couldn't gauge his reaction. I remembered the conversation I overheard in the car in which Eamonn alluded to the fact that Con had never wanted kids. Had that been the truth or just an inside joke between brothers? If he really didn't want kids, I guess I didn't have to worry too much. He might even be relieved—a possibility that irritated me for some irrational reason.

But what if Con *did* want children? It was easy to picture. He would make an incredible dad, and any kids he had would be the absolute luckiest. If that was what he wanted, was he now rethinking our relationship? Maybe even that very moment, as he sat next to me, driving the car and looking serious?

The mere thought made my stomach lurch. Looking down at my claddagh ring—already the most cherished thing I'd ever owned—I couldn't help but question whether he regretted giving it to me.

I wondered how Con felt about adoption. Of course, that option wasn't guaranteed either, as I knew from friends who'd gone through the process—some successfully, some not. At least it was a possibility, though. Unlike me getting pregnant, evidently.

As we drove along, Con glanced over at me. Doing a poor job of trying to hide his concern, he asked, "Are you all right?"

"Yeah, I'm good," I lied. "Just a little worried about Deirdre."

Back at the Airbnb, I had shown him pictures of her on social media so we both knew what she looked like. Then we'd taken Eric up on his offer to contact his hacker colleague, Banshee, who'd agreed to help us. As a first step, she pinged Deirdre's cell phone. It had been powered off since Friday night, but its last location was Max's house.

"There are plenty of hours between now and sunrise," Con reassured me. "We'll get to her."

He didn't finish the sentence, though.

"Before Max 'sacrifices' her?"

"That's not going to happen." He slowed the car

down and drove onto the shoulder. "Not on our watch."

He turned onto a boreen, which he explained was the Irish word for a narrow, one-lane country road, usually gravel, with "the distinguishing feature of a strip of grass running down the middle." He and Banshee had spent some time mapping out Max's property and surrounding areas and spotted this particular boreen close to the house. It was a good place to stash the car—close, but over a hill so it couldn't be spotted from the "Right Kip"—Irish slang for a "real dump" and our new code name for the house.

After coordinating Con's plan with Banshee, we placed a call to Agent Banai. He agreed to call Sergeant O'Leary again and ask him to have our backs if we called for help. As Con predicted, though, when Agent Banai called us back, he said that due to the entirely informal nature of the request, the sergeant had agreed only as a favor and a goodwill gesture, and only if he made the independent judgment that the situation justi-fied gardaí intervention. Sergeant O'Leary also reiter-ated to Agent Banai that he'd ordered Con to stay out of trouble, so he would be very surprised if we had need to call the gardaí at all. From that, we understood that he would be supremely annoyed if he did end up hearing from us.

Agent Banai then asked to speak to Con privately. Con took him off speakerphone and had a very low volume, serious-sounding conversation as I retreated to the kitchen to put together some snacks. After he hung up, I asked him what that was all about.

"Quid pro quo" was all he said, but he promised to explain everything in detail after the Max and Deirdre situation was dealt with.

Con seemed confident that his plan would work and we would be able to rescue Deirdre or whatever "sorceress" Max had in his so-called dungeon. It did seem like a solid plan, but while I apparently had "diplomatic immunity," I couldn't help worrying that one way or another, Con could end up in jail—and that an additional "get out of jail free" card from Agent Banai might be too much to hope for. Still, we couldn't sit on our hands and wait until the gardaí examined our evidence and built a case. That could take days, or longer. By then, Max could have killed someone and done God knew what else. As long as Max was roaming around free, Ciara wouldn't be a hundred percent safe—and Con, Eamonn, and I might not be either.

We'd spent quite a bit of time on the phone with Banshee, hashing out how she could help. Con told me a banshee was a spirit creature from Celtic folklore whose mournful screaming foretold a death, so I was expecting Eric's friend to be intimidating. But hacker Banshee was the exact opposite. With a warm, melodic voice, she sounded bright and cheerful over the phone, unbothered by the grave nature of our call. To each request or idea from Con, she responded, "Sure-sure-sure, no bother." We told her a little about Max and the situation for context, and she replied, "Well, he sounds fecking charming!"

I liked her immediately, and we were both grateful for her can-do attitude and impressive technical skills. There seemed to be no potential obstacles to which Banshee couldn't find a creative solution. I could see why she and Eric were friends, and why he told us we could trust her.

Finally, we'd gone out for supplies—or so I'd thought. Instead, Con took me to an after-hours outpatient clinic to get my head injury checked yet again. When my name was called, he came with me into the exam room to describe what I'd been through in medicalese. The doctor said I looked fine and displayed no concerning symptoms.

Taking advantage of the situation, I announced that we weren't leaving until someone looked at Con's leg. Before he could escape, he was descended upon by the doctor and two nurses, all of whom showed such genuine concern that he couldn't brush them off. He kicked me out of the exam room, though, and he was only in there for ten more minutes before they released him, loudly voicing their misgivings. Before we left, the doctor handed him a piece of paper with the address of a nearby pharmacy that also sold medical equipment, strongly advising him to get a temporary replacement for his leg brace.

I convinced Con to do just that by promising that if he didn't follow the doctor's advice, he would never, ever see me naked again. Within an hour, he'd been fitted with a soft brace that went from midthigh to midcalf and bent at the knee. The pharmacist said it would give him some stability and hopefully keep the damage from getting worse. Con didn't say a word about it after that, but I could tell that, although he found the brace irritating, his pain wasn't as pronounced.

After our medical excursion, he dropped me off at the Airbnb, which I wanted to clean a bit before we left, and went off on his own to pick up some things we needed. An hour later, he was back with a few bags, the apartment was presentable again, and we were packed and ready to go. We each had a new backpack full of supplies.

As we said goodbye to the Airbnb, I felt an unexpected hitch of regret in my chest. Maybe it was nostalgia over our make-out session on the couch, or maybe it was simply because I knew we were safe there. I couldn't say the same about where we were headed.

The rain made the drive to Max's house hard going for Con, who had to squint to see through the windscreen, even with the wipers on full blast. Once we finally reached the boreen, he stopped the car, unlatched his seat belt, and turned to face me. His expression was ever-changing, shifting between worry, determination, and high alert.

"Are you ready?" he asked.

I nodded. "Yes, I'm ready."

Con pulled out his burner phone and called

Banshee. She'd managed to hack into a communications satellite and point its cameras in the vicinity of Max's house. Those images confirmed there were two SUVs parked in front of the house, but she couldn't see any people or other movement outside.

Then it was time for me to make a call. Con handed me the phone and the piece of paper with my talking points. With a deep breath, I tried to calm the butterflies fluttering in my chest as I dialed the number for the garda station.

"Inveran Garda Station, Garda Jensen speaking."

I put the phone on speaker. "Garda Jensen," I said, and it didn't take much effort for me to sound distressed. "I'm so glad it's you. This is Neve Keane. I was at the station last night with Dr. O'Brien. Something's happened, and I need your help."

There was a slight pause, and I thought I heard a sigh. I guessed Sergeant O'Leary had told her about his conversation with Agent Banai, but they were all hoping we wouldn't call. "What's happened?"

"We heard Max Hinsen had kidnapped someone and was holding them at his house with the intention of killing them," I began.

I could hear papers rustling and the click of a pen. "And where did this information come from?"

Con and I had decided the best way to protect Eric was to leave any mention of a source out of the story completely. "That's not what matters right now. What matters is that Con believes it, so we're at Max's house now."

"You're there *now*?" There was a distinct note of alarm in her voice. "Where, exactly, and what's happening?"

"Con parked the car down the hill from Max's house," I said, trying to sound breathless. "He hand-cuffed me to the steering wheel so I couldn't follow him. He said he didn't want me to get hurt. But he's heading up to the house on foot right now to try to rescue the victim."

I winced as muffled cursing came across the line. Con gave me a thumbs-up.

"Just a moment," Garda Jensen said.

As expected, the next voice I heard was Sergeant O'Leary's. "Miss Keane, tell me again what's going on?"

I explained it again, answering additional questions like was I hurt (no); did Con intend to harm Max (not if he could help it); did Con have a weapon of any kind (no); and did we know who the alleged kidnapping victim was (no, but we had an idea it was a young woman).

"All right." Sergeant O'Leary's voice was muffled, as though he'd covered the mouthpiece and was speaking to someone. After a moment, he came back and said, "Miss Keane, we listened to the recording you gave us."

"You did?" I asked as Con and I exchanged surprised looks. We weren't expecting such quick results.

"Yes. The sound quality isn't perfect, and the

recording is garbled in places, but we heard enough to give us a definite interest in interviewing Mr. Hinsen. We were waiting to see what they pulled off the HD card, verify the recording, and corroborate your claims before we moved on him, but under the circumstances, we can expedite that interview by sending a car up to Mr. Hinsen's house right now."

"Oh, thank you," I said with genuine relief. "Please come quickly. And you might want to send more than one car. Con said he heard there may be a group of people involved."

"He heard that, did he?" I could almost imagine Sergeant O'Leary shaking his head. "We'll have to talk later about where Con hears these sorts of things, but for now, leave it with us. Are you all right where you are?"

"Yes, I'm fine. Just please help Con and that kidnapping victim."

"All right. We'll come get you as soon as we're able. In the meantime, stay put and call again if anything changes—sorry, I guess you don't have much of a choice but to stay put."

"Unfortunately," I said, hoping my smile didn't come through in my voice. "Thank you so much, Sergeant."

"We're on it." And with that, he hung up the phone.

"Well, that went well." I grinned at Con, who was rummaging around in his backpack. "Couldn't have gone better, in fact. What do you—what—hey!"

He grasped my wrist and took the phone out of my

hand. Before I knew what happened, he'd pulled me forward and, with a pair of actual handcuffs that came out of nowhere, hooked me to the steering wheel.

I yanked on the cuffs, gaping at him. "What the hell?"

"I didn't want to make a liar out of you," he said as he reached down and began zipping up his backpack.

He must be joking. This must be a joke. If he *wasn't* joking, he was at risk of making me so angry I would never forgive him for the rest of eternity. "Very funny. Hilarious, in fact. Uncuff me now."

Con stopped midzip and looked up at me, his brows pulled together into a dark line. "You'll be safe here. I'll be back soon."

"That's not the *plan*!" I wrapped both hands around the chain portion of the cuffs and yanked several times, but they weren't budging.

As I struggled, Con slapped a second pair of cuffs onto my previously free hand, latching it to the steering wheel, as well. "That's *my* plan."

An explosion of anger demolished my composure. "So you're just doing this, and it doesn't matter what I say? What happened to our listening pact?" I shouted, placing my feet against the console for leverage and pulling back as hard as I could on the cuffs. "Ow!"

He shook his head. "You're going to hurt yourself, love. And the listening pact doesn't apply to *raiméis*."

"You can't call me 'love' and also keep lying to me!"

"I didn't lie to you," he said matter-of-factly. "You

asked to stay with me, and you will—within two kilometers. That fits my definition of 'with.'"

"*Your* definition?" I stopped pulling when the bite against my wrists became too painful to bear. "And you get to define what is and isn't *raiméis* too?"

Con grasped my forearms, holding me still. "Yes. I'm the one who speaks Irish."

"You… you… *jerk*!" There were worse names I could have called him, but I was still holding out hope that he'd change his mind. I tried to pull away from him to no avail. Hot tears pricked the backs of my eyes, and I hated myself for wanting to cry in that moment. In fury and despair, I slumped sideways against the seat. "You can't go up there alone with no one watching your back!"

Slowly, he released my arms. "I'll have help. Let's call her." Picking up the phone again, he dialed.

Banshee answered. "Is it time?"

"It's time," Con said.

I still couldn't believe he was actually doing this. I screwed my eyes shut as we listened to Banshee hum softly, clicking away on a keyboard. After a few minutes, as predicted, she announced, "Done. Security systems down, internet and mobile phone signals scrambled. The Right Kip is blind, deaf, and dumb. You're good to go in."

"Well, *I'm* not!" I cried, hoping to gain some sympathy from Banshee, at least. "Con's handcuffed me to the steering wheel!"

"She's safer here," Con said, like that was some sort of complete explanation.

There was a slight pause, and then Banshee said, "Sorry, I have a policy not to get involved in domestics. Need anything else?"

"We're good," he said. "Thanks for everything. I owe you a pint or three."

"Send Eric the price of it in cryptocurrency and we'll call it even. Call me if you need anything else, lads," she said, then hung up.

Ignoring the poisoned, flaming arrows my eyes were shooting at him, Con donned his new black knit cap, smoothed it down over his head, and strapped on the night vision goggles he'd bought for both of us—as a ruse, apparently, since only one of us would be using them. After turning them on and testing them, he pushed the goggles up onto his head, opened the car door, and stepped outside.

In one final, desperate attempt to make him see reason, I asked, "So you're allowed to worry about me and be my backup, no matter how dangerous the situation, but I'm not allowed to worry about you walking into the lion's den alone?"

When Con leaned into the car, his eyes held a fury so cold it froze me in place. "Max got one opportunity to hurt you. That was one too many. He won't get another."

"But what about you?" I couldn't lose him; I just couldn't. The tears I'd been holding back began to fall. "Why not just wait for the gardaí?"

"You know why." In his voice, I heard the swell of emotion he was trying to control. "It will take them twenty minutes to get here. If Max is holding Deirdre in a hidden room or somewhere off-site, the guards could come and go without ever finding her. Even if they take Max away, Lord knows what his minions might do with her. Not to mention, once they get here, they'll take over the scene, and I won't be allowed near Max. I've got to get to him first and make him tell me where she is."

"By yourself? With two carloads of people there?" Beads of perspiration broke out on my face. "What if they have guns?"

"I can't imagine why they would, but Banshee killed the lights and the security cameras," he said, tapping the night vision goggles on his head. "They can't shoot me if they can't see me." Con pulled the hood of his rain jacket up over the gear. "The guards will be here soon enough to back me up. I just need a few minutes with Max."

I could see it in the set of his jaw—he was going, and there was nothing I could say to stop him. But I still couldn't help trying. "But what if they have night vision goggles, too, for some reason? What if this whole thing is a trap to lure you out here? What if…?"

With each question, Con drew closer, finally cutting me off with a kiss. The sensation of his warm, rough lips on mine forced my eyes closed and sent my pulse thumping through my veins. He wrapped his hand around the back of my neck, pulling me toward him as his tongue urged my mouth open, meeting very little resistance. As outraged and terrified as I was, his kiss still had the same effect as always, igniting an inferno deep inside me. As the blaze rose, he swallowed my pleading whimper. Then he pulled away.

With his eyes locked on mine, he rasped, "Stay here. Don't move."

Before I could utter another word of objection, he was gone. The car door shut, and I heard the dull click of the doors being locked remotely.

"Really?" I shouted at his large shadow as he disappeared into the rain. "You locked the doors? I'm handcuffed, for God's sake!"

But Con didn't turn around. He just kept moving down the boreen. My eyes remained glued to him until he was completely out of sight.

He's going to get himself killed. The thought landed on my heart in the most frightening way possible: softly, quietly, and with deadly certainty. My tears fell in earnest, blurring my vision. I tried to dry them on my sleeves as I wrestled with my boots, managing to untie them and kick them off, along with my socks. Then I used my toes to unzip my own backpack and turn it upside down, dumping its contents onto the driver's seat. There in the middle of the pile was my burner phone.

"Thank you, God," I whispered as I twisted around. Slowly and painstakingly, I used my foot to lift the phone into my cuffed hands. With extreme care, wary of dropping the phone and having to start all over again, I dialed Banshee.

"That you, Neve?"

"How did you know?"

"I've got both your numbers. What can I do for you?"

"I'm so glad you asked," I said, breathing through my tears. "I need you to help me figure out, with the things I can reach, how to get out of these goddamn handcuffs."

CHAPTER 28

CON

Con didn't know whether to curse the rain or be grateful for it.

The storm provided a plausible explanation for the power cut and gave him decent cover. But he'd been away from Ireland so long, he'd forgotten a person could get soaked to the skin even wearing a waterproof jacket. A welcome rush of adrenaline dulled the ache in his leg as he pushed up over the hill to Max's house.

He didn't spot anyone guarding the front of the house—unsurprising in that weather. The outbuilding was quiet except for the hum of an engine. From the pitch and quality of the sound, he guessed it was coming from a large generator. So while there were no lights visible, electricity was going somewhere—possibly to a hidden basement.

Earlier in the day, Banshee had pulled the house's records. There was no space under the original structure, but Max had built on an extension. That seemed like the most likely place to find a "Dungeon beneath the Grand Castle."

Con made his way slowly around the perimeter of the house but saw no sign of anyone. Then he settled in behind one of the vehicles in the drive and watched. It wasn't long before a bright green spot flared in his goggles, coming from the window to the right of the front door. It looked as though someone was in there shining a torch around the place. Then the door opened, and Sean from Wicked Games stepped out, zipping up his mac. This langer was popping up everywhere. Con wondered if he was "TOT," Max's cult hobbyist partner from the dark web discussion board.

He followed from a safe distance as Sean walked around the property, looking for something—probably the cause of the power outage. Sean examined the satellite dish on the raised concrete platform, then went back in through the front door. Con saw the light of Sean's torch move toward the back of the house. He followed it to the new extension, then watched as it lowered toward the floor and gradually disappeared. That could be the entrance to a basement.

Time was ticking, and the gardaí were on their way. He had to move.

As his stiff, uneven gait took him up to the front door and freezing rivulets of rain drenched his shirt, Con cursed his aching leg and thought, *I didn't go to medical school for this.*

When he left Ireland, he'd thought Eamonn had

grown up enough that Con would never again have to step in on his behalf and give someone a clatter. And yet here he was. The saying was true: "we make plans, and God laughs"—maniacally, most likely. When Con died, he would have quite a few stern words for the Almighty.

He grasped the handle of the front door and pressed down on the lever. It moved freely. *Perfect*. Sean hadn't locked the door, so he and Max must not be too concerned about unexpected visitors. If it was just the two of them in there, with the element of surprise on his side, Con shouldn't have too much trouble handling the situation.

He pulled the door nearly closed behind him, leaving it half an inch open so Sergeant O'Leary could see it was easy to enter. He wiped the rain from the lenses of his goggles. Listening carefully for any sounds, he followed the path Sean had walked toward the back of the house. Just as he entered the extension, he felt a rhythmic thumping coming from the floor. Backing up, he could see a slight glow at a spot near the edge of an area rug.

He lifted the rug. The glow was in the shape of a square, like the outline of a door. Feeling around the edges, he found a piece of metal about six inches square. It was flush with the floorboards except for the slight indentation where a finger could be inserted to pull up a latch.

This must be it.

Con shed his soaked jacket and removed his night

vision goggles, setting them off to the side and giving his eyes a moment to adjust before he opened the hatch.

The image of Neve cuffed to the steering wheel flashed through his mind. *She's going to kill me when this is over.* But Neve was the last person he needed to be thinking about right now. That was the second reason he'd left her in the car, the first being to keep her out of harm's way. Not that it hadn't pained him. A part of himself had been torn away as he ended their last kiss.

Even if he had considered letting Neve come to Max's with him, what happened earlier that afternoon would have nixed that idea. While he gave her the news from her medical report, Con watched her face crumble over and over, like dozens of eggs cracking in slow motion. He refused to allow one more thing to happen to her that required her to be brave. Not one more thing.

Not to mention, with everything she'd lived through over the past couple of months, the last thing she needed was to be put in another potentially dangerous and violent situation—even if Con was inflicting the violence. Especially then, in fact. That was why he'd wanted to leave her behind at his parents' house in the first place. Neve had thwarted that plan, but by God, she wasn't getting in the way of this one. She didn't need any more ugly images in her memory bank, and she didn't need to see in living color the things Con was capable of.

Max did, though. Max definitely did.

Con unsnapped the leather sheath clipped to his belt

at the small of his back. He fingered the handle of the knife with the seven-inch blade—the one Neve didn't know he was carrying. He took three quick, hard breaths. Then he slowly pulled up on the door latch, relieved when the hatch opened smoothly and quietly.

Music boomed out from the opening. So far, all he could see was a wooden ladder built flush against a concrete wall. It led down into a darkened space. *Not optimal.* It would be quicker and easier to climb down the ladder without his new leg brace. He quickly pulled apart the Velcro tabs that held it in place and laid it down next to his jacket and goggles.

A male voice shouted over the music, followed by a woman keening. The chilling sound of her cry propelled him forward. Con lowered himself onto the first step of the ladder, praying whoever was down there was too occupied with what they were doing to see him. Two more steps, and he was able to duck his head down and see a bit more.

To his relief, there was a black curtain hanging between the ladder and the rest of the room. Knowing Max, he wouldn't want to ruin the dungeon-like atmosphere by leaving an escape route visible. At any rate, Con was grateful for the cover as he made his way down.

Once his foot hit the floor, he looked around quickly, trying to get a better grasp of his surroundings. Bright light shone out from the edges of the curtain; that area must have been powered by the generator. Other than the ladder, there was nothing else behind the curtain but a folding table leaning against the wall and a few metal chairs stacked beside it. He could use one of those. Fighting in his younger years had accustomed Con to improvising.

Trying as hard as possible not to make any noise, he lifted the top chair off the stack, made his way to the far wall, and peered through the narrow opening at the edge of the curtain.

Fecking hell. It was Deirdre.

Con recognized her from her social media photos. Just in front of the curtain, Max had built a six-foot version of his eight-spoked wheel and tied her to it, spread eagle. She was wearing a long white robe and was tied to the wheel with ropes at her waist, wrists, and ankles. Con couldn't see any blood on her from where he stood, and her eyes were open, if barely. But there was significant bruising around the ropes on her extremities, and her face was red and swollen. No wonder, because the sick maggot had built the wheel onto a platform and rigged it to turn, and Dierdre was currently hanging upside down. God knew how long she'd been in that position.

Suppressing the impulse to rush in, Con took in the rest of the scene. The basement looked to be the same size as the extension, about five hundred square feet. The whole floor was tiled in black, and every wall was covered with the same type of black curtain he stood behind. At the far end of the room was a built-in bar, stocked with numerous bottles and illuminated by recessed lighting.

In front of the bar was a large folding table holding a desktop computer with a camera hooked on the monitor. Two bright LED lights on tripods stood on either side of the table, pointing at Deirdre. A man Con had never seen before sat at the table, staring at the screen while banging on the keyboard and cursing. Banshee's scrambling of the internet must have been holding fast. The man was broadly built and appeared tall, judging from the way he was hunched over the table.

Pushed against the side wall close to Con was a long leather couch. Sean reclined on it, bobbing his head to the god-awful music as he sipped something from a highball glass. Max was notably absent. Con thought it best to dispense with these two before the man of the hour appeared.

With a roar, he came out from behind the curtain, swinging the chair. Sean was so stunned he didn't even drop his drink until Con hit him on the side of the head with the metal frame. Falling to the ground and wailing, Sean tried to reach for Con, but he flipped the chair over and slammed it into the back of Sean's head, putting enough power behind the blow to knock him out for a while at least.

There was a loud crash, and then the music stopped. Con looked up, ready for an attack by the computer operator, but none came. The table was overturned, and the computer equipment had hit the floor. Meanwhile, the man had disappeared—probably behind the bar, the only place in the room to hide.

"Come out and I won't hurt you," Con bellowed. "I'll just tie you to the fecking wheel!"

Then he heard the distinct, metallic *click-click* of a bolt-action rifle being loaded.

Jaysus, he thought as he lowered himself to the floor behind the end of the sofa. *Neve was right. They* do *have guns.*

"I'll blow your head off!" the man called out from behind the bar. "I swear I will! Get the hell out of here!"

Con wasn't an expert in American accents, but if he had to bet, he'd say the man was from New York or New Jersey. He was also drunk and scared, a combination Con could recognize in anyone's voice.

"Gladly," Con called back, "but I'm taking the girl with me. And if you try to stop me, you'll find out what it feels like to bleed out and die a long way from home."

That seemed to give his opponent pause. Con could almost hear the man's thoughts spinning, probably wondering who Con was and if he had a gun too. Hopefully he was considering the deal he was being offered and would decide it was worth Max's wrath to take it.

If Con could get out of there with Deirdre, that would be mission accomplished. As much as he wanted to beat Max to a pulp, he would be willing to let the gardaí handle that arsehole.

Another *click-click* froze him in place. This time, the sound came from a few feet behind him.

Deirdre's gaze darted behind Con, and her eyes

popped open as she screamed. That told him exactly who was pointing the rifle.

"Max," Con snarled.

"Dr. O'Brien," Max replied with a strained laugh. "The police let you out already? I'm surprised but glad you could join us. We made such memories back in the cave." He took a step closer. "Clasp your hands behind your head. Slowly. Good job. Ryan, you can come out. The situation's under control. Bring me some rope, will you?"

Con turned to give Deirdre what he hoped was a reassuring look. "A gun for every man," he observed coolly. "Is that an American thing?"

Ryan emerged from behind the bar and approached Con cautiously. He held a coil of rope in one hand but dangled the rifle in his other, as though it were a snake that might bite him at any moment. Ryan wasn't comfortable with guns, then. He moved awkwardly, Con observed, like he was a stranger in his own body, so while his size might make Ryan a handful, Con wasn't too worried about him otherwise.

"I grew up hunting my own food," Max replied. "Now I shoot clay pigeons. It pays to have those kinds of skills. You never know when they might come in handy. Ryan, toss me the rope and pat him down."

Ryan followed orders. As Con felt Max loop the rope around his wrists, Ryan laid his rifle down on the ground and stepped forward.

Con knew the chances of getting himself and Deirdre out of there uninjured would decline dramatically once his hands were firmly tied and both men had their rifles back. The guards were coming, but the entrance to the basement was well concealed. He wouldn't have found it himself without the night vision goggles. If the hatch was closed, the rug was in place, and Max kept things quiet in the basement, the guards likely wouldn't find them on a first sweep. No doubt after locating Con's car, they would come back at Neve's insistence and do a more thorough search. But God only knew what Max would have done to Deirdre and him by then. He had to move. Now.

Using all his strength, Con yanked his hands up over his head, throwing Max off-balance. He heard the rifle clatter to the ground as he threw his body back and to the side, knocking Max into the wall. With one eye on Ryan, who was scrambling to get a hold of his own rifle, Con swung around and smashed his half-bound fists into Max's outraged face. The blow made a satisfying crunch, followed by a yowl as Max frantically tried to hit, kick, or scratch Con anywhere he could reach. But Con had him pinned so tightly against the wall that he couldn't get any leverage, so his attacks were ineffective.

Ryan either didn't really know how to shoot or he'd lost the nerve, but it seemed he'd seen enough movies to know the butt of a rifle also made a good weapon. He charged at Con with the gun raised over his head, but just as he swung it down, Con ducked. Ryan's blow hit Max squarely in the jaw. There was a loud crack, and Max slumped to the ground.

As Ryan stood there gaping, Con turned and swept his good leg out. Although his hands were still tied, he managed to grab the barrel of Ryan's rifle as the man stumbled and tried to keep himself from falling.

Quickly, Con stepped away from both men. He was ready for another attack, but Ryan hesitated, giving Con the opportunity he needed. He pulled his hands free from the loosened knot and lifted the rifle. In one smooth motion, he tucked it against his shoulder, checked the bolt, and pointed it straight at Ryan.

For once, he was glad he knew how to shoot. He hated to admit it, but Max was right—you never knew when those skills might come in handy. Recognizing that Con knew his way around a gun, Ryan slowly raised his hands in the air.

"Take that gobshite over to the bar and sit on the ground. Take the rope with you," Con said, tossing it over. "Tie his wrists and your own, then tie both of you to the footrail."

Trembling, he did as told. Although Max was conscious and able to stumble along with Ryan's help, he wasn't going to be a threat to anyone anytime soon. Once they reached the bar, Ryan gave his full concentration to his knot-tying task. Still, Con kept one eye on them as he turned his attention to Deirdre.

"Deirdre, I'm Con. Everything's going to be okay now. I'm getting you out of here." Slowly, he turned the wheel until she was upright. When he pulled the knife out from behind his back, she started gasping like a fish pulled from the water. "It's all right," he said, backing away from her. "I'm just going to cut the ropes, okay?"

Eyes wide, she paused for a moment, then nodded. He knew her thoughts must be muddled if it took her more than a second to decide whether she wanted to remain tied up, but she could easily be in shock. God only knew what Max had done to her down there.

Gingerly, he approached her, glancing back frequently to check on Ryan's progress. He started with her ankles, cursing when he saw the skin was rubbed raw. He sawed at the ropes until they fell apart, then moved up to her waist and wrists.

"Your legs might not work straight away," he warned her as he cut away her bindings. "Just fall on me, okay? I'll catch you."

She nodded, her eyes red and swollen from crying. As the second wrist was cut loose, she pitched forward off the wheel. Con caught her and eased her down. Once her feet were on the ground, she tried to put her weight on them, but her legs gave way.

"You'll be all right." He dropped the knife, scooped her up, and carried her to the couch. "Just rest here while I take care of those two." Then he stepped over Sean's motionless form to check on Ryan and Max.

The knots weren't pretty, but they would do the job. "Decent work there, Ryan," Con said. The man looked relieved by the praise, if a bit anxious as Con tightened the ropes.

"You're not going to kill us, then?" Ryan asked, his voice wavering.

"Like I said, I just want the girl. The guards will be here soon for the two of you. Just stay put and you'll be fine."

That elicited moans and curses from Max, who spat at Con's feet with a pinkish mixture of saliva and blood. "He's going to rape you, Dee!" Max yelled. "He had you in the cave, and now he wants you all to himself!"

What the hell is he on about? Con wondered as he stood up and turned toward Deirdre. *Surely she doesn't think I'm here to harm her? I freed—*

But Deirdre was standing, holding Max's rifle and pointing it straight at Con.

He raised his hands. "Wait—"

Bang!

Con lurched to his left as something hit him in the shoulder, hard. The momentum flipped his body around and slammed him against the bar. He couldn't move his left arm, but he grabbed the edge of the counter with his right hand, getting just enough purchase to hold himself up.

He turned back to look at Deirdre. Logically, he knew she must have shot him, but he didn't feel any pain. Maybe he was already bleeding out. That would explain why he was hallucinating Neve. In his dying vision, he imagined her creeping up behind Deirdre, holding a large object in the air, and then, with a scream, bringing it down hard on Deirdre's head.

That image put a smile on his face as his eyes closed like leaden shutters. Con felt his body sliding down the side of the bar until he was sitting on the ground.

So this is how my life will end.

Consciousness was slipping away from him so quickly he didn't even have enough time to feel one way or another about it. The only emotion he had was relief that at least Neve was back in the car, where she'd be safe.

As his connection to the world was severed, Con sent God a silent prayer of warning: *You'd better watch over Neve, because I'm on my way up there.*

CHAPTER 29

NEVE

Okay. Con was right. This sucks.

Now I had some idea how he'd felt, sitting by my bedside in the emergency room after I was stabbed, not knowing—

Snap out of it, I ordered myself. I scooted my chair even closer to the side of the hospital bed and slid my hand under his, careful to avoid the IV tubing. His skin felt cool. I hoped my touch would warm him up a little.

If I closed my eyes, I could imagine we were at Capitol Hill General. It was somewhat comforting to think of us being back in our second home together. I could picture us both standing over the bed of a mutual patient, smelling the same sharp scent of disinfectant, hearing the same steady beeps from machines measuring vital signs. And every so often, there was the low hum of the blood pressure cuff inflating, then deflating, followed by a loud beep to announce it had a satisfactory result.

But we weren't at Capitol Hill General. We were at St. Vincent's Hospital in Galway. And we weren't at a patient's bedside. I was at Con's.

And I couldn't afford to close my eyes, because then I might miss something—maybe the moment he woke up. When he opened his eyes, I wanted to be the first thing he saw.

There was a light knock on the door. Eamonn walked in with two cups of coffee. He handed one to me and sat in the chair on the other side of the bed. "Relax, would you?" He gave me a tired smile. "He's going to be fine. He's just having the best sleep of his life right now. Once the anesthesia wears off...."

"I know, I know." I turned my head and leaned down, resting my cheek on the bedrail. "It went right through. Nothing major was hit."

"Yeah. Not to mention he's a huge lout, and the bullet was only a .22."

Eamonn was right; the doctors hadn't given us any reason to worry. In the basement, when I saw Con collapse as quickly as he did, I was sure the bullet must have severed an artery. I didn't know how much time passed between that moment and when the doctor told me Con would be fine. But somewhere in there, I felt like I had aged twenty years. Apparently it was the shock of the bullet combined with the severity of the pain from Con's injured leg twisting as he fell that had caused him to lose consciousness.

The gardaí had arrived just minutes after I knocked Deirdre over the head with the lamp I grabbed on my way to the basement. I was shocked by the lack of hesitation I felt in attacking her, especially since I knew she was one of Max's victims. But when I saw she'd shot Con and was still pointing a gun at him, something primal took over and I acted without thinking. Then I ran to Con and stayed with him, not even sparing a thought for poor Dierdre until help arrived. I still wasn't sure what to do with that new piece of self-knowledge, but I decided it could wait.

Max had left the hatch wide open when he went down after Con, probably because he wasn't expecting any additional visitors. Garda Jensen was one of the guards who responded and the first one down the ladder. After taking one look at me and the rest of the scene, she shouted up the hatch for someone to call the ambulance service.

They let me ride with Con, who regained consciousness on the way to the hospital. I was so relieved, I almost passed out myself. At first, he was confused, asking where we were, why he couldn't sit up, and why I was there. I explained as gently as I could that he'd been shot, then watched his face cycle through a number of emotions as everything came back to him. Finally, his expression settled on "furious," and he nearly launched himself off the stretcher, roaring about handcuffs and staying in the car. Fortunately, the EMT was ready for him and quickly jabbed him with something that settled him right down. Lord knew I was as frustrated with Con as he was with me, if not more so.

But my anger didn't even touch the abject terror I felt, not knowing….

But I couldn't let myself think like that, so I shut down all my emotions and let the nurses take over when we got to St. Vincent's. When Con went into surgery, I took their suggestion to call a family member. Eamonn left right away, and by the time Con was out of surgery, he was with us. Knowing Con was going to be okay and having his brother nearby, my numbed heart slowly began to thaw.

Now, Eamonn was doing his best to cheer me up. To show my gratitude, I tried to smile. "I know he'll be okay, because he has to be okay." I looked down at my claddagh ring, twisting it around my finger. "He *has* to."

"Kiss me."

"What?" I squinted at Eamonn, but he looked just as shocked as I did. Then I realized the voice had come from the bed.

Jolting upright, I stared at Con, but his eyes were still closed. My voice trembling with hope, I whispered, "Did he say something?"

I jumped again as Con cleared his throat. Then, with eyes still closed, he spoke again, louder this time. "Kiss me."

Unsure what to do, I glanced over at Eamonn. But he just offered an uncertain shrug. Slowly, I leaned over Con and softly brushed my lips against his.

Then I yelped in surprise as his hand darted up to the back of my neck and tugged my head forward, pressing my mouth firmly against his. He released his grip as I pulled back, half because I'd nearly lost my balance and fallen on top of him and half because I didn't want to make out with him in front of his brother.

"Ahh," Con moaned on a long exhale, like he'd just chugged a cold soda on a hot day. "Now *that* was the kiss of life."

Eamonn snorted with laughter while I flapped my arms, wanting to smack something but finding no appropriate target. I sat back down in the chair and ordered Con, "Open your eyes!"

Warily, he opened one, then the other, looking at me the whole time.

Once I was certain he could see my face and fully experience the impact of my words, I demanded, "The kiss of life? How can you even *joke* about that?"

"That's my signal," Eamonn said, trying to stop himself from laughing even more as he headed for the door. "I'll be back when you're done."

"Done what?" I asked, but Eamonn didn't answer, just closed the door behind him.

Con reached up and took my hand. "I think he meant when I'm done making inappropriate jokes, and you're done being angry with me about it."

His tired smile softened me in an instant. I folded his hand between my palms like a prayer book. "Are you okay? Are you in pain?"

"I'm fine." He grasped my hand and squeezed. "After all, Eamonn was right. It was only a .22."

"What about your leg? The doctor said—"

"My leg has come back from much worse, and it'll get better again."

He was trying to minimize his injuries, just like he tried to minimize every bad thing that happened to him. But it hadn't just happened to *him*. I was in love with him, so it happened to me too.

Now I understood how devastated he must have been those few times recently when I'd been hurt. "I'm so sorry," I whispered as hot, heavy tears streamed down my cheeks.

"Hey." He tried to sit forward, but when his shoulder prevented him, he pulled me toward him. As he reached up to wipe my tears, he said, "What are you sorry for? You saved me."

"No, I mean…." I sniffed a few times and took a deep breath. "I'm sorry I ever made you feel the way I'm feeling right now."

"Come here. Come."

From where I was sitting, I could only lean forward at an awkward angle. Con helped, guiding my head down onto his belly, where I could rest it comfortably. Then he began stroking my hair. "*You* never made me feel that way," he murmured. "Don't be daft. The people who hurt you—*they're* the ones who made me feel that way. The only reason they could is that I love you so deeply, I want to spend the rest of my life with you. And loving you is the best thing that has ever happened to me. Nothing else even comes close." Softly, his finger traced a line down my cheek. "So no matter what, I'm coming out so far ahead. Miles and miles. Light-years, in fact."

My tears kept falling, but now for a different reason. Ever since the shooting, my mind had been completely occupied with worrying about Con. But hearing him talk about the future brought thoughts about my medical report back to the fore. I'd barely had a chance to process how I felt about my diagnosis, let alone think through all the implications. Surely he hadn't had time to consider it fully either.

Fear and uncertainty pummeled me like a hard rain. If there was a chance Con might change his mind about being with me, I had to know. I was too deeply in love with him to just go on as we were, pretending everything was okay, unsure if or when he would deliver the bad news, shattering my heart.

Pushing past my terror of the potential worst-case scenario, I dried my eyes on my sleeve and asked, "You're sure you still want to spend the rest of your life with me?"

"Hang on." Con stopped stroking my hair and reached over to the electronic controls on the side of the bed railing. I sat up while he experimented with pushing the arrows until the back of the bed came forward, bringing him into a sitting position. His eyes locked onto mine, holding my gaze as a torrent of emotion flowed between us. "Of course I want to spend the rest of my life with you. I want to marry you, Neve. That's what the claddagh ring means. Why would you ask that?"

Because my body doesn't work properly. It's profoundly faulty. It isn't capable of doing the single most important and miraculous thing evolution designed it to do. But it had taken all my courage to ask the question. I didn't have enough energy left to explain.

Forcing a smile, I said, "It's nothing. We can talk about it later. You just got out of surgery, for goodness' sake! You need rest."

"I'm perfectly well rested, thanks to the anesthesia." He reached over, laying his hand over mine. "But while we're talking, I do have a confession to make."

Relieved by the change of subject, I asked, "What is it?"

Con looked down for a moment, and I could tell whatever it was, it was serious. In the tension of the moment, the sounds around us seemed to grow louder: the hum of the fluorescent lights, the beeps from the heart monitor, the muted bustle in the hallway outside. Finally, he met my eyes again but with a grave look this time. "For the past two years, I've been selfish, and I've been afraid."

What is he talking about? I couldn't imagine Con being either of those things. The only time I'd seen him afraid was when a patient's life hung in the balance. And selfish? He was the most selfless person I'd ever met. Turning my hand over, I gave his a reassuring squeeze.

"Two years ago, I met *you*," he continued. "And as you know, I've been all in from the first. I was willing to wait as long as it took. I knew eventually that gobshite you were dating would screw up so badly you'd leave him, and when my chance came, I grabbed it with both hands."

My heart swelled as I listened to him tell the story again. But his expression was hard and pained. He had something to get off his chest. I remained silent, listening.

"In all the time I've known you, you've never said anything about wanting to be a mother," he said. "The selfish part of me hoped that meant you didn't want children. But the fearful part of me was terrified that you might."

Confusing clouds of emotion roiled inside me. "Terrified why?"

Con's eyes broke away from mine as he looked down at the claddagh ring, touching it gently. "Because I've never wanted children. I've been very open about it. You can ask my family."

So he *did* know why I asked if he still wanted to spend his life with me. He knew exactly what was weighing on my mind and heart, just like he always did. I threaded my fingers through his.

"For one thing," he continued, "unless they're patients, I never know what to say to children, how to be around them. Add to that, I have a mighty temper when it gets going at all—don't shake your head, it's true. I would never want to burden a child with that, or with this," he said, gesturing at his injured leg. "I can't even keep up with you sometimes, let alone a small one."

My heart lurched as though it wanted to jump out of my chest and dive into his. "Con, that's ridiculous—"

"I'm not looking for soothing words," he insisted. "I know you don't believe my injury is an issue—"

"Because it isn't!"

"Perhaps not." He squeezed my hand. "But in any case, that's only half the story. I've been with enough parents bringing their children to our clinic to know what they say is true: when you become a parent, it means your heart is walking around out there on two legs, outside your body and your control, for the rest of your life." He looked up, his gaze shot through with pain. "I was selfish, dreading the possibility that once I finally got you, if you *did* want children, I would have you all to myself for only a short time before a little one came along and stole your heart."

"Oh, Con. Nothing could ever…." Overwhelmed by feelings I couldn't name and searching for words, I reached out and touched his cheek. "I mean, I don't think that's how it works."

"Be that as it may," he continued, laying his hand over mine, "when you showed me your operative report, I was upset on your behalf. You were learning that something was wrong with you physically, which is never easy. But I also didn't know if it might represent the end of a dream for you."

Con fell silent then, as though waiting for me to respond. He was sharing his feelings so openly, so bravely. As hard as it would be, I had to reciprocate.

I swallowed hard. "Honestly? I keep cycling

through different feelings about it. I can't remember ever actively wanting to be a parent. My desire, my focus has always been on caring for my clients. And then I was with my 'gobshite of an ex,'" I said, smirking at Con's perfect description of Stephan. "Not only was he indifferent about having children, but he also demanded so much of me, I knew I could never be with him and also care for a child. So I gave up on the idea of being a mother, and while it feels kind of... I don't know, taboo or unnatural to say this, the truth is the only real pain that thought has ever caused me is when I think about what it means for my parents."

As I thought of them, tears sprang into my eyes. "I'm their only child," I said, blinking rapidly. "If I don't make them grandparents, no one will. And I know they would be the best grandparents. They have so much love to give. But when I was with Stephan, I think they knew it wasn't in the cards. They went out of their way to reassure me that it was okay with them if I never had kids. But they *would* say that, you know?" Sniffling, I dried my eyes. "I love them so much, and it crushes me to think I might disappoint them."

"Neve." Con took my tearstained hand in his. "I've spent time with your parents. I've seen how much they love you, and I can't imagine any circumstances under which you could possibly disappoint them."

His words acted as a soothing balm on my heart. The pain was still there, but it was more bearable. "Thank you. That's really sweet of you to say."

"It's not sweet," he replied gruffly. "It's the truth. Which brings me to the last part of my confession."

Relieved to be off the hot seat, I nodded.

"I would do anything to make you happy, Neve. Anything." His eyes met mine with urgent determination as he grasped both of my hands. "If you ever decide you want to try to adopt, I'll be with you a hundred percent. I'll fix whatever about me needs fixing so I can be the man you need me to be."

How could he possibly think...? "You've always been the man I need you to be, Con, times a thousand. A million! And so much more than that."

He gave my hands a gentle squeeze. "Neve, serious talk here."

"I am being—"

"No, listen."

His expression was grave. I pressed my lips together hard.

"The standards for adoptive parents are very high. You, of course, would exceed them effortlessly. But when I was eighteen, I was convicted of assault. Thinking about your situation, I did a bit of internet research last night, and with adoption agencies, my history could be a deal-breaker."

"Wait, what? You were convicted of assault?" While that news surprised me, I knew the last thing Con needed as he lay there in a hospital bed was a dramatic reaction from me. It *did* explain the degree of tension in his parents' kitchen when Jack brought up "all the fighting." Mostly, though, I was just grateful he was opening up and trusted me enough to tell me. Careful to keep the shock out of my voice, I asked, "What happened?"

Con closed his eyes, blowing out a hard breath before he spoke. "I broke someone's nose—that was the worst of it, luckily. A boy in my class. Seventeen years old and already a menace. He would pick a girl, play on her affections, and, once she was smitten, talk her into meeting him behind the school's equipment shed. Then he'd put his hands... well, everywhere he could before she ran." His face twisted in disgust. "Afterward, he'd brag to all his friends about it in vivid detail. I was half ready to get into it with him regardless—somebody had to—but then I found out he'd decided to go after Una."

My hand flew to my mouth. "Oh no."

Con's eyes opened, and I could see the rage and horror he felt then as he recalled the situation. "I ignored it at first, hoping she wouldn't fall for him. But then he started winning her over. I tried to warn her against him, but that only drove her to him more. Eventually, Una agreed to meet him behind the shed after school. But I was keeping my ear to the ground, so I got wind of it. I found them there just as he was starting to back her up against the shed, trying to cage her in. I lost the head altogether." Frowning, he dragged his hand slowly across his face. "When it happened, I had just turned eighteen, so that made the legal situation more serious. Fortunately, the investigation showed the guards what a vicious arsehole he was. Una told them what happened, and some of his friends gave statements about his plans for her and his past behavior. As a result, I got off relatively easy. I had to pay restitution and do community service but no jail time."

"Always rescuing someone," I whispered, recalling Imogen's words. At eighteen, Con was already a hero.

"Ah, no," he said with a dismissive wave of his hand. "Just being a big brother. And I shouldn't have lost control. It was foolish." He raked his hand roughly through his hair. "Before now, it never occurred to me that it might affect you. I planned to tell you at some point, of course—certainly before we made anything legal, so there wouldn't be any secrets between us. But I was also putting it off as long as possible, until I knew you were certain you wanted to be with me—"

"Well, we're there!" Exasperated, I held up my ring finger, the claddagh catching the light.

Con's eyebrows shot up at that proclamation, but it didn't break his train of thought. "I was afraid once you knew about that side of me—which you do now, I suppose, after seeing the mess I left in Max's basement —you might run for the hills."

"Oh my God, seriously?" I closed my eyes and sighed. "Okay, first of all, I *vaguely* remember seeing a few guys with blood on them lying around that basement. But frankly, my whole focus was on you and whether you were okay. I'm not sure what it says about me, to be honest, but I didn't care *at all* whether those other guys were okay, or even alive. And I won't say I'm glad you broke that kid's nose—I would have rather the story ended with him in jail—but I certainly understand why you did it, and I love you even more than I did ten minutes ago, knowing you defended your sister like that. Maybe that makes me a bad person. I don't know. But if you want to talk about a history of violence, let's not forget I'm the one who hit Deirdre over the head with a lamp!"

"And thank God you did." Con cupped my cheek. "Neve, no matter what, you could never be a bad person. You're the opposite. You were my guardian angel last night. If you hadn't stopped Deirdre, she might have taken another shot at me, tried to finish the job."

As the potential consequences of that sank in, silence fell over us. I closed my eyes and nuzzled my cheek against his palm.

Quietly, he asked, "Is she all right, by the way?"

"Yes, thank goodness." A small bit of tension left me. "It was like when the ladder hit me in the head. She was disoriented for a few minutes, but now she's fine. Either I'm not that strong or the lamp wasn't that hard, fortunately." With a sigh, I added, "The other guys will live, too, by the way, if it puts your mind at ease."

"I won't lose a moment's peace worrying about those bastards." Con shook his head. "But I *will* lose peace knowing that, should you ever wish to adopt, I could be a liability to you. I appreciate you being so understanding about my past, but it's something you need to think through—and take all the time you need. I'm not pressing you for an answer. I do wonder, though, knowing all of this, do you think there's still a possibility, however small, that you might consider marrying me someday?"

Unbelievable. First of all, how could he possibly ever think of himself as a *liability*, for God's sake? But more to the point, over the past two years, and the past few months in particular, Con had *become* my life. I'd barely begun to process my infertility, let alone think about what it meant for the future. But I did know that whatever challenges were to come, I only wanted to face them with Con by my side. We would just have to work all of those things out together, because I couldn't be apart from him. I just couldn't. Didn't he get that?

It was clear I would have to explain it to him using language he understood. "Do you know what that is, that question you just asked me?"

With a cautious eyebrow raised, he asked, "What?"

"It's a bunch of *raiméis*." I beamed, proud of my spontaneous use of the Irish word.

He narrowed his eyes at me. "I'm being serious here, Neve."

"I am too!" Making a fist with my left hand, I held it up right in front of his face so he could get another good look at the claddagh ring. "You gave me this ring, Con, and I'm not taking it off—not now, not ever. You can't get rid of me, do you hear me? And you could never be a liability. You're my *everything*."

I was surprised to hear myself say those words, but once spoken, their truth was undeniable. Con *was* my everything. I couldn't imagine "me" without him anymore. And not in an unhealthy or codependent way.

Rather, it was like we'd developed a complete symbiosis, almost magical in nature. In other words, it felt like love.

"And you're mine," he replied, his voice rough with emotion, "which makes me the luckiest man on God's Earth." He grasped my fist and kissed my finger where the ring sat. "So that's how it is, is it?"

"Yes, as a matter of fact, that's how it is." I felt something between us shift. It was like we'd been standing in the quicksand of dreams, and in that moment, it sucked us in just a little bit deeper. "Out of curiosity, what would you have done if I'd run for the hills?"

With a thoughtful frown, he murmured, "Well, I would have had to run after you, possibly stalk you—with Eric's help—kidnap you and tie you to my bed, and somehow convince you to change your mind." His eyes flashed. "In other words, a lot of unnecessary drama."

"A bed, hmm? That seems like a pretty specific choice. Not a chair or a sofa?"

"Well, I'd want you to be comfortable."

"That's very thoughtful of you." I couldn't suppress a smile. "I almost feel like I missed out now."

Con narrowed his eyes at me and, in a warning tone, said, "Don't tempt—"

Before he could finish that thought, there were two light knocks at the door. Eamonn's weary voice asked, "Are you two done yet?"

Con murmured quietly, "Promise me you'll keep talking to me—about everything we've been discussing, or anything at all, anytime, for as long as you like. For the rest of our lives, if needed. I'm here for you, and I'll do everything I can to make things right, and to make you happy. Promise me."

Just when I thought it wasn't possible to love him any more…. "I promise."

Con lifted my hand to his lips and kissed my palm. The gleam in his eye revealed that he knew exactly what that would do to my body as he called out, "Come on in, Eamonn!"

"I'll get you back for that," I muttered.

Then he threw my own words back at me. "Promises, promises."

CHAPTER 30

NEVE

Eamonn found a hotel in Galway and booked us two rooms. Their parents had wanted to come as well, but Una and Yasmine had arrived. Eamonn convinced them all that Con was going to be fine, so they agreed to stay home and keep an eye on Ciara. His brother also conveyed a stern message from Con that plenty of Black Jack bars had better still be there when we got back. Meanwhile, I spent every moment I was allowed in the hospital by Con's bed.

The next day, his surgeon said the bullet wound was healing nicely with no signs of infection. The same was true of the cut he'd sustained on his shoulder as he swam me out of the cave—no lingering issues. An orthopedic specialist did a full evaluation of his leg and endorsed Con's earlier prediction that it would eventually heal back to where it was before it was reinjured. A physical therapist came by for an initial session and shared some new techniques that might even help him regain more function with less pain than he had previously.

Since Con was doing so well, I kept expecting someone to start talking to him about discharge planning, but no one mentioned it. When I asked him about it, he explained that Irish hospitals tended to keep patients longer than hospitals in the US. Then he really shocked me by saying the cost of his stay would be capped at seven hundred and fifty euros. When I mused that our hotel rooms would cost more than that, Con called Eamonn and insisted on paying for them. I was learning what to tell Con and what not to tell him.

His third day in the hospital was a bit quieter. All the initial evaluations had been done, so he only had a quick check-in with the doctor in the morning, the usual nursing evaluations throughout the day, and an hour with the physical therapist. Aside from the injuries slowing him down, Con was fully back to himself, and the fist of worry that had been clenched around my heart began to loosen. But the frequency with which he napped throughout the day showed his body was still healing from the trauma.

That first night after he got out of surgery and the hospital sent Eamonn and me away, I had called Sergeant O'Leary to update him on Con's condition. Part of our plan before going to Max's was that Banshee would find a way to anonymously email those dark web account numbers Eric had found for Max to Sergeant O'Leary. The sergeant told me he'd received an email with Max's name and a bunch of numbers and asked me if I knew anything about it. I pleaded ignorance.

Now that Con was feeling better, he called Sergeant O'Leary himself for an update. Along with Sean and Ryan, Max was now in jail on several different charges, from the attempted murder of Con and me to Deirdre's kidnapping. While they hadn't yet found any proof that Max intended to murder Deirdre, he was also charged with some things we hadn't anticipated, including blackmail and coercive control. Apparently, the HD card Con took from Max's video camera was full of explicit videos taken without the subjects' consent. Each video showed Max and Sean looking on while a different man had sex with Deirdre on the stone slab in the sea cave. Max began each video by telling them it was a ritual initiating them into the top tiers of the *Temple of Taranis*. Deirdre told them that Sean had coerced her into participating in these "rituals" at Max's behest.

Sergeant O'Leary said the account numbers showed payments by the videotaped men into Max's account. While Max insisted the payments were "tithes," each of the men the guards had contacted so far said Max told them if they didn't pay, he would post the videos online and send links to their families and schools or employers.

"Max said he had 'insurance policies' on his followers," Con said. "Sounds like he meant the videos."

"That tracks," the sergeant agreed. Apparently the

same threat to release the videos, compounded by threats of violence, were hung over Deirdre's head should she ever tell anyone what was happening to her.

All at once, everything Max had said to Deirdre in the basement made sense, along with her extreme fear of Con.

"Christ, the poor girl," Con said. "She was right to shoot me. For all she knew, Max was telling the truth, and I was there to abduct her. It was my own fault. I didn't introduce myself properly."

"That seems to be the story," Sergeant O'Leary said. "Deirdre believed that by shooting you, she was acting in self-defense. For that reason, we haven't charged her with anything, but if you decide to press the matter, that's a different story, of course."

"No, certainly not. She was the victim in that room, not the perpetrator. And God knows she's been through enough."

"That was our conclusion as well. When we interviewed her, she told us she and Max recently had a falling-out. She'd been keeping an eye on your brother's fiancée—Ciara, I believe—and feeding information back to Max. But when she saw how sick Ciara became because of what Max had done to her, and Max refused to help… well, Deirdre genuinely cares about Ciara. She told Max she wanted out. He corroborated her version of events, by the way, albeit with a much different take on things."

"Let me guess," I said. "He's the victim of disloyalty? Both Ciara and Deirdre betrayed him and deserved to be punished?"

"That's the long and short of it." To our relief, he told us that Deirdre was receiving mental health services to help her recover from her trauma. Also, she and Ciara had spoken and were now supporting each other through their respective recoveries.

Meanwhile, Eamonn was happy to report that Ciara was getting better by the day. The call with Deirdre had also clarified a lot of information for Ciara and her treatment team. One of the things Deirdre explained was that Max had taken the handfasting seriously and still viewed himself as married to Ciara. Horrified, Ciara told Eamonn all about the ceremony then, but her understanding was that they were just play-acting for the gamers' weekend on the island. None of us were at all surprised to hear that "marriage" had been all in Max's head.

In even better news, Eamonn told us Ciara was going to be released from the hospital at the end of the week. She would still go back a few days a week for treatment, just until they were sure she was in the clear. She'd been devastated to hear what had happened to Deirdre, and it was a struggle in many ways for her to learn so much new and terrifying information about Max. But she was elated about her impending release and looking forward to being home with Eamonn for the weekend. She was even talking about throwing herself back into wedding planning, something to help keep her positive and focused on the future.

With so much good news floating around, it seemed even more depressing that Con still had to stay in the hospital, especially because the better he felt, the grumpier he became about being confined. To cheer him up, I found a good fish and chips restaurant nearby and brought Con a slab of cod and some vinegar-soaked french fries for dinner. Seeing the immense pleasure he took in eating his favorite meal—one I knew he'd never found the equal of in Washington—delighted me so much I thought my heart would burst.

After dinner, Con invited me to lie down on the hospital bed next to his right side, the "uninjured" one. As he tugged on my hand, I asked, "Is this safe for you? Won't the doctor be mad?"

"Neve," he reassured, "I have great expertise on the subject of 'angry doctors.' Let me worry about that."

Content enough with that answer, I climbed in beside him. It was a tight fit and I ended up half on top of him, but he assured me he didn't mind in the slightest. Once I was tucked in against him and the rough hospital sheets, he said he had a burning question for me. "How in the hell did you get out of those handcuffs?"

A grin spread slowly across my face. I'd been waiting for him to ask. "I had help from Banshee."

"Banshee? That traitor! But how did you actually do it?"

Smiling at his mock-outrage, I said in a singsong voice, "Oh, you know, Banshee just looked up some videos on YouTube and told me how to make a shim using a pen clip. Then it was just a matter of pushing it in, jiggling it around, applying pressure in the right places… and click! I was free."

I only realized I had acted out the word "jiggling" when Con's eyes dropped to my chest. He cleared his throat twice. "Are you trying to plant scandalous thoughts in my head? In a hospital?"

"Those were her actual instructions!" A furious blush made me uncomfortably warm. To get Con's mind off salacious topics, I said, "Banshee said I was a natural. She thinks I should get a handcuff *tattoo*!" I knew how strenuously he would object to *that* idea. Con knew about the one tattoo I already had—a sadly mushy pair of butterflies on my shoulder—and he'd lectured me once before about the dangers of tattoos, complete with warnings about infections, diseases, and heavy metals in the ink.

He shifted his good arm beneath me and snaked it around my waist, pulling me hard against him. With our faces so close, I had no choice but to look him in the eye as he scolded, "I hope to God you're joking after everything Ciara just went through."

I tried to pull back, but he held me in place. "I hope to God *you're* joking. You're not seriously trying to draw an equivalency between Ciara's horrifying experience and the ill-advised body art of my twenties?"

A muscle in his jaw ticked. Clearly Con was putting forth a good deal of effort to hold back from giving me yet another lecture. "Of course not," he finally conceded. "There's no comparison between the two.

That said, I would *strongly* prefer it if you consulted me before getting any more... what did you call it? Body art? That way I can make sure it's done by a qualified individual in a manner that is least likely to lead to scarring, neurological problems, or the contraction of hepatitis."

By the time he reached "hepatitis," I was barely suppressing laughter. "Don't worry, Doctor. I'll invite you to accompany me on any future body art excursions. But now you have to answer *my* burning question."

With a sigh, he closed his eyes. "I'd be delighted if it leads to a change of subject."

"Okay, then. What were you and Agent Banai talking about during that private conversation of yours Sunday afternoon?"

"Ah, that," Con said, opening his eyes. "You'll be pleased to hear he's sending us to Cork for a week on the Secret Service's dime. All expenses paid."

"He's what?" That sounded suspicious, even to me. "As... a gift?"

"In part." He drew his hand across his jaw. "But he also wants me to do something for him."

A weighty sigh escaped me. "I'm afraid to ask."

"Don't worry, it's nothing bad. There's an endocrinology conference happening there. He wants me to give a presentation."

That made no sense at all. I mean, Con giving a presentation at a conference made sense. He was one of the foremost experts on treating comorbid endocrine and psychiatric disorders. But what could that possibly have to do with the Secret Service? "Is the president coming or something?"

"No, but it's a favor for him. His goddaughter is in her third year at university studying Irish folklore, and she's spending a year abroad in Cork. Recently, she's been struggling with some issues that appear psychiatric in nature, but there's a possibility of endocrine system involvement. She's in treatment and still managing school for now. Someone must have told the president about my specialty, though, because he wants me to look over the case."

News of the young woman's problems tugged at my heart. "That poor girl, going through something like that—and especially on her year abroad, away from home. That's got to be hard."

Con nodded. "But the president is worried his goddaughter will balk if she suspects he sent someone all the way from the US to check in on her. He thinks she might agree to let me talk to her treatment team, though, if I'm a friend of his who 'just happens' to be in town for a conference."

All I could do was shake my head. "He really thinks she won't see through that?"

He squinted at me. "You think she will?"

It seemed neither he nor the president was familiar with the intelligence level of twenty-year-olds. "It's a strong possibility."

Con shifted around until he was lying on his right side and we were facing each other directly. He laid his hand on my cheek. "Would you be willing to help me, then? I have a feeling you'd be better at talking to her than I would, especially if she's resistant."

"Hmm." I smiled. "Did Agent Banai ask you to seduce me into helping?"

"He better *not* mention you and seduction in the same sentence." With narrowed eyes, Con slid his hand behind my neck and began drawing small circles at the nape. "He said he'd call you after the crisis here was over and ask you himself. He didn't want to give the impression that any quid pro quo was expected from you. You're free to say no. I, on the other hand... well, he got me out of jail, and I'm not a US citizen, so there was really only one answer I could give. Don't look like that." He leaned forward and placed a soft kiss on my neck, just beneath my ear.

I bit my lip. "Like what?"

"Like you dropped your ice cream on the sidewalk." He kissed me again in the same place. "It will still be a romantic getaway. I'll only need to spend one morning at the conference. Then we'll devote half a day to this young woman's case, a full day at most. After that, our time is ours to do with what we will."

It was becoming increasingly difficult to form thoughts as Con placed kiss after tender kiss on my neck. "Well, it's not like I'm letting you out of my sight." Quoting his own words back at him, I said, "You have a 'surprising propensity for putting yourself in harm's way.'"

"Oh, really?" He reached down and grabbed my

backside. When I yelped and tried to squirm out of his grasp, he squeezed. Cocking an eyebrow, he asked, "You're on board, then?"

"Ow, yes!"

Grinning, he released his hold.

I shot him a sharp look. "I happen to like the president. I don't mind doing him a favor."

Con lifted his hand to encircle my wrists. "I'm glad to hear that because I'm not letting you out of my sight either. After we've done this favor, I'm not even letting you out of my bed." Drawing my hands up to his lips, he then placed slow, sensuous kisses on my palms—first the left, then the right.

"Cut that out!" I pulled my hands away. He was trying to distract me with seduction, and if I wasn't very careful, he would succeed. As my body bloomed with heat, I asked, "And what happens to your plan if Agent Banai puts us up in a hostel somewhere, or student accommodations?"

Con tipped my chin upward, forcing our eyes to meet. With a sexy rasp in his voice that told me we were both suffering from the same affliction, he told me, "He said we can pick any hotel we like. I have a few luxury options in mind."

He slid his right hand around the back of my neck again while his left began to stroke up and down my waist. I froze, unable to do anything but look into his eyes as I imagined it: Con and me, alone in a hotel room with no one and nothing to disturb us.

"We wouldn't even have to leave the room," he

continued, fleshing out the fantasy. "Room service for every meal. We can relax on the balcony while they clean for us. Nothing to do but indulge."

"In... in...." I had to clear my throat to speak. "Indulge? In what?"

With a grunt, Con used his injured arm to tilt my body closer again to his. Not wanting him to hurt himself, I finished the job, scooting up to him until our torsos were flush against each other. He tilted his head, placing his mouth close to my ear. "Indulge in whatever we like."

Then he nipped my earlobe.

I squealed softly as, cell by cell, the surface of my skin ignited.

He whispered, "I believe you know what I'd like. I've told you what my plan is when I finally get you into my bed. What we'll do for days." An earlobe kiss. "Weeks." Another soft nip. "Months, even." Then he pulled my earlobe between his lips and slowly ran his tongue along the edge.

That was my body's breaking point. I arched my back, pressing myself into him, then wrapped my arms around him and began to devour the spot where his neck and shoulder met. Con held me against him, and we melded together like two red-hot iron rods.

The corner of the bedrail bit into my back, reminding me where we were. That realization compelled me to pull my lips away from his skin long enough to ask, "But what'll we do until then? I mean, you're in the hospital. You're injured. And then we'll be back at your parents' house."

"Hmm." Con's torso vibrated against mine with the depth of his moan-like hum, plunging me even further into flame. "I guess we'll just have to behave ourselves —somewhat, anyway," he said, placing his lips near the corner of my mouth. "Exercise some discipline."

"Discipline?" I asked, aghast. My whole body silently screamed in rebellion at the concept. I tugged the bottom of his T-shirt up until I was touching the hot skin on his lower back. Helplessly, I pleaded for an answer—from Con, from the universe. "How?"

His body shook against mine as he chuckled, driving me to distraction. Holding his lips a hairbreadth from mine, he murmured, "I know you know how to exercise discipline."

The thought of doing anything other than going to a hotel room with him immediately and staying there forever was unbearable. Untenable. Completely unacceptable. Frowning deeply, I shook my head.

"Of course you do," he insisted. "Surely you coach your clients on this."

I froze in place as Con ran the tip of his tongue along my protruding lower lip. When he stopped, I leaned in for a kiss. But he pulled back, leaving me in dismay.

Sliding his arm out from under me, Con grasped my chin between his thumb and forefinger and held my face just far enough from his that my searching lips encountered nothing but empty air. "You build discipline through *practice*."

He would deny me a kiss, knowing very well the explosive state I'm in? The thought both enraged and inflamed me. I struggled to pull my chin from his grip so I could attack his mouth with mine, lighting the fuse that lay between us.

Bringing his other arm up as well, Con cupped both sides of my face, holding my head firmly in place and just out of reach. But I could see it in his eyes—he burned with desire too. He wanted this kiss as desperately as I did. For God's sake, he even licked his wicked lips while I watched.

He sucked air in through his teeth as I dug my fingernails into the flesh of his back. "What are you doing?" I demanded in a voice that sounded to me like a stranger's, harsh and commanding.

Amusement flashed across his wanton expression. "Practicing."

He's torturing me. He's actually torturing…. "You bas—"

But before I could finish, Con pulled me in and finally gave me the potent kiss I'd been longing for. As our lips met and our tongues began their ravenous dance, we were consumed by white-hot flame. We burned there between the rails of the bed, combusting with such cosmic force and heat that the whole of the room, the hospital, the entire city of Galway, and the rest of the world dropped away and spun out of existence.

My mind disappeared, and I transformed into an inferno fueled by a wild heart. His touch, his kiss, his love had turned me into this. Whether any living creature could survive such incandescence, I had no idea. But I did know one thing: Con was a man of his word. And that meant we would have the rest of our lives together to find out.

————

Thank you so much for reading *Dead Keen*! I certainly hope you enjoyed it. If you'd like to help spread the word, please consider telling a friend, or taking a few minutes to leave a review on your favorite book website. Reviews really do help readers discover new books they'll love. Thanks again for your support. It is deeply appreciated!

Sign up for my newsletter, read about my work, and more on my website:
HTTPS://ANISEEDEN.COM

ABOUT THE AUTHOR

Anise Eden writes suspense novels with thriller, romance, and paranormal elements. She is the author of DEAD SOUND, the first book in the Things Unseen series, an Amazon bestselling thriller and winner of an FCRW National Excellence in Romantic Fiction Award. Anise also wrote the multi-award-winning Healing Edge Series. Originally from the US, she now lives in Ireland with her husband and her small but mighty canine writing companion.

facebook.com/authoraniseeden

twitter.com/aniseeden

bookbub.com/profile/anise-eden

ACKNOWLEDGMENTS

First and foremost, I would like to express my gratitude to my wonderful readers. Your love for the first book in this series, DEAD SOUND, inspired and encouraged me so much as I wrote this sequel. From my heart, thank you!

I am deeply grateful to my wonderful editor Kristin Scearce, Rebecca Johnson, and the rest of the extraordinary team at Tangled Tree. Thank you so much for the brilliant support you have given me in so many ways and for your ongoing belief in my writing.

I would like to thank the following people for their special contributions to this book:

Sergeant Eileen Kelly of the Mallow Garda Station for so generously sharing your valuable time, knowledge, and experience to assist with my research into arrest procedures in Ireland.

Dr. Jean Ayers for your expert suggestions and thoughtful feedback on the medical aspects of this story (and for lending me your keen literary ear!).

The folks at T. Dillon & Son in Galway for your warm hospitality. It was such a pleasure to meet you, and a joy to include your beautiful claddagh ring store in this story.

Bubz at Lux Ink Tattoo and Beauty in Mallow for so graciously answering my endless questions and lending your expertise to my tattoo research.

My perfect and brilliant nephew, Jimmy, for teaching me about online gaming.

Much gratitude, as well, to two extraordinarily gifted writer friends: Nicole E. Kelleher for so kindly reading and giving me your feedback on an early draft of this manuscript, and Lisa Fahy for sharing your insider knowledge of Galway (and for our lovely writing weekends!).

I began writing this book before the first lockdown in Ireland and only finished it after the last. Heartfelt thanks to all of those whose friendship, love and support sustained me through those challenging times. Special thanks for creativity-themed coffees (both real and virtual) to dear and fabulously talented friends: Lisa Barrett and Joanna Foley (my generous Irish subject matter experts), Rosanna Leo, Rose O'Driscoll, Sarina Prabasi, and Shannon Rowan.

My deepest gratitude goes out to my beloved parents and family for your unconditional love, support, and belief in me. Thank you so much for the countless ways in which you keep me going every single day. You are my true north, and I hold you in my heart always.

And finally, to my husband (and genius plot doctor). Every day, you make me even more grateful that we both chose to climb all those stairs! If you catch glimpses of us in these pages, it's because every book I write is an extended love letter to you.

ABOUT THE PUBLISHER

Tangled Tree Publishing loves all things tangled and aims to bring darker, twisted, and more mind-boggling books to its readers. Publishing adult and new adult fiction, TTPubs are all about diverse reads in mystery, suspense, thrillers, and crime.

For more details, head to www. TANGLEDTREEPUBLISHING.COM

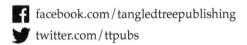 facebook.com/tangledtreepublishing
twitter.com/ttpubs

Milton Keynes UK
Ingram Content Group UK Ltd.
UKHW012131160823
426962UK00001B/4